MEMOIRS OF A TOURIST

STENDHAL

Memoirs of a Tourist

Translated by Allan Seager

With Illustrations by Roger Barr

NORTHWESTERN UNIVERSITY PRESS

First Paperback Printing, 1985

Printed in the United States of America

Translator's *Acknowledgment*

I SHOULD LIKE TO EXPRESS PROFOUND THANKS to M. Monnerot-Dumaine, Clos des Fréres Gris, Aix-en-Provence, and to Mr. M. D. Elevitch of Boston. Between bouts of cutting firewood against the mistral, M. Monnerot gave me invaluable help with difficult passages. Mr. Elevitch is the editor of *First Person*, and by his splendid presentation of excerpts from this translation in his magazine, he called it to the attention of its present publishers.

A. S.

Translator's *Preface*

THIS IS A CUT VERSION of *Mémoires d'un Touriste.* While I have retained some, the most amusing, I did not feel that every single one of Stendhal's *anecdotes d'amour* was worth reprinting, nor did I believe that his splenetic animadversions on the Jesuit schools in France in the reign of Charles X were of sparkling contemporary interest. Several mere lists of paintings in provincial museums have been excised as dull. It might be thought that the minor works of a great man could be handled with confidence simply because they are minor. I do not feel this confidence. Greatness lurks, springing out on you when you least expect it, and I have probably made mistakes.

However, the facts are these. Stendhal undertook the writing of *Memoirs of a Tourist* for the money there was in it. He was living in Paris during an extended leave from his consulate at Civita Vecchia on half-pay of five thousand francs a year, and he had expensive tastes. Despite or perhaps because of his big belly and his tousled dark-brown wig, he insisted on dressing in the height of fashion, and this kept him in debt to his tailor. A man fifty-four years old who in his heart does not really believe he is too old to fall in love needs all the help a tailor can give him.

Stendhal wrote the *Memoirs* by fits and starts in 1837 and

1838. Simultaneously he was translating and polishing his Italian tales, "Vittoria Accoramboni" and "The Cenci," working at his life of Napoleon and at his unfinished novel, *The Rose and the Green*. The *Memoirs* were accepted by an editor named Dupont who was later to publish *The Charterhouse of Parma*. He gave Stendhal fifteen hundred and sixty francs for them and published them in June, 1838, in two volumes. Stendhal's name was not on them. The title-page read, "Memoirs of a Tourist by the author of The Red and the Black," hardly a recommendation to a public who had ignored the novel. The reviews were as usual few and bad. The critics seemed to think Stendhal had cynically maligned both France and the French. They were acute. He had. He wrote to a friend, "What is there so imprudent in the Tourist? To please fools while proving to them for seven hundred pages that they are fools is an impossibility in any case."

Stendhal had hoped to make money nonetheless because travel books were popular in France at the time, but they dealt chiefly with what the traveler would see, the art and the monuments. Stendhal shifted the emphasis to the tourist. The *Memoirs* is a book about a man traveling through France. The pictures, the statues, the great buildings are all there, but so are the towns that contain them and especially the people in the towns.

Who is this tourist? Stendhal, of course, but he finds it necessary to pretend otherwise. In a long Introduction, he establishes the character of a commercial traveler for an ironworks who has lost his wife, made money, and wishes to end his days in the colonies, Martinique probably, where he spent his youth. It occurs to him that in spite of all the business trips he has made, he has never really seen France. Before he leaves it forever, he makes this long journey to acquaint himself with his homeland and enjoy himself while doing it if possible, a journey made by private carriage, public stagecoaches, river boats, even by the new railroad, from the Channel to the Mediterranean, from the Atlantic to Strasbourg, with side trips to Geneva, Genoa, and Barcelona. It is this tourist whose memoirs we have, but the disguise is thin. Stendhal comes bursting through.

Now this is very interesting. Why did Stendhal have to invent a commercial traveler? Why couldn't he have given us his own memoirs? Throughout his life Stendhal gave signs that his sense of his own identity was feeble. He used over fifty pseudonyms in his writing. When he was forty-nine years old, musing about his life on the Janiculum Hill in Rome, he said, "Have I had a talent for anything? Am I clever or a failure? What have I really been?" It bothered him. There seem to be three reasons for this chronic indecisiveness about himself. The first may lie in the death of his adored mother when he was seven and his lifelong hatred of his father. We already know the old Freudian formulae to explain situations like this. While possibly true, they are boring to explicate. A second influence may have been the times he lived in. He could remember the liberty cap on a pole in the Place Grenette in Grenoble at the beginning of the Revolution in 1789, and he lived through six more changes in government, hopeful only of the young Napoleon, alienated from all the rest, a man of aristocratic tastes who could not bear the company of noblemen, who stood for democratic ideals but would not associate with the masses, a bourgeois who hated the middle classes because they were money-grubbers. Confused by his origins, he was further confused by the social and political turmoil of his time. The French *maquis* used *The Red and the Black* as a handbook on how to live in enemy country. The third reason is possibly only tangential to Stendhal's private and social life. It may lie in the conscious use of the fundamental artistic device of the novelist, the adoption of a fiction as a way of revealing truth, a device of power and intensity which elicits its power and intensity from the reader, who, if his interest has been aroused, must then follow, unravel, and interpret the fiction and when its truth breaks over him feels the thrill of discovery as if he had done it all himself. Stendhal had been thinking about the arts all his life as his letters show and his works prove. He had written poetic plays before he was twenty. He had taken acting lessons—partly, it is true, to get next to a handsome young actress. He had written about music, painting, the drama, and by the time he produced the *Memoirs*, he had finished two novels. Thus it is probable that these disguises, these pretenses about himself, the perennially displaced person, were deliberate and made in the service of truths he was reluctant to reveal in other ways.

It is a book of great charm. I have seen the French staring at their own monuments with it in their hands. Not that it is wholly reliable as a guide book. Stendhal used his own wide experience as a traveler, but he also used other people's memories, newspapers, gazettes, any source where he could find material, and sometimes his sources are wrong. He was writing his friend Baron de Mareste in June, 1837, "Il me faut trois ou quatre anecdotes d'amour. . . . relisez vos mémoires," and in October, "Donnez-moi vite Marseille et Nîmes." The charm lies in this: you have as a traveling companion a man who is, very likely, more observant, wittier, more intelligent, more responsive than you are, responsive not only to the relics of the past but especially to the resonances people evoke from him—people like the girl, for instance, carrying a superb peacock in a basket on her head or the Americans at Le Havre. Scenes of nature he describes dryly, accurately, unromantically, partly in reaction against the florid romantics of his time like Chateaubriand, possibly also because he had been stunned by the magnificent scenery around Grenoble as a boy and had had enough of it.

What is chiefly interesting are his opinions, always striking, always penetrating, drawn from an experience more profound than any other novelist's, almost any other writer's. Who else has made the retreat from Moscow *and* been a wholesale grocer? Who has headed the occupation of the Duchy of Brunswick and won a mathematics scholarship at the Ecole Polytecnique? Who has held an empress on his lap when she was a great big girl of thirteen, taken acting lessons, served as consul in Italy, been a correspondent for the London papers and a good wing shot, to boot? And he did all these things honestly, that is, to make a living or because they interested him and not with any thought of writing them up later.

He was a little man with a big head, not handsome, vain of his small hands and feet, boilingly emotional and trying to control it with *logique*, a word he always pronounced in three syllables. In this he did pretty well, for he had a full set of prejudices and he hated all the right people for his time, and, with his candor, he might very well have ended in jail. (He often cautions himself that the most exhausting thing is useless hate.) He was incessantly in love, and he tinkered away at a logical method for the seduction of women, but it seemed usually to develop bugs at crucial moments. However, when he did succeed, he wrote the date on his suspenders.

It is a cliché to say that he had the most original and prophetic mind of his century. A great man, he is almost unfailingly, except with women, intelligent, and even them he could write about intelligently. All he was trying to do was to be happy, a gigantic task considering the array of tastes he had to satisfy.

André Gide said he wrote the greatest French novel, and Stendhal would be the first to appreciate what the French have done with him. He lies in Montmartre Cemetery in the dark under a big steel railroad bridge called the Pont Caulaincourt with a dusty bunch of crockery violets (Parma violets) at his feet and a stone at his head with this inscription:

Arrigo Beyle, Milanese
Visse, amo, scrisse.

Perhaps it serves him right for calling himself an Italian.

ALLAN SEAGER

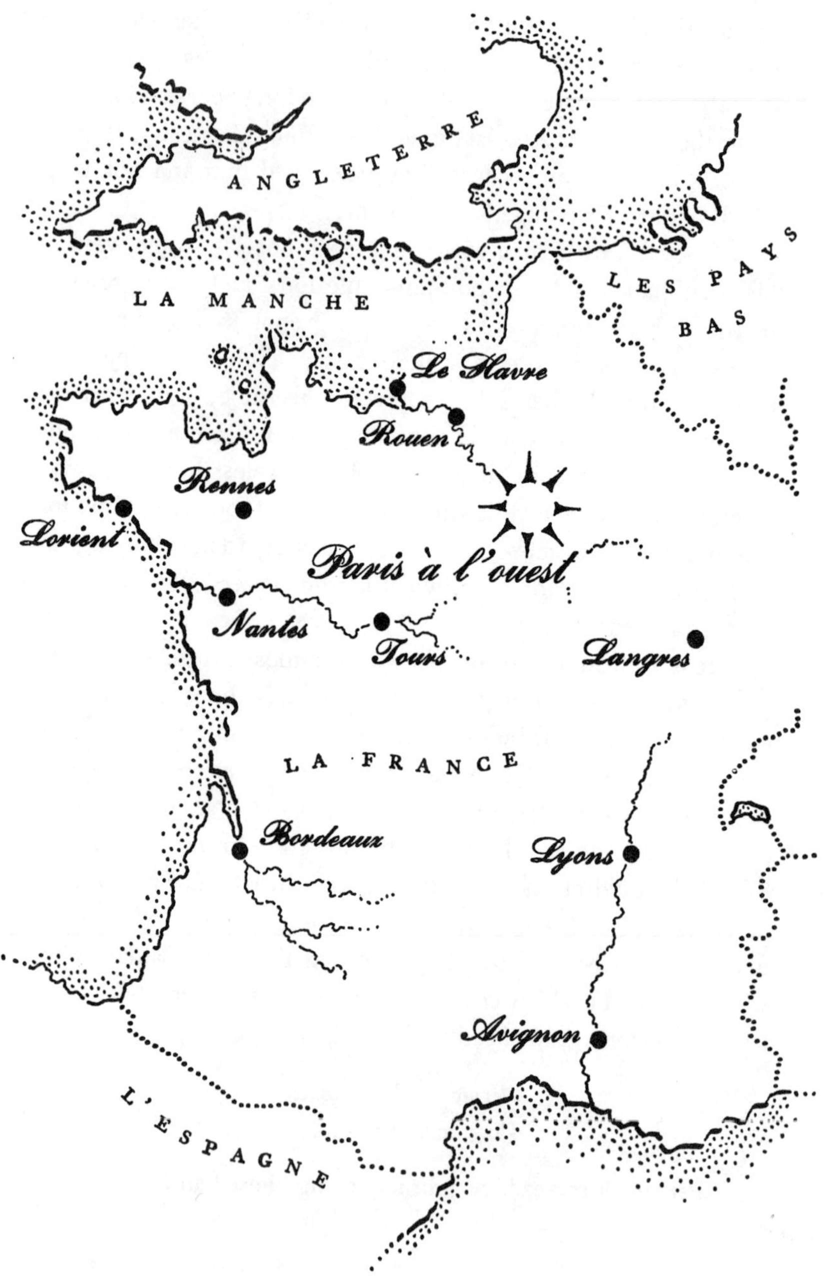
ANGLETERRE
LA MANCHE
LES PAYS BAS
Le Havre
Rouen
Rennes
Lorient
Paris à l'ouest
Nantes
Tours
Langres
LA FRANCE
Bordeaux
Lyons
Avignon
L'ESPAGNE

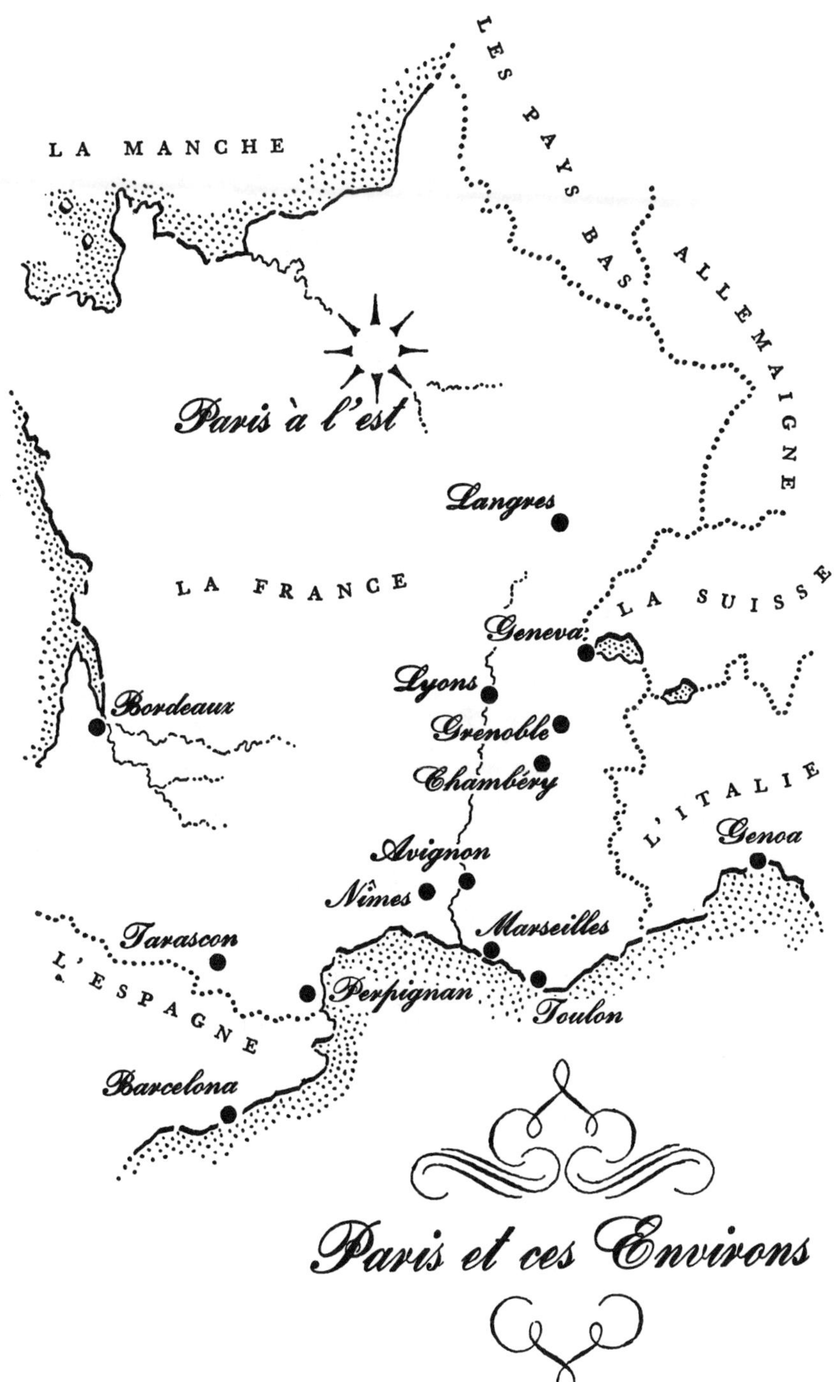
LES PAYS BAS
LA MANCHE
ALLEMAIGNE
Paris à l'est
Langres
LA FRANCE
LA SUISSE
Geneva
Lyons
Bordeaux
Grenoble
Chambéry
L'ITALIE
Genoa
Avignon
Nîmes
Marseilles
Tarascon
L'ESPAGNE
Perpignan
Toulon
Barcelona
Paris et ces Environs

MEMOIRS OF A TOURIST

Foreword

THE MANUSCRIPT JOURNAL of Mr. L——, commercial traveler in hardware, forms the basis of the book you are about to read. It is Mr. L——'s shortcoming to call a few too many things by their right names, and this could blacken his character and give a very wrong idea of it. He has asked me to correct his style, and I answered that I very much needed someone to correct my own. I hate and detest the academic style.

Since Mr. L—— is accustomed to speaking Spanish and English in the colonies, he has included a great many words in those languages as more expressive.

"Expressive!" I said. "Undoubtedly, but only for those who know Spanish and English."

The whole of my slight effort in the editing of the following pages has been to point out little mistakes like these. I have had to cut out a quarter of the manuscript which consisted of anecdotes and reflections. He might risk publishing this part later if, in spite of its candid tone, his *Journey in France* should find some readers. I doubt whether it will; the author does not spare any group. In my opinion, everything that could displease the Faubourg St. Germain or the *National* ought to be cut out.

My own political opinions are different from those of the author and wiser, but he wouldn't stand for having his softened a bit.

H[ENRI] B[EYLE]

Introduction

I AM GOING TO TELL what I have done, or, rather, what has been done to me in the nearly thirty-four years I have been on this earth.

My father, a harsh man who had succeeded in making a name for himself in a learned profession by hard work, reminded me every day that I was poor and had me given an excellent education, not without trouble, at least for me.

As a child I never had any fun at all, and my life was always hard. When I was ten years old, I was working ten hours a day at Greek, Latin, and mathematics. It was with great distress that this paternal strictness allowed me to study music and drawing and only on condition that I get up an hour earlier every morning. The upshot was I got hardly any sleep.

At sixteen I worked in a Customs office. The manager was a friend of my father's, and I had four or five hours a day in which to finish my education.

My father said that in this slipshod century everything tended to make a man mediocre. "I don't know whether you are destined to be a distinguished man," he added. "At least you will be an educated man."

After following such a system so exactly, I had no time to be young. At eighteen, the office took up all my time and kept me busy ten or twelve hours a day. As I look back on it now, I suppose my father took care to leave me no time to go wrong. The fact is, I was a victim of work.

I had been three or four years in the Customs when suddenly I was sent to practice my trade in the colonies. I don't know the idiot who denounced me as a *liberal* to the manager, but he outdid himself and sent an abominable note to Paris about me. It stated that I was a man of very dangerous opinions. At nineteen, after working eight hours in a stuffy office, God knows whether I ever thought about anything but getting one of the lovely girls I happened to meet to look at me. But I don't want to complain. These gentlemen had all the intelligence of their government.

Thus I arrived in this colony labeled a dangerous fellow. What struck me the most about the place was that they woke me up in the morning to give me coffee. To revenge myself on the government that exiled me, I learned English and set myself to study liberalism.

Living in that country (which I ended by liking very much), I twenty times over blessed the slick-haired manager who had sent me there in exile. Often I commandeered one of the little Customs boats and went from one island to another. I made friends with some merchant captains who in this warm climate led happy lives. I even had the honor of drinking punch sometimes with officers of the Royal Navy. But I committed some indiscretions. They were not political, but they were serious enough otherwise. One day when I was working in the sun, I caught such a violent inflammation that the manager sent me back to Europe without waiting for any word from the Ministry, merely out of kindness. He was a good man who, for fear of compromising himself, never had an idea in his life, and in him this impetuosity was sublime.

When I was halfway there, the fresh winds from Europe brought me back to health at once. In France I went back to my father's house and all the pettiness of bourgeois life: the smoke

from my cigar discommoded the maid. I was a man who knew how to make other men obey, and my father treated me exactly as if I were fifteen years old.

I was afraid I was turning into a monster, of having to admit that I did not adore my father. In the midst of all his gruffness he kept repeating an idea that often struck me. "Just what the hell are you going to do with yourself? What is the cart you can pull until you are fifty so you can get a pension of nine hundred francs?"

He suggested that I resign my job in the Customs and get married. I didn't dare refuse him. I could see very clearly that he would not give me the small sum necessary to refurbish my equipment so I could return to the colonies when my leave was up.

I went into my father-in-law's hardware business and went on the road as a commercial traveler, buying and selling merchandise. My father-in-law liked to look busy, but he was the laziest of men. Finding me willing to work, he let me do everything. I prospered.

As a result of many different circumstances in which chance took a much bigger part than my own skill, our business grew and grew, and my own fortune improved considerably. People thought I was happy. Everyone would have sworn that nothing was lacking, but happiness was the farthest thing from my mind!

I am so bold as to think that my wife blessed her condition in life. At least I went to any length to anticipate her wishes, and I believe she was happy, but it turned out that I didn't really care anything about conjugal love. On the other hand I had only respect for my father. Was I a monster, then, I asked myself. Was I fated never to love anyone?

The gods punished me by giving me what I asked. At thirty I was a young man. My ideas changed completely. It was the same with my feelings.

The strongest perturbation that gave me a new way of life was the misfortune of losing my wife, and I had the consolation that she never suspected any of the things that would have given her pain. I wept for her sincerely. A profound disgust for everything seized me.

In the first three or four months that followed this cruel separation, I retired to Versailles. I came to Paris only three times a week to spend an hour at my business. My despair annoyed my father-in-law. A lady-friend of the family, quite a schemer, spoke to me of marrying again.

That day I was on guard duty at Chateau d'Eau on the boulevard, for, no matter how unhappy and absent-minded I was, I had to do guard duty. I didn't return home until I had finished my turn at two o'clock in the morning, and I remember I spent the whole night in deep thought, sitting in a straw-bottomed chair in front of the guardhouse.

I was sure that my father-in-law had put Mme Vignon up to suggesting that I re-marry. Maybe she had spoken only because he had urged it. I marry again? If I did, I would be resuming the kind of life I had led for six years.

I had begun my matrimonial career with an act of ferocity. I knew only too well what it was to eat my dinner every day with a father or father-in-law. I wanted to have a home of my own.

Soon, as our business improved, I had to give dinner parties. Now, because of the fine wines, giving dinners is a very expensive pleasure. Not only that; it is a terrible bore.

Winter had come on. A gratifying result of our dinner parties and one that I had not foreseen was that my wife was invited to quite a few balls. I had to play écarté. When there were more than seven or eight five-franc pieces on the table, there was always one missing when it came time to pay up. This sort of thing disgusted me profoundly. I blushed to the whites of my eyes as if I were the thief. Then I blushed because I blushed. Games with these swindlers was a worse torture than the dinners.

The hardware business had continued to prosper. I worked

hard at it so that I wouldn't have the embarrassment of changing jobs a second time in the middle of my career. Many is the time I had to lock in my desk one or two thousand-franc notes. I admit I was childish enough to regard them with a certain self-satisfaction. I had never had so much money, and this money was pure profit on deals I had cooked up myself. I said to myself, "I have made this money, and, the way things are going, I shall earn more in the future." I was frugal by nature, and I confess that I looked as lovingly as a miser at those paltry thousand-franc notes.

My wife had soon found a way to use them. We were constantly giving some dinner parties and consequently meeting a great many more people. My wife even spoke of having me appointed lieutenant of my company. She exclaimed one day as if she were inspired, "People who come to dinner at our house must say, 'How do they give dinners like this? They must be hard-up, judging by their furniture.' You must admit, my dear, that our furniture no longer matches the position you have reached in the world." I made some resistance, naturally, but in the end, that year, in fact, it was not two thousand francs but seven or eight that went into furniture. It is true that my father-in-law who garnered about sixty per cent profit in our business made a gift of three thousand francs to his only daughter. I forgot to say that in order to have an apartment worthy of our furniture we moved into the second floor of my father-in-law's house. We gave a house-warming in stunning good taste.

It was a year and a half later that I was so unfortunate as to lose my wife. Since I had no children, I thought of returning to the colonies. Of course my father-in-law knew this, and he began to love me with a passion. One fine day, to console me a little, he said, he had presented to me a signed contract which allowed me half the profits as a reward for my hard work. A mutual friend of ours told me that I would be a monster if I abandoned this unhappy father in his grief. I did not answer at once for fear I would be taken for a monster. This good old man was concerned only with his health, which, it is true, was very feeble. He had not felt any sorrow whatever at the loss of his daughter.

We had reached this point when they began to talk up a second marriage to me, and it was these ideas I turned over in my mind all one night, sitting in my chair before the guardhouse of Chateau d'Eau. I weighed, I analyzed every eventuality. I asked myself very seriously, "At the time we were buying new furniture and changing from mahogany to rosewood, was I happy?"

As the reader foresees, the upshot was that, less than a year after my wife's death (to whom I had been a good husband as she had made me an excellent wife), I discovered one thing that made me terribly ashamed at first. This was that, except for the first moment of anguish, which was terrible, I was happier alone. I was so ashamed of this discovery that I became a louse for the first time. I turned into a hypocrite; and two days later I declared to my father-in-law, in a tone that approached the tragic, that I would preserve an eternal fidelity to the adorable wife heaven had snatched from me.

"In that case," he replied with an air of great tranquillity, "we will have to fire Augustine with a present of fifty crowns and get a housekeeper who understands domestic affairs a little better. Saturdays when she puts clean sheets on my bed, they are always damp."

And not a word about his daughter. I nearly burst out laughing at my own silliness which banished my sorrow entirely.

We hired a housekeeper who had worked for a peer of France, and I looked after my father-in-law. Nothing could be easier. I personally verified the state of dryness of the sheets when they were put on his bed.

The good old man was aware of my solicitude and embraced me, weeping. "Promise me never to abandon your wife's unhappy father." I promised, and he insisted on drawing up a deed which not only gave me the right to half the profits but in case he died before me, I could if I wished take possession of the warehouse, whatever was in the till, and all the business except for the sum of one hundred thousand francs payable to a person named in his will.

"And that person will be you, my dear Philip," he often told me fondly, but I didn't believe a word of it. I had often made deals which were too risky to suit him, and I had been obliged to force his consent a little, something the vanity of a Parisian could not forgive. But by this time I had an aim in life. I liked money, and for nearly two years I had had a taste for it. "I'll nurse my father-in-law along," I thought, "so that he can't get along without me, but I am rich. If he dies, I'll sell the business and go back to the colonies. I haven't enough intelligence to spread it over every little action of the day as you have to do in Paris." It looked as if I were going to get very rich. Since I didn't care at all for business in general or hardware in particular, I always behaved with perfect *sang-froid.*

Now that my father had heard that I was the best in my line of work, he began to have some consideration for me, and if I had wanted to push myself into the higher ranks of the National Guard, as I well could have, he would have spoken to me respectfully. But this sort of thing never entered my head. I ask nothing of men, father or anyone, except that they leave me in peace, and perhaps I would have ended by establishing myself in the colonies, where, I find, men are much more philosophical. To have to wear a straw hat and a linen jacket nine months of the year is a great protection against the conceited foolishness which is the sin of our time. It could be said that naturalness and simplicity of costume influences actions. Besides, I believe happiness is contagious, and I have found that a slave is a thousand times happier than a peasant in Picardy. He is fed, clothed, and cared for when he is sick. He hasn't a care in the world and he dances every evening with his love. It is true that this happiness will cease the day Europeans teach him he is unhappy. I would not, myself, retard their emancipation by one minute. I am even a little sorry for the preceding phrase. Regard it as unsaid, O reader. I do not mean to tell you that a life habitually spent among slaves has made me at all unhappy. Here, as with so many other things, I think that what commonly passes for truth is utterly false.

But I only write these things. If I said them, I would be disgraced in the eyes of my confrères, the money men. They regard me very highly. They think I am a fine fellow, only a little stupid. If I showed that I had any ideas and talked about those ideas, I would be a horrible Jacobin to them, an enemy of the present government, etc.

This notion which is still barely fixed in my mind of going to end my days in Martinique or at least to spend there the eight or ten years still left me before old age sets in prompted me to make some comparisons.

A week ago, I said to myself, "I am going to leave France, perhaps forever, and I don't know her."

I see that I have forgotten to say that, two years after my marriage, a bankrupt whom we put on trial in Leghorn and whose dividend was settled by bills on Vienna, gave me the chance to see Italy, Austria, and Switzerland without my wife's being able to tax me with idle curiosity.

In Italy at this time I bought some pictures. A taste for the arts which at first was only a way of consoling myself, actually the only one I could afford, soon took possession of a heart that long had known no other emotions than the deepest sorrow. I believed that if I let myself sink unchecked into grief, a certain lady would find me only a gloomy old man if fate ever permitted us to see each other again. This idea changed my whole being.

I understood my strict duty. It was to take the place of the daughter he had lost with my wife's old father. Now M. R——, brought up to be a businessman, had no other happiness in life except buying and selling. We had to keep the business going, then, and fate, having refused me happiness of spirit, persisted in giving me a fortune. I had no children. When it was no longer necessary for me to take care of him, I thought I might find some pleasure in spending a year or two in those lovely regions where once I had found a youth so gay and so free from care.

"But, see here," I said to myself, "am I going to leave Europe, perhaps forever, without really knowing France?" I had given it only the hasty glances of a traveling salesman. Why couldn't I travel now and look around me? But I was by no means master of my time. The great age of my father-in-law filled him with a nervous timidity that made him unhappy whenever I was not near him to prove to him that our speculations were going well.

My father, seeing me rich, was happy. He was a member of the Chamber of Deputies the last fifteen years of his life, and he left me some small parcels of land worth one hundred fifty thousand francs, encumbered with eighty thousand francs debt. He was a hard, honest man who gloried in his poverty.

Memoirs of a Tourist

Verrières, Near Sceaux

I DO NOT SAY "I" out of any egotism. It is only that there is no other way of telling things quickly. I am a merchant. While traveling in hardware through the provinces, I took the notion of writing a journal.

There are hardly any *Travels in France*, and that is what encourages me to have this one printed. I see the provinces for a few months, and I write a book, but I don't dare talk about Paris where I have lived for twenty years. To know that city demands a lifetime of study, and it takes a pretty hard head to keep from concealing realities because they might be out of fashion, which in this country more than ever before lays down all truths.

In Paris you are assailed by ready-made ideas on every subject. You might say that willy-nilly they want to save us the trouble of thinking and leave us only the pleasure of talking well. In the provinces, unfortunately, it is just the opposite. You pass a charming spot or some ruins that are a striking expression of the Middle Ages. Well, you can't find anyone to tell you ahead of time that there is anything there worth seeing. Your provincial, if his countryside has some reputation for beauty, brags about it in terms that are equally exaggerated and devoid of ideas—in fact, poor copies of Chateaubriand's pomposity. Or, on the other hand, if the newspapers have not warned him that he has a fascinating landscape a hundred yards from his country house, he will tell you when you ask if there is anything worth seeing in his neighborhood, "Ah, Monsieur, how easy it would be to cut an income of a hundred thousand francs out of woods full of timber like that!"

Fontainebleau, April 10, 1837

At last I am on my way. I am taking my time in a fine open carriage I bought second-hand. My only company is the faithful Joseph who with great respect asks permission to speak to me and makes me impatient with him. From Verriéres, where there are some pretty woods, to Essones, I have thought only about myself and even then in the dullest way. If I happen to travel in a carriage of my own another time, I shall take a servant who doesn't know French.

I am getting over some frightfully ugly country. Long grey dull paths run to the horizon. In the foreground, absence of any fertility, trees stunted and cut to the quick for kindling wood, peasants poorly dressed in blue cloth, and it's cold. Moreover, this is what we call *La Belle France!* I am reduced to telling myself, "She is morally beautiful. She has astonished the world with her victories. This is the one country of the universe where men make one another the least unhappy by their mutual activities," but I must admit, at the risk of shocking the reader, that nature has not placed a very lively source of happiness in the souls of the north of France.

The wise government of a king who is a superior man does not permit the rich to be insolent to the poor as in England or the impertinence and pretensions of the priests as in the days of Charles X. So I said to myself when I saw Essones before me, "Maybe this is the one town in the world where the government does the least harm to the governed and best guarantees safety on the highways and justice when they take a notion to bicker among themselves. Further, the government amuses them with the National Guard and its tall fur hats."

The tone of these half yokels–half bourgeois whose conversation I overhear along the road is cold and reasonable. It has that touch of joking malice that shows they have never had any great sorrows or deep feelings. This scoffing tone does not exist in Italy at all. Instead, there is the fierce silence of passion, a language full of images, and the jokes are bitter.

At Essones I stopped for a quarter of an hour at the home of one of our firm's representatives to verify this observation. He thought I stopped to show him I was driving a carriage this trip. He gave me some excellent beer and talked to me seriously about the municipal elections. Climbing back into my carriage, I wondered whether the practice of having elections, which really begins in France only this year, is going to force us to court the lowest class of people as in America. If so, I shall become an aristocrat very quickly. I don't want to pay court to anyone but still less to the People than to a Minister of State.

I recall that in the Middle Ages women's breasts were not in fashion. Those who were so unfortunate as to have them wore corsets that pressed them down and concealed them as much as possible. The reader may find this recollection somewhat indecorous. I don't take this tone because I am affected and want to show my wit, God forbid, but I do claim some freedom of language. I have tried to think of a paraphrase for twenty seconds, and I haven't found one that's clear. If this freedom puts the reader's back up, I invite him to shut the book. As I am dull and stand-offish in my warehouse with my colleagues, the money men, so I intend to be simple and natural evenings when I write in this journal. If I should lie the least bit, the pleasure would fly away, and I would not write any more. What a pity!

Our rash and wayward gaeity, our French wit—will they be crushed and destroyed by our having to butter up uncouth and bigoted mechanics as they do in Philadelphia? Will democracy gain this triumph over our nature?

The common people are superior to the well bred only in spiritual crises, when they are capable of generous passions. Too often the upper classes show their self-conceit by acting Robert-Macaire.* What has become, they say, of the great personages of the Revolution who did not know how to make money?

If the government instead of [discouraging?] mediocre and worn-out people allows anyone who feels a talent for eloquence to gather into a chapel all those who are bored and have no money to go to the theater, soon we will be as morose and bigoted as they are in New York. What am I saying? Twenty times more. It is our privilege to push everything to excess. For polite conversation in Edinburgh, young ladies speak to young men only about the merits of this or that preacher and quote bits of his sermons. That is why I love the Jesuits whom I hated so much under Charles X. Isn't the greatest crime against any people to deprive them of their gaiety every evening?

I shall not live to see our genial France so degraded. This triumph will hardly come before 1860. But what a pity it is for the country of Marot, Montaigne, and Rabelais to lose its natural piquant spirit, wanton, critical, spontaneous, the friend of gallantry and imprudence! Already it is hard to find in society, and in Paris it takes refuge among the street urchins. Good Lord, are we going to turn into Genevans?

It was at Essones that Napoleon was betrayed in 1814.

Before reaching Fontainebleau there is one place, only one, where the countryside is worth looking at. It is the moment when all at once you see the Seine winding two hundred feet below the road. The traveler is on a wooded slope forming the valley at the left, but it is too bad that there are none of those venerable elms, two hundred years old, as in England. This mis-

* A figure taken from a French comedy, Robert-Macaire was embellished, enlarged upon, and immortalized in the lithographs of Daumier, who used him to inflict all kinds of satire on the foibles of the *Juste Milieu.* He was a fancy-talking swindler, promoter, and crook. Thackeray devotes most of an essay to him in *Paris Sketches.*—Tr.

fortune which destroys any depth of feeling the countryside may give is general in France. Whenever a peasant sees a big tree, he thinks of selling it for six louis.

The road from Paris to Essones was filled this morning with several hundred soldiers wearing red trousers, marching in twos, threes, and fours, or resting stretched out under the trees. It made me angry. It was despicable to see them straggling along like lost sheep. What a thing for Frenchmen to do who are already so slovenly! Twenty Cossacks would have routed the whole battalion, which was on its way to serve as guards for the court during the marriage of the Duke of Orleans.

A little before Essones I met the vanguard of the battalion which had halted to rally part of the command and enter the town with some decency. At the sound of the drum, I saw the young girls of the town come running out of doors, beside themselves with joy. The young men gathered in clumps in the middle of the street. Everyone watched the battalion form up at the end of the street toward Paris and, since the road was inordinately wide, everyone could see very well. I was reminded of the tune of Grétry:

> Nothing is so pleasing in girls' eyes
> As the courage of the warriors!

This is wonderfully true in France. The women love courage that is foolish, adventurous, not the high-minded, tranquil bravery of a Turenne or a Marshal Davoust. Anything profound is neither understood nor admired in France. Napoleon knew this well; hence his affectations, his comic airs which would have ruined him before an Italian public.

Dined very well in Fontainebleau at the Hotel de la Ville de Lyon. It is a snug hotel (calm, quiet, full of engaging faces) like Box Hill near London.

I went to the chateau at the end of the Rue Royale and found it shut. Very simple—they were busy with preparations for the wedding. But I had made my inspection of Fontainebleau some time before. Then an employee gave me the chance to cast a friendly glance at the Court of the White Horse, which takes its name from a plaster model of the horse of Marcus Aurelius which Catherine de Medici had placed there. (The original is in the Capitol at Rome.) At heart an Italian princess always loves the fine arts. This plaster model was not removed until 1626. An Italian, Sebastiano Serlio of Bologna, designed and built this courtyard in 1529.

I ran into some hussars of the Fourth, the model regiment. The hussars are very proud because they are the only French soldiers who may wear sky-blue trousers with red dolmans. All honor to the brass who know how to give such infinite value to such little things! I saw a fractious horse being shod. A hussar fascinated him with a glance and held him motionless. A hussar can saddle his horse, accouter himself, and make the sparks fly in two minutes.

Since I couldn't go into the chateau, I asked for some post-horses. I would have liked to see certain paintings of Primaticcio's which they say are very well restored—that is a fine word. How is our starchy and mannered taste going to be able to make the simplicity of this good Italian last? Besides, our painters don't know how to do the female figure. Probably I missed nothing but some shrugs.

It is in pamphlets like Voltaire's and, when the writers are sprightly, in the articles in the *Charivari* that we are unbeatable. Even if all the wits in Germany, England, and in Italy to boot should band together, they still could not produce such articles. But to restore a fresco of Primaticcio's! That is another matter. Even the Germans would beat us at this.

The chateau of Fontainebleau is very badly situated in a dip of land. It is like a dictionary of architecture. Everything is there, but nothing is impressive. The rocks of Fontainebleau are ridiculous. What makes them fashionable is that they have been talked up so much. The Parisian who has never seen anything imagines in his astonishment that a mountain two hundred feet high is part of the great chain of the Alps. The forested land is insignificant except when there are trees eighty feet high, and there it is impressive and beautiful. The forest is fifty-five miles long by forty-five wide. Napoleon had seven hundred and fifty miles of road opened here for galloping. He thought the French liked kings who hunted.

I certainly prefer having a prefect of police, who sometimes, it is true, examines my papers, to having to go around armed all the time. My life is pleasanter this way, though I am worth less because of it, I am less a man of heart because of it, and I pale a little in the face of danger.

Montargis, April 11

A PRETTY, INSIGNIFICANT LITTLE TOWN. It has been much beautified since 1814 through being able to enjoy the reforms introduced by Sieyés, Mirabeau, Danton, and other great men whom, among today's pygmies, it is smart to slander. A good supper at the Hotel de la Poste, which is very well furnished. I didn't meet a dishonest postilion all day. I pay fifty sous. Many of them mount a horse badly, which displeases me. I had thought, if the Prussian soldiers, pushed by the Russians, attacked us, the postilions could be conscripted. Before leaving, I went to see the promenade that runs along the banks of the Loing and the Briare canal. It wasn't much.

Neuvy, April 12

I HAVE JUST CROSSED a dreary stretch of country before going down into the Loire valley. I think it is called the Gatinais. After you leave Briare, you go up and down a succession of fertile slopes that all lead toward the Loire. They should at least have placed the road to the river on the embankment.

Memoirs of a Tourist

Cosne, April 12

As I approached the Loire, the trees began to show buds. The countryside loses that look of profound aridity that depressed me in the Gatinais. As I was passing through a big town on the Loire, I grew thirsty. I went looking for water in a stinking café, and it was atrocious. It would be a good idea to buy eight square bottles like the ones that hold Turin liqueur and put them into a compartment under the seat. In this way you would have both wine and water, and you could refill the water bottles at every well.

I slept at Cosne, a filthy town and a filthy inn, but I had to see the factories along the Loire where they make cast-iron anchors. On the walls of these ironworks I saw the flood-marks of the river, and I was surprised to see how high they are.

I saw a suspension bridge over the Loire. The people around here say it is ugly—I don't know why. The French have some ludicrous notions. Maybe the engineer who built the bridge wore his cravat too high, and it made him look conceited, or maybe he wounded the vanity of the small-town bourgeoisie by some other equally grave offense. The wooden roadway over one of the arches of the bridge fell one fine day because one of its supporting piers broke, and three people were drowned. It should have been made of iron from La Roche in Champagne. Perhaps they inadvertently used the brittle iron from Berry. However no one can predict the weaknesses in iron. Suddenly a bar of the best forged iron breaks off sharp. Is it the effect of electricity?

This unfashionable bridge leads to one of the Loire islands. There are so many islands in this river that it's funny. An island ought to be the exception with a well-bred river, but with the Loire it is the rule, so that the river is always divided into two or three branches and lacks water to fill it. This unfortunate bridge leads, then, to a road that crosses a cut-over island that could be charming. It is claimed that many people in the neighborhood are angry at the bridge. This is the misfortune of the provinces, to get out of temper. In the colonies they do not lose their tempers at all.

To fill out my picture of the town, I went into the shop of a little grocer who sold me some raisins. A peasant with a stupid face and dressed in blue cotton passed over the bridge. The grocer told me that this man ate meat only eight times a year. Ordinarily he lives on cottage cheese. During the heavy labor of the harvest, the peasants take the liberty of drinking *piquette.* This potion is made by pouring water over the grape-skins as they leave the press, and we say we are better than Belgium or Scotland! The negroes in the colonies are happier. They are well fed and dance with their girls every evening. Such frugal peasants as these ought to be glad to get into the army, but they aren't at all. Their morale is the same as their physiques. The puniest are the most wretched when they draw a bad number, but, at the end of six months, they are singing in camp.

Memoirs of a Tourist

La Charité, April 13

I WAS PASSING THROUGH the little town of La Charité at a fast trot, when, to punish me for having thought too long this morning about the diseases of iron, the axletree of my carriage broke clean. It was my own fault. I had promised myself that if I ever had a carriage of my own, I would personally superintend the forging of a fine axletree made out of six bars of soft iron from Fourvoirie.

I examined the grain of the iron in my axletree. Apparently it had seen a great deal of use, for it had become coarse. I weighed the character of the blacksmith, and he pleased me. Without saying anything, I sent out for four bottles of wine, one for each of the workmen. This got me their good will, I could tell by their eyes. In one moment I was the boss.

The great and fundamental difference between Paris and a little town like La Charité is that in Paris they read about everything in the newspapers, while in La Charité the bourgeois sees with his own eyes and examines with the deepest curiosity everything that happens in the town. In Paris, if a crowd has gathered at the end of the street, my first thought is that they will get my white trousers dirty and so make me go back into my house. If I see one slightly civilized person, I find out the cause of all the racket. "It is a thief," I am told, "who has just jumped out of a window with a clock in his arms."

"That's good," I say to myself. "Tomorrow I will read all about it in the *Gazette*."

One of the great misfortunes of Paris, one of the great misfortunes of civilization, one of the most serious obstacles to the increase of happiness among men is *uniformity of opinion*. This uniformity has advantages only on the political side. It harms the arts and letters. Journalism is excellent. It is necessary to political interests, but it poisons literature and the fine arts by its charlatanism. As soon as a man made great by the newspapers dies, his fame dies with him. In towns not subject to journalism, Milan, for instance, everyone goes to see the picture before reading the article about it, and the journalist had better take care not to be ridiculous when he writes about a picture on which everyone has an opinion. It is because newspapers are *politically* necessary in big cities that this gloomy compulsion toward *phoniness* arises, *the one and only religion of the nineteenth century.*

What decent man does not admit that he is embarrassed because he has to be a phony to get ahead? This comedy of necessity glazes the social habits of Parisians and gives them I don't know how much falseness and even wickedness. There simplicity undoes a man. Those who are clever fancy that a simple man hasn't enough brains to play even a little bit of the necessary comedy.

Yes, necessary. You like to hold your head up, and so you appear on the boulevard with too high a cravat, and everyone says you are insolent. It is impossible to uproot this truth. But, politically speaking, our liberty has no other guaranty except the press. It is by the mechanism I have just pointed out that liberty will kill, perhaps, literature and the arts. We are falling into the class of boors and I can see three or four causes for this fall. Are we going to break our necks?

Nevers, April 14

I ARRIVED AT NEVERS as early as eight in the morning. It is only fifteen miles from La Charité, but the people with whom I do business are in the country, and I am somewhat in the same situation as I was yesterday at La Charité; that is, I have to kill time although I have some important business to do here and in the ironworks nearby.

Nevers is built on a hill in the form of an amphitheater at the confluence of the Loire and the Niévre. The cathedral and the chateau are at the top of the hill, and the streets go down it.

As ugly as they may be otherwise, this gives the houses an air, at least.

Always anxious to learn, I luckily found Caesar's *Commentaries* at the bookseller's. Caesar set up the treasury of his army at Nevers (Noviodunum). Caesar's is the only book you would have to take along, traveling in France. He refreshes the imagination when it is fatigued and irritated by the outlandish arguments that occur on all sides and which you have to pay attention to. His noble simplicity is a perfect contrast to all the contorted civilities that abound in the provinces.

I went to see the royal cannon foundry which turns out two hundred and thirty cannon a year. I went up to the town library, where I hoped to find some extensive relics from the Roman period. There was nothing there that was worth anything.

St. Stephen's church rather pleased me. One must go down several steps to get inside. It was built in 1063. Fashion has not yet destroyed all the souvenirs of ancient art. This is a Romanesque church, and the nave is wide compared to its length. What moved me deeply and proved to me that I do not have true Christian taste is that the narrower the nave of a church and the more closely it is shut in by high pillars, the more it represents unhappiness.

St. Stephen's is a Latin cross. Square pillars with an engaged column on each face divide it into three naves. The distinctive characteristic of Romanesque buildings, or those erected by timid architects who still kept some memory of Roman monuments, is solidity. The choir is enclosed by round pillars joined by round archways. The round arch occurs everywhere and in my opinion banishes any idea of hell and unhappiness. Does the reader feel this way?

In the upper part of the choir there are some quite barbaric columns which have capitals almost as long as the shafts. The transepts, the crossbars of the crucifix, are separated from the nave by a wall that touches the vault, but it is opened at the bottom by a large arcade surmounted by five smaller ones.

Nivernais, April 18

The beautiful rose-windows, so remarkable in St. Ouen at Rouen, were still, when this church was built, only a very small bull's eye.

There is nothing poorer than the facade and ornamentation of St. Stephen's.

There are some curious sculptures at Holy Savior's; another Romanesque basilica miserably transformed today. The top is now a hayloft and the ground floor a shop where they sell wagons. Provincials paint all their buildings over with a dreary whitewash the color of *café-au-lait* like Notre Dame, St. Sulpice, and others in Paris. If you take a cane and hit the whitewash of Holy Savior's a few whacks, it will scale off, and you can see that the walls and the shafts of the columns were originally covered with a thick coat of brilliant red. Some of the capitals were painted a beautiful green and in certain places gilded. Above the choir is a Gothic steeple, built much later than the church.

St. Genest's, adjoining Holy Savior's, has been turned into a brewery. This church which is in the form of a Greek cross with the four branches equal shows the transition from the round to the pointed arch. Some of its details are elegant. I should place it at the end of the twelfth century.

Nivernais, April 18

In one of the little towns I have just passed through, I found an old man with a great reputation as a wit. He is the eagle of the district. I had the pleasure of dining with him, and, since I am a Parisian and, moreover, a Parisian traveling post, he condescended to tell me the remark that brought him so much fame. Listen to something very dull.

In 1815 or 1820, Robertson, the physician, conjuror, and inventor of the "phantasmagoria" gave a soirée in this old gentleman's town. In the middle of his lecture, he took up in a tragic manner a cup of colored glass. "This cup, gentlemen," he said to the spectators, "brings back memories of a time very sweet and very bitter to me. By means of my science, this cup that you see, this simple cup, contains all that remains on earth of my dear third wife. After her decease I had her carried to a funeral pyre where she was burned in the ancient manner. Through my science, I have vitrified the ashes, and every time I drink from this cup, I think with pity of my dear third wife."

"Hey, Monsieur, did you bottle the first two?" cried M. de C——.

There is the remark, the poor remark, the glorious remark that changed his life. The applause was tremendous. Since the great day, he raises his voice, cuts through all questions, and, in his presence, no one dares doubt anything he puts forward.

If your provincial is excessively timid, it is because he is excessively conceited. If a man passes him on a road twenty paces away, he believes that this man is busy watching only him, and if by any chance this man laughs, he swears eternal hatred for him.

I give up. No matter what style I employ, what striking turn of phrase I may invent, I shall never be able to give any idea of the triviality of provincial conversations, of the numberless petty things that make up the life of even the most elegant provincial gentleman. You refuse to believe that reasonable beings could interest themselves in such things, but then, one day, you perceive the abysmal boredom of the provinces, and you understand it all immediately.

A sensible woman of my acquaintance was traveling from Nevers to Orleans, and one of her trunks was only half full. She was afraid that the clothing she had packed in it would be disarranged by the jostling. I suggested the brilliant idea of packing some waste paper in the corners. "Stop right there," her husband said to me. "They will laugh at us in Orleans. 'Look,' they will say, 'These people didn't figure out how many trunks they needed for their things, and here they are bringing us scraps of waste paper!' "

Since 1815 and especially since 1830, there has been no

more society. Each family lives isolated in its house like Crusoe on his island. A town is a collection of anchorite cells. After a year of this kind of life even the most united families find they have long since talked themselves out. Some poor woman fakes astonishment and smiles for the hundred-and-fortieth time at the story of the frock coat stolen off some friend's bed, which her husband gets ready to tell to a stranger.

Nivernais, April 19

OPEN THE ROYAL ALMANACH FOR 1829, and you will see that the nobility occupied all the positions [in the government]. Now they live in the country, consume only two-thirds of their revenues, and improve their estates. It is a pleasure to meet them. In their houses you find an air of exquisite politeness you would look for in vain elsewhere, especially among the newly rich. But if the form of their conversation is light and pleasant, it ends gloomily, for at bottom they are somewhat ill-tempered.

In the position they have made for themselves since 1830, the most agreeable men in France see life pass them by, but they do not live it. The young men are not fighting at Constantine, the men of fifty are not administering prefectures, and France loses; for many of them know the laws and regulations very well, and they all keep pleasant salons and are not boorish unless they want to be. For a well-born man, to be impolite is like speaking a foreign language which he has had to learn and which he never speaks with ease. With what rare facility do people in high places speak that language today!

Here follows a *historic* dialogue between the division chief of a large prefecture and a country mayor, which M. de N—— told me; but in his character as a man of wit, he has doubtless embellished it:

DIVISION CHIEF: Well, Mr. Mayor, you are going away happy.

MAYOR: This time, at least, the business of my commune is done. It took some trouble, though.

DIVISION CHIEF: You might very well send me something.

MAYOR (with a more eager politeness): Sir, I shall take the greatest care in discharging the commissions you have laid on me.

CHIEF: You don't understand, Monsieur. Isn't your commune famous for its cheeses? Send me two dozen.

The Mayor was indignant. He had nothing better to do when he returned to his little town than to repeat this dialogue and to hurl condemnation at corruption, the effrontery of clerks, etc. The sensible men of the neighborhood spoke among themselves. "But what does it mean, except that we pay two hundred and forty francs? After all, we do a lot of business at P——." The matter was placed in deliberation. They wrote out the proceedings on a loose sheet of paper and decided not only to send the cheeses but also to pay the freight on them. The total expense came to two hundred and fifty-two francs, including the box.

Nivernais, April 20

Here is a story that was told this evening at a fine chateau. It is a grisly experience that overtook a M. Blanc, one of the notaries of the locality, an honest man, undoubtedly, but one who is always dying for fear of compromising himself.

One evening, eight or ten months before, he was called in by a rich country landowner who had fallen ill in town with pneumonia while he was visiting his daughter, a woman of the greatest piety. The sick man had just lost his power of speech. In such cases the law allows a man to manifest his last will by the use of signs, but there must be two notaries present, so M. Blanc had brought a colleague with him. After they had been made to wait for some time, these gentlemen were taken into a terribly overheated little room, kept that way, they were told, to keep the sick man from coughing. What's more, the room was badly lighted.

M. Blanc approached the patient and found him very pale. There was a strong odor over the bed, which was placed in a sunken alcove and almost hidden from sight by full curtains. The notaries sat down at a small table not over two steps from the bed.

They asked the sick man if he wished to make his will. The sick man lowered his chin on the coverlet and made a sign, yes. They asked if he wished to give one-third of his fortune unencumbered to his son, and he made no move at all. When they asked if he wished to give his third to his daughter, he made the sign, yes, twice repeated. Just then a house dog came into the room and started to bark furiously. He threw himself against the notaries' legs trying to get at the bed. They quickly drove the dog out. The will was read to the dying man, who by many repeated noddings indicated that he approved everything.

The will finished, the notaries rose to go away. Notary Blanc's handkerchief had fallen to the floor when the dog burst in. He stooped to pick it up, and, as he did this, he saw very clearly under the bed the legs of a man without shoes. He was greatly astonished, but he went out with his colleague just the same. However, when he reached the foot of the stairs, he told him what he had seen. Great embarrassment for these poor fellows. The sick man's daughter, whose home they were leaving, was a superior woman, highly regarded in the town. They felt they would have to go back upstairs, but how were they to explain why?

"But, my dear colleague," said the second notary to M. Blanc, "what's the connection between the legs of the peasant and our drawing up of the will?"

These notaries were certainly honest men, but they were horribly afraid of offending the dying man's daughter, who was the curé's niece and president of two or three societies devoted to good works.

After an anguished conversation, they resolved nevertheless to go back up the stairs. They were received with marked astonishment, and this increased their embarrassment. They didn't very well know how to explain their return, and at last the second notary asked how the sick man was. The notaries were taken to the door of the room and shown the closed curtains. Making his will had tired the sick man. They were given many details of the symptoms of the illness which had increased since midnight, and while this talk was going on, they were conducted gently toward the door. The poor notaries, finding nothing to say, went down the stairs a second time, but they were hardly a hundred yards from the house when M. Blanc said to his partner, "We have got ourselves into a peck of trouble here, but if we don't take sides, we will reproach ourselves to the end of our days. The son is away, and they're going to skin him out of a capital of eighty thousand francs."

"But we'll see our efforts come to nothing," said the second notary. "If this woman decides to persecute us, she'll give us the reputation of shysters."

However, the more time passed, the sharper became their remorse, and at last the notaries were so worried that they had the courage to climb the stairs again.

It turned out they had been spied on from a window. This time they were received by the sick man's daughter herself, a woman of thirty-five, famous for her virtue and one of the great talkers of the neighborhood. She took the notaries in hand, cut them off when they tried to explain, and made herself mistress of the conversation. When they tried to override her, she dissolved in tears and began to hold forth on the virtues of the excellent father she was threatened with losing.

After great trouble the notaries succeeded in getting another look into the dying man's room. M. Blanc stooped down. "What are you looking for?" tartly asked the woman so renowned for her great virtue. From the moment she spoke so angrily, the notaries saw with horror the full extent of the danger they were rushing into. They stood abashed. They took fright and let themselves be shown out after a scene lasting three-quarters of an hour. But they were barely in the street when M. Blanc said to his colleague, "She showed us the door just like schoolboys."

"But, good God, if this bitch starts to persecute us, we are ruined men," said the second notary with tears in his eyes.

"And you think she hasn't noticed why we kept going back up there? In two days the old fellow will be dead if he isn't already. She will be out of danger, and then she will triumph. We'll have her whole clique at our heels, and they'll play every trick in the book on us."

"What enemies we're going to make!" sighed the second notary. "Mme D—— has heavy backing. Only the Liberals will be left for us, and Liberals don't make wills. They haven't a sou, and they're smart fellows."

However, remorse worked so keenly on these two poor honest men that they went to the house of the King's Attorney to ask his advice. At first this wise magistrate feigned not to understand, then he seemed to be as embarrassed as they were and made them repeat their story three times. He claimed that, in as serious a matter as this, when as honored and as honorable a woman as Mme D—— was under suspicion, he could not lawfully act unless she was denounced in writing. The notaries and and the King's Attorney, seated facing each other, were silent at least five minutes. Perhaps the notaries were only asking to be shown the door.

Meanwhile the Police Commissioner came in, humming to himself. He was a young dandy who had come from Paris only six months before. Almost in spite of everyone he made them tell the story again.

"Why, gentlemen, this is that scene from *The Legatee,*" he said, laughing.

The notaries and the King's Attorney were disconcerted by this excessive levity.

"But perhaps you don't know, sir," said the second notary, trembling all over, "that this woman is Mme D——?"

The dandy did not condescend to reply.

"If the King's Attorney sees fit to give me the authority," he said, "I shall go with these notaries and present myself at the home of this terrible Mme D——. In my presence, M. Blanc will speak of the legs of the man he saw under the bed. I shall ask, 'Why these legs?' and take charge from then on."

So it was done. The woman changed color when she saw the Police Commissioner, who immediately took a commanding tone. He said there were certain crimes, without any doubt, that lead people to the galleys and even to public exhibition in chains and the loss of all civil rights. Mme D—— fainted. Her husband turned up and ended by confessing that his father-in-law had been dead two hours before the notaries' arrival, but he kept saying that the old man had wanted everything to go to his daughter, etc., etc. During this long recital of the old man's goodwill and its causes, of the misbehavior of the son who was a great spendthrift, etc., etc., the son-in-law began to take heart again. The Police Commissioner cut him off short and spoke again of the galleys and the iron collar. At last after a scene briskly played by the dandy who was delighted with his role, the son-in-law begged the notaries in a barely audible voice to give the first draft of the will to him to tear up. The Police Commissioner forced the son-in-law to confess that it was a tenant-farmer of his, who, seeing their grief at the sudden death of the father-in-law (who would certainly have drawn his will in their favor), had the unfortunate notion of crawling under the bed. They had taken two planks out of the bottom of the bed. The bold farmer sat on the floor and with his two hands had easily made the old man's head move.

I am like the reader. I find this grisly anecdote quite long when it is written out. Told, it goes very well. What is important in situations like this is to keep the dog out.

Moulins, April 21

A MAN WITH GOOD SENSE WHO, moreover, has acquired several millions by this same good sense said to me this evening, "The markets are glutted. Too much is being produced. Since you have an Academy of Moral and Political Sciences, why not ask them how you prevent a man who has only a hundred thousand francs from borrowing two hundred thousand?"

I admit that nothing would be more difficult when it is only a question of a private individual. You would be accused of violating the secrets of private life. That I can't accept at all. Inspection would take place at the moment a certain paper fabricated *ad hoc* is sold.

But how much easier it would be to pass a law as soon as a company of capitalists was involved, organized by a charter signed before a notary and properly recorded. Make haste to understand what is happening in the United States and lay down the principle of a law before there come to be what your Robert-Macaire calls vested interests.

The law should go something like this. ARTICLE 1: A company of capitalists may issue stock only for the amount actually held in cash. ARTICLE 2: Each stockholder of the company will be allowed to contest its validity if the company does not conform to ARTICLE 1. ARTICLE 3: The facts will be determined by a special jury chosen by lot from the two hundred landlords and the two hundred merchants most heavily taxed in the department.

There are other provisions for catching up with shares which have been sold through exaggerated representations. Often the scandal of a suit will be enough by itself to intimidate the petty crooks.

Moulins, April 22

MOULINS HAS NOTHING REMARKABLE except the tomb of the Duc de Montmorency whose head Cardinal Richelieu had cut off in 1632. In Toulouse we shall see the little cutlass that had that honor.

The presence of a provincial guide, a low braggart, makes me take the things he shows me with a grain of salt. This is one of the things that convinces me that I am not destined to write a travel book about France, and the only value these memoirs will have is to serve until something better comes along.

All in all, I prefer the provincial who is ignorant of the beauties of his region to the provincial enthusiast. When an inhabitant of Avignon cries up the Fountain of Vaucluse to me, it has the same effect on me as a blabbermouth who comes to talk about a woman I find pleasing and who commends in pompous terms precisely the beauties she has not got and condemns her for the absence of those I never dreamed she had. His praise becomes a hostile pamphlet.

The horror I have for this rude and gabby sort of thing almost made me miss seeing the admirable church of St. Menou, about twelve miles from Moulins. It has some fine columns in imitation of the Corinthian and some large Romanesque parts. It is about to fall down because of the unequal thrust of the arches.

There are some Romanesque sections and some others that date back perhaps to the eighth century in the magnificent church of Souvigny, nearer Moulins, one of the oddest in the province. It was rebuilt in 919 by the Chevalier Aimard. The tombs of the Ducs de Bourbon can be seen there. The nave is Romanesque, the choir Gothic. Some parts are florid Romanesque.

I have just been carried away by writing the words "Romanesque" and "Gothic." May I explain myself?

The Romanesque is the earlier in point of time. It followed after the complete barbarity of the year 1000. It is very solid, very timid, and uses poor materials.

The Gothic style, which followed it when the clergy were even richer and could make the peasants work by paying them with indulgences, seeks first of all to astonish and seem daring.

It supports very high vaults with frail columns. It enlarges the windows excessively and divides them by mullions so thin that the eye can hardly believe in their solidity. It employs the pointed arch more frequently than does the Romanesque.

The Gothic style seeks to surprise the imagination of the faithful *who are in the church*, but on the outside it is not ashamed to surround the building with flying buttresses that support it in all directions; and if the eye were not accustomed to it, it would have the appearance of a ship about to fall apart. It is only all-powerful habit that keeps us from recognizing this ugliness. It prevents us from even seeing the evidence we have learned from infancy to deny.

Here is a little chronological list which I intend to learn by heart so that it will help me to play the role of a savant:

After the year 1000 at the end of the extreme barbarity of the tenth century, the *Romanesque* style. Then:

1050 Ornate or *florid* Romanesque.

1150 to 1220 Transitional period.

1200 Gothic.

1260 Ornate or *florid* Gothic.

1350 The beginning of the *flamboyant* style. (The contours of the decorations—tracery—set on the vertical divisions of the windows resemble a capital S formed by the flame of a burning fagot.)

1500 The transition from the Gothic to the Renaissance. (It is called the style of Louis XII in France.)

1550 The Renaissance well-established.

The eighth century and the beginning of the ninth are distinguished by the *cubic* capital, but this is found only near the banks of the Rhine.

Burgundy, April 26

I HAVE JUST CROSSED a very depressing region. I stopped a few days at the chateau of a friend of mine, M. Ranville, an intelligent man who is getting some woodland ready for sale and consequently is very much interested in getting a certain road built. The Chief Engineer is excellent. Besides, he is the most likeable man in the province. This uncommon engineer is a fine young fellow, very well trained, enthusiastic about his work, who comes to his road with a piece of bread and a book and spends whole mornings there. From the midst of the country, this young engineer has just been sent to the other end of the realm.

My friend Ranville was very angry at this transfer, and he said to me, "This is a ruined countryside!" He was even more enraged against a foreman who stole. I said to him, "Why do you get so worked up? Why the devil do you let your happiness depend on others? It would be less silly to fall in love with a pretty young woman. Then you would have to struggle against the whims of only one person. In this business of the road you have to contend not only against the real interests of about a hundred of these provincials but still more against all the idiocies they think are their interests."

I went with M. Ranville to the sub-prefecture. The Chief Engineer had made an excellent road plan. This plan had been deposited three years before at the sub-prefecture along with a big book of white paper where objections to the plan could be set down. I proceeded to read the objections. They would make anyone die laughing. The Prefect had appointed a commission to pass judgment on them, but, not wanting to offend two members of the General Council of the department who lived in the region, he had put these members on the commission. It should be made clear that in the provinces the General Council is to the Prefect somewhat as the Chamber of Deputies is to the Ministers in Paris. One may jeer at them, but they must be won over.

These two members of the General Council didn't want to offend the voters with whom they had to deal nor their parents. The public who gathered in the local pothouses announced that they were strong against the Chief Engineer's plan which had no other merit except that it was reasonable. He was going to level an abominable hill which the same peasants had cursed for thirty years.

The engineer had made his road go past the last house of one of the villages. They forced him to make it run through the village so that the unlucky road had to make two right-angle turns where it should have gone along the outskirts. I would never finish if I wanted to tell all the absurdities they committed against this great work at that time. Such are the effects of a *pothouse aristocracy*. We are already like America here, obliged to pay court to the most unreasonable part of the population.

Burgundy, April 27

Mme ranville has excellent tea. About eleven o'clock this evening a collation was served. After it everyone left very quickly and went off in their carriages. Eight or ten of us remained, guests of the house and a chateau nearby. We said how gay the old times were, and Ranville went to look for a bottle of Clos-Vougeot, the real stuff and almost unique. Only six bottles were left from that year (1811). We didn't go to bed until about one o'clock. We shared that bottle among the nine of us, and we were very lively; but I was the youngest, and I am thirty-four. At the beginning of the evening all the young fellows were very serious and professed never to find any pleasure in the society of women. Some charming ones had been present, but these gentlemen had gambled all the evening among themselves and left the field free to us old fellows.

I found in my room a volume of Balzac's the *Abbé Birotteau* of Tours. How I admire this author! How well he lists the evils and petty concerns of the provinces! I would prefer a simpler style, but, if he wrote that way, would the provincials buy him? I would think that he writes his novels twice: the first time rationally, and the second time he dresses them up in this beautiful neological style, full of the sufferings of the soul, "it snows in my heart," and other fine things.

Burgundy, April 28

We rode horseback this morning. To divert my poor friend a little, who was crucified by the road which will enable him to exploit his timber, we talked about flirtations, chastity, and the ladies of the provinces.

"Out of six women of the neighborhood," Ranville said with great composure, "there is perhaps one who has had any tender moments of frailty. There is a second who would cry out like the Marquise de Marmontel, 'How fortunate!' But there are four who are worthy of all our admiration." I explain this phenomenon in the same way as chastity in London: if a man pays a visit to any house three times in succession, the whole neighborhood is scandalized, and the poor woman who suffers from it is warned before she falls in love.

Ranville gave me ten examples, the best of which cannot be reported here. They resurrected the scandal of the locality. To this great question, "Is there any passionate love in the best society in Burgundy?" the answer is absolutely negative.

However, the lover of one of these society women either fired a pistol himself or was shot at one night about eleven o'clock when the husband was in the next room. The guess is that the husband, who was very indifferent, did not get up at all. The lover had the sense to hire a sort of gamekeeper who appeared the next morning with a sheepish story of how his gun happened by chance to fall out of his hand, just under Madame's window, and how he, afraid of a reprimand, took to the woods where he spent a wretched night. He had seen wolves coming for him, and his gun was not loaded, etc.

Another one of these ladies had a jealous lawyer for a husband. He always made her travel with him in a wicker carriage. She fell ill at a little inn twenty-five miles from the court where her husband spent all his mornings. She had the courage to stay in bed for six weeks. The lawyer spent all his Sundays at this abominable inn. He brought in famous doctors who, quite naturally as a result of their skill, found the lovely woman gravely ill. Imagine what followed. The lawyer was warned of what was going on by one of his clients who lived nearby. He was very friendly with two Deputies who arranged with the Minister of War to have the officer sent to Algiers, where he was killed. Notice how nothing in the world equals the ignorance and lack of curiosity of some provincial doctors.

In Paris servants live at the top of the house. True love rarely descends below the fifth floor, and then sometimes it jumps out the window. It is perhaps a little less rare in the provinces. It can sometimes be found in the middle classes who are not well-off—among the women, of course, for, since 1830, love is one of the worst disgraces for a young man.

Autun, April 29

In Burgundy as everywhere, the constant subject of young men's jokes is the love-match. They talk all the time about the amount of money they will require from the woman they condescend to marry. One of Ranville's neighbors, a fellow of boisterous habits and a great braggart in front of his dirty hangers-on (the beau of the province), asserted when he was twenty-five that he wouldn't marry any woman who didn't have three hundred thousand francs. At thirty he came down to a hundred and fifty thousand, and just now he has ended by marrying a woman with only eighty thousand.

Young men spend their lives at the café, smoking cigars and talking to each other about schemes to make money. Every scheme has to be sharp and quick. The luck of a certain artillery lieutenant has driven all Frenchmen crazy for at least half a century. This year, Ranville told me, these young men who want to make a fortune without working have begun to talk a great deal about the elections and the railroads which were voted down by the laziness of the Chambre. If a Mirabeau or a Danton rose among them, his eloquence might lead them into the greatest follies.

"Speaking of boredom, what about literature?"

These gentlemen can't understand the feigned unbridled passion of the modern novel, and they understand still less the tender exaltation of novels that drove us mad when we were their age. No one reads *La Nouvelle Heloise* any more or the novels of Mme Cottin or those of Maria-Regina Roche, translated by the Abbé Morellet. Young men's literature in 1837 hardly rises above the *Mémoires* of Mme Dubarry or of Mme de Pompadour, de la Contemperaine, de Fleury, etc., etc., which deal with people who make a lot of money and whose lives sometimes are embellished by nice, licentious parties. They believe in the existence of a Mme de Créquy. Balzac's *Peau de Chagrin* has created a furore. Everything written in a simple style they find cold, and the neologism is the very crown of wit for them. The most distinguished of these young men at the café is reading the *Memorial of St. Helena* and seems to be furious about the Emperor. Hasn't he found out how Napoleon endowed General Marchand with an annuity of eighty thousand francs because he behaved well at Eylau?

At bottom quick fortunes raised by the caprice of a king suit the foolish hopes of these present-day republicans much better than the moderate fortunes they could make for themselves under a well-run government.

Ranville consoled me somewhat when he said, "It is our luck to live in a century when a man who has opinions of his own will not be listened to. What they no longer see at all is that it is the fools, the lazy, and the timid who repeat the fashionable opinions."

What a splendid solitude it would be that would encourage a young man of Semur or Moulins to form his own opinions on five or six subjects! How rare, how distinguished, and, when he spoke, how soberly attended to would be a man who at twenty-five had an opinion of his own under five or six headings!

In Paris distractions are too continuous. Even for a young man of twenty who is so lucky as not to count on any inheritance, how many sources of pleasure there are! How many things besiege his attention every day! Who is the twenty-year-old in Paris who has read the eight volumes of Montesquieu, seeking out and finding the errors in them?

You might think that, running around as I do, I haven't time to see either provincial society or its young men. All these judgments were given me by a man of a deep, sharp intelligence who has lived in this region since 1830. In nearly all the towns where I have stopped briefly—Lyons, Marseilles, Grenoble—I have had glimpses of young men who seemed extremely promising to me. In fact, I think that in 1850 the men of merit will for the most part originate far from Paris. To become a distinguished man, the youth must have at twenty that warmth of heart, that credulity, if you like, that can hardly be found except in the provinces. He must also have instruction which is philosophical and devoid of any falseness, and that is to be found only in the best Parisian colleges. But the faculty of will is more and more lacking in Paris. They don't read the best books seriously: Bayle, Montesquieu, Tocqueville, etc. They read only this modern nonsense and then only to be able to make conversation about every book when it comes out.

I have just written all this to divert myself from a violent fit of anger. On arriving at Autun I found I had lost the keys to all the boots of my calash, and I am writing while Joseph tries to pick the locks with a locksmith. As this operation is not finished, I am going to tell the history of Autun which I studied in M. Ranville's library.

Everyone knows that here we are in the famous Bibractus, capital of the country of the Aedui, whom Pomponius Mela calls the most illustrious of the Celts (or Gauls) and of whom

Caesar speaks so often.* Caesar, who attacked the Gauls with a bravery equal to their own and the superior intelligence of more advanced civilization, sought to divide these infant peoples. He aroused the private jealousies of the inhabitants of Autun, drew them over to his side which was that of the foreigner, and these poor people of Bibractus, pushed by the fatal pleasure of humiliating the Allobrogi and the Arverni, joined with the Romans. As a reward for this folly, they received the title of brothers and allies of the Roman people.

They owned the territory between the Loire and the Saone, and, to Caesar's good fortune, they were very rich. The people of Autun, having lost their liberty, debased themselves so far as to flatter Augustus and to give their town the Latin name of *Augustodunum*. Under Constantine they changed the name again, but the one it now bears is an abbreviation and an eternal reminder of their first flattery of the foreign tyrant. Endowed with such an ambitious spirit, the town made its fortune and became one of the most beautiful and important cities of Gaul. Tacitus tells how they sent young Gauls there as early as the reign of Tiberius to have them instructed in Greek and Latin literature. Its splendor was still unimpaired three hundred years later under Constantine. It had been horribly burned and pillaged at the end of the third century when the Bagaudes revolted, but Constantine repaired it.

Attila seized it a hundred and fifty years later and after the custom of his people destroyed everything that bore the least appearance of civilization. The Burgundians and the Huns wrangled among the ruins of Autun. Finally Rollo and his Normans appeared and completed the destruction of the little that was left.

* Caesar VI, XII, *et passim.* To be thought learned in 1837, one must believe that the Celts came from Asia and had themselves conquered the Gauls. It is obvious, say the Germans, that the Romans came from India.—H. B.

In spite of so many misfortunes Autun is one of the most curious cities in France. Its citizens have many fine qualities, but they certainly care nothing for antiquities. As late as 1762 they built a seminary out of the stones of their amphitheater. In 1788 they used what remained to repair the church of St. Martin, destroyed a short time ago. The amphitheater was built perhaps under Vespasian.

Autun is perched on the brink of a steep hill near a stream called the Arroux at the foot of three hills that conceal it from the east and south. When I arrived in Autun, I had the keen pleasure of walking on the stones of a Roman road. The street is steep, and horses can hardly stand up on these blocks of granite.

Autun, May 1

THE EVENINGS, which are so pleasant in Paris, are the hard part of travel, especially if you are so unlucky as not to like café life or to find happiness at the bottom of a champagne bottle. I read Caesar, and I am going to copy out what Napoleon said of this great man. It seems very discerning to me.

Caesar, buried under debts in Rome, a man of the most distinguished family, and famous as a youth for his boldness and knavery, began the war with six legions. The number was later increased to twelve. If I am not mistaken, a legion was composed of five thousand, five hundred soldiers of all arms.

"He made eight campaigns among the Gauls," Napoleon says, "and during these, two invasions of England and two forays on the right bank of the Rhine. He fought nine great battles in Germany, laid three great sieges, and reduced five hundred miles of country to a Roman province. Through the usual taxes this enriched his treasury by eight hundred millions" and gave him the means of buying all the citizens of Rome who were for sale, that is, the immense majority.

In the less than six years the war lasted, Caesar reduced or took by assault more than eight hundred towns. He subjugated three hundred tribes. In his different battles he defeated three million enemies, a third of them killed on the field of battle, another third enslaved. "If Caesar's glory were founded only on the Gallic Wars," Napoleon says, "it would be questionable."

The Gauls were full of fire and showed an astonishing bravery, but, divided as they were into so many tribes, they hated one another. A town would go full tilt to war against a neighbor merely out of jealousy. Lively and irascible, fond of anger, they rarely listened to the voice of prudence.

Their ignorance of all discipline, their dissensions, their scorn for military science, the inferiority of their means of attack and defense, their habit of never profiting by a victory, the rivalries of their chiefs as hot-headed as they were valiant, delivered them over successively to an enemy as brave as themselves and at the same time abler and more persevering.

Only one Gaul understood the advantages of unity. This was Vercingetorix, the young chief of the Auvergnats. Florus says, "On feast days as well as council days when the Gauls gathered in crowds in their sacred woods, his speeches, full of a fierce patriotism, exhorted them to reconquer their freedom."

Caesar understood the danger. He was at Ravenna, busy raising troops. He crossed the Alps, which were still covered with snow. He had with him only some light-armed troops. He assembled his legions in the twinkling of an eye and appeared at the head of an army in the middle of Gaul before the Gauls believed he had crossed their frontiers. He laid two memorable sieges and forced the Gallic chief to come and beg mercy of him. Vercingetorix appeared as a suppliant in the Roman camp. He threw his horse's harness and his arms at Caesar's feet. "Brave man," he said to him, "you have conquered."

Nowadays they think they can write history by exaggerating the nuances they find in the old writers, and they have been so bold as to write, "The name of Vercingetorix was never pronounced in Rome but with terror." Some historian of the same stripe, seeking the same kind of fame, will say, two thousand years from now when he is speaking of the nineteenth century, that the very name of Abd-el-Kader made Parisians go pale.

The use of trickery was very often enough for Caesar against these Gauls, so brave but so naive, who imagined that mere courage sufficed to win victories. To snares and betrayals their savage vanity revealed them willing to oppose only their invincible bravery. This kind of enemy seemed to be made to procure glory wantonly for a Roman general who was a past master of all deceit.

Caesar who wanted above all to make a big name in Rome, employed against the simple Gauls an astonishing profusion of bold and magnanimous actions. He went bare-headed ordinarily, with only one soldier behind him to carry his sword. He made a hundred miles a day when he had to, swimming alone across any rivers he came to or crossing them on leather bottles filled with air, and often he arrived before his couriers. Like Hannibal he always marched at the head of his legions, oftenest on foot, bareheaded in spite of the sun and rain. He kept a frugal table, and this roué, worthy of our own century, had a slave beaten with sticks before his soldiers for serving him better bread than the army got.

He slept in a carriage and had himself waked at all hours to visit a camp or siege operations. He was always surrounded by secretaries, and when he had no more military orders to dictate, he composed literary works. Thus, when he was crossing the Alps from Lombardy into Gaul, he dictated *A Treatise on Analogy*. He composed his *Anti-Cato* some time before the battle of Munda, where they say he nearly gave up his role when he saw victory about to escape him. Suetonius tells us that he wrote a poem called *The Journey* in the twenty-four days consumed by his expedition into Spain.

Here are some details. The Gauls were then very rich, and

Caesar carried off everything they had, but after paying off his private debts, which came to thirty-eight million francs, they say, he formed the habit of distributing among his soldiers all the money he amassed. In this way, little by little, the soldiers of the Republic became the soldiers of Caesar.

Here is the portrait left us by Suetonius in the manner of Tallemant des Reaux, a very low style. Caesar had a delicate white skin. He was subject to frequent headaches and even to attacks of epilepsy. He had a frail body that did not show its strength. He was an excellent horseman, and he thought it useful to parade his skill before his soldiers. On his marches he liked to put his horse into a fast gallop and ride with his hands clasped behind his back.

In each man Caesar valued only the quality that made him useful. He wanted courage and bodily strength in his soldiers, and he troubled himself little about their morals. After a victory he allowed them unbridled license, but when the enemy approached, they recovered themselves at once with the strictest discipline. He rudely upbraided any soldier who pretended to guess at his plans, and he kept them ignorant of the roads they were to take and the battles they were to fight. He wished that at all times, in all places, they would be equally ready for combat or marching. By these means and others of the same kind, Caesar succeeded in diverting his legions and making them fear him. In a word, he knew how to arouse their enthusiasm. It should be pointed out that all the enthusiasm that was useful to him originated in himself alone, while Bonaparte profited by the beginnings of the enthusiasm created by the Revolution.

I have gone into these details to justify Napoleon's lies and the other means through which he gained success. His success saved the country at Arcola, for instance, and now it unfortunately scandalizes certain prudish and eminently moral writers —brave fellows who have never seen or done anything that matters but who nevertheless want to direct public opinion with authority.

They speak of the three days of rain and wretchedness at Mascara. What would they have to say about the fifty-four days without eating on the retreat from Moscow? What would Napoleon have said, what would the public of 1812 have said, if there had been complaints after a week of retreat? *

Chance showed us a war thirty-eight years ago like the one Caesar fought against the Gauls, the campaign in Egypt. The Mamelukes had the extreme, thoughtless bravery of our ancestors. All the moderate dangers suffered by the army in Egypt sprang from their separation from their homeland, but when Caesar judged it necessary, he went to gather recruits at Milan and Ravenna, and if he had been beaten, he would have had a safe retreat through a fertile country.

Napoleon was right, then. The Gallic Wars do not place Caesar in the rank of Hannibal and Alexander. Caesar learned war in Gaul. He found enormous sums of money there, trained his soldiers there, and played there a comedy with such rare talent that he went back to Rome covered with glory and defended by the enthusiasm of his legions. With these advantages he launched the great war, the real war, Pharsalia, Munda, and against troops who knew as much about it as his own.

In 1796 General Bonaparte, unknown, of obscure birth, fought his finest campaign, his first, against the best troops in Europe, commanded by the most celebrated generals. The priests and nobles of the country where he fought were against him. He had to obey the orders of an imbecile government, and with his army always inferior in numbers he destroyed four Austrian armies.

* The private opinion of a single individual about Napoleon means nothing. If I may be permitted to express my own, it is that I am going to write a life of this great man, and it is better that the reader recognize the author's opinion at the start. Napoleon saved the Revolution in 1796 and in 1799 on the 18th Brumaire. Then he tried to destroy the Revolution, and he would have been worth more to the happiness of France if he had been killed in 1805 after the peace.—H. B.

Chaumont, May 3

Business has quickly taken me from the foundries of the Nivernais to the factories near Chaumont. This part of the country is very rich in iron, but actually it is so ugly that I had rather not talk about it. I would be taken for a bad Frenchman. The disadvantages of France suit me. I think I would angrily defend my country if a stranger attacked her, but, all the same, I prefer an intelligent man from Granada or Königsberg to the intelligent man from Paris. Him I know rather too well. The *unexpected*, the divine unexpected, is better found elsewhere. Personally I feel none of the English kind of patriotism which took pleasure in burning all the towns of Belgium merely to increase the prosperity of one section of London.

Chaumont is situated on a flattened sugar loaf. From the window of my inn I see only dry, arid slopes and three stunted trees, not more, that decorate these slopes. There is not even any water. You can find neither a fowl nor a hot pastry to buy. Every townsman gets his provisions from the country, but there are so few strangers that a pastry cook would die of hunger. Roe deer, boar, and game of all kinds flourish in the forests that cover the soil of this department, but they all fly away from the house of Mme Chevet. It's too bad that Chaumont is not in the middle of one of these forests.

I was told this morning that the "assembly" would be at Mme So-and-So's this evening. At this gathering there was a good deal of talk about the savage conduct of the Allies who occupied Chaumont in 1814 at the time of the campaign in France. Those people are decidedly less civilized than we are. In Germany around 1806 or 1809, some of the occupation officers, left in the rear, were made to pay forty francs a day by the council of the town they themselves commanded, and they had a big dinner party three times a week and gave picnics all the time in the country round about. Finally on the day of their departure they had to borrow ten louis from one of their new friends, and many pretty eyes were filled with tears. A German saves his money.

From Strasbourg to Besancon and to Grenoble, the most noble patriotism distinguished this eastern frontier.

The mineral wealth of the department of the Haute-Marne is so great that it has led to a division of labor. There are people who clean the ore and sell it to the foundries. And everywhere nature has placed forests above the ore.

Here is all I have found of literature in the Haute-Marne. Beneath a small badly-drawn portrait of a handsome young man who comprehends no other pleasure in life than the killing of roe deer, a woman whom perhaps he neglected has written in pencil some barely visible lines of the ancient Voiture:

> His pleasure is in conquest and not in being loved,
> And in his vain caprice, after a victory
> He scorns the fruit and wants only the glory.

Since I had to hurry on my way to Chaumont, I stopped only an hour at Dijon, the time it took to climb the old tower of the former palace of the Dukes of Burgundy which M. de Barante made fashionable some years ago. This square tower was completed under John the Fearless. He increased its height considerably during his struggles with the people of Orleans. He wanted to look over the flat country from a distance and guard against surprises.

On the keystone can be seen the carpenter's plane the Prince chose for his device after the Duc d'Orleans (who was later assassinated) chose a stick covered with knots for his.

Witty like all the Dijonnais, the man who showed me the tower offered to take me through the museum although it was only half-past five in the morning.

In the museum in the midst of many mediocre things I found seventy little marble figures, all a little more than a foot high. They were monks of the different orders. In their expressions the fear of hell, the feeling of resignation, and scorn for earthly things is really wonderful. The heads of many of the monks are hidden by their cowls, and their hands are in their sleeves. Nothing naked can be seen at all, and in spite of this, the faces are filled with a grave and sincere expression. Religion is beautiful in these marbles.

A statue like one of these would have astonished Pericles. These little figures surround the tombs of the Dukes of Burgundy at the Charterhouse in Dijon. There is a very curious St. Michael. It is the way he is armed.

Among the pictures I looked quickly over a "Death of St. Francis" by Agostino Caracci, a "St. Jerome" of Domenichino's, and a landscape by Gaspard Poussin which might well teach our landscape painters to be less affected. One only that I admired made the trees that he drew recognizable, but now M. Marilhat has gone to study the palms of Arabia.

I noticed a good copy of "The School of Athens," that sublime fresco which we know in Paris from the excellent copy M. Constantin has done on porcelain.

Here is an incident I was mixed up in day before yesterday. A rich banker sent off a bag containing fifty thousand francs by a little country stagecoach, but, to lessen the duty he had to pay, he declared only ten thousand francs at the stagecoach office. When the coach arrived at its destination, the bag was gone. The banker, a member of the Legion of Honor, mayor of the town, very close to the Prefect, etc., etc. hurried to the town where he had sent his bag. He is a man of a large build and very important looking. He kicked up a row at the stagecoach office, claimed that they had to pay him fifty thousand francs, that he was going to bring suit, that he was hiring a lawyer from Paris, that he would spend another fifty thousand francs if necessary to recover the first. In brief, he made himself important in the most comic fashion. All the same, he gauged them correctly. They were terrified.

An Italian postilion there took the terrible banker's servant off to one side. "Is it really true that there were fifty thousand francs in that bag?" he asked.

"Certainly," said the servant. "I saw it counted myself."

"It was very small, though."

"That's because it was in gold."

"All right. Go tell your master that if he wants to stop all this chasing around, I'll find his money for him in exchange for some nice writing on a paper stamped by a notary."

Three hours later the fat banker had his bag back. The postilion, pretending that one of his horses cast a shoe, had buried the bag at the foot of a tree in some woods the stagecoach had passed through during the night.

This man had enough nerve to steal ten thousand francs, but he couldn't get used to the idea he had safely stolen fifty thousand.

Langres, May 5

On the road from Chaumont to Langres.

In my mind I have always split France into seven or eight big divisions which in the main do not resemble one another at all and have in common only the things that appear on the surface. I want to talk about that which originates in the government.

I would first single out Alsace and Lorraine as openhearted regions of an ardent patriotism with something serious in the affections. Although it is horrible, I even like the German spoken in Alsace.

Then follows Paris and the vast circle of egotism that surrounds it for a hundred miles in every direction. Except for people of the lowest class, Parisians try to take part in the government, whatever it may be, but to make a stand to defend or change it is held to the height of credulity. Thus there is nothing so different as the environs of Paris and Alsace.

Moving westward, around Nantes, Auray, Savenay,

Clisson are found the Bretons, a people of the fourteenth century, devoted to their curé and holding their lives as nothing when it comes to avenging God.

Further north appear the Normans, sly, shrewd, never giving a straight answer to any question. This division if it is not the most intelligent in France seems to me far the most civilized. From St. Malo to Avranches, Caen, and Cherbourg, this region of all France is the one most adorned with trees and has the prettiest hills. The countryside would be entirely admirable if there were some large mountains or at least some hundred-year-old trees, but, on the other hand, it has the sea, the sight of which throws so much seriousness into the mind. The sea, by its dangers, cures the bourgeois of the little towns of half his pettiness.

After the four divisions of the north—the generous Alsace, Paris and its circle of egotism two hundred miles in diameter, devout and courageous Brittany, and civilized Normandy—we find Provence to the south with its somewhat uncouth candor. Party politics yield murders in this part of the country . . . Marshal Brune's, the Mamelukes of Marseille in 1815, the massacre at Nîmes.

Then we come to the great division of Languedoc which extends, I think, from Beaucaire and the Rhone to Perpignan. There is something of wit and delicacy in these regions. Love there has not been replaced by calculation. Toward the Pyrenees there is even a tinge of romantic gallantry and a taste for adventure that foretells noble Spain.

Going north from the Pyrenees we come to that happy country where the people comb their hair so beautifully and doubt nothing. Gascony from Bayonne to Bordeaux and Perigueux has supplied France with two-thirds of her marshals and celebrated generals . . . Lannes, Soult, Murat, Bernadotte, etc., etc. I find a great natural wit at Villeneuve d'Agen and Bordeaux but, on the other hand, very little education. The peasant is wholly barbarous around Rodez and Sarlat, but nothing can equal his natural spirit. He could read *Don Quixote* with pleasure where a Norman would notice only a few of Sancho Panza's sharp ideas. In all this region the middle classes are mad about property. If a man has an estate worth eighty thousand francs, he will buy a field next to it for thirty thousand and expect to pay for it by little economies, with the result that all his life he won't have any money. However, being a Gascon, bragging is enough for him. He calls his house a castle, says he is a great landowner with every breath, and ends by believing it.

We have left toward the southeast that country of fine intelligence and enlightened patriotism, Grenoble, which on July 6, 1815, twenty days after Waterloo, when all France was discouraged and Grenoble was abandoned by Marshal Suchet and the troops of the line who had retired to Lyons, wished nevertheless to defend herself. Grenoble fought bravely against the troops from Piedmont who were none other than those excellent regiments raised there by the Emperor. This quality of civic courage even more than the military in a France crushed by Waterloo is unique in the history of our revolution.

In the provinces the government is the Prefect. He is almost the same everywhere. However, I shall have much to say under this head.

There are departments of the South where the government has hardly any influence on the moral nature of the people. It is based on barbarism or the passions of the inhabitants and the Prefects' lack of ability. These gentlemen hand out rewards at random, and, besides, they are replaced every three or four years, that is, when they have begun to learn a little something about the country under their jurisdiction. Most of them even after many years in office have no inkling of what goes on around them. They are mixed up in the passions of some secretary-general or councillor of the prefecture they think the finest fellow in the world and who actually has the elevated views and general character of a sly and greedy lawyer. Before 1830 these Prefects could not flatter themselves that they controlled the will of a single person in their departments. At best they bought them by handing out medals and licenses for the sale of tobacco, and all the while the deputies were not disconcerted and did not call them to account.

If the elections are ever conducted more honestly than they were before 1830, these southern tribes will begin to take some interest in the government. Up to 1830 they regarded it as an all-powerful enemy which exacted taxes and conscription from them but with whom they could sometimes make a good bargain by making it pay for sending the deputies it demanded to Paris.

The people were electrified by Napoleon. After his fall, the crooked elections, and the other things that followed his reign, the nasty egotistical passions resumed their sway. I hate to say this, I hope I am deceived, but I see nothing generous any longer.

Everyone wants to make a fortune, an enormous fortune very quickly, and without working. Out of this, especially in the South, springs an extreme jealousy of the man who has hooked the government out of a job worth six thousand or even three thousand francs. They do not consider that he has exchanged his work or his time which he could have spent making money in business or the law. They regard every public functionary as a crook who swindles money out of the government.

You rarely meet this ridiculous point of view in the civilized part of France, which I place north of a line extending from Dijon to Nantes. South of this line I see no exceptions except Grenoble and Bordeaux. Grenoble is raised somewhat above the surrounding prejudice by her profound good sense and Bordeaux by sallies of wit.

But even if you ignore the effect of government on the seven or eight great divisions of France, you would have to spend at least a year in each one of these divisions to know them even moderately well and still longer to be a Prefect or an Attorney-General.

What makes this study infinitely more difficult for us Parisians is that nothing prepares us here for the way things are in the provinces. Paris is a republic. The man who has something to live on and who asks nothing never encounters the government. In Paris who would dream of inquiring into the character of M. le Prefect?

There is more: when a minister gives a cross to a fool who is notoriously inept, in Paris we smile. There would be nothing to laugh at if the cross had been given to someone who deserved it. In the provinces they grow angry at such a spectacle. They become profoundly disaffected. The provincial still does not know that everything in life is a comedy.

Department of the Haute-Marne, May 6

Some men like to ponder over the moral conclusions they have drawn from a fact, but they are so unlucky as to be unable to remember any figures or proper names. Men like this are apt to be brought up short in the midst of a lively discussion by some idiot who knows a date. A watch could be made with an enamel dial on which to write necessary figures for ready reference.

Yesterday in a salon filled with very distinguished people, they took pleasure in speaking very ill to me about the economic report of the King's government.

I answered in an oracular tone: "The general commerce of France, that is, the value of what leaves and what enters the country, was more than 1,866 millions in 1836. In 1828 it was only 1,216 millions. The difference in favor of Louis-Philippe's reign, 650 millions. In 1836, Paris exported 134 millions; in 1828, only 67 millions, and, moreover, Paris is where the riots have taken place. In 1836 agricultural France exported 70 millions in wines. In 1836 France sent 159 millions and to England alone 66 millions. Now proclaim a republic or recall Henry V, and you will understand your customs-house figures."

Langres, May 5

Langres, May 9

WHILE CLIMBING UP THE MOUNTAIN to Langres the postilion told me that after Briancon it is the highest town above sea level in all France. I found that it resembled what they say of Constantinople. Langres is very jealous of Chaumont.

My business finished, the very cold wind made me take refuge in the cathedral. I began to read Caesar there at once. When I had revived a little, I pondered over Gothic art and on the ogive, which properly speaking is not at all an exclusive feature of the Gothic, which was born in 1200.

The ogive has existed in Egypt at all times. The bridge over the Jordan in Syria has pointed arches. In the tenth century the Arabs brought the ogive into Sicily.

What I am more certain of because I have seen it is that the vaulting of the outlet of the Lake of Albano, built, they say, during the siege of Véies, is ogival. Nothing is more natural. It is the strongest vaulting and the one that first occurs to the mind. What could be simpler than to make an ogive merely by overhang?

Romanesque architecture, then Gothic developed little by little among people who were bored by Greek architecture and its younger sister, Roman, or who despaired of equaling it.

The society of the tenth century bears a strong resemblance in one particular to that of Paris in 1837. The conquerors from the north had just invaded the elegant society of Rome. (Plain columns were no longer enough for them. They wanted columns ornamented with mosaics; see Ravenna.) Elegant, I say, but weak and sickly, without a sincere taste any longer for anything that demanded consistency, no longer able to be aroused by irony, that species of pleasure that demands of the intelligence only a single moment of attention.

Without the press which permits a wild craftsman like J. J. Rousseau to speak and get himself listened to, good society, since Marshal Richelieu took Port Mahon by assault, has been so far as the passions go in the same degree of utter clumsiness as the Rome Petronius gives us in his novel.

The mixture of these barbarians with this enervated society produced long and frightful convulsions and the complete barbarism of the tenth century, but at last an amalgam was made, and the social entity called France was born.

Today, through the effects of the Revolution, our people are energetic—witness the suicides—and a third of the rich people who take boxes at the opera would be hard put to prove that their grandfathers could read.

It is this energy that is trying to break out in the literature of 1837 to the horror of the Academy and a few soft elegant men born before 1780 or accustomed to the habits of that period.

The principle of energy was stronger in tenth century society than now. The son of the Roman knuckled under to the son of the barbarian everywhere.

Sicily, less devastated by the northern tribes, bored itself with Greek architecture and, step by step, invented Gothic architecture. Then came the twelfth and thirteenth centuries who blushed for their barbarity and were passionate builders. This is proved by the cathedrals of Strasbourg, Reims, Rouen, Auxerre, Beauvais, Paris, and the thousands of Gothic churches in the villages of France.

For cold, egotistical tastes, it is the complicated, the difficult that is beautiful. Now Gothic architecture makes everyone give himself a bold air. This explains the success of Alexandrine verse in tragedy. Souls made for the arts applauded:

> Eh quoi! n'avez-vous pas
> Vous meme ici tantot ordonné son trépas?
>
> *Andromaque*

They were struck by the genius it took to find a situation so cruel. You can see, they said, that Racine loved passionately, and besides, the way it is said pleases them. The vulgar, the pallid people, the pedants admire the richness of the rhyme and the difficulty in finding it. If they dared, they would blame the thought as gross and too simple.

French literature, then, can hope for a fine period of energy when the grandsons of those who were enriched by the Revolution come to be born.

The streets are quite pretty in Langres. Walking through them and seeing the cutlery shops everywhere, I could think only of Diderot. Undoubtedly he was bombastic, but in 1850 how far superior will he seem to our contemporary bombast! His bombast did not come from a poverty of ideas and a need to hide it. Very much to the contrary, he was embarrassed by all that his heart furnished him. Six pages of *Jacques the Fatalist* must be torn out, but, once this purification has been accomplished, what work of our own time is comparable to it? At the age of twenty it was part of Diderot's talent to have the pleasure of paying court to a fashionable woman and the boldness to appear in her salon. His bombast disappeared. It was only a relic of his provincial manners.

Perhaps he also thought, like Voltaire, that it was better to strike hard than accurately. Doing this you please a large number of readers, but on the other hand you offend mortally the spirits who have some feeling for Mozart and Corregio. Diderot could reply that such spirits were very rare in 1770, but I would answer that in 1837 the tragedies of Voltaire bore us to death. In 1837 they worship Diderot in Madrid and St. Petersburg. They hate him for a vile libertine in Edinburgh, and twenty years from now he will have his rights even in the Rue Taranne.

On the Road from Langres to Dijon, May 10

A LITTLE WOODED HILL, which was only a pretty sight as I left Chaumont, here seems sublime and enchants the eye. What an effect Mount Ventoux would make here or the lowest of the mountains they scorn near the Fountain of Vaucluse!

Unfortunately there are no high mountains around Paris. If heaven had given this region a lake or one passable mountain, French literature would have been far more picturesque. In the great days of our literature, La Bruyére, who speaks of all things, hardly dares mention in passing the profound impression that a view like the one at Pau or at Cras, in the Dauphinate, leaves on certain minds. There is a depressing compensation for this: all the dull writers of our own day speak of these things without shame and without measure and spoil them as much as they are able.

Like good coaches and steamboats, the picturesque comes to us from England. Like his aristocracy, a good landscape has something religious in it for an Englishman. It is the object of a sincere emotion for him.

The first trace of attention to nature I have found in the books that one reads is that row of willows where the Duke of Nemours takes shelter when he was reduced to despair by the beautiful interdiction of the Princess of Clèves.

France is wrinkled by five mountain chains. The two chains of hills that serve as buttresses to the Seine seem like swaths at a certain elevation. They have to be seen from the bottoms of their little valleys. From a fair height, there is nothing uglier. Mt. Valerien seen from the top of the pretty hill at Montmorency says nothing to the spirit. What a pity some good fairy does not bring here some of the terrible mountains from Grenoble!

If this fairy had separated France from both Spain and Germany and poor Italy from Germany by arms of the sea ten miles wide, Europe would be two centuries nearer the happiness civilization can give. This does not keep people who are paid to do it from talking incessantly to us about the goodness of fairies. Think of the Rhine, the Vistula, the Po, and the Ebro as twenty-five miles wide at their sources. How then would Russia be able to threaten civilization and parade her Cossacks in the middle of Europe?

Beaune, May 12

As for myself, I was in Königsberg last year, and I know Russia hasn't the twenty millions it would take to give her troops this fine trip but that some of the middle class have let themselves be frightened by the terrible and well-paid articles that the *Gazette of Augsburg* translates from the Russian.

Beaune, May 12

When I went through Dijon, I visited the museum for a half-hour. An exhibition of pictures from the region is in preparation. They will be stiffer and even more exaggerated than those in Paris. The art of the provinces can be judged by the literary articles in the *Review of the Two Burgundies* which I have just bought in Dijon. In it I found nothing in French except the letters of President de Brosses.

There are, it seems to me, two very distinct races of men in the streets of Dijon. The Francs-Comtois, tall, slender, slow in their movements, drawling their words; these are the *kymris.* They make a perfect contrast with the *Gaels* whom I have often recognized here by their round heads and gay looks.

Dijon, which has no rival in France for intelligence except Grenoble, is a town made up of pretty houses built of little square stones but they have barely a second floor and a small third one. This gives it the air of a village. They are healthier and more convenient than five-story houses, but there is little that is serious or stylish about them. They are like village houses. I wanted to see the pretty little marble monks ten inches high (in the museum). You have to look for their faces in the depths of their cowls (like the statues at Notre Dame de Brou).

During the past year I have become convinced that, from Lyons to Marseilles, to a man who spends the whole day speculating in pepper or silks a book written in a simple style is obscure. He really needs the commentary and the explanation his newspaper gives him. He understands a pompous style better. Neologisms astonish him, amuse him, and seem beautiful to him.

In order to judge sanely of the perfection of a language, there is no need to take the masterpieces. Genius breeds illusion. To my notion, perfect French is to be found in the translations published about 1670 by the solitaries of Port Royal. Very well. It is precisely this kind of French that the businessmen of Marseilles and Lyons understand the least. Besides, they are afraid of praising something that seems so easy to them.

The men I pass on the roads near Dijon are small, spare, lively, ruddy. You see that their good wine governs their whole makeup. So, to make a superior man, a logical head is not enough. There must be a certain fiery temperament.

As I left Dijon I stared hard at the famous Côte d'Or, so celebrated throughout Europe. I had to recall the verse, "Are witty people ever ugly?" for, without its wonderful wines, I would find nothing uglier than the Côte d'Or. According to the system of M. Elie de Beaumont, it was one of the first mountain ranges to emerge on our globe when the crust began to cool.

The Côte d'Or, then, is only a small mountain, quite ugly and barren, but they mark the vineyards with little stakes, and at every instant you find an immortal name, Chambertin, Clos-Vougeot, Romanée, St. Georges, Nuits. With the aid of so much fame, you end by getting accustomed to the Côte d'Or.

When General Bisson was a colonel, he was on his way to join the Army of the Rhine with his regiment. As he was passing the Clos-Vougeot, he made them halt, ordered them left into line of battle, and made them present arms.

As my fellow traveler was telling me this honorable anecdote, I saw a square, walled enclosure of about four hundred acres sloping gently to the south. We came to a wooden door which bore in rough, ugly characters "Clos-Vougeot." This name was furnished by the Vouge, a brook that winds a little way away. This immortal enclosure once belonged to the monks of the Abbey of Citeaux. The good fathers did not sell their wine. They gave away what they did not drink. No merchant tricks in those days.

This evening at Beaune I had the honor of taking part in a long discussion. Should the Clos-Vougeot grapes be gathered in transverse strips parallel to the road or in vertical strips from the road to the top of the hill? They had tasted the 1832 vintage produced by one of the procedures and the 1834, I believe, by the other.

Each year has its special characteristics, or, rather, successive characteristics. For instance, the 1830 wine could be inferior to the 1829 wine when it is three years old, that is, tasted in 1833, and it could be superior in 1836 when it has come to its sixth year.

By the end of the session, which lasted more than two hours, I was beginning really to perceive the difference between certain qualities. Everyone knows the *Wine of the Comet* that announced the fall of Napoleon in 1811. Every five or six years there is a superior year.

Generally the wines of this region are drunk in Belgium. The proprietor of the Clos-Vougeot could deceive his customers, he would only have to spread horse manure on his vineyards, and they would produce much more, but the wine would be of an inferior quality. A bottle of Clos-Vougeot that would be sold for ten francs in a Paris restaurant is not sold on the premises here but is *obtained* by a special favor at a price of fifteen francs. I must admit, however, that nothing is comparable to it. This wine is not very pleasant in its first or even its second year, thus the proprietors always keep a hundred thousand bottles in reserve.

The charming exaggerations of poetry have overwhelmed this subject so dear to the Burgundians, and this evening my agent at Beaune promised to let me drink a bottle of Clos-Vougeot that came from Citeaux Abbey. But how can I believe in this venerable antiquity when this wine begins to go off after twelve or fifteen years?·

In the days of the monks, who were great connoisseurs and no salesmen, the enclosure produced less and the wine was worth more, but nowadays how is the temptation to manure the vineyards a little going to be resisted when each bottle sells for fifteen francs? It is quite true that they give the grape-pickers excellent dinners and especially dishes to which they are not accustomed so as to kill the notion of eating the grapes.

The wines of Nuits have become famous since the illness of Louis XIV in 1680. The doctors ordered the king to drink the old wine of Nuits to recover his vitality. This order of Fagon's created the little town of Nuits.

Beaune is situated in chalky soil. A pretty promenade has been made along the ramparts, and the Bourgeoise, a very clear little stream, full of big green plants which float with the water, crosses the town. The courtyard of the hospital offers some fine remains of Gothic architecture. Nicolas Rollin, chancellor of Philip, Duc de Burgundy, founded the hospital in 1443. It was very proper, said Louis XI, that Rollin, who had made so many people poor, should build a hospital to lodge them in.

One day about 1803 the Beaunois found a great many gold medals in the bed of the Bourgeoise. They were worth, so the report went, twenty thousand francs. A collector offered to pay for the gold by weight, but the Beaunois answered that they had rather melt the medals down.

On my way to Chaumont I had passed by Pommard, Volnay, and Meursault, but only today do I learn the secret cause of the wealth of those celebrated places. They produce a white wine which has the property of mixing with red wines and giving them fire without altering them. I saw Mt. Blanc very clearly from Beaune.

Chalon-sur-Saône, May 14

A MATTER OF TWO HOURS' BUSINESS called me to Autun, but I allowed myself the pleasure of spending half a day before its admirable monuments. What sublime simplicity! Even from the period of Diocletian, the antique elevates the soul to a serenity very near to perfect virtue which makes sacrifices easy. But whose soul is moved by simplicity today?

If some poor young man could be found in Paris gifted with a horror of vaudeville and with that private disposition, cousin-german to foolishness, which makes one love fine architecture, he ought to come to Autun if he cannot go to Nîmes. In the presence of these two triumphal arches, almost whole, he would find the reason for his horror of all those "Gallo-Greek" buildings called "magnificent" in the official publications.

Thirty years ago they applauded Lainé at the Opera. Today they applaud M. Duprez. They built that warehouse fifty years ago (this edifice will be passable when it is in ruins); they build the Madeleine today. That's progress for you. Let us take one more step: when a little church is wanted, let us copy a temple at Athens or the Pantheon at Rome or at least the Maison Carrée. But it would be overwhelmed by the height of our houses.

What a contrast there is to Autun! The character of a brave Gaul furious against Caesar's Romans and the character of a bourgeois in gold lace mounting guard before the Porte d'Arroux!

And for all that, the sixtieth ancestor of this pitiful bourgeois was a Gallic citizen of Bibractus. There, you must agree, is one glorious result of our modern civilization! It produces the Diorama and the railroads. Birds and plants can be modeled admirably from nature. In twenty-one hours a Parisian can reach Marseilles, but what kind of man will this Parisian be?

I had some business today with a young lawyer from Macon. He owned a house he rented out for five thousand francs a year, and he had made ten thousand more working. He was only thirty years old. He had good hope of dying a peer of France and a millionaire. He was complaining of his lot while I maintained that he was the happiest man in France. He acts. He would be better if our institutions were stronger. Then he would be a Fox or a Pitt. In the Emperor's day he would have been a Councillor of State like Chaban and administered the province of Hamburg.

But, barring a miracle, can a young man be born nowadays with twenty-four thousand a year private income and, if you please, a title? Under Napoleon he would at least have been forced to be second lieutenant or one of thc guards of honor.

As this town of Autun from which I escaped this morning is dead, so does Chalons seem to me full of activity, youth, and life. It is maritime activity, a foretaste of Marseilles. The town is filled with big four-story hotels where they treat pretty carelessly the fish they have caught in their net. I complained to the man next to me at the table d'hôte, and those are the terms he used.

"Alas, sir," I said. "It's just like Paris."

A café owner lays out a hundred thousand francs to decorate his cafe, but it does not occur to him to pay a Venetian, a pupil of Florian's, fifteen hundred francs for knowing how to make a cup of coffee.

All the uncomfortable hotels in Chalons have immense signs.

Chalons is one of the most commercial towns in France. A man who works hard can make 15 per cent on his capital without risk.

At Chalons I met M. D——, one of the chief economists in France. He comes from Besancon. Never in my life have I stopped in Besancon except to do business.

I began and ended my excursions around this town by going into the cathedral, where there is an excellent "St. Sebastian" by Fra Bartolomeo. Opposite is the "Death of Saphira" by that steadfast colorist, Sebastiano del Piombo. Sometimes Michael Angelo furnished him with drawings so as to play tricks on Raphael's pupils. This great man (del Piombo), protected by by his uncle Bramante, a schemer of the first rank, got some sharp advantages for himself from Michael Angelo. It was the old Corneille eclipsed by the sensitive Racine.

Part of the Besancon bridge is of Roman construction. The houses are all built of a fine ashlar, and I would like to visit the Granvelle palace. Besancon, M. D—— tells me, is still Spanish. It is a serious and deeply Catholic town.

On the Steamboat, May 15

I HAVE COMMITTED AN ACT that would disgrace me forever in the eyes of my wise father-in-law if he ever heard of it. My valet annoyed me by talking like a gentleman, so I sent him to Lyons in my carriage, and I boarded the steamboat with no other luggage than my cloak and Baudry's big Shakespeare. Joseph, in spite of his deference from which I do not permit him to deviate, gave me significant looks. He was sure his patron had some lady in mind. Would to heaven I had!

I would like to be madly in love and to make love again and again with the ugliest peasant woman on the boat! That says a great deal. But, alas, I embarked only because this agent I spoke of earlier told me that the banks of the Saône recalled those of the Guadalquivir and are charming from Trévoux to Lyons.

After Chalons (the dome of the hospital, built in 1528, makes quite a nice effect from a distance) the steamer glides through the middle of immense meadows that are too often flooded by the waters of the Saône, a stream that now seems asleep. These waves put me in mind of the wonderful source of the Doubs where I saw them spring forth from the rocks.

Macon has a pretty quai that serves as a promenade for society. We saw there a tame lioness which a young officer had brought from Africa. This is a wonderful war and not too expensive at twenty million francs a year. It shows the Cossacks what kind of people we still are and singles out for the nation's respect generals like Duvivier and Lamoricière.

Macon is proud of its big bridge, long, massive, very useful undoubtedly but hardly prepossessing. This bridge leads to one of the strangest and most backward areas in France, the country of the Doubs.

The peasants there are stupid, and they have fever six months of the year. By way of using the land, they make ponds on it seven years in a row, which gives them plenty of fish. Then they draw off the water, and they get, without fertilizer, three or four magnificent crops. In the Doubs country five-sixths of the population believe in sorcerers, and every three or four years they have a handsome miracle. This condition of the lower classes is quite pleasing to certain people the reader will name for me. As I was saying thoughtlessly that France ought to make a gift of twenty thousand francs a year to this unhappy region to pay teachers to teach them to read and put the sorcerers out of business, M. de M—— cried passionately, "Take care, sir!"

For my part I judge the political morality of a man by his hatred or his lack of hatred for education. In cultivated areas where, to keep their jobs, they don't dare hate education, they hate wit anyhow and protect the scholars. Here is a second imprudence of mine: they will say I am no good, a gloomy fellow. Alas, every day I see I am on the wrong side.

The same M. de M—— who protested against the education I wanted to give the peasants of Doubs knows the country very well since it is his own. He has a dry, precise, but very cultivated mind. He had rather talk about the physical or historical circumstances of the region than the moral. He told me that Tournus like Chalons has it antique column, fished out of the Saône some years ago.

As we were passing Macon, someone on the boat told in a loud voice the adventure of the mistress of the Wild Ox Inn (that fire that burned up a room where the young traveler no longer was). Next came the famous witticism that is the pride of the region and its revenge on the pretended superiority of Paris. Someone mentioned the *Saône* in front of a Parisian who

was showing off the knowing simplicity of his manner on the pretty quai at Macon.

"In Paris we call that the *Seine,*" he said, smiling.

Trévoux, built in tiers on the left bank of the Saône, looks very pleasant. It is one of those little towns La Bruyère speaks of. It looks as if you could spend six weeks there very pleasantly, and all the inhabitants are burning to get away from it. There, a hundred and ninety seven years after Christ, a bloody battle decided who would be master of the world, the great, cruel emperor Septimius Severus or the rebel, Albin. Fortune favored the worthier.

Lyons, May 15

I DEBARKED AT THE HEAD of Ile Barbe where an iron cable bridge joins it to the bank. M. S—— had not deceived me. Five miles above Lyons, the banks of the Saône are picturesque, unusual, very pleasant. They remind me of the loveliest hills of Italy, those of Desenzano, immortalized by the battle Napoleon dared to launch there against Marshal Würmser and the advice of all the knowledgeable generals of his army. On these Saône hills the silk-weavers of Lyons have built their pleasure-cottages which are as ridiculous as the ideas they have of beauty. In every particular they have retained the grand tastes of the period of Louis XV, but the natural beauty of the countryside gets the better of all their Chinese pavilions with which they pretend to embellish it. There are some pretty tree-covered crags which precipitate themselves, so to speak, into the course of the Saône, forcing it to make some quick detours.

I believe that somewhere near here at a place probably called Neuville the woman I respect most in the world had a small estate. She intended to spend the rest of her days there quietly, but the Revolution called all the capable men into public life, and ministers like Roland replaced ministers like De Calonne.

I spent two very pleasant hours, two—why blush and not say the word?—two very delightful hours on the roads and paths along the Saône. I was absorbed in contemplating the heroic times of Mme Roland. We were as great as the first Romans then. As she was about to go to her death she embraced all her cell-mates who had become her friends. One of them, M. Reboul, who told it to me, burst into tears.

"What's this, Reboul?" she said. "You weep, my friend? What weakness!" She herself was animated, smiling. The sacred fire shone in her eyes.

"Very well, my friend," she said to another prisoner, "I am going to die for liberty and my country. Isn't this what we have always wanted?"

It will be some time before we see such a spirit again!

After this great character came the women of the Empire who wept in their carriages on the way back from St. Cloud because the Emperor had found their gowns in bad taste; then followed the women of the Restoration who went to mass at Sacré Coeur so as to make their husbands prefects; and finally, the women of the *Juste-Milieu,* models of naturalness and amiability. After Mme Roland, history can barely name only Mme de la Valette and the Duchesse de Berry.

At last I entered Lyons on foot, and I saw that I had not escaped the scorn of even the little boy I paid to carry my cloak and my Shakespeare. I offended the god of the region, money. I looked poor.

When I said I was going to stay at the Hotel de Jouvence next to the post office, he said with his drawling accent, "But that's a very expensive hotel, sir!" Without my astonished glare, I believe he would have finished his thought, "Too expensive for you."

Now I am in this hotel, and I am writing this in a beautiful room hung with crimson damask from gilt rods. Half the circumference of the room is lined with wooden paneling painted white shading into blue and varnished, which gives it a look at once dirty and gloomy. I walk on a well-waxed parquetry floor with square insets in an intricate pattern whose name I forget, and it squeaks as I walk. The hangings in my room are surrounded by gilt moldings, damaged, it is true, and tarnished in twenty places, but when I asked for a mosquito net to throw over my bed to keep off the mosquitoes that would keep me awake, the bell-boy smiled with an air of interior satisfaction and answered with all his Lyons pride that they did not keep such things in the hotel, and no one had ever asked for one before. All this bogus luxury, all this self-defeating civilization depressed me with its pettiness and harmless stupidity. It was like being present at a discussion in the Dutch legislature about railroads or customs-houses.

It is impossible that a town of a hundred and sixty thousand souls like Lyons should not contain a great many men of true worth, but I have never met them, and I beg the pardon of any of them for what follows.

I had visited Lyons five or six times, always by mail coach. I was always very busy, and I did not even have time to go up to the museum in the Place de la Terreaux.

Every time I got out of the coach I was met by M. C——, a cousin of my father-in-law's. He has Barême's face to the life and Barême dissatisfied because he has just suffered a loss of twenty francs.* You should have seen his anxiety as he threw himself at me and interrupted me as I was telling a man from the station to take my valise and carry it to my cousin's house. He was afraid I would pay too much for this little service.

"And for that you want a twelve-franc piece!" he said to the man with marked agitation. His face grew more bad-tempered. The man complained and was almost insolent. I acknowledge my own weakness. From that moment my heart became incapable of any pleasure in Lyons, and I wanted only the happiness of leaving it.

* Francois Barême, an arithmetician, achieved almost incredible renown in the reign of Louis XIV.—Tr.

First thing today, M. C—— told me that the sumptuary laws since 1830 which forbade the Tunisians any luxury in dress gave a fatal blow to his business. And when he said that, he made an unbelievable face. M. C—— is a very worthy fellow, very honest, excellent father, pays his taxes promptly, but, my God, what a face! Like his colleagues, the traders, he hires as workers silk-weavers they call *canuts*, and each of them works in his own room. I would, myself, extend this name to the traders themselves. All that this small business—which demands patience above all, a constant attention to detail, the habit of spending less than one makes, and the fear of anything unusual—can produce in the way of egotistical silliness, of pettiness and bitterness concealed by the fear of not making money, seems to me to be summed up in the word *canut*. The Lyonnais themselves apply it to the lower classes of their town.

Now the character of the lower classes where pride does not set an impassable barrier, as in Paris, very quickly forms the character of the upper classes. This combination of habits and ways of looking at things that amazes you in your child and which you call his character is first given him by his nurse and then by the society of servants. Please notice that your child is always a slave in your presence. With servants he regains his equality. What am I saying? He is superior. Now no creature on earth loves superiority like a child. Also see the lightening of heart with which a youngster of seven runs to the ante-room or the stable when he has a moment free. The most subjugated of parents are obliged to make a formal defense in the face of this.

The French Revolution raised the character of servants. Many have been soldiers or think it a noble profession. A little later the savings banks gave them habits of rational thought. Also children are no longer exposed to all the platitudes that spoiled our childhood twenty-five years ago. Sometimes I find running through my head some very absurd idea. After hunting around, I find that this phrase originated with Barbier, my father's favorite servant.

Lyons, May 16

To get any idea of the Lyonnais character you must listen to these traders gossiping among themselves in a café. Find someone in Lyons who will go play a game of dominoes with you.

The girls of the lowest class in Lyons are tall and well made. In Paris they are four feet high.

Lyons, May 16

In general the chief traits of the Lyonnais are fairly high-minded. A man retired from business with six thousand francs a year affects a majestic movement when he walks, carries his head with respect, and looks around in a kind of noble way. I recognize the portraits of the Louis XV period. With all this he still looks like a man who is ill-humored in the evening because he did not make twelve sous in the morning. I see faces of this kind in Paris occasionally, and I would bet they came from Lyons. A simple manner, the ideal of the Parisian and which he goes to so much trouble all his life to hit, seems low and not worth much to a Lyonnais.

But here, as elsewhere, *noblesse oblige*. The National Guard of Lyons lost twelve hundred men in its admirable defense of the town in 1793. (In Lyons they say fifteen thousand.) These men were commanded by a host of emigré officers and by the brave Précy. The leaders knew how to fight, and the men had the enthusiasm. Here is the fine side of the Lyonnais character: to be susceptible to an enthusiasm which will last two months. In Paris it lasts six hours, as could be seen when Napoleon presented his son to the National Guard in the great hall of the Tuileries.

The National Guard of Lyons seems to me worthy of sustaining a comparison with Vienna's, which twice, in 1797 and in 1809, furnished a corps of volunteers who six weeks after they were formed had to be killed to the last man by the French armies. In the 1809 campaign on the banks of the Traun, the

Vienna volunteers, dying under Masséna's grape-shot, fell some forward, the others backward, but what was most remarkable was that the wavy line formed by their boots was not more than eight feet wide. A man who had a Grand Cross was a corporal there and, what's more, got himself killed.

I have often come to Lyons on business, but all the time I am in this town I want to yawn, and the most beautiful things have no effect on me. True, I have always stayed with that fatal cousin on Money-bags Street. This is the first time I have dared set myself up at an inn, but—and I beg pardon of the worthy people of this region—the habit of being bored is very strong. I would willingly shut my eyes because everything I see adds to my disgust, and this makes me resentful. Even the shape of the iron balconies irritates me: the lines are heavy and tormented. I need to try to overcome my interior disposition and admire the Quai St. Clair on the Rhone, but I still can't admire it. I judge that it is admirable.

Once when I was young and overwhelmed with disgust, I had an hour to myself, and I went to a bookseller's to buy a book: I was so sleepy I didn't know what to ask for. Finally I asked at random for *Jacques le Fataliste* or the novels of Voltaire. The bookseller fell back a step, assumed a gloomy look, and read me a sermon on the books I had spoken of. He ended by offering me *Le Spectacle de Nature* by Abbé Pluche. At first I was annoyed by the impertinence of this giver of advice, but as he preached to me, he had so *canut* a manner, so vacant yet so important, that he finished by amusing me. I wanted to verify whether he was acting out of a pure mercantile spirit. Maybe he had Pluche in his shop and not the novels of Voltaire. He had them all right, the monster, but, since I seemed so young, he was determined not to sell them to me. This evening I told my cousin C—— about this business. He got red and claimed that I had exaggerated. In a word, the municipal honor was wounded, and he didn't say a word to me all the rest of the evening. There I caught a glimpse of one of the charms of the Lyonnais's character. He takes offense easily. These people imagine that others are thinking about them and about humiliating them.

Lyons is paved with little pointed pear-shaped stones. It is absolutely impossible for me to walk on them. I look as if I had the gout. This large city, the second in France, is built at the confluence of the Saône and the Rhone whose course forms a capital Y.

Lyons, May 18

THE FORMER NAME, *Lugdunum*, contains the syllable *Lug*, which according to the alleged scholars meant "mountain" or "stream" among the Gauls. Leide and Laon were also called *Lugdunum*.

Strabo, who lived under Tiberius, says that Lugdunum was exceeded only by Narbonne in wealth and importance. Lutetia (Paris) was still a village, straggling and ignored. Augustus, that skillful man, lived for three years in Lyons and made it the metropolis of Celtic Gaul. Claudius was born there. A great fire reduced it to ashes in Nero's reign, and Seneca made a Phrase about it, "There was only the space of one night between a large town and none" (*Una nox fuit inter urbem maximam et nullam*). Nero hastened to send a great deal of money. Trajan, the only man of antiquity after Alexander and Caesar who reminds one of Napoleon, had several buildings erected there.

Lyons was the cradle of the Christian religion among the Gauls and it is still, I think, our most devout city. It does not have a keen fanaticism like Toulouse. There is a self-abnegation and an utter confidence in the priest that always astonishes me. I know twenty rich individuals who give a tithe of their income to the good cause.

Under Henry IV and Louis XIV Lyons formed a separate state. The ruling family was named Villeroy, and often a Villeroy archbishop was simultaneously governor. The story of Count Villeroy is well known, the lieutenant-general who succeeded his uncle as governor of Lyons who had been archbishop and governor himself. The new governor, getting into his coach on the day of his accession, began to give benedictions right and left, and when someone hazarded an objection, he said proudly, "I have seen my uncle do it," and continued.

The Lyonnais like all devout populations are very charitable, and the virtue is needed in this region. I have never thought it wise to base the prosperity of a town on its manufactures. A government that had time to consider its duties ought to arrange matters so that the number of factory workers did not exceed a twentieth part of the population.

My honorable friend, M. Rubichon, the only man of great intelligence, I think, who loved the Restoration, told me that the amount of money a silk-worker in Lyons received for his day's work represented much less than he could buy in Colbert's time in terms of bread and meat. The successors of this great minister have not understood that Italy grows silk and has begun to make very good silk fabrics at San Leucio near Naples and at Milan, and with England drawing on the silk textiles of China, who will soon supply America with them as well, it is necessary to encourage by all possible means young people of sixteen to apply themselves to the silk-worker's trade. Tunis and Morocco prefer the light Italian silks to ours.

Lyons, May 19

Three days ago, Mr. Smith, an English puritan who had lived here for ten years, judged it apropos to quit this life. He swallowed an ounce of Prussic acid. Two hours later he was very sick, but he was not dying at all, and, to pass the time, he was rolling around on the floor. His landlord, an honest shoemaker, was working in his shop in the room beneath. Startled by the odd noise and afraid that his furniture would get broken, he went upstairs. He knocked. No answer. He went in then by a door that had been boarded up. He was terrified by the plight of his Englishman, and he sent for M. Travers, a well-known surgeon and a friend of the sick man. The surgeon came, dosed Mr. Smith, and brought him very quickly out of danger. Then he said to him, "What the devil have you been drinking?"

"Some Prussic acid."

"Impossible. Six drops would kill you in the twinkling of an eye."

"They certainly told me it was Prussic acid."

"Who sold it to you?"

"A little apothecary on the Quai de Saône."

"But ordinarily you go to Girard, there across the street, the best pharmacist in Lyons."

"That's true, but the last time I bought some medicine there, I had the idea he was charging me too much."

Lyons, May 20

I WENT TO THE CHURCH OF AINAY built at the confluence of the Rhone and the Saône near the spot where sixty Gallic tribes in common (I regret to say) raised an altar to Augustus. Their justification lies in the word "sixty." What could sixty nations do against only one and that guided by aristocratic chiefs preserved from the puerility of the lords of Venice by three hundred triumphs? Caesar was the roué *par excellence* of that Roman civilization.

At the museum they will show you a famous bas-relief that once decorated the facade of the church of Ainay. It represents three women (mother-goddesses.) The one in the middle holds a horn of plenty.

Near the sanctuary you must examine the four enormous granite columns, which, before they were sawed, formed two columns about twenty-five feet high. But have they been sawed? Every scholar makes fun of the one who preceded him and says the opposite of what he said, and so it goes until the end of the world or the academies. I advise the reader to believe only what he sees, the material fact. Everything else changes every thirty years, according to whatever is the reigning intellectual fashion. These columns belong, they say, to the altar raised in honor of Augustus by the sixty tribes. Sacrifices were made here on August 10 in the 742d year of Rome, eleven years before the Christian era.

The mixture of these noble fragments of antiquity with the Gothic always induces in me a feeling of contempt, a disagreeable thing. I am not enough of a Christian.

Caligula began or re-established the games celebrated around this altar of Augustus, and if Suetonius and Juvenal can be believed, it was here he placed the seal on his folly. Prizes for eloquence were distributed here, but the losers were obliged to furnish the prizes and present them to the winners. Then they had to recite harangues in praise of the winner. (What torture for these jealous men of letters!) But that was not all the danger they ran, either. If their works seemed unworthy of the gathering to which they had dared present them, the unlucky authors had to efface their productions *with their tongues* or at least with a sponge. Then they were beaten and thrown into the Rhone.

Lyons, May 24

M. S——, AN INTELLIGENT ENGLISHMAN, asked me how a stranger could become acquainted with France. "I know only one way, and it is fairly unpleasant. You must spend six or eight months in a provincial town where they aren't used to seeing many strangers. And what is most difficult for an Englishman, you must be genial, a good fellow, and not collide with anyone's self-esteem. If you want to know the modern, the civilized, the steam-engine France, pitch your tent north of a line running from Besancon to Nantes. If it is the original, the spiritual France, the France of Montaigne you want to see, go south of that line.

"I don't forbid you to come to Paris every two months to

breathe for a week, but, on your return, you must be sure to swear to your provincial friends that you infinitely prefer the town you have chosen to Paris. Add that you go to Paris only on business.

"When you first come to the little town, you must fall quite sick and choose the doctor who is the glibbest talker. The absolute pinnacle would be to have a lawsuit with someone.

"Remember that what fools scorn as gossip is, on the contrary, the only history in this century of affectation that really combs a region over. You will find that all small towns of ten thousand inhabitants, especially in poor districts, are animated by a great hatred for the Sub-Prefect. He gives two balls every year, and the people he invites to them have great contempt for the others, whom they call servile, but it is only during the elections every four years that they really fight.

"You can live twenty years in Paris, and you will not know France. In Paris the bases of all stories are vague. No one is ever absolutely sure of any slightly ticklish fact, of any anecdote whatever. What is sworn to for six months is contradicted the next six. You can personally observe on the Bourse and in the Chamber of Deputies; everything else you read in the papers. On the other hand, in your little town of ten thousand, you can, if you're clever, get to be sure enough of most of your facts so you can base a judgment on them. Since you must get along well (which is not easy for a stranger, because you will have to swallow a number of disappointments and not become annoyed at the absurd rumors that circulate about you), you will manage not to be too bored. In the south you can pick Niort, Limoges, Brives, Le Puy, Tulle, Aurillac, Auch, Montauban, or, well to the north, Amiens, St. Quentin, Arras, Rennes, Langres, Nancy, Metz, Verdun."

The great difficulty is to find some plausible reason for staying there. Many English men have chosen Avranches because they like to fish.

At M—— about 1827 there was an apothecary who made

some lucky speculations in drugs, got rich in six months, and turned out to be more conceited than is permissible even in the Midi. He couldn't walk down the street without giving himself all the graces of a drum major. One fine night, six of his friends (a man's friends are always the most indignant at his good fortune: look at the people who read the newspapers after a promotion), six of his friends, then, broke into the apothecary's shop at two in the morning. They went up to his room, woke him, bound and gagged him, and carried him into his shop. There they danced around him rejoicing in his good fortune and finished (I don't know if I even dare say it) by begging him to accept a warm-water cure from each one of them. As they left they promised to do it again if he kept showing off in the street. This is perfectly true. It's the kind of joke they like in the South.

If I had some anecdotes about love that were even a little moving, I don't think I would put them in this work. Love is no longer fashionable in France, and women nowadays get barely any courteous attention. Any man who marries except through the mediation of his family lawyer is looked upon as a fool or at least a madman who should be pitied, a man who might ask to borrow a hundred louis from you when he woke up from his folly.

The chief merit of the few anecdotes that could make the jump from manuscript into print would lie in being *perfectly true,* which means that they would not be very piquant.

Lyons, May 29

I HAVE THOROUGHLY EXAMINED the style of a curious fragment of an antique statue.* It is a horse's thigh in gilt bronze. This fragment has a history: for a long time the boatmen and

* By the style, or the way the muscle attachments were rendered, their refinement, the veins, etc., the period of a statue can often be determined within fifty years.—H. B.

fishermen had noticed in the Saône near the Ainay bridge a kind of landmark they called *le tupin de fer*, that is, the broken iron pot. The fisherman avoided it so they would not tear their nets, but the boatmen set their hooks on it to help them get up the river.

On the fourth of February, 1766, the water was low and frozen hard, and a boatbuilder named Laurent tried to pull out the *tupin de fer*. He got one of his friends to help him. As they were not strong enough, they called several stevedores, and finally, after they had loosened it with a cable, they pulled up this horse's leg which was probably attached to the body of the horse itself. They offered it to a Lyons burger for eighteen francs, which he refused to give them. Then they took it to the Town Hall and received two louis from the Provost of Merchants.

It is odd that no one had the idea of excavating on that spot in summer when the water is often very low. They could have used a cofferdam and a little steam pump.

The gilt bronze on this statue may have the thickness of a cord. The inside was filled with lead. The bronze was not cast whole. It is composed of little pieces which were cut to dovetail and fit together. The colossal arm in the very finest style that was recently found in the "Darse" at Civita-Vecchia was made in this way. It is now in the Vatican Museum in Rome.

Lyons, June 2

The lyonnais have never opened their minds to anything connected with the fine arts, and this is so in spite of the nearness of Italy, with which they have had such long and frequent relations in the silk business. (See Cellini's *Memoirs.*) A lucky accident, a fire, I believe, disembarrassed them of their big theater, an enormous heavy building of the period of Louis XIV. It was just opposite the Town Hall, and it smothered it. It is a spot where you can't see clearly even in the middle of the day: witness the reading room where I was reading the newspapers only half an hour ago. The question of building a new theater came up. Some quite reasonable sites were proposed, for instance, that of the Boucheries near the Saône. But not at all. They preferred the old location, and the town is forever uglified.

Only a step from Lyons, Italy offers four hundred ready-made models for theaters and of all sizes from that of the one at Como to the one at Genoa. This kind of finished design is preferable to a plan, but the bourgeoisie of Lyons took great care not to go see the Fenice theater in Venice or the new theater at Brescia or the Scala. As a crowning silliness, at a house where I spent the evening, a solemn man claimed that certain people had made a lot of money out of re-building the theater. In the South they hurl this accusation whenever the government or the towns spend any large sums. It's envy again. They said this evening that the Jesuits ruled Lyons from 1814 to 1830. They quickly made conquests of the public officials, and if any were so unwise as to resist them, these were promptly sent away.

I know of only one thing they do well in Lyons. They eat wonderfully and better than Paris in my opinion. Vegetables especially are divinely prepared there. In London I learned that they grow twenty-two different kinds of potatoes. In Lyons I have seen twenty-two different ways of preparing them, twelve of them, at least, unknown in Paris.

On one of my journeys, M. Robert of Milan, a businessman and former officer, a man of heart and intelligence, gained my eternal gratitude by introducing me to a society of men who knew how to dine. These gentlemen, ten or twelve in number, give dinners four times a week, each taking his turn as host. Anyone who fails to turn up pays a fine of a dozen bottles of Burgundy. They have female cooks, not male. At these dinners, there are no impassioned politics, no literature, no demonstrations of wit. Their only business is to eat well. If a dish is excellent, they keep a religious silence and busy themselves with it. Moreover, each dish is severely judged without any regard for the host's feelings. On grand occasions they have the cook come in to receive their compliments, which are not often unanimous. It was a touching sight, one of these girls, a fat slut of forty, weeping with joy when they had a duck with olives. Believe me, in Paris we know only a copy of this dish.

A dinner like this where everything must be perfect is not a small matter for the man who gives it. Granted that the preparation must begin two days before, even so, nothing can give you any idea of such a repast. These gentlemen are rich merchants, most of them, and they think nothing of going two hundred miles to buy a famous wine. I have learned the names of thirty different kinds of Burgundy, the aristocratic wine *par excellence*, as the excellent Jacquemont says. What is so wonderful about these dinners is that, an hour later, your head is as clear as it is in the morning after your cup of chocolate.

Lyons abounds in fish, all kinds of game, and in the wines of Burgundy. With money, like everywhere else, you can have excellent Bordeaux wines also, and finally Lyons has vegetables that have only the names in common with the insipid weeds they have the nerve to serve us in Paris.

M. Robert, former captain of the Army of Italy in 1796, not only knew how to get ahead in the world, he concocted amusing ideas.* For instance, when he introduced me to these wonderful men who know how to live so well in the midst of the prevailing gloom, he gave me a part to play without warning me—he knew how to lie about me so well. In spite of my ignorance, I was not too offensive, and I was insanely amused making his lies good. It was conquer or die.

I had the honor of being invited many times. Owing to these gentlemen, I can praise something in this region without restraint.

After dinner you generally go to play *boule* at the Brotteaux.

* Is this Robert of *The Charterhouse of Parma?*—Tr.

Lyons, June 4

SOMETHING THAT ALWAYS SADDENS ME in the streets of Lyons is the sight of the unfortunate silk-workers. They get married, counting on wages that stop suddenly every five or six years. Then they sing in the streets. It is an honest way of asking for charity. I pity these poor people, and they spoil nightfall for me absolutely, the most poetic moment of the day. It is the time when their number doubles in the streets. In 1828 and 1829 I saw Lyons workmen better dressed than we are. They worked only three days a week and spent their time gaily playing *boule* in front of the cafés of the Brotteaux.

A government with any courage would prevent the Lyons clergy from pushing poor workmen into marriage. Instead, they do just the opposite. They preach nothing else at the tribunal of penitence.

These workmen manufacture fabrics of wonderful freshness and brilliance in the rooms where they lived surrounded by their poor families. All day the youngest partner in every Lyons silk firm runs from room to room (there are about fifteen thousand of them) and pays the workmen for what they have finished. At this job, the partner makes six thousand francs a year. He, his wife, and his children eat up five thousand francs, and they put aside a thousand francs, which after forty years of work becomes a hundred thousand. Then the father of the family retires into some country house, ten or twelve miles from his birthplace, but if anything comes to distrub such a tranquil life as this, your Lyonnais fights like a lion. This soft life, prudent, regular, without any novelty whatever would certainly kill me after a couple of years, but it enchants the Lyonnais. He is in love with his city. He speaks enthusiastically of anything to be seen there. It is in this spirit that I have been taken to see something marvelous. It is a big room on the Quai St Clair where six hundred people drink beer together every Sunday.

Lyons, June 4

The misfortune of this city is this: they get married much too thoughtlessly. Marriage in the nineteenth century is a luxury and a great luxury. It is permissible only when you are quite rich. And, too, what a mania they have for creating children who will be quite miserable! For in the end the son of a burgher, a "gentleman" as they say in Lyons, will never become a woodworker or a cobbler. As long as the Emperor waged war, people could avoid this patriarchal taste for having children without too much inconvenience, but, since 1815, providing an estate for a young man sixteen years old is quite a business, and this kind of trouble for the fathers of families can very well become serious trouble for the government. The simplest thing would be to have the priests make a sin out of this mania for calling into existence beings who cannot be fed, but these gentlemen work in precisely the opposite direction.

In the United States they marry unwisely, but the young American always has the resource of buying fifty acres of woods for two hundred and fifty francs, a slave for two thousand, farm implements and food for six months for another thousand, and, after this petty expense, he, his wife, and children can go hide their misery in the virgin forest that borders their country and gives it its only singularity. It is true that the settler should be a carpenter, a woodworker, a butcher, and during the first year of his settlement he and his wife have to sleep under the stars, but he has, almost certainly, the prospect of leaving a fine farm to each of his children.

Compare this situation in life with that of a Lyons merchant's son, unhappy young man, very pious, knowing Latin, having read Racine, used to wearing broadcloth, who at twenty, when his father dies, finds himself thrown into the world accustomed to all the pleasures of life and with eight hundred francs' income. This will make for a bad marriage in the nineteenth century. In France only the peasant can get married. Under another name he is in the same shape as the American pioneer. His little seven-year-old son is already earning something. This is the reason he doesn't want him taken away and taught to read.

But these are distressing ideas.

When you meet an old man in Lyons, you must get him started on the famous siege of 1793. If the Allies, the enemies of France had had even the shadow of military talent, they could have gone up the Rhone from Toulon and come to the aid of the Lyonnais. Fortunately, at that time only men of genius knew how to make war.

After Lyons was taken, about fifty Lyonnais were led out two by two, tied by the arms, to the Brotteaux plain and shot. On the way one of these brave men managed to get his right arm, which was tied to the left arm of his companion in misfortune, half-untied.

"Get yourself untied," he said in a low voice, "and when we come to a cross street, let's run like hell."

"What are you talking about?" said his indignant companion. "You're trying to compromise me."

This joke shows the mutton-headed courage of the period and how seldom anyone used his head midst the dangers an exhausted civilization loosed on France. They did not act this way in the days of the League: see the naive and wonderful journals of Henry III and Henry IV. They speak of a different people.

Walking along the banks of the Saône this evening, I heard a Provencal song, sweet, gay, wonderfully original. Two Marseillais sailors were singing in parts with a woman from their region. Nothing shows better how far it is from Paris to Marseilles. French intelligence *understands* everything admirably, and in music this leads the French to perform very difficult things, but since they lack absolutely the musical feeling that lies in a sense of rhythm and in being horrified at everything harsh, they take delight in hearing the frightful music I have seen applauded in Lyons.

A people who can listen to such things with pleasure can

boast of occupying a wholly distinguished position. Not only do they have no taste for the good, they love the bad. The French musical instinct is for quadrilles, waltzes and military tunes. Further, their intelligence leads them to applaud any difficulty overcome. For some years they have judged it proper to their vanity to have some enthusiasm for Rossini and after that for Beethoven. I agree that the combination of his skillful and almost mathematical harmony gives a hold to that faculty of comprehension which so eminently distinguishes the French genius. The result has been that two or three years after they paraded this unutterable enthusiasm for Beethoven, this great composer has actually begun to give them some pleasure.

It is a little different with painting. France has produced Lesueur and Prudhon and, in our time, Eugene Delacroix. The French are not entirely lacking in a glimmer of natural taste for this art. When the Academy does not close the Louvre, they judge the pictures there with a certain independence. Thus the tolerable copy of Michael Angelo's "Last Judgment" by M. Sigalon which was exhibited in August, 1837. Had the painter who composed the fresco been unknown, the "Judgment" would have been hissed. There is nothing simpler: the French love little well-licked miniatures, spiritual ones.

Lyons, June 7

THIS MORNING I WENT TO SHOW the antiquities of Vienne to an English officer, a friend of mine who is so courteous as to believe that I know more than he does because I have sold some hardware in Italy. We went very briskly by steamboat and returned by stage coach.

Traveling, it is the evenings that are hard. When it strikes ten, I confess that I miss certain salons in Paris where there is some naturalness, where money and credit with the ministers are not the only gods. (They *are* gods, however.) I spent yesterday evening very pleasantly with my English friend, who laughed sometimes if it can be called that. People who know him are not at all surprised by the respect I have for his words. We were arguing about future wars, which will be short. After two campaigns the House of Commons, who do the paying, will no longer be angry, and, particularly, no matter what happens, England will never again be angry with France. When the Roman Senate saw the common people obstinate about demanding a reasonable reform, they got a war started. The Tories would be willing to imitate this good old tactic but the freedom of the press would upset their fine phrases about love of country, duty of revenge, etc.

After we had discussed these big questions thoroughly, we came to the little, less serious details. "What embarrasses us quite a bit in England," said my friend, "is the flogging which is customarily administered to delinquent soldiers."

"You know, Parliamentary inquiries are serious things with us. The Duke of Wellington, a man dedicated to power whatever it may be and a better prop to despotism in his way than Metternich, answered during an inquiry, 'If you suppress flogging, you must make officers of all soldiers who conduct themselves well as is the custom in France. If our soldiers no longer have fear, they must have hope, for, without one of these two incentives, a man won't march."

"So far, when a young man wants to be an officer in England, they ask for proof that he belongs to the middle aristocracy, that is, they make him buy his commission with a certain amount of money. The whole present system will be destroyed if you make an officer out of a common soldier who has distinguished himself. With us, the army does not think at all. That is its chief merit. It is not the army that has any aversion to flogging. It is the nation which has suddenly begun to hate it and be scandalized by it as it was formerly struck by a hatred for slavery. With occasional floggings and good rations every day, you will have an excellent English army.

"The best army that ever existed *with no enthusiasm for*

anything—notice this point, so consoling to certain people—was the English army that fought at Toulouse. With an army like that and a few millions furnished by the privileged classes, Russia could annihilate freedom in Europe.

"Every man who fought at Toulouse had entire confidence in the man next to him and boundless respect for his colonel. Ten years ago soldiers fought under the same generals. More than that, they were sure of the countries they left behind them.

"The English army at Waterloo did not know its generals and was quite inferior to the one at Toulouse. Nevertheless the Prussian army lost a quarter of its strength marching from Waterloo to Paris (this is the Duke of Wellington speaking), and the English army did not lose two hundred men. The Prussian army was forced to evacuate certain departments of France because it could not live off them. The English corps that replaced the Prussian regiments subsisted there very well because of the great effect of discipline, that is, of flogging."

Colonel Fitz-Clarence is a good officer, very brave and often wounded, but, in the end, it seems that you cannot be the natural son of a king with impunity. One day at the common table of the regiment—the "mess" (*sic*)—a young ensign undertook to cut up a pheasant and was making a botch of it.

"I have always agreed with my father," said the colonel, the king's son who often spoke of his father, "that you can always tell a *gentleman* by the way he carves."

"Please tell me, colonel," said the young ensign, stopping short, "what does Madame, your mother, say to that?"

A young man from Grenoble said to us this evening, "They say poets are greatly puzzled when they try to describe Paradise. For myself, I would ask only a few things of God. First, my health as it is today; second, to forget Italy every year. Then every year I would go see Milan, Florence, Rome, Naples again. Third, to forget *Don Quixote* and *The Thousand and One Nights* every month."

I have spent twenty-five days now in Lyons, and I haven't

dared present myself at the dining club. It would have looked too much as if I were begging an invitation, for, with connoisseurs of this rank, it is out of the question for me to offer them a wretched dinner at some commonplace inn.

What is especially lacking in the Lyonnais character is what might have excused my gastronomic advances, a spirit of daring, a reckless imprudence, the presence of wit, the gaiety of a Paris gamin. It is not that the character of the Paris gamin pleases me. Although still a child, he has lost the child's sweetness of manner and especially his naiveté. He calculates just how far he can profit from his youth to let himself be impertinent. Such is the twenty-five-year-old Parisian. He uses his position coolly and skilfully to get the advantage over anyone he deals with, and his self-assurance wilts if he ever finds any resistance. It is not my ruffled vanity that abhors the Paris gamin. It is rather my love for the graces of childhood that suffers when I see them degraded.

Hazlitt, an intelligent Englishman and a misanthrope, asserts that naturalness no longer exists in Paris even in an eight-year-old child. In Lyons, you still see the gamin. In Marseilles we are in the midst of naturalness. The child there is rude already, hot-headed much like his father, and, further, he has all the graces of childhood. The children of the Dauphinate are completely natural.

I write these somewhat too serious lines before a window that overlooks the Place Bellecour and the statue of Louis XIV which has to be guarded by a sentry. To all intents and purposes this statue of Louis XIV is very dull, but it is a perfect likeness. It is very much Voltaire's Louis XIV, the farthest thing in the world from the natural and tranquil majesty of the Marcus Aurelius at the Capitol. Chivalry passed that way.

Nowadays there are two very hard trades, that of prince and that of sculptor. To make something out of majesty that will not be ridiculous is a tough job. You make certain gestures. You raise your head to give me, the mayor of a little town, the idea that you are a prince. You wouldn't trouble to make these gestures if you were alone. It is only natural that I should say, "Is this how this comedian works it? Is this what I find majestic?" This one question destroys the whole feeling.

A long time ago they did not make gestures, and there was no natural behavior in good society. The more important something was to the man who said it, the more impassive he kept his manner. Poor Sculpture lives on gestures; what was she to do? She lived no longer. If she wanted to represent energetic action in the great men of the day, she was oftenest reduced to copying an affectation. See the statue of Casimir Périer at Père-Lachaise. He speaks with affectation. He is wearing his cloak over his uniform as he speaks to his colleagues in the Chamber. This would give the idea, if this statue gave any idea, that the hero was afraid it was going to rain on the rostrum.

In Ingres' painting, notice Louis XIII's gesture at the moment he is placing his realm under the protection of the Holy Virgin. The painter wished to give him a passionate gesture, and in spite of this painter's great talent, it became only the gesture of a stevedore. Calamatta's sublime engraving could not conceal the defects of the original. To look grave and dutiful, the Madonna pouts. She is not *grave-in-spite-of-herself* like Raphael's virgins whom Ingres is imitating.

Notice the Henri IV on the Pont Neuf. He is a recruit who is afraid of falling off his horse. The Louis XIV of the Place des Victoires is more skilful. He is M. Franconi putting his horse through its paces before the whole barracks.

Marcus Aurelius, on the contrary, extends his hand as he speaks to his soldiers, and he has no idea whatever of being majestic to make them respect him.

"But," triumphantly remarks a French artist, "the thighs of Marcus Aurelius go back into the sides of his horse."

I reply, "I have seen a letter of Voltaire's with three spelling mistakes in it."

The Louis XIV in the Place Bellecour is a squire who sits

his horse quite well. Perhaps some Minister of the Interior posed for the statue.

This Place de Bellecour, so renowned in Lyons, is vacant rather than large. The "facades" of Bellecour, as they say, pompously in this region, are particularly inhabited by the nobility, who are very devout and not very gay. There is nothing gloomier than the Place de Bellecour.

When, unfortunately, I have no business to do and I am ready to give myself to the devil out of boredom, I go hire a *brèche*, if the weather's good, on the Quai de la Feuillé on the Saône. The quai on the Saône is well situated, surrounded by hills and buildings of some character, and it represents summer in Lyons. As for the quai on the Rhône, it is modern insignificance and *winter*.

I got carried away by my sentence, and I forgot to say that a *brèche* in Lyons is a little boat covered by a round frame with a canvas over it, rowed by a young girl whose grace, elegant cleanliness, and almost virile strength recall the blooming ferry-women of the Swiss lakes. You ride down the Saône toward Ile Barbe.

Sundays and holidays especially, all the boat-women sit on the parapet of the quai, ranged in order of their arrival, but the prettiest know very well they will be chosen first by strangers. They call out boldly, talking up the pleasure of the trip, describing the enchanting places they will take you.

The waters of the Saône flow down so slight a grade that it is often hard to tell in what direction they are going and whether one girl has enough strength to row a *brèche*. You must pick two boat-women, pay them a little more than usual, and set up a sort of rivalry between them.

Vienne, June 9

HERE I AM AT VIENNE, come by an abominable road all uphill and downhill. Two or three times my poor little calash just

missed being broken up by the enormous six-horse carts coming from Provence, and, what is worse for a man of spirit, I could not revenge myself. The least sign of resentment on my part would have gotten me lashed by the whips of two or three Provençal carters, the roughest and most quick-tempered in the world. It's true I have some pistols, but the carters are quite capable of not being frightened until after I had fired. What frightful lengths to have to go to!

I shall make the same remark here as I did in the Gatinais: why not put the main road from Lyons to Vienne on the right bank of the Rhone where there are no mountains? It enters Vienne over the pretty suspension bridge I have just crossed. The road could, I think, also follow the left bank.

Vienne, June 10

The people of vienne are affable and not at all afraid of compromising their dignity by speaking to an unknown traveler. We are twenty-five hundred miles from Paris. I have been presented to M. Boissat, notary, the most influential man in Vienne and one who rules by kindness.

The modern town is very ugly but, to make up for it, has an admirable site. I much prefer this sort of luck to a well-built town set in a low place like the Chateau of Fontainebleau, for example.

Vienne, which the Romans called "The Beautiful," today lies half on the hillsides that overlook the Rhone, half on a little tongue of land that projects between the river and the hills. It is surrounded by mountains, some bare, others covered with brush. Their varied profiles mark the horizon in an odd fashion.

A guide took me to what they call "The Needle" here. It is a pyramid erected in a field some distance from the suburb toward Valence. This monument is really ancient, but it is very ugly. The first thing you notice is a four-sided pyramid, hollow part of the way up. It is set on a square base held up by four archways under which you can pass, and they are less ugly than the pyramid itself. There are engaged columns at the four corners. The top of the pyramid is seventy-two feet from the ground.

Since the capitals of the columns are only rough-hewn, I don't believe that this monument, whatever it may be, was ever finished. It is known that the Romans chiseled architectural details on the spot. The pyramid of Vienne has at least the merit of having been built out of enormous stones, perfectly joined. No trace of cement is visible, but, as in the Coliseum at Rome, there are deep holes gouged out by the barbarians, apparently so they could steal the clamps.

This monument might have been erected by one of those emperors whom the Praetorians hurled from the throne after a few months' reign. The emperor's death would have kept it from being finished.

One fine day at ten o'clock in the morning a strapping young man came running out of one of the finest houses in Vienne. He was barefooted and in his shirt. Blood was streaming from his cheeks.

Luckily he had no idea that he might be suspected of murder. Here is what we learned the next day. A very bellicose husband pretended to go hunting, planning to return and surprise his wife *in flagrante delicto.* He had been tipped off by another aide-de-camp, a rival of the young man's. When he came to the stubble-fields near the town, his dog put up some quail, and, in spite of his anger, the husband couldn't resist having a shot at them.

He didn't return home until ten o'clock, thinking that he would have to save the surprise for another time, but no, he found the young man sound asleep in his bed, and he was not alone. The furious husband struck him a blow with his sword that pierced both cheeks. The sleeper was awakened by the cold steel passing over his tongue. An interested party who found herself nearby siezed the sword just as the husband drew back to launch a second and better-directed thrust at the offender's breast. He ducked under the husband's arm and reached the street in the simplest apparel.

Another young man of this same southern town was even more heroic. To save the honor of a woman he adored, he undertook to descend from the sixth floor with the help of a single bed-sheet, which meant that he jumped down into the street from the fifth floor and broke both his legs. A milkman passed at five in the morning. He gave him some money to carry him five hundred yards down the street and lay him under the windows of an inn. The young man is still very lame. What is odd is that she still loves him.

St. Vallier, June 11

AT ST. COLOMBE opposite Vienne begins the Côte-Rotie, famous for its red wines. Every hamlet in the neighborhood gives its name to a celebrated wine. Who does not respect the Ermitage wines, those of Ampuis, of Condrieux, etc.? The soil of the left bank of the Rhone which follows the Marseilles road is covered with such a prodigious quantity of pebbles that you can hardly see the ground, and to the left of the road, the countryside is planted with mulberry trees so close together that it looks like an orchard, and in the shade of these trees, wheat grows wonderfully well. I was deafened by the cicadas.

From Vienne nearly to Avignon the peasants build their houses of earth or puddled clay. The road leading to Grenoble is lined with chestnut trees which antedate the road and make it very picturesque.

Ampuis produces perhaps the best melons in the South and those excellent chestnuts known in Paris as "*marrons de Lyons.*"

On the right we see in the distance a fine suspension bridge that stands out above the trees. It is the fourth or fifth iron-wire bridge over the Rhone, which is so wide and rapid here. The impetuosity of its current doubles the impression of the victory man has gained over nature.

Why must the ugliest iron bridges in France be those in Paris precisely? Have the engineers' brains been iced over by fear of the ridicule the newspapers heaped so lavishly on the first unsuccessful bridge?

About twelve and a half miles from Vienne I passed over the famous gradient of Revantin which once used to hold up the big wagons from Provence for hours at a time. You know that under Henri IV all the roads in France were only muletracks. This prince and Sully, his minister, began to widen them, and they are still called Henri IV's roads. They were built by the inhabitants of one village so they could communicate with the next. Some of the grades were terrible, but what's a grade to a mule? Louis XIV and Louis XV widened them further. Few new roads were made under Louis XIV, many under Louis XV who waged no big wars and was able to employ two talented men, Péronnet and Trésaguet. The provincial establishments, especially Languedoc, Brittany, and Burgundy, made many roads. As for those of Flanders, which are still the best, they antedate Louis XIV and were made by the municipalities. As is well known, there was a moment at the end of the Middle Ages when liberty seemed to want to establish itself in Flanders. At once it produced its miracles. The vile hills you still have to climb in France are the remnants of those mule-tracks built by Henri IV.

The gradient of Revantin, which I have just come down at a trot, slopes thirteen centimeters in every meter and is nearly a mile long. There is a company that has worked out a grade of only four centimeters if they build just fifteen hundred meters more road. It is easy to see that the road was laid out by mere chance in the first place. The toll the company would charge to reimburse itself would last only eleven years and seven months. After that the road would be free like all the others. The toll, I think, would be six sous a horse going up and three sous going down, and the toll would cost less than the extra horses hired. Here is the degree of civilization we have reached as far as road-making is concerned: today in France a horse can pull about a ton and a half on level ground.

Valence, June 11

THE GOOD HUMOR, the naturalness I thought I had already noticed in Vienne bursts out still more in Valence. Already we are really in the South. I never could resist this impression of joy. It is the antipodes of Parisian politeness which, above all, should summon up the self-respect of the person you are speaking to as well as what he demands from you. When he begins to speak, everyone here thinks only of satisfying whatever emotion is agitating him at the moment and never in the world of building up a noble character for himself in the mind of the person who is listening, still less of paying the respect that is owed to his social position. This is surely what Talleyrand was speaking of when he said, "In France they no longer respect anything."

A kind of native delight winds through the actions of these men of the South which seems coarse to a half-consumptive youth brought up in good Parisian society.

I wander through this little town under the burning sun. I go up to the citadel begun by Francis I, a beautiful view. An old corporal calls to my notice on the opposite bank of the Rhone the slope of St. Peray, the home of the good wine of that name. The artillery range, remarkable for its beautiful plane trees, makes me think of Napoleon's youth. The most distinguished woman of the town received the young lieutenant kindly and became his guiding genius. His vanity suffered cruelly, and she soothed it. His comrades had their horses and carriages, and the small allowance his family promised him was seldom paid. Nevertheless his family decided on the painful sacrifice of selling a vineyard to be able to pay the allowance.

Napoleon's weakness for the aristocracy came to the surface in Mme du Colombier's salon (as General Duroc tells it).

It was there that Napoleon, who, no matter what anyone says, had received a very imperfect education in the military schools of Brienne and Paris, drew most of his opinions other than those on mathematics or the art of war. How much difference it would have made to France and to himself if he had read Montesquieu in Valence! The emperor never saw anything but disorder, foolishness, or rebellion in the operations of a deliberative assembly. His executive genius never saw any source of legitimacy for law. His admirable Council of State did not deliberate; they consulted as to the best way of executing a decision already fixed in the First Consul's head.

I talk freely with ordinary men. What for me is such an arduous duty elsewhere, cultivating my company's representative as I pass through, I do not have to do here.

This southern state of mind which has surrounded me for some hours now has plunged me into a sweet serenity. It falls like a half-transparent veil over three-quarters of the worries I would take to heart in Paris, and the absence of these worries makes my happiness perfect. I am enjoying life. Going for a walk on the banks of the Rhone, I stop under a magnificent willow.

I know that nothing is in worse taste than expounding one's way of life. Explaining it almost destroys it, but I ask nothing from the society of Paris. Soon I shall be in America, and if anyone pushes me, I shall give this explanation to that critic of the period: "Why should I flatter powerful salons if I ask nothing from them?"

I went to see the church of St. Appollinaire, rebuilt in 1604, the bust of Pius VI, and the tomb of the Mistral family (an ill-omened name in this region). The house of M. Aurel is a strange monument of fifteenth-century architecture. The common people love the four enormous heads on the facade which represent the four winds.

Here are the ideas I had when I visited St. Appollinaire: the ogival arch is depressing, while, I don't know why, the round arch gives the idea of a force employed to defend you. I admit that Gothic architecture is like the sound of a harmonica to me. It makes an astonishing effect the first time you hear it, but it has the defect of being always the same, and it is no good in the hands of a mediocre player. Thus the church of St. Ouen in Rouen, the cathedral at Cologne, and the one in Milan give me an impression something like those of the Maison Carrée at Nimes or St. Peter's in Rome, but the vulgar Gothic churches—for instance, the cathedrals of Lyons, Nevers, or Valence—are like mediocre pictures to me, and when I see a scholar work himself up about them, he gives me the impression of a man who wants to make the Academy quickly. Do you feel this way?

The only mediocre Gothic that has any effect on me is some poor little chapel in the middle of the woods. It is pouring rain. Some poor peasants drawn together by the little bell come to pray to God in silence. During the prayer no other sound is heard except the rain falling, but this is the effect of music, not architecture.

This evening at the table d'hôte of the Valence inn which is in the suburb on the road to Avignon, my neighbor, a fat fellow whose name I didn't know and with whom I had been speaking of one thing and another, suddenly said to me, "You must be really an idiot to spend your money on the coach from here to Avignon. Stuff your carriage into the boat which passes here at ten o'clock tomorrow morning and at three, you will be in Avignon."

This thirty-year-old fat man would have been amazed had I replied, "Pray keep to yourself, sir, the offensive designations for the things you do yourself. I thank you for your advice, but either retain it or give it to me in other terms."

I was brought up in the South myself, and I wasn't very much annoyed really. I said quite simply that I would profit by his advice, and after dinner I offered my new friend some cigars such as no one, probably, had ever seen equaled in Valence. He accepted them with pleasure, but he soon confessed that they seemed *pretty weak* to him. "What about these?" he said, sticking some cigars under my nose. They were made of Sardinian tobacco, I think, and strong as the devil.

On the Steamboat Opposite Montélimar, June 12

THE BANKS OF THE RHONE ENCHANT ME. The pleasure makes me take heart. I hardly know how to find terms prudent enough to describe the growing prosperity of France under the reign of Louis-Philippe. I am afraid of being taken for a paid writer.

I see masons at work everywhere. They are building a tremendous lot of houses in the cities, towns, and villages. Streets are being straightened everywhere. In the fields all the slopes are being tiled, walls built, hedges planted. I could fill four pages with details about the prosperity of France, especially in the departments north of a line drawn from Besancon to Nantes. Even the stick-in-the-mud South begins to rouse itself. Algiers revives Marseilles. If that great city votes against the present government, the fault lies with the confessional, but fundamentally she is not dissatisfied.

Everywhere the nobility economize and improve their lands, exactly the opposite to what they did before 1789.

This prosperity amazed an Englishman, a sensible man with whom I drank tea yesterday evening. It can be explained a priori. History has never presented the spectacle of a people who have five million property-owners out of a population of thirty-three million. This is what no counter-revolution can destroy. A Russian army could camp on the heights of Montmartre, but it could not change the distribution of property.

By the democratic law which shares out estates, the number of property-owners tends to augment itself to infinity. A return of '93 would alarm all property-owners but, in view of this fact, how can it be feared? Consider the fact that the peasant who has only one acre clings to it more tenaciously than his moneyed neighbor does to his two-hundred-acre park.

On the Steamboat Opposite Montélimar, June 12

What a magnificent omen for our future prosperity! In France no one can become an imbecile with impunity. The four sons of a man who has an income of eighty thousand francs know very well that their fortunes will be only twenty thousand francs apiece, and, unless they add to them either by their own abilities or what people are contemptible enough to call a "good marriage," their children will have to become doctors, lawyers, or cloth-manufacturers to make a living. (To my notion but not to theirs, these are the patterns of life that offer the most chances of happiness.)

What shocked my Englishman most in France was that they marry for money here. "How dare you speak of tender sentiments?" he said.

Memoirs of a Tourist

Avignon, June 12

Before reaching the village of Rochemaure on the right bank of the Rhone nearly opposite Montélimar, I tried to see the famous spires of basalt. Suddenly we saw them very distinctly. They stand alone, quite close to one another, and almost in a straight line. In fact, they are detached from the limestone mountain but from a distance they seem joined to it. The mountain is covered with vines and olive trees that are always green. There are even meadows at the foot, and the view from that spot is very pleasant, they say, with the magnificent Rhone in the foreground and the Alps of Dauphiné in the distance. The tallest of these needles is three hundred feet high and is reputed to be inaccessible.

The sight of these fine volcanic products livens up the whole landscape. We saw the two craters of Rochemaure and Chenavari in the distance. Would to God that one of these grand volcanoes of the Vivarais would begin to erupt!

Once Vesuvius went eight or ten centuries without giving a sign of life. To everyone's great astonishment, it started up again only in the year 79 in the eruption that smothered Pliny.

In Avignon I started off in a bad temper. Eight or ten huge porters hurled themselves on my baggage and made off with it in spite of me. I was enraged, but I didn't say a word. Joseph, who is more natural than I am, gave and got some pretty good shoves.

Going into Avignon you would think you were in an Italian town. The workingmen have fiery looks. They are tanned, and they sling their jackets over their shoulders. They work in the shade or sleep lying in the middle of the street; for here, as on the banks of the Tiber, they are not acquainted with ridicule, and if they think they see it in their neighbor, they do not fear his epigrams, but they regard him as an enemy.

I took lodgings at the Palais Royal Hotel. I was covered

with dust. The bootblack, rendering me his little services, changed all my thoughts. "Do you know, sir, that Marshal Brune was killed in this hotel in 1815? The proprietor doesn't like to have it talked about, but if you ask Jean, the servant, he will tell you all about it." I had this gloomy curiosity. I crossed the floor of the room where the Marshal was shot, but I shall not do the reader the disservice of recounting in detail what I saw. The floor was covered with fleas. This filth increased the horror of the act I was thinking about. I saw more clearly the grossness of the assassins. But who paid them? History will tell. A commercial traveler found the body of the Marshal stuck in some reeds on the Rhone near Arles.

I saw Marshal Brune exiled by the Emperor at Méry in Champagne. He was six feet tall with most imposing features. Every Sunday he went to mass in full uniform. (He began as a Republican and a printer.)

To forget these black memories, I had myself taken to the museum. The pictures are charmingly hung in some huge rooms that give on to a solitary garden which has some fine trees. There was a profound stillness there that reminded me of the beautiful churches of Italy. The mind, already half-separated from the vain interests of the world, is prepared to feel sublime beauty. I found many pictures of the Italian School there, a Luini, a Caravaggio, a Domenichino, a Salvator Rosa, etc., but the French public hardly likes to hear these things talked about which they understand so little.

I spent two delightful hours daydreaming in this museum. How different from the one in Lyons! Avignon would undoubtedly gain by exchanging its pictures for the ones in the Saint-Pierre Palace, but in Lyons the silk-weaving atmosphere dessicates the heart. When the imagination is stimulated a little, it fears being wounded by something ugly or appalling, and when you are surrounded by money-grubbers, you have to make yourself tough.

The Avignon museum has twelve thousand medals. With a

child's curiosity I examined the great bronze collection of Roman emperors—Caesar, Augustus, Tiberius, Vespasian—who will always be personages different in our minds from Charles V, Charles VII, Henri II, and all the faded kings of our history.

After the first Caesars the election was military. Still, it was an election, and incompetency was punished by death, hence the succession of great men who led this great empire of a hundred and twenty million subjects: Trajan, Hadrian, Marcus Aurelius, Septimius Severus, Diocletian, Julian.

I admired first an excellent little Caracalla caricature showing a pastry merchant; second, a Roman sign in bronze, very well engraved. It was made of two circles that touched each other and a mosaic showing a bird's-eye view of a town or fortified camp with square towers. The museum also contains some bas-reliefs in a good style, once tomb ornaments, and a life-size bas-relief done under the direction of Good King René. The faces are very ugly and remind me of the German manner.

I crossed the Rhone to see Villeneuve and its beautiful tower. I found the Gothic tomb of Innocent VI, a beautiful "Descent from the Cross" by an Italian master, a "Last Judgment," and finally the admirable portrait of the Marquise de Ganges as penitent by Mignard, the excellent copyist of Italian painters.

Avignon, June 14

I have just come back from the Fountain of Vaucluse, so dear to the people who read Petrarch's sonnets, but they have made so many fine phrases about this celebrated spot that I shan't say anything about it except that the trip takes ten hours.

Avignon, June 15

This morning I was taking a walk on the road to Orange with young Count de Ber——, who is barely nineteen years old.

Avignon, June 15

A young girl had just passed, riding on a donkey. A twelve-year-old boy took the donkey by the tail and jumped on behind. It didn't bother the girl. There was a huge wagon coming down the middle of the road. The driver, an enormous fat Provençal, threatened the child, and, as the donkey went by at its little trot, carrying its double load gaily, the driver let go a lash of his whip at the child, who gave a cry.

Count de Ber—— shuddered. "What a cruel thing to do!" he said.

"I'll give you another, you shrimp," shouted the carter, swearing and coming toward us.

Quick as a shot, the young count jumped on the gigantic Provençal, seized him by the throat, and choked him so hard that he grew pale and blood covered his lips. After he had gone about twenty paces, the Count threw him back his whip which he had picked up. I shall love this young count to the end of my days. He is not at all stupid even if he is rich.

The women of Avignon are very pretty. As I was admiring the truly oriental eyes of one of these ladies shopping in the square, I was told she was Jewish.

I found a magnificent view from the top of the limestone mass of the *Dons* where the Palace of the Popes was built in the fourteenth century. It was a fortress and was so considered by the anti-pope Benedict XIII (Pierre de Luna), who withstood a prolonged siege there against Marshal Boucicaut. Today the palace is oddly ruined. It is used as a barracks, and the soldiers detach heads from the Giotto frescoes on the wall and sell them to the well-to-do. Despite these degradations it still lifts its towers to a magnificent height. I noticed that it was built with all the Italian mistrust. The interior is as well fortified against an enemy who penetrates into the courtyards as the exterior is fortified against the enemy who is settled outside.

I went over all the different floors of this singular fortress with the keenest interest. I saw the stake (called an "awakener") on which the Inquisition made the ungodly sit who were unwilling to confess their crimes, and I observed the charming heads, the remains of Giotto's frescoes. The red contours of the original drawings are still visible on the walls.

Everyone knows that Philip the Fair, a prince who could use his will, had Bertrand the Goth appointed Pope. He took the name of Clement V, and in 1309 he transferred the Holy See to Avignon where it remained until 1378. The papal court, then the world's foremost, civilized Provence, which, thanks to Marseilles, had never been so barbarous as Picardy, for instance.

John XXII needed money. He invented the *daterie*, a kind of budget of ways and means composed of levies called first-fruits, reservations, provisions, exemptions, expectancies, all paid by the Christian kingdoms. By means of the *daterie*, this pope left a treasure of eight million gold florins (equal to two hundred million in 1837) and a personal estate estimated at seven million florins. It pleased me to notice that the tomb of this intelligent man was spared by the Revolution.

The adroit and powerful men who made up the court at Avignon did not need to check or dissimulate their passions, for in that century, they had passions. In my opinion, this goes far to justify the cruelties and the injustices. Moreover, it was a long time still before Luther and Voltaire.

I recall those Latin letters of Petrarch where he speaks without reserve of what happened in the brilliant days of that court. There is nothing more curious, but the Latin is obscure. It must be agreed that they are concerned with actions very different from those that occupied Rome in the time of Cicero, whose style Petrarch copied as well as he could. In these letters we see an old man, very intelligent, very dignified, who puts a red biretta on his head in order to accomplish the seduction of a fourteen-year-old girl.

The view from the top of the *Dons* is one of the most beautiful in France. To the east you see the Alps of Provence and Dauphiné and Mt. Ventoux as well. To the west, you can follow a large part of the Rhone basin. I find that the course of the river gives an idea of its power. Its bed is strewn with willow-covered islands. This verdure is not especially stately, but in the midst of this dry, stony country it delights the eye.

Beyond the Rhone and the famous Bridge of Avignon, half of which the Rhone carried away in 1664, rises a hillside crowned by Villeneuve and the fortress St. André. Their walls are surrounded by woods and vineyards. The county (Venaissin) is so thickly covered with olive trees, willows, and mulberry trees that some parts of it could be called forest. Through these trees the handsome ramparts of Carpentras can be seen in the distance.

The view of the nearby islands of the Rhone is not bad. I have honestly judged all these views to be pleasant, but I haven't enjoyed a single one of them. I'm in no condition to enjoy anything. A furious mistral began again this morning. It is the great *drawback* [*sic*] to any pleasure you can find in Provence.

Strabo called this terrible wind *melanborée,* the black north wind. The Dauphinois still call it that, but in Provence it is the mistral. Strabo and Diodorus Sicilius assure us that its violence is so great that it carries away stones and upsets chariots. It wasn't two weeks ago that the stagecoach crossing the Beaucaire bridge had to be held upright by eight men hanging on to ropes hitched to the top. It looked as if it were going to fall into the Rhone.

The north wind strikes the long river valley which runs north and south, and the valley acts as a pair of bellows that redoubles the wind's force. When the mistral is blowing in Provence, no one knows where to hide. As a matter of fact, the sun may be shining brightly, but this cold and unbearable wind penetrates into the most tightly locked rooms in a way to throw the bravest into an unreasonable gloom.

Avignon, June 16

Rabelais calls Avignon "the town that rings," and you do see a host of belfries there. Myself, I would rather call it "the town of pretty women." At every turn you see eyes the like of which you never see near Paris. The streets are sheltered with canvas during the hot weather. I like the practice and the half-light it produces. The natural indolence of the traveler lost me an hour inspecting a certain ivory crucifix, much talked up, quite mediocre, and you had to get permission to see it, too. A nun displays it with great ceremony.

Countess Jeanne, Queen of Naples, famous for her beauty and her adventures, sold Avignon to Pope Clement VI for the sum of twenty-four thousand gold florins. What sweetened the bargain was a little absolution for the murder of her first husband, and the Queen forgot to ask the Pope for the twenty-four thousand gold florins.

I meet many old soldiers. There is a branch of the Hotel des Invalides here. Nothing could be more sensible. The only treasure a poor man of sixty can have is fine weather. Three-quarters of the veterans' hospitals in France should be set up at Antibes, a league from Var and from the frontier, which these brave men can defend if need be. Bread, wine, and meat are cheaper there than in Avignon, and Strabo's black north wind is less terrible there.

A Corsican, a sensible man, M. N——, said to me, "French history begins only with Louis XI. From then until now there is continuity. Before Louis XI there are some anecdotes about Charlemagne, Charles V, the Maid of Orleans. Some intelligent man like Vertot should translate the scholar Sismondi into French."

Mme d'Arsac of Avignon used to say to her daughters, "Ladies, you must never believe in 'very' (in the 'very' beautiful or the 'very' wicked). There is nothing but mediocrity in this world."

Just when I thought I was going to spend a fortnight traveling in this lovely Provence (whose mistral is all I have seen of it), I receive all at once some letters telling me that our business in Algiers does not require my presence in Marseilles and other letters from Paris that prove to me how feebly and clumsily business has gone in my absence. This evening I leave again for the Nivernais where business is terrible. Happy is the man who has something to live on or who is sure, at least, that he will never be sorry if he is stopped on the road to a little fortune.

Nivernais, June 18

I PASSED THROUGH CLERMONT, and I was quite annoyed that I couldn't stay there. What a magnificent location! What an admirable cathedral! What wonderful *breezy* heat!

My stay in Clermont, brief as it was, still was long enough to be defiled by complaints. I was in heaven. Then some demands made by a firm owned by friends of ours on another house equally friendly made me fall in the mud. When shall I be rich enough so that I won't have to put up with forced relations with any man? Posterity will say, "The *envious* nineteenth century." That is the sad epithet it deserves in France. All our present worries spring from envy.

If I had a week, I think I might very well spend it in the Cantals in the neighborhood of St. Flour. There are some lonely places there worthy of the minds who read Petrarch's sonnets with pleasure, but I shall not point them out any more distinctly than this, and thus they will be protected from the ready-made phrases and unfortunate superlatives of the humbugs who write articles for the reviews.

If you want to have the reputation of a capable fellow in France nowadays, you must speak solemnly, never collide with any general ideas, and treat with respect the five or six idiocies that are the false gods of every career. You might say that *not being important* is an insult to all who are. I am very much afraid that in the next four or five years these gods will fall flat. This misfortune will occur when public affairs are controlled only by men born after 1789.

I foresee a second cascade in the very distant future, say thirty years from now, when things are taken in hand by the men who were fifteen years old in 1828, that fatal epoch when the gentry dared bring reason to bear on the most venerable old rubbish. But at this distant time even the sons of upstarts will know how to read. Their voices will count in literature, which will offset the torrent of innovation.

To go back to my little room at the inn and write this journal is a more active pleasure to me than reading. It is an operation that effectively scours my imagination clean of all notions of money, all the filthy suspicions we adorn with the name of prudence. Prudence—how necessary it is, and how queerly it weighs on those who were not born with a little money, on those who neglect it, and on those who invoke its aid!

Nivernais, June 19

"Would to God that fire was consuming the four corners of Paris!" I heard this said quite seriously this evening at a fine dinner. A rich businessman from the Midi made this charitable wish. Not only is every man envious of every other in this gloomy nineteenth century, not only does every banker or rich businessman loathe M. Laffite, but even Toulouse, Bordeaux, etc. grow thin from the prosperity of Paris. They envy Paris, first, for the speculation on its stock exchange (clandestinely, a man with no reputation as a plunger can take the keenest pleasure in the most foolish speculations); second, they envy Paris its revenue. There are sixty thousand Parisians sharing in this income and not four thousand in the provinces. It is very hard to make land pay more than 2½ per cent, and money in Paris bonds returns 4¾. "Yes," the bondholders could reply, "but owning land indulges one's vanity and makes one a captain in the National Guard with a bearskin bonnet." Third, all big business can't avoid being organized in Paris. The only known exceptions are some second-rate deals arranged in Lyons.

Nivernais, June 19

"Whose fault is it?" I asked all the petty *hatreds* who would classify everyone who was able to live in Paris as deserters from the provinces. For, since I didn't want to seem cowardly, I was obliged to speak pretty coolly. "But, gentlemen, this is the fable of the limbs revolting against the stomach. Do you want to be a withered country like Spain, with no capital at all?" They listened, quivering with hatred. Then I gave myself the pleasure of really distressing their envy, "But are you acquainted with Paris, gentlemen? After the census of 1800 had revealed only four hundred and sixty thousand inhabitants, the First Consul said, 'The capital of France must have half a million souls,' and he gave special weight to the half-million. In 1837, the actual count was nine hundred and twenty thousand, independent of the suburbs like Vaugirard, Les Batignolles, etc. that touch Paris on all sides. Twenty rich persons from my department have taken refuge in Paris because there is less hate and envy there than in the provinces, and, however much you want to, you cannot hate someone you do not know."

This dinner was excellent but boring. The guests were newly and very rich. A lord of recent date, a very handsome fellow, all garnished with gold chains and very proud of a ribbon two days old, thought it a good idea to monopolize the conversation. He seemed to be reciting a lesson learned by heart. "Our revolution of 1830," he cried, "had a sublime mission, and it has well fulfilled it. Let us honor, let us bless the memory of those whose virtue and genius have made France independent of neighboring kings and free and virtuous within herself, but let us by no means try to imitate these sublime men, for they have left us nothing to do but to enjoy the fruits of their labors in peace. Let us take care not to upset the equilibrium of things, let us not be so unwise as to awake the spirit of emulation in the populace. That, especially, is the danger. More mutual education, more big schools are what we want." Everyone laughed loudly at this because this gentleman had made his fortune from the sciences and the big schools. He was stung to the quick. His wounded vanity had thrown him into imprudence. The laughs redoubled, and you might say he was jeered at as far as politeness allowed. Like so many others, M. N—— wanted to enjoy his own position and at the same time to find in the salons that profound consideration, that unanimous benevolence he had met there formerly. This is the kind of torment suffered by the men who have made their money in the last seven years.

"It is a true European malady," he said moodily, "this need the masses have to mix in public affairs and to intervene in the exercise of sovereign power. To be well used, this power must have nothing but moral barriers; otherwise your opposition will be distracted by it, perhaps even angry, and it will not be able to devote itself to the high and arduous mission it received from heaven. . . ." (I have put the style in order, which was bombastic in quite a different way.)

At these words everyone allowed himself to poke fun at the great man, even young fellows who were just making their social debuts. Such was my evening. Not a single little amusing anecdote.

Bourges, June 20

The la Charité stage stopped a moment at Rousselan. This station is a single house in the middle of a field surrounded by thick woods. Few places have given me more the feeling of complete isolation. I spent a quarter of an hour there, walking along the woods, a hundred paces from the farm. I was happy. I had all the troubles of the world at my feet.

A few miles farther on, crossing the gloomiest of plains with the wretched horses that have to do a relay of fifteen miles; I caught sight of the tower of the famous cathedral of Bourges. This tower, the object of all my wishes, disappeared many times behind ridges in the terrain. At last we reached certain little bogs, immediately surrounding the town, where they grow cabbage. The local people find it beautiful.

The coach set me down at the best inn of the region halfway down a main street as you come from Paris. A servant in a cotton cap who seemed half-asleep carried my valise up to my room, but I was hardly there when I was seized by a pang impossible to describe. The idea struck me of sending someone to look for a post-horse and of leaving at once for Issoudun, which is on the road to Tours. I was suffocated by the feeling of bourgeois pettiness.

To prevent the possibility of giving in to such a silly repugnance, I dashed out of my room (a frightful place), but there was an uneven step in the middle of the landing of the winding wooden staircase. I just missed falling. The staircase is of such venerable antiquity that I was afraid the banister I hung on to, made of little worm-eaten columns, would come away in my hand.

I left the inn swearing loudly, I confess, against all provincials. I wanted to go to the cathedral, but I think I would have died sooner than ask one of these fine people the way. I felt that an answer that was just a little too ridiculous would make me turn sharp into a street where, on my arrival, I had noticed a post where horses could be hired.

I have thought that the people of the thirteenth century showed rare good sense as long as the aforesaid good sense was not eclipsed by their religion. If they wanted to build a celebrated church in the middle of a vast plain, they chose the highest part of town. I started to follow the gutters upward in the middle of these gloomy streets, formed once by garden walls and now by mean little two-story houses. After five minutes I found myself at the foot of the square tower of the cathedral. Seen up close, the tower does not have a good effect. The contour that stands out against the sky is uneven. This serious disadvantage is produced by the leaning figures of saints which are protected by ogival canopies plastered against the tower.

Luckily the door of the cathedral was still open. They were restoring the big Gothic portal and doing it very well. It was nearly night. I hastened to enter the church for fear it would be closed. As a matter of fact, as I went in, they lighted two or three little lamps in this immense emptiness. I admit I experienced an odd sensation: I was a Christian. I was thinking like St. Jerome whom I was reading yesterday. During one full hour my mind no longer felt the torment of the petty annoyances I had suffered since my arrival in Bourges.

I sense the complete impossibility of giving any idea of this church; however, I shall never forget it. It has only one tower. It has the form of a playing card. It is divided into five naves by rows of enormous pillars excessively elongated. Begun about 845, it is nevertheless Gothic. The two magnificent north and south portals whose architecture I can never tire of admiring seems to me to be of an earlier period. Notice the wooden door toward the south, covered with capital R's.

All I can say of the interior of this vast cathedral is that it accomplishes its aim perfectly. The traveler who wanders among its immense pillars is seized with respect. He feels the nothingness of man in the presence of the Divinity. If there were no revolting hypocrisy and no political end hidden under this pious word, this feeling would last several days.

I was lucky enough to be almost alone, and night was rapidly falling. After some time, I saw the porter making big circles around me, and seeing finally that I did not understand, he advanced to meet me with a resolute air, which was only timidity perhaps, and told me it was time to leave.

I suddenly gained his friendship with my generous ways. In a moment he had given me a number of details that aroused my keenest interest. He told me that there was a subterranean church (or crypt) under the choir.

Since it is beyond my powers to give an intelligible description here, I am going to fall back on the historic, as those elegant and stupid writers are always doing when they have to review an opera or a picture.

St. Etienne is this cathedral's name, one of the most beautiful in France. It was begun in 845 when the arts had a certain glimmer of prosperity under Charlemagne. It was not finished for many centuries. The portal, reached by a flight of a dozen steps, is a hundred and sixty-nine feet wide. The bas-relief above the main door represents the Last Judgment. During the religious wars of the sixteenth century, the Protestants broke the heads of most of the saints on the facade. The principal nave is a hundred and fourteen feet high and thirty-eight feet wide. The building's total length is three hundred and forty-eight feet. The great rose window, adorned with twelfth-century stained glass in brilliant colors, is not less than twenty-seven feet in diameter.

At my urgent request the porter went to get a lantern, and I went down into the crypt with him. There I saw the tomb of Jean I, Duc de Berry. His big head had a proud and wicked air. Shall I speak of the pleasure it gave me to go through this immense edifice, lighted only by our lantern and two little lamps on the altars? I tasted with delight a child's joy.

I arranged to meet the good porter at eight the next morning. He pushed kindness so far as to take me to the fashionable café. When I said, "Fashionable café," he did not understand. Then I asked him for the café where the proprietor made the most money, the one that drew the most people, finally, the officers' café. At this last word, the porter's anxious face brightened, and we set out.

The place was not up to much, but it was full of people who talked very loudly, and there were artillery officers in brilliant uniforms who played cards with all the fire of youth, shouting over each trick. All this revived me.

To crown my misfortunes this evening, after I had drunk my chicory coffee, I intended to return to the café at the inn in the hope of supper, and I got completely lost. It was the disgraceful hour of ten o'clock, and there were a lot of little streets, all curved and forming a labyrinth, and there was not a soul in any of them. Every few minutes I would come to a little square planted with trees. At last I found a toper, the oddest in the world, profoundly drunk but who could still talk well enough and who got huffy because I spoke to him. He kept saying, "Pooh, what's it to me if you got to town two hours ago and can't find your hotel?"

He was really funny when, out of charity and with deep scorn, he would name me the streets I didn't know. When he saw that I didn't budge but kept on questioning him, he said banteringly, "Go that way. You'll find the post that'll take you where you want." He laughed a great deal at this sally and went off repeating it and bumping against walls.

As for me, I walked quickly away. I had noticed the posting station on my arrival at Bourges. In five minutes I had found my inn again, where a fat maid put a stinking candle in a dirty candlestick into my hand, and I am writing this on my chest of drawers.

Tours, June 22

At nine o'clock in the evening I embarked in a stagecoach that strongly resembled Noah's ark. Outside, the top was filled with hunting dogs that seemed quite discontented with their lot and attested it loudly. This first kept me from eating supper and then from sleeping very well as far as Issodun. Around midnight I walked a hundred paces in the main square of this little town which they say is very pretty. At five, I mean five in the morning, we arrived at Chateauroux, which I was very glad of.

When it struck a quarter past five, I went to finish waking up a brave café owner who was opening his shop which had a little alley of young trees in front of it. He told me that the milk didn't come until six. Then I told him how religious scholars had discovered that it could be replaced by the yolk of an egg. This great secret had not penetrated as far as Chateauroux. The good café owner gave me an egg and some brown sugar and watched attentively what I did.

The chateau that gave its name to the town, which Ralph the Bold ordered built in 940, still exists, perched on a hill where its towers overlook the Indre. I admired the beautiful view. The town is surrounded by pretty meadows. The houses are ancient, it is true, but full of character. They haven't the wretched air of the houses in Troyes. I got the church of St. André opened, but the beadle of St. Martial's kept a deaf ear. Then I ran quickly back to the new inn. The fifty minutes the driver had given me had expired, but nothing was ready for departure. Two or three burghers of Chateauroux had only just realized at a quarter to six that they wanted to go to Tours. From the top of my compartment I assisted in loading their trunks and in worrying about their health. It was a pitiful spectacle. A fop arrived unexpectedly, singing, and took a seat beside me. He amused me as far as a village fifteen miles down the road to Tours. He took infinite pains to tell me, without seeming to do so, that he had some horses and, further, that these horses were coming to look for him. I did not understand it, myself. When we came to this village whose name I have forgotten, there were no horses whatever. The fop disappeared like magic. I read Caesar as far as Chatillon. In my mind I quarreled with George Sand who has given us such lovely descriptions of the banks of the Indre. It is a pitiful stream which may be twenty-five feet wide and four feet deep. It winds through a fairly level plain bordered at the horizon with low slopes where grow some walnut trees twenty feet high. I looked with all my eyes for that beautiful Touraine about which the authors who wrote a hundred years ago speak so emphatically and the ones today who copy them. I was not destined to find it. That beautiful Touraine does not exist.

The country became more fertile as we drew near Loches. The banks of the Indre were covered with paltry little walnut trees fifteen feet high. The main road never runs far from the stream, whose waters make willows and some poplars grow in the neighboring meadows.

Suddenly I perceived on top of a slope at the left two high towers joined by a wall and cut off sharply and horizontally as if by a saber stroke. It was the Tower of Loches. There perished after twelve years of captivity inflicted by Louis XII that distinguished man Louis the Moor, Duc de Milan, the friend and protector of Leonardo da Vinci. He had found the secret of gathering at his court the most remarkable men of his time, and with them he had what he called "duels of wit." They discussed all sorts of subjects freely and at any length. What court can say as much today? I still remember the amiable cast of countenance on his marble statue that I saw at the Charterhouse near Pavia. It's true that he was a rascal, but that was pretty much the misfortune of all the sovereigns of his period. He had his nephew poisoned in order to succeed him, but he did not have two thousand of his subjects burned alive like our brilliant Francis I in the hope of wangling an alliance with a foreign ruler.

At last we came to some big trees where the road goes down the southern spur of the Cher opposite Tours. Soon after the bridge over the Cher we entered the magnificent street of Tours. It seems as wide as the Rue de la Paix, and this is astonishing in the provinces where you are smothered by shabby bourgeois. This street runs in a straight line to the famous bridge over the Loire.

I put up at the Grand Hotel de la Caille. My room does very well, but I nearly died of hunger because of the meager dinner at the table d'hôte. There were two or three English guests who patiently endured this scarcity, which proves that the dinner is usually as magnificent as this. It lasted not less than an hour and a half. I fled before the dessert to go see the bridge that is the pride of Tours.

Like everything made in France in the last fifty years, this bridge is very convenient and lacks any character whatever. It would take a paid journalist or the editor of a departmental yearbook to have the face to call it beautiful. The smallest of the hundred or so bridges Napoleon had built in Lombardy give a lively feeling of grace or beauty, but those people did not take Constantine by storm like us.

Since I knew no vestige remained of the famous church of St. Martin of Tours, I was reduced to the beauties of nature, and I went over the hill to the north of the bridge with interest. It has the finest site in the world, full south with the view of the big river and a fertile countryside.

It was dark when I got back to Tours. I went to see what are claimed to be the remains of the famous church of St. Martin. There were about a hundred English there, less haughty than usual. In earlier trips around France they have found that a better French is spoken in Tours than in Paris.

I was dead of fatigue. I climbed the stairs to a reading room that occupied a second floor on the beautiful main street. During the whole year I had not felt so cruel a cold. There was an abominable north wind, and the Tours readers thought it a good idea to keep the windows open. I bravely resisted wanting to ask to have them closed. I feared some stupid retort.

I returned shivering to my inn, scared to death of taking cold. It is the only misfortune I dread. It puts me in a bad humor every evening for three weeks. And what's left to the poor traveler if he loses his good humor? I asked for some boiling water. I had taken a teapot from the kitchen myself, and I went up to my room to make my tea. It's incredible, but three times in a row these provincial monsters brought me water that was not even warm, and finally the servant got angry with me. I was frozen, and I flew into a rage. Luckily I understood that I was a fool to have polite manners in the midst of the surrounding barbarians. I rang hard enough to break the bell. I kicked up a row like an Englishman. I demanded a fire, and I got it, that is, my room was filled with smoke, and an hour and a half after I asked for the hot water, I was able to make some tea.

Cured of my cold and discomfort I went to smoke some cigars on the sidewalks of the main street like a true soldier. I drew a tart moral on the ease with which I grow angry: *Ira furor brevis* ("Anger is a brief madness"). If this tendency grows with age, I shall soon be a grumpy old bachelor.

By chance I passed a hardware dealer's. "And my package of books!" I said to myself. This idea changed everything. Two hundred paces from there, at the obliging M. D——'s, I found a package of a dozen books that had arrived for me the day before.

Ten minutes later I was the gayest of men, settled in my room, before a good fire, cutting the pages of a fine copy of Gregory of Tours, just published by the historical society of France. The abominable tallow candles of the provinces made me remember where I was. I went down to the kitchen and took the last remaining scullion off to one side. I made him a present of ten sous and asked him very humbly to go buy me a pound of wax candles. He accomplished this little commission perfectly, and at two o'clock in the morning I had to exert all my good sense to get myself to go to bed.

Never in my life have I had so many ideas as reading Gregory of Tours. What candor! And he was a bishop! How different from our over-subtle historians who pretend to genius and new points of view, sold, as everyone knows, in the hope of a seat in the Academy or for some financial advantage!

Tours, June 23

AT TEN O'CLOCK I WENT TO THE CAFÉ and found myself in the midst of about thirty officers in full uniform. I had brought my own tea, which made the mistress of the house look sulky, but it didn't matter. All relations are broken off between the provincials and me. I almost had to get angry again to get some boiling water. The ill humor of this shrew in the café did not keep me from tasting the excellence of my tea. Ten years ago my heart would have been corroded with anger.

I had *Quentin Durward* in my pocket. Reading, I went on foot to the village of Riche, twenty minutes from Tours, where some remains of the castle of Plessis-lez-Tours are still visible. It was built of brick. In the end, Louis XI's fear turned it into a fortress. The dungeon is all that remains of the old building.

Hidden in the palace, this melancholy Louis XI had all those he was afraid of hung from the nearby trees. There he died in 1483, sighing and trembling at the idea of death like the last man in the world, making his doctor rich and summoning a saint from the depths of Calabria. To me, this king was Tiberius with the fear of hell added.

When I came back to town, I went to see the cathedral which I had heard greatly talked up. After it had been twice destroyed by fire, they began to rebuild it toward the end of the twelfth century, but the region lacked piety, perhaps, for it was finished only in 1550. The rose-window is admirable as are the towers which are quite high. The canons, men of taste, have had the bases of the Gothic pillars in the choir covered with wainscoting. I saw the library and the wretched museum. Leaving the cathedral I found quite a pretty street, but the houses are too low to have a style that says anything to the passerby except, "You are in a village." This old Tours is very badly built.

Since I am so bored in Tours, what I write must be very colorless. How much more pleasant and easy it would be to write of a journey in Italy! This beautiful land with its sublime countryside, its lakes in Lombardy, its Vesuvius, the pictures by Raphael, and the music. It has the spirit of its inhabitants. In Italy my soul is filled with incessant wonder. Nothing unfeeling there.

In an Italian peasant's house, you find at every moment, instead of the foolishness so characteristic of Champagne and Berry, that profound common sense, a consequence of the republics of the Middle Ages and the admirable rogueries through which about thirty powerful families succeeded in stripping the people of any power, the Medicis, the Malatesta, the Baglione.

Further, what music engenders, that is, a naturalness of life, has set in all hearts the love of love. Elsewhere for half the inhabitants, love is only the occasion for the pleasures of vanity. The peasant of the Papal States has white bread, meat, and wine at every meal.

The arts were born in Italy about the year 1400. They ininherited the fire the medieval republics had left in the hearts of the people. This sacred fire, this passionate generosity breathes through Dante's poem begun in the year 1300, and it formed the soul and mind of Michael Angelo.

What is found in France in the year 1300, in the year 1400? Some petty tyrants who gloried in their bewildered serfs and in not knowing how to read. The consequences can be seen in the peasants of Berry, in the Doubs country, etc. They believe in sorcerers, and they don't read the newspapers.

Out of necessity the arts were born in France at the same

time the Cid was alive. The religious wars had inflamed souls weakened by the long, ignoble years of feudalism. The intrigues of the Fronde had sharpened their wits. The French had done some fine things, but in spite of the foolishness expressed by these words, "The Century of Louis XIV," this prince soon quenched the sacred fire that made him afraid. The foolish passion that adores one's country and all that is great inflamed Corneille while it was no more than a point of view to the elegant Racine. The last dupe of this nobility, henceforth ridiculous, was Marshal Vauban.

In 1837 France has only one superiority for herself, immense in its truth. She is the Queen of Thought in the midst of that poor Europe still under censorship. Italy herself is only one of France's subjects. As soon as a printer in Brussels learns that a work has been a success in the reading rooms in Paris, he prints it, and, in spite of all the police, this work is read with avidity from Petersburg to Naples. Ask the Belgian pirates for a list of the works that have been the most useful to them, and you will see that France is Queen of Thought precisely through works that have shamed the French Academy. Has there been a tragedy by one of these gentlemen performed in London or Vienna in the last ten years?

Nantes, June 25

There is nothing in France more unpleasant than the moment a steamboat arrives. Everyone wants to get at his trunk or his parcels and pitilessly upsets the mountain of baggage piled high on the bridge. Everyone is grumpy, and everyone is rude.

My poverty saved me this bother. I took my dressing-case under my arm, and I was one of the first to cross the plank that set me on the pavement of Nantes. I had not gone twenty steps behind the porter who was carrying my valise when I recognized a large town. We went along a beautiful grillwork enclosing a garden on the quai in front of the stock exchange. We went up the street that led to the theater. Although most of them were closed at nine o'clock, the shops were prepossessing. Some of the jewelers' shops were still lighted, and they reminded me of the fine stores on the Rue Vivienne. Good Lord, what a difference from the dirty tallow dips lighting the dirty shops of Tours, Bourges, and most of the towns of the interior! To return to the civilized world brought me back my philosophy, somewhat altered, I admit, by such cold weather for June, and, besides, the pleasures of the eye had not taken my mind off the ills of the body.

I had expected something comparable if not to the banks of the Rhine near Coblentz, at least to those wooded ridges on the Seine near Villequier or the Meilleray. I found only some green islands and wide meadows ringed with willow trees. The Loire had a reputation made for it, and this reputation shows clearly the lack of taste for the beauties of nature characteristic of the Frenchman of the Old Regime, the man of wit like Voltaire or La Bruyére.

I stayed at a magnificent hotel in a fine room overlooking the Place Graslin where the theater is. Five or six streets entered this pretty little square which would be remarkable even in Paris.

This morning not much after six I was waked up by the servants beating all the clothes in the house in front of my door, whistling as loud as they could. I had taken my room on the third floor in hopes of avoiding this racket, but provincials are always the same. It is vain to think of escaping them. As I was leaving, I said to the head valet very pleasantly that perhaps they could use a room on the ground floor to beat the clothes in. He gave me an atrocious glance and did not reply. Like a true Frenchman, he will be angry with me all his life because he couldn't think of anything to say.

Luckily our correspondent in this town is a former Vendéean. He is still a soldier and not at all a merchant. I accepted his invitation to dinner this evening with a great deal of pleasure.

Full of ideas about the civil war and not about business already done, I went to see the Duchesse de Berry's hiding place. It's astonishing that they didn't find this heroic princess sooner. All they would have had to do was measure the house outside and then inside as the French soldiers did in Moscow when they were looking for hiding places. On many places on the fortress I noticed the cross of Lorraine.

I went up to the promenade which is quite nearby. It overlooks the citadel and the course of the Loire. The view is quite pleasant. I watched a steamboat come in from St. Nazaire, twenty miles away on the sea. I spent two hours on this height. There are several rows of trees there and some statues that are beneath criticism. Below toward the Loire I noticed two or three houses that a town as rich and beautiful as Nantes should have kept from being built, but the magistrates who run our towns are not strong for beauty. Look what they allow to be put up on the Boulevard in Paris! The smallest towns in Germany have something charming about them. They are decorated in ways to make the best architect envious, and this without walls, without construction, without any great expense, simply by using trees and the sunlight. This is because the Germans have a soul.

The trees of the Nantes promenade are puny. You can see the soil is worthless. I am going to set down an idea that will horrify the magistrates of Nantes if it ever comes to their attention. It is to make some trenches ten feet deep in the side lanes of their promenade and fill them with the excellent black compost found on the banks of the Loire.

You could die of hunger in the main dining room of my hotel which is so proud of its grand stone staircase and its fine Louis XV architecture. There are some English here who eat with unpleasant vulgarity, but I have discovered quite a passable restaurant opposite the theater. The mistress of the house, a comely young woman with a simple pleasant manner, advises you on the dinner menu. She told me that my big hotel was founded about twenty years ago by capital the shares of which were invested in a tontine, and the survivors still draw only 5 per cent.

The chief café beside the eight big awkward columns of the theater suits me very well. It is the center of gay civilization and the society of the local young men like the cafés in Italy. There I began to catch a glimpse of the excellent Brittany cream. I dined there at length, reading the paper, and I was amused by the smiles and remarks from the little tables nearby, much less dignified than in Paris.

But I would be unjust to the young men of the highest Nantes society if I didn't hasten to add that these gentlemen held their heads erect with all suitable stiffness and that these heads are adorned with a too strongly marked parting of the hair, but these young men, insofar as they wish to be correct, do not appear at the café. "Before 1789," Count de T—— told me, "a well-born young gentleman would not have appeared in a café for anything in the world." In our day what is more gloomy than luncheon at home with one's grandparents and the table surrounded by servants to whom you give orders and who grumble all the while you're eating? As for myself, I am never bored at a café. There the unforeseen happens. It is a place not under my orders.

Nantes, June 28

YESTERDAY ABOUT FOUR O'CLOCK of a superb afternoon as the boat going rapidly up the Loire was passing the houses of the countryside, the low rows of willows and monotonous acacias that grow near the river, we stopped to give audience to a little boat which brought us some passengers. The first was a priest in a little collar, then came two more or less elderly

women. The fourth person was a young girl of twenty in a green hat.

As I looked at her, I was stupefied and motionless. Hers was nothing less than one of the most beautiful heads I have ever seen in my life. If she resembled any paragon of beauty already known to me, it was the most moving of the Virtues with which Michel Colomb adorned the tomb of Duc Francis in the cathedral at Nantes.

I threw my cigar into the Loire, apparently with a silly movement of respect, for the old women were watching me. Their astonishment reminded me to be prudent, and I arranged myself so I could contemplate the Virtue of Michel Colomb without being annoyed by the spiteful glances of ordinary beings. My admiration increased continually. Her naturalness, her noble ease, evidently the result of force of character and not the habit of high rank, were beyond all praise.

This face is a thousand leagues from the petty affectation of the noble demoiselles of the Faubourg St. Germain whose heads change from a vertical axis every moment. She is still further from the beauty of Greek forms. On the contrary, the features of this beautiful Breton were profoundly French. What divine charm, not to be a copy of anything in the world, to give an absolutely fresh sensation to every eye! Since my admiration for her did not diminish, I felt completely mad. The two hours this girl spent on the boat seemed only ten minutes to me.

I was scarcely able to form this judgment: that my admiration was based on novelty. Until this girl accompanied by the priest and the two old women disembarked at Nantes with everyone else, I was unable to feel any sensation except the keenest wonder mingled with profound astonishment. In vain my reason told me that I had only to say the first thing that entered my head to the priest and soon I would be talking steadily to the ladies. I lacked courage. And, if I were going to concoct the polished twaddle suitable for a priest, I would have to turn away from this lovely creature who was warming my heart.

I confess that, as we were getting off the boat, I had to restrain myself to keep from following these ladies at a distance to see the green ribbons of her hat a few moments longer. Here is the perfect woman one so rarely finds in France. She was quite tall with a beautiful figure, except that perhaps she will put on weight in time.

The chief reason which, rightly or wrongly, deterred me from following these ladies a little way was that I saw very clearly that the girl in the green hat was aware of the close attention I was paying her though I sought to hide it as well as I could. Sooner or later I would have had to leave her and without her esteem.

Here are the fruits of a long evening: all the commonplaces of Parisian conversation are eagerly hashed over in the provinces, where they exaggerate everything. I saw this very clearly in the conversations about the play. They were giving the first performance in Nantes of *Camaraderie*. I was in a loge with some people I knew. Profound astonishment of the provincials. What! They dared talk this way about the Chamber of Deputies, that Chamber which before 1830 distributed all the little posts worth a thousand francs and barbarously raised to twenty years the term of service for everyone who did not have a vote to give? After the stupefaction, which lasted well over a minute, they applauded crazily M. Scribe's naive epigrams. Without admitting it to themselves, these provincials are sick and tired of what they praise most emphatically, these plays hacked out of the old pattern which never weary of imitating Destouches and *The Domestic Tyrant*. They admire but still do not praise the one man of this century who is bold enough to paint, in rough sketches, it is true, the manners they meet in society and does not imitate Destouches and Marivaux every time. This evening they reproached *Camaraderie* for showing an election arranged in twenty-four hours. The police cut the play off short.

In Molière's time the middle class dared insult the ridiculous. Louis XIV wanted no one thinking without his permission, and Molière was useful to him. He inoculated the middle class with timidity, but since they overestimate the power of ridicule, comedy no longer has any freedom. Under Louis XVIII all the counter-jumpers wanted to beat up Brunet, and there was a cavalry charge in the Passage des Panoramas. We lag far behind what Louis XIV permitted. One detail will prove my point: isn't it true that an exact and even satiric depiction, if you like, of all the sleight-of-hand tricks that filched an election before 1830 would offend fewer people now than the actions and gestures of *Tartufe* who, under Louis XIV, exposed and embarrassed the petty affairs of a whole class of society? *Tartufe* was so dangerous and struck so exactly at the way this class got rich that the celebrated Bourdaloue grew angry, and La Bruyère, in order to please his protector, Bossuet, was obliged to censure Molière, at least according to literary report.

Thus, a curious thing and one which would have shocked D'Alembert and Diderot, you must have a despot to have any freedom in comedy as you must have a court if you are to have any very clear and very comic absurdities. In other words, since there is no longer a model for each caste, a model which everyone wishes to imitate and which is approved by the king, you cannot show the public any people who are amusingly wrong in thinking their manners are perfect. Everyone combines against laughter, even the carping half-peasants who are scandalized by *improbability*. An election improvised in twelve hours! And by a newspaper! I say, gentlemen, it takes a newspaper with eight thousand subscribers only six months to make a great man.

Day before yesterday I was made to go to dinner with a herculean man, a rich plantation owner from near New Orleans. He is like a simpleton. He hunts thrushes and takes off their heads with one shot. "So as not to damage the game," he says; I pride myself on being a good shot, and I didn't believe a word of this story. The American noticed it, and this morning we went out together. He killed seven sparrows or finches, a clean shot every time. He took off the heads of two blackbirds, but, since the balls carried a long way, we regretted we were not in a New World forest, and my new friend stopped using his rifle. The barrel is very long, and the balls of very small caliber. It can be loaded quite quickly. With a fowling-piece and some small shot, the American killed every snipe that showed itself. I didn't see him miss a single shot.

M. J—— was seventeen years old in 1814 when the famous battle of New Orleans was fought where five thousand militia put to flight an army of ten thousand English, the best soldiers in the world, who had recently fought many years against the French under Napoleon.

"We put ourselves in a line of skirmishers," said M. J——, "and less than an hour later, all the English officers were killed. The English, always stuffy, said that this kind of war was *immoral.* The fact is, they never took the trouble to relieve their sentries. We hit them all while they were walking their posts, but our people had to go on their hands and knees through the mud to get within striking distance, and the English, not content with the reproach of *immorality*, still call us *dirty shirts.*

"On the day of the battle only one single man of the English army (Col. Regnier, born in France) was able to get as far as our trenches. He turned around to call up his troops, and he fell stone dead. That evening after the battle had been won, two of our militia were arguing over the glory of having killed this brave man.

" 'There's a simple way to tell,' cried Lambert. 'I shot him in the heart.'

" 'And I shot him in the eye,' said Nibelet.

"They went over the battlefield with lanterns. Col. Regnier had been shot in both the heart and the eye."

Nantes, July 1

One of the fearless acts of Gen. Jackson was to have two Englishmen shot who had just been acquitted by a court-martial. They said these men pretended to be fur-traders but were leading Indians into fighting the Americans. The fact is that the next day the English discharged the Indians, who did not dare show themselves against the Americans.

On the day of the battle Gen. Jackson was daring enough to give the command of all his artillery to the brave Lafitte, a French pirate who asked if he and his five hundred filibusters could fight for him because they held such a grudge against the British for what they had suffered on their prison ships. A price had been put on Lafitte's head by the American government. If he had betrayed Jackson, Jackson would have had no other choice but to blow out his own brains. He told Lafitte so candidly when he handed over his artillery.

My hunting companion gave me a great many other details, and I listened to them with the keenest interest. I am going to write them to the brave R——, my friend in Lausanne. The Swiss ought to use these long rifles if they are ever attacked by some army like Xerxes'. But where will you find a man in Switzerland who knows how to exert his will? Are there still any men like Jackson in Europe? Undoubtedly there are some brave and wonderful talkers like Robert-Macaire, but in difficult circumstances the man *without conscience* suddenly lacks force. It's a poor horse that falls on the ice and doesn't want to get up.

Nantes, July 1

NANTES IS THE PLACE where I keep running into people. At the Stock Exchange I found a ship captain who was once my companion on a Customs cruise in Martinique. He had just spent three years in the Baltic and St. Petersburg.

"Are we going to be Cossacked?" I asked him.

"The Emperor N—— is an intelligent man," he replied, "and he would be very distinguished as a private person. He is the handsomest man in the empire as well as the bravest, but he is like the hare in La Fontaine—fear gnaws at him. In every intelligent man, and there are many in St. Petersburg, he sees an enemy, so difficult it is to have the force of character to resist the possession of absolute power."

1. The Czar is furious against France. Our freedom of the press gives him convulsions, and he hasn't twenty millions to spend to soothe his anger. Kankrin, the Minister of Finance, is a talented man. He is barely able to make both ends meet, and he makes everyone scream doing it.

2. The Emperor doesn't want any husbands deceived in Russia. If a young officer sees an attractive woman too often, the police call him in and warn him to discontinue his visits. If he ignores the advice, he is exiled. An extremely passionate love affair can end in Siberia. Nothing annoys the young nobility so much. Customarily absolute sovereigns know that they can maintain themselves by sharing with their nobility the enjoyment of vice. Saint-Simon tells us that Louis XIV gave huge pensions to his whole court, and, although ridiculously pious himself, he never pretended to put any obstacles in the way of husbands being deceived. The Duc de Villeroy, his most intimate courtier, had a public liaison with the governess of the king's children.

It must be added that the Czar, personally very handsome, is a little like our French prefects who preach religion in their salons and never go to mass.

3. Russia does not want Serbia to enjoy the charter that Prince Milosh wants to give her. Of all the rulers beyond the Rhine, the Prince is the one who knows his business best.

4. There are many intelligent people in Russia, and their self-esteem peculiarly suffers because they have no charter when Bavaria, even Wurtemburg, no bigger than your hand, both have them. They want a Chamber of Peers, made up of nobles who have a real income of a hundred thousand roubles (deduction made for debts), and a Chamber of Deputies, composed,

the first third, of noblemen, the second third, of officers, and the third, of businessmen and manufacturers; and they want the two Chambers to vote the budget annually. In Russia they don't like freedom as we understand it. The nobleman understands that sooner or later it will deprive him of his serfs (who, moreover, are very happy), but his self-esteem suffers because he can't come to Paris and see himself barbarously treated in the most insignificant little French newspaper.

"I don't doubt," said Captain C——, "that in twenty-five years Russia will have something like a charter, and the crown will be buying orators with crosses."

"In Peterburg they say that General Yermolof is the man of greatest merit, perhaps a man of genius. They would like to see him Minister of the Interior. General Jomini is training some very knowledgeable officers as the next war will show, but these officers do not want to be regarded as more simple-minded than the Bavarians.

"Russia absorbs three-quarters of the French books pirated by the Belgian publishers, and I know twenty young Russians who are better informed than you are about everything that has been published in Paris in the last two years."

Nantes, July 4

For several years now Le Havre has been the port for Paris and has secured the business that once was the glory of Nantes and Bordeaux. In these towns the descendants of men who made very considerable gains every year now make only moderate ones; yet they claim to have a luxury their fathers never knew. They exist in a state of permanent anger.

"Are we pariahs?" they asked me this evening. "Should Paris have it all? Must we exhaust ourselves to realize 5 per cent for sixty thousand investors in Paris?"

The inhabitants of Nantes and Bordeaux blame the Chamber of Deputies who, they say, were unwilling to vote in railroads in 1837 because this would give the provinces some of the advantages of Paris.

This arduous day would have been frightful for me, even to the point of disgusting me with travel, if it had not ended with one of Bouffé's performances. I expected to spend only half an hour at the play, but the manner of this excellent actor's playing was so true, so little conceited that it held me to the end. We were horribly uncomfortable in the orchestra. Everyone was complaining. During the intermissions I felt like a fool for having stuffed myself in there. One of the causes of the decadence of dramatic art is that theaters are so uncomfortable they are disappearing.

For people who read, novels and newspapers are replacing the theater by half. Sixty years ago it would have been social life. The great change which is coming about has many causes. (1) *The general unsociability*. People prefer domestic pleasures. As soon as they leave their own homes, they must take part in a tiresome comedy or lose something of their reputations. (2) They have seen Talma in *Andromaque*, and they don't want to spoil a brilliant souvenir of genius. (3) They are frightfully uncomfortable in Parisian theaters. Since gaiety has fled, we hold on to our comfort now. Perhaps thirty years will elapse before fashion thinks of commanding theatrical entrepreneurs to furnish their theaters like the Italian Opera in London. There they have armchairs set wide apart. (4) The play and the dinner hour are at war. You must eat your dinner in haste and run from the table to shut yourself up in a hall overheated by people's breath. For many people this reason alone is enough to paralyze the mind and make it incapable of enjoying any pleasure whatever. (5) The few who have some imagination prefer to read *Andromaque* and to choose a moment when the mind is tranquil and can rule the *tattered garment* to which it is joined. When one is so unlucky as to know by heart fifteen or twenty good tragedies, one reads novels which have the charm of the *unexpected*. What is left to dramatic art is, I think, only the kind of comedy that

raises a laugh. Laughter comes from the unexpected and from the sudden comparison I make between myself and someone else. My enjoyment is quadrupled by that of my neighbor. In a hall that is packed to the rafters, where the audience is already thrilled, the buffoonery of a popular actor intensifies the really comic tricks of the play twenty times. The comedies of Regnard must be seen and not read. *Prosper and Vincent, The Debutante's Father,* all the farces, and certain little modern plays besides, *Michel Perrin, Poor Devil, Monsieur Blandin* must be *seen.* With just about this one exception, the theater is disappearing. (6) I merely remind you of the *too-clear introductions* and other vulgar things forced on us by the presence of the newly rich.

About 1850 we will go to a theater because it will offer us seats—seats two feet wide separated by real armchair arms and the spectator will not have to pull back his legs at all when his neighbor returns after the intermission. He will be free to take the air in an immense foyer any time. He will be sure of not inconveniencing his neighbors when he goes back to his seat. Half the loges will be little rooms shut off by curtains like those at St. Charles, at the Scala, and in all the theaters of any country whose civilization did not spring from feudalism and which does not derive all its pleasures from one single passion, *vanity.*

After the spectator's comfort has been assured through these simple precautions, he will be offered a musical number which will last an hour, an hour's pantomime mingled with dances like Vigano's, and finally a last musical number lasting an hour and a quarter.

On great occasions the play will end with a comic ballet that will not last more than twenty minutes. All its melodies will be taken from famous operas. This will be an occasion for the public to hear the delightful cantilenas of Cimarosa, Pergolese, Paisiello, and other great masters whom our taste for orchestral din makes us find cold. In the days of those great painters Coypel and Vanloo, Raphael was accused of being cold.

Admitted to this model theater will be voters, members of

the Institute, officers of the National Guard, and finally any persons who will offer certain guaranties on condition that they pay a moderate annual subscription. From this it will come about that they meet at the theater for all sorts of affairs as they do in Milan. The ladies will receive visits in their loges. The price of the tickets will be five francs.

The sixth loges which will be reached by a separate stairway will cost fifty centimes (like the *loggione* in Milan.) All noisy people will go to the *loggione.*

Vannes, July 5

AT SEVEN O'CLOCK THIS MORNING I left Nantes by stagecoach, well satisfied with such a great and noble town. It is built on a hill, and this gives many of its streets a slope, admirable for healthfulness as well as beauty. Although Nantes hasn't the fine Gothic monuments that teem in Rouen, she has an infinitely more noble air.

Leaving Nantes on the road to Vannes, you stop seeing country houses and find yourself on a vast, perfectly sterile heath. Across it we made the gloomiest forty miles in the world to La Roche-Bernard. I despaired of the countryside and no longer took the trouble to look at it. I was sombre, discouraged, and lackadaisical about what I was going to see when the driver asked if I would get out for the crossing of the Vilaine.

It was already five o'clock in the evening. The sky was heavy with black clouds. When I got out of the coach, I saw nothing but ugliness. A mean house was in front of me. I went in to get warm. They offered me a glass of cider which I took to pay for the inconvenience I caused them.

I had not gone two hundred paces when I was surprised by one of the most beautiful natural scenes I had ever encountered. The road descended suddenly into a wild and desolate valley. At the end of this narrow valley which seems a hundred leagues from the sea, the Vilaine was rapidly being driven back by the

rising tide. The spectacle of this irresistible force, the sea overrunning the narrow valley to its limits combined with the tragic appearance of the bare, rocky crags that hemmed it in threw me into a state of animated reverie very different from the languour I had felt since Nantes. It goes without saying that I felt the effect and enjoyed it fully before I saw why. Soon the most beautiful descriptions of Sir Walter Scott returned to my memory, and I enjoyed them with delight. The very misery of the country contributed to the emotion that it gave, even its ugliness, I would say. If the countryside had been more beautiful, it would have been less terrible; part of the mind would have been busy feeling its beauty. The sea was nowhere visible, which made the appearance of the tide more strange.

By such an end to such a dark and gloomy day, a serious and ugly danger seemed to be written on all the little crags tufted with scrubby little trees that surrounded this muddy river. The boatmen had a lot of trouble getting the heavy stagecoach on their little boat. Because the rise on the Vannes side of the river is quite steep, I saw that I could have the pleasure of being alone for quite a while still. Two very pretty women of the rich working class had also made the choice of going up the slope on foot, but I prefer the wealth of sensation a cigar gives me, and I purposely kept fifty paces from them and the old kinswoman who served as a chaperon. The older, a widow of twenty-five, had a very sharp eye, however, and a strong inclination to talk, and, had I been ten years younger, I would not have preferred the tragic sensations given me by memories of Sir Walter Scott's novels. I have seen nothing more alike than Scotland and the country around the ferry-crossing of the Vilaine, desolate, gloomy, puritanical, fanatic, so much so that I had imagined it before I saw it, and I prefer the picture I made of it then to the reality. Dull reality, made wholly disgusting by the love of mere money and advancement, cannot destroy the poetic image for me.

From the Vilaine to Vannes, the country is quite pretty.

There are bright green trees, and on the twenty-five miles of road we often saw the admirable bay of Morbihan. Although I was tired out when I reached Vannes, I asked where the canal was that leads to the sea. Its course is picturesque. The road hugs an old fortification in the town and a ditch which is twenty feet lower down. When I came to the canal, I started out boldly. I wanted to see the sea, but I was so tired that I nearly lay down on the ground. I kept saying to myself that when I reached the little port I would hire a horse or a donkey for the trip back. A long way away I saw a woman who was evidently out walking with a man she was sweet on. Night fell. There was not another living soul under the trees along the canal. Therefore I was obliged to ask the gentleman in my pleasantest tone what I would find when I soon got to the sea. He answered that I still had about four miles to go.

I confess that I was absolutely stunned by my ignorance. I would have said that Vannes was near the sea. I sat down on a big stone in despair. "When you are as ignorant as this," I said to myself, "you must at least have the courage to ask questions of the passersby." But I have to confess to a kind of disease: I have such a horror of vulgarity that I lose the thread of my feelings when I am in a strange countryside (and to see strange countrysides is why I travel) and have to ask my way. Even if the man who answers me is only a little ridiculous or pompous, I think he is making fun of me, and my interest in the countryside vanishes forever.

On the banks of the lonely canal at Vannes I would have given a lot of money to see a cart coming. I couldn't have taken a hundred steps. If the canal banks had not been so damp, I would have taken a fifteen-minute nap. I really had to go back up to the town, but I did it by sitting down every five minutes. I found a sailor who was cleaning up his boat. I think he took me for a robber when I begged him to sell me a glass of wine from the bottle I saw in the boat. I was much too tired to be polite, and he acted quite surprised when I paid him.

Auray, July 6

THIS MORNING AS I LEFT Vannes for Auray it was genuine Druidic weather; besides, the fatigue of the day before disposed me wonderfully to a feeling of sadness. Big clouds running very low in a profoundly darkened sky were swept along by a high wind. A cold rain came in gusts and almost stopped the horses. This put me into a deep sleep. At Auray I found a little cabriolet which did not protect me at all from the frightful weather, and the driver was even more depressing than the weather. We started on our way. From time to time I saw a desolate beach and a grey sea broken in the distance by huge sandbars, images of misery and danger. You must agree that a Corinthian column would have been out of place in the midst of all this, yet when we passed a dreary little church, we heard the organ somewhat indistinctly modulating one of Mozart's plaintive cantilenas.

My guide, morose and silent, directed his cabriolet by the clock-tower of the village of Erdéven. The general aspect of the country is dull and gloomy. Everything is poor and calls to mind the extremes of misery. It is a plain, and some parts of it are under cultivation. The plots are surrounded by little walls of loose stones.

Five hundred paces from the woebegone village of Erdéven you begin to see over the hedges and the stone walls blocks of granite. As you approach, your mind is overwhelmed by intense curiosity. You are in the presence of one of the strangest historical problems in France. Who has set these twenty thousand blocks of granite in systematic order? Soon we came to several parallel lines of these granite blocks. With the cold rain hitting my face and running down inside my cloak, I counted ten avenues formed by eleven lines of blocks. (The isolated block is called a *pulven.*) The largest ones are fifteen or sixteen feet high. Toward the middle of the avenues they are barely five feet and most of them won't stand above three feet, but often in the midst of these pygmies, you suddenly find one nine or ten feet high. None of them has been worked. They lie on the ground. Some have been sunk five or six inches into the earth. Others seem never to have been moved. They have been left piercing the soil where nature cast them. It should be remarked that this arrangement didn't take too much work. The Erdéven district like that of Carnac is a vast bank of granite covered with a little vegetative soil.

These ancient processions of stones add to the emotion given the neighborhood by a gloomy sea.

We went in the never-ending rain to the wretched village of Erdéven to light a fire and give some handsful of grain to the unfortunate horse. From there, the wind and rain redoubling, we reached Carnac. I found there some other rows of granite blocks so much like those at Erdéven that I would have to use the same words to describe them. They go from west to east. Perhaps the region of Carnac and Erdéven was holy ground.

The people around here seem glum and sad. I asked one of them what he thought of such a strange monument. He answered as if it were something that had happened yesterday that St. Cornely, pursued by an army of pagans, saved himself from them at the sea's edge. When he found no boat there and was about to be seized, he changed the soldiers who were following him into stones.

"It would seem," I replied, "that these soldiers were pretty big, or else they swelled up a lot and lost their shape before they were turned into stones." At which I got a scowl.

None of the scholarly explanations are less silly than the peasants'. Fashion, which bestows a scholar's reputation on the inventor of the reigning absurdity, today in England decrees that these avenues are the remains of a vast temple, the monument of a religion that ruled over the whole earth, the cult of the *serpent*. Unluckily for the supposition, no one up to now has ever heard tell of this universal cult.

Since all religions except the true one, that of the reader,

are founded on the shrewdness of a few and the fears of the majority, it is quite easy to see that crafty priests chose the serpent as an emblem of terror. Actually the serpent is found among the first words of all histories of religions. It had the advantage of astonishing the imagination, much more than Jupiter's eagle, the Christian lamb, or the lion of St. Mark. It had in its favor its strange shape, its beauty, the poison it carried, its power of fascination, its always unexpected and sometimes terrible appearances. For these reasons the serpent has entered into all religions, but it has not had the honor of being the principal deity of any.

Supposing for the moment that the *Ophic* religion did exist, how can it be proved that the long ranks of granitic blocks at Carnac and Erdéven form a *dracontium* or temple of that religion? The answer is overwhelming and quite simple: the sinuosities of the lines of *pulvens* represent the undulations of a crawling serpent. Thus the temple is at the same time an image of the god.

It is very odd that Caesar, who made war in the neighborhood of Locmariaker, does not mention the lines of granite at Carnac and Erdéven. It is in the letters of bishops who proscribed them as monuments of a rival religion that history finds its first mention of them. Later there is a decree of Charlemagne requiring them to be destroyed.

Are the monuments of Carnac and Erdéven anterior to Caesar? Are they anterior even to the Druids?

Yesterday evening when I arrived in Auray, I noticed several country gigs loaded down with whole families, sometimes as many as six people. One unlucky horse with a long dirty mane pulled each one. A mattress would be tied up behind and a cooking-pot balanced on the axletree while three or four would be attached to the sides.

"Is it moving day?" I asked my guide.

"Oh, no, sir. This is for grace received.

"What do you mean?"

"It is, sir, a pilgrimage to our patroness, Ste Anne."

And then the guide gave me the history of a little chapel, a few miles from Auray, dedicated to Ste Anne, to which they come from all parts of Brittany.

This evening while she was assisting at my supper, the landlady explained to me that Brittany owed the few good harvests she had in these wicked and unhappy times to the protection of her good patroness, Ste Anne, who watched over the land from heaven. "Because of her the Russians did not come and pillage us in 1815. Who else kept them from reaching here?" she added.

The part of Brittany where they speak Breton, from Hennebon to Josselin and the sea, lives on buckwheat pancakes, drinks cider, and keeps itself absolutely under the curate's orders.

Lorient, July 7

EARLY THIS MORNING I was on the road to Ste Anne's chapel. It is a bad road and the chapel insignificant, but I shall never forget the expression of deep piety I saw on all the faces. There, a mother cuffing her four-year-old child has the look of a believer. It is not that you see anything fanatical or dazzling in their eyes as you do in Naples before the images of St. Januarius when Vesuvius is threatening. This morning I saw among my neighbors the dull, resolute eyes that mark a stubborn mind. The costume of the peasants has the right look for such sentiments. They wear blue pantaloons and jackets of immense breadth, and their pale blonde hair is cut off around their heads at the ear lobes.

Those young Parisian painters who believe in nothing and who receive from a ministry as firm in the faith as they are an order to make some pictures of miracles which will be judged at the Salon by a society which believes in nothing but politics ought to look for models here. The expressions of character even more than the passing emotions which I have noticed in the chapel of Ste. Anne can be compared to certain faces breathing a cruel and resolute fanaticism that I have seen in Toulouse.

I was well satisfied with the countryside from Landevan to Hennebon and Lorient. I often saw forests in the distance. This damp, very green Breton country reminds me of England. In France the contour traced by forests against the sky is composed of a row of little points. In England the contour is formed by great rounded masses. Would this be because there are still old trees in England?

Here are the ideas that occupied me in the stagecoach from Hennebon to Lorient. I don't know whether the reader will share my opinion that the great misfortune of the present period is anger and impotent hatred. These gloomy emotions eclipse the natural gaiety of the French temperament. I ask whether one might cure one's self of hatred not out of pity for an enemy one is able to harm but out of pity for one's self. Care for our own happiness cries out to us, "drive out hatred, especially hatred that is powerless."

I heard the celebrated Cuvier say during a curious evening when he had mingled his French friends with the pick of his foreign ones, "If you wish to cure yourself of the quite widespread disgust inspired by worms and big insects, study the way they make love. Come to understand the day-long actions they engage in before your eyes to get their subsistence."

From this indication by an especially reasonable man I have drawn this corollary which has been very useful to me in my travels," If you wish to rid yourself of the disgust inspired by some turncoat sold out to the powers that be who examines your passport with a shifty eye and tries to say something insulting to you if he cannot succeed in annoying you more seriously, study that man's life.* You will see that, drenched with scorn, pursued by fear of a stick or the blow of a dagger like a tyrant

* What ages most women of thirty are the hateful passions that war in their faces. If women in love with love age less, it is because this dominant emotion preserves them from hatred.—H. B.

but without a tyrant's pleasure in giving orders, he does not stop thinking of the fear that gnaws at him except when he can make someone else suffer. Then, for an instant, he feels himself powerful, and the sharp steel of the fear stops pricking his loins.

I'll admit that not everyone is exposed to the insolence of foreign policemen. One cannot travel or limit his journeys to the friendly T——. But since the battle of Waterloo has launched us on the road to liberty in France, we are very much exposed among ourselves to the frightful and contagious malady of impotent hatred.

Instead of hating the little bookseller of the neighboring town who sells the *Popular Almanach,* I tell my friend Ranville, "Apply the remedy suggested by the celebrated Cuvier. *Treat him like an insect.* Find out his means of subsistence. Try to divine his ways of making love. You will see that if he is absolutely at the end of his tether complaining against the nobility, it is quite simply in order to sell popular almanachs. Each copy sold brings him two sous, and in order to get his dinner which costs him thirty, he must sell fifteen almanachs a day. You don't think of that, Ranville, you with your eleven servants and six horses."

I would say to the little bookseller who reddens with anger and glances at his National Guard musket when the chambermaid from the chateau retails to him the jokes that the brilliant Ernest de T—— made yesterday about men who work for a living, "Treat the brilliant Ernest as an insect. He tries to pull off these bright, witty phrases because he is trying to please the young Baroness de Malivert for whose hand he is struggling with the Engineer of Roads and Bridges, employed by the district. The young baroness who is quite high-minded has been reared in an extremely *ultra* family, and, besides, by trying to make people who work for a living look silly, he has the fun of taking a devious crack against his rival, the Engineer."

If the little bookseller who sells *Popular Almanachs* in this little town of fourteen hundred inhabitants has had the patience to follow my reasoning and to recognize the truth of all the facts I have cited one after the other, at the end of a quarter of an hour he will find that he has less of this *powerless hatred* for the brilliant Ernest.

Further, M. Ranville cannot get rid of the bookseller any more than the bookseller can get rid of him. They scowl at each other all their lives and do each other bad turns if they can. For instance, the bookseller kills all the hares he can find.

I think of all these things since I have tried hard not to lower myself by feeling anger against poor devils who spend their lives eaten with scorn and who examine my passport when I go abroad. Consequently I have tried to destroy in myself the powerless hatred for well-mannered people I meet in society who earn their living or who please beautiful women by making jokes about the verities that seem most sacred to me, about the things that are worth the pain of living and dying for.

There are many sorcerers in Brittany, or at least I am led to believe so by almost universal testimony. A rich man told me yesterday with ill-dissimulated bitterness, "Why should there be more magicians in Brittany than anywhere else? Who believes in these things now?" It is easy to see how many Bretons whose father did not have a thousand francs a year income when they were born might have some belief in sorcery. The reason for it is that these gentlemen who sell land in an unknown part of the country are not bothered by the customary beliefs of the neighborhood. Terror renders the common people docile.

How can you not believe in sorcerers on that terrible Ushant coast by St. Malo? Storms and dangers appear there nearly every day, and the brave sailors spend their lives face to face with their imagination.

At Lorient you must go to the Hotel de France. It is far and away the best I have encountered this trip. The proprietor, an intelligent man, gave us an excellent dinner at a table d'hôte set in the middle of a magnificent dining room. (Five casement windows filled with beautiful glass from Paris. At the table d'hôte they talked constantly about how much these cost.)

One sees that Lorient has been built by the hand of reason. The streets run straight, and this keeps them from being very picturesque. In 1720 the India Company set up its warehouse at the mouth of a little stream called the Scorf. As the tides come in with some force there, it was easy to make the place a big naval base. They build a great many ships there, and I should undertake the chore of a visit to the yards and warehouses as at Toulon. May God preserve the traveler from such a pleasure!

You can't see the base at all from here. It lies to the left of the promenade and is separated from it by one of the town's long streets. My sailor explained every part of the base as he rowed me to the sea. Every minute he was naming ships of seventy or eighty guns, and he was scandalized by the coolness with which I greeted these large numbers of cannon. Myself, I thought he pronounced their names with ridiculous self-conceit.

"There it is," I said to myself, "that *esprit de corps* so necessary to the armed forces but so ridiculous to the spectator. It would be unlucky for France if this man spoke to me about these ships like a cold philosopher. Do I dare hazard a vulgar word? This class of people has to have this *gab* so they can stand the boredom of long voyages, but my boredom standing in a glacial wind in the middle of these vast sandy beaches only makes me take a dislike for Lorient's stream. I couldn't have been more bored where I was. That's why I determined to go see the naval establishment.

This chore finished, I asked for the big café, and they told me it was the one by the Comedy. A pretty little boulevard leads up to this theater. The trees are forty feet high and the houses thirty. The theater is well arranged, small, tranquil, silent, *snog* [*sic*]. This word *should* have been invented by the English, a people so easy to offend, whose frail happiness can be destroyed by the least threat to their social position. The *brio* of the people of the Midi does not know the *snog* which, in their eyes, would be the *sad.*

I have hardly any *brio*, and, as I was leaving the State hemp warehouses, I was delighted by the situation of the Café de la Comédie. I saw a brave naval officer who, I think, had no arms or legs. He drank his beer gaily, hailed everyone who came in, and asked them to drink beer with him.

I was served a sublime cup of coffee with cream such as you get in Milan. I saw a copy of the *Siécle* across the room, and I read it with great care, even down to the advertisements. The customarily good articles of this newspaper seemed admirable.

At the end of an hour, I was another man. I had forgotten the rope-walk and the State warehouses entirely, and I began to saunter gaily around the town.

In Brittany, July

In a village nearby they make a practice of shutting up madmen in the crypt of the principal church. "And are they cured?" I asked the beadle.

"In my time, sir, they have put only three of them down there, but it didn't work. They yelled a lot, and one of them got crippled up with rheumatism, and they had to take him out."

Rennes, July

I must confess that the dark grey color of the little square bits of granite out of which they build Rennes houses doesn't make a bad show.

They were building a bridge over the Vilaine, which is quite a small stream there. (I think it has fallen since.) The promenades of the Tabor and the Mall pleased me very much. The red trousers on the conscripts who were learning the manual of arms looked very well in the setting sun. It was like a picture by Canaletto.

I hurried to get into the museum before the light was gone. The pictures are hung in a large hall on the ground floor. A big church nearby cuts off the sunlight completely. It is also very damp there, and the pictures decay rapidly. I saw a Guercino almost wholly ruined by the damp. In two or three little rooms adjacent where pictures and engravings are piled up for lack of space, one can have the pleasure of exploration. I found there a pretty collection of the mistresses of Louis XIV. They have strange eyes, well worthy of being loved, but, because of the dampness, one cheek of Mme de Maintenon has just detached itself from the cloth. I remained in these rooms until night drove me out entirely. The concierge, a very intelligent man, was led to settle in Brittany by the capture of Mayence. Once, at Bologna, as I was moving some pictures heaped up like this, I discovered a pretty little portrait of Diane de Poitiers, who, strongly presuming, as it seemed, on her personal charms, had had herself painted as Eve before the Fall.

I hear with respect details of the frank and loyal character of the Bretons, who, moreover, will fight for what they love. I am touched by the "Calvaries" they erect everywhere. "Calvary" is the name the Bretons give to a crucifix surrounded by the instruments of the Passion. Sometimes the Madonna, St. John, and the Magdalen are represented by rough statues of wood or stone. This fashion could have caused the birth of sculpture. It was the same way when it was born in Italy about 1231. At the time they were making such ugly things in France, Niccolo Pisano made the tomb of St. Dominic at Bologna.

St. Malo

THE REALLY SUBLIME PROVINCIAL INNKEEPER is the one who makes you miss the stagecoach and forces you to spend another twenty-four hours in his hovel. They tried to make me a sublime victim, but I rebelled and left Rennes, such an aristocratic town, perched on top of the stagecoach to the great astonishment

of that knave of a landlord. I was even better placed to enjoy the truly remarkable countryside between Rennes and Dol.

You have to go a quarter of a league from Dol to find the famous rock of Champ-Dolent. Does this name recall human sacrifices? My guide solemnly told me it was placed there by Caesar. Was it then in the midst of the forest? Now it stands full in the center of a cultivated field. This *menhir* is twenty-eight feet high and ends in a point. The way I measured it, its base is eight feet in diameter. To sum up, it is a block of greyish granite with the shape of a slightly flattened cone.

It should be noted that this granite is only found three-quarters of a league from the town at Mt. Dol, a hill surrounded by marshes which was probably an island once. The rock of Champ-Dolent rests on a mass of quartz which it has penetrated to a depth of several feet. By what mechanism did the Gauls, whom we consider so little advanced in the arts, transport a mass of granite forty feet long and eight feet thick? How did they set it up?

Caesar has told us how great was the power of the Druids. These clever priests ruled the Gauls absolutely. By directing the attention of their people constantly toward one single object, they made them lose *in this respect* the quality of savages. These Gallic monuments marked places of rendezvous in the midst of the boundless forest. Denmark, Sweden, Norway, Ireland, even Greenland show similar monuments. Did the Druids rule in all these countries, or were these blocks of granite raised by some power other than the Druidic religion? Sioborg informs us that in Scandinavia tradition indicates a different custom for each monument.

There were customs related to the cult everywhere, for the Christian synods showed great jealousy of them. They forbade their prayers and also the lighting of torches in front of stones (*ad lapides*).

The Druids' power lay partly in the belief that the soul changed bodies after death. On the other hand, Aristotle believed the soul to be mortal. The Celts and the Germans were thus better prepared for the Catholic faith than the Greeks and the Romans. The habit of terrified obedience to the Druids prepared our ancestors to obey their bishops. The priests' sanction was identical: excommunication.

Mont St. Michel issues from the waves like an island with the shape of a pyramid. It is an equilateral triangle of increasingly brilliant red verging on rose that stood out against a grey background. We left the sea, then we saw it in front of us. As it sank just at that moment, we saw on all sides little islands hacked out of blackish granite protruding from the sea. St. Malo is built on the largest of these little granite islands, and, as is well known, it is joined to the land at high tide only by the main road.

Going into St. Malo and approaching the fortified gate, we had the open sea on our right and at the left an immense basin of damp mud where every hundred paces some poor ships lay on their sides. They were waiting for the tide to lift them up again, and this continual exercise strains their ribs.

Since I have been in Brittany, some truth besets me every hour of the day. The petty bourgeois of Autun, Nevers, Bourges, of Tours is a hundred times more behindhand, more stupid, even more envious than the bourgeois who lives ten miles from the coast and who has a cousin drowned in a storm from time to time.

The gallantry of the young Breton boys from the Morlaix coast who hide themselves on the boats that go to fish for cod on the Grand Banks of Newfoundland! They are called the "found" (found on board the boat when it is far out at sea). An Imperial Guard could be raised here from the sailors.

Under the Empire the Breton privateers used to wait to set out until a storm kept the ships of the English blockade away from their masses of black granite. What a difference it would have made to Napoleon if, instead of building a fleet, he had equipped a thousand privateers. What couldn't he have done with the Bretons!

I don't know how I was drawn into losing two days in this strange, unfriendly town. Actually it's a prison. What a noble, exaggerated idea I got of St. Malo from the bold privateers! Will I always make this mistake? What childishness I still have in my head! I have seen only moneyed faces. In the whole art of painting is there anything uglier than the shape of a banker's mouth who is afraid of losing his money?

In the midst of this spiritual aridity, I found only one *intonation* that moved me. It was when a postilion said to me, "Ah, sir, when you come in this direction, you always have to take the same road back. You can't go any farther." In that last word, and such a common one, there was by chance all the deeply felt sadness of an islander or a prisoner.

Here is what I found in my journal under the heading of St. Malo: "They don't know how to do anything well in the provinces, not even die. A week before his end, the unhappy provincial is warned of the danger by the tears of his wife and children, by the awkward remarks of his friends, and finally by the terrible arrival of the priest. At the sight of the minister of the altars, the sick man takes himself for dead. It's all up with him. At this moment, heart-rending scenes begin, repeated ten times a day. At last the poor man heaves his last breath in the midst of the cries and sobs of his family and the servants. His wife throws herself on his lifeless body. They hear her dreadful cries out in the street. This does him honor, and she gives the children a lasting memory of horror and misery. It is a frightful scene."

A man in Paris falls gravely ill. He closes his door. A few friends get in to see him. They take great care not to speak gloomily of his illness. After first remarking on his health, they tell him what goes on in the world. At the last moment, the sick man asks his nurse to leave him alone for a moment; he needs rest. Sad things occur as they always have, without our foolish customs, in silence and in solitude. Watch a sick animal. He hides himself and finds the heaviest thicket in the woods to die in. Fourier died hiding behind his portière.

Since the idea of an *eternal* hell has left us, death has become a simple matter again as it was before the reign of Constantine. This idea will be worth millions to the law, to masterpieces of the fine arts, to the depths of the human spirit.

Granville

THERE IS NOTHING MORE OBLIGING than the inhabitants of Granville. In places where there is a businessman's club, cafés don't subscribe to Paris newspapers. It would be too big an expense for their slender receipts. So I was quite annoyed in Granville this evening. Since, coming from St. Malo, I was reconciled to Paris, I was piqued by quite a silly curiosity. I would willingly have stopped passersby to ask them, "What's new here?" At the café I found only the *Gazette du Département* in which I had read the news in St. Malo. I went gloomily back to my rooms. I tried reading, but I have never succeeded in reading by force. As I left to saunter through the streets, I found the courage to speak of my difficulty. The waiter at the hotel quite simply led me to a club founded a short time before at the end of a new promenade formed by some pretty, very bushy trees. Three years before there was nothing there but a dismal beach covered with pebbles. In a region where there is progress, there one is happy; consequently there one is kind. As I came into the clubrooms, a very courteous gentleman without saying a word placed at my disposal three or four newspapers that had arrived from Paris within the hour. When I left after having devoured them, the concierge told me on behalf of these gentlemen that the club was open every morning at seven. It seems to me that it is impossible to do better even in Paris. Granville has doubled in the last ten years, but, as Figaro says, with any kind of wealth, it is not the possessing that makes for happiness, it is the acquiring. The businessmen of Granville are prosperous, from whence it follows that they are happy and polite and undoubtedly less wretched and cantankerous than the bourgeois of so many little French towns who don't know what to do with their time and complain of their eighteen hundred livres of income.

Since I left Dol I have been traveling alone in the coupé of the stagecoach with an extremely beautiful peasant woman forty years old. She has Roman features and very distinguished manners, and, what surprises me, I find in these manners an ease and naturalness that many of our great ladies might envy. She has none of the airs of an actress giving a close imitation of Mlle Mars.

Every so often this noble peasant took from her little basket an *Imitation of Christ*, very well bound in black, and read for a while.

I rashly supposed that, because of her great beauty, she had had some occasion in her youth to mingle with good society in England. (Her manner was somewhat serious. She is like a heroine of the Abbé Prévost.) That when she had come to a certain age, she had married and had reached the position of a rich peasant woman. I didn't particularly want to talk, but a conversation was begun between us, so well and with so much respect on my part that I was able to tell her a little of the novel I had been imagining about her. She laughed good-naturedly and told me with perfect ease that she was the wife of a fisherman on the island of Jersey. While her husband was at sea, she kept a little shop full of hardware and everything poor sailors might buy. She told this as well as Mme de Sevigné could have done it.

"Your story is charming," I told her, "but let me tell you that it isn't convincing, even if it is enchanting."

This forty-year-old peasant woman is unquestionably the most distinguished woman I have met in my travels, and, as for beauty, she follows just after the adoráble girl who came aboard the Loire steamer in the green hat.

While I was having lunch in the inn at Avranches, I learned that this district is haunted by a crowd of Englishmen, but they are continually on the move because they are so unfortunate as to fish too well with hook and line. They use artificial flies that deceive the foolish fish too expertly, whether salmon or trout, I don't know. The good luck of the English has excited the Normans to the highest pitch of jealousy. They have broken off all social relations with the fishermen, and, as I understand it, are thinking of having the law on them.

Even if I am not a fly fisherman, I would stay at Avranches or Granville in spite of this Norman "politeness," if I were ever condemned to live in the provinces anywhere near Paris. At first glance, it might be tempting to go and settle toward the south near Tours or Angers so as to escape the hard winters, but the difference in the state of civilization carries more weight than two degrees of latitude. Your neighbor at Tours or Angers shows a hundred times more provincial meanness and irritating curiosity than at Granville or Avranches. One must always come back to this axiom," Nearness to the sea destroys pettiness." Every man who has sailed the sea is more or less exempt. Only, if he is a fool, he goes on about the storms. If he is a slightly conceited wit from Paris, he denies they exist.

The fortified town of Granville perches on a cliff. I climbed up to the town. The houses, black, dreary, and very much alike have only two low stories. They very much resemble the houses of English small towns. In spite of the height and the view of the sea enjoyed by all those on the right side of the street as they go to church, the characteristic that marks this ancient town is a somber gloom. I went to the end of the cape where there is a big meadow surrounded by the sea on three sides. One of the local children said, "You hear so often of the end of the world. Well, look. There it is." This is a fairly appropriate idea.

In this meadow are some unhappy sheep tormented by the

wind. I found there an iron twelve-pounder abandoned in the grass and the remains of a battery. When I returned to the town, I went into the church, a wonderfully depressing place. About twenty young girls were bringing there the mortal remains of one of their comrades. There were no other men present except the beadle who looked drunk, the old priest who was cold and in a hurry, and myself, the spectator. How much wiser they are in Florence! All this kind of thing happens at night.

A coach drawn by some excellent horses took me to Honfleur very speedily, but on this road I did not find any longer the lovely green Normandy of Avranches. It is a cultivated plain like that near Paris. There was a fair at Pont l'Évêque. You should see the faces of the Normans driving bargains. It is really amusing. There is room there for a new Teniers. They would snatch up his works by the hundreds in the elegant chateaux that throng Normandy.

On my arrival at Honfleur I found that the boat for Le Havre had gone two hours before. The landlady announced with an indulgent air that it would return in the evening perhaps. It was a pleasure to see through this Norman shrewdness. By giving me this foolish hope, the landlady wanted to keep me from taking a little boat that would easily carry me to Harfleur in two hours. I could see the smoke of its factories.

Le Havre

I TOOK A FINE ROOM at the Admiralty Hotel on the third floor overlooking the harbor, which fortunately was empty. I am separated from the sea, that is, the port, only by a very narrow little quai. I can see all the steamboats arrive and depart. I have just seen the "Rotterdam" come in and the "London" go out. As you know, entry to Le Havre is quite difficult. You have to pass opposite the Round Tower built by Francis I. When I was settling into my room, the port under my window and the atmosphere as far down as the rooftops was full of brownish smoke from the steamers. This deep obscurity caused by the coal smoke reminded me of London and with real pleasure at a moment when I was saturated with the shabby bourgeois meanness of the interior of France.

All activity pleases me, and Le Havre is the most exact copy of England in this way that France can offer. Nevertheless, the Liverpool customs-house sends off a hundred and fifty ships a day, and at Le Havre they don't know which way to turn if they handle twelve or fifteen. This is an effect of French urbanity. In England, not a useless word. All the clerks are installed in booths that open into one big room. They go from one to another without raising their hats and even without speaking. The manager has his office on the second floor, but it has to be a pretty serious case for a clerk to tell you, "Upstairs, sir."

My walk was interrupted by the dire necessity of going back to the hotel at five o'clock for the table d'hôte dinner. I took a seat near the door at a horseshoe table where there was some hope of getting a little air. There were thirty-two Americans at that table, chewing away with extraordinary rapidity, and three French fops with irreproachable complexions.* Opposite me were three quite pretty young women with awkward manners, come the day before from overseas, and speaking timidly of the events of the crossing. Their husbands were beside them, not saying a word. Their hair was much too long; now and then their wives looked at them with fear. Because I was bored, I wanted to attract everyone's attention, and I ordered a bottle of iced champagne and complained grumpily because the ice had not been chopped fine enough. Every eye was turned on me, and, after a brief moment of admiration, all the rich ones in the party,

* Americans are merely the quintessence of the English, harder workers, greedier, more pious, on the whole more unpleasant. I am not talking about Americans from Carolina or other slave states. They are Creoles, gay, carefree, enemies of all work, and marvelously cruel as soon as anyone speaks of freeing their slaves.—H. B.

whom I recognized by their air of importance, ordered French wine, too.

Rouen

What is admirable in Rouen is that the walls of all the houses are formed by wooden beams set vertically a foot apart. The space between is filled with masonry, but the beams are not covered with it. Acute angles and vertical lines can be seen on all sides. These acute angles are formed by slanting cross-pieces that strengthen and unite the uprights, and the outline of the beams looks like a capital **N**.

When the Gothic was fashionable, Rouen was the capital city of some very wealthy princes, men of wit, and still overcome with joy at the conquest of England which they had just brought about as if by miracle. Rouen is the most beautiful town in France for its medieval things and its Gothic architecture. I have made a forty-page description of it which I take care not to print here.

1. Who does not know St. Ouen, built by Richard II of England?

2. The cathedral?

3. The charming little church of Saint-Maclou?

4. The big Gothic house in the square facing the cathedral?

5. The Hotel Bourgderoulde and its magnificent bas-reliefs? Only there can a clear idea be gotten of how society looked at the end of the Middle Ages.

Who does not know the dull statue of Joan of Arc in the same square where the cruelty of the English had her burned? Who does not understand how absurd it is to use a Greek style to portray a character so eminently Christian? The most spiritual of the Greeks would have tried in vain to comprehend her character, a unique product of the Middle Ages, an expression of its follies as well as its most heroic passions.

St. Ouen is longer and narrower than the cathedral and beautiful in quite another way. My guide called the rose-windows to my attention. As I was admiring the beautiful greyish black color of the church's interior, he said to me, "Alas, sir, it is one of the outrages of the Revolution. The Jacobins set up an armory in our church, but as soon as the foundation has enough money, they will have it whitewashed." "In that case," I told him, "the English will no longer tip the porter. I warn you that somber colors are fashionable with these gloomy people, and already, I foresee, the amateurs of Paris are beginning to share this taste."

Paris, July 18

What I like about traveling is the wonder of the return. Full of admiration, my heart swelling with joy, I run about the Rue de la Paix and the Boulevard, which, on the day I left, seemed merely places I was used to.

Now I make up for the dragging days I spent at Auray, observing the customs of the Bretons or beating about the ocean in a boat at St. Malo as in the lovely idle days of my youth. In Paris I don't sleep two hours a night.

I thought my travels would end when I came back to Paris, but chance decided otherwise. The able, excellent young man who was going to represent us at the Beaucaire fair is ill, and I leave again this evening for the banks of the Rhone which I count on seeing again within fifty hours.

Tarascon, July 27

It was impossible for me to do any writing at Beaucaire. There was no place for it. One night, when I wanted to get a good night's sleep in spite of the fleas and their cousins, I went a league out of town. The day of my arrival I was so flabbergasted by the incredible racket that it was several hours before

I knew what was going on. Every minute some friend of mine was shaking hands and giving me his address.

In all the streets that run through the meadow on the bank of the Rhone, the crowd is continuous. Every moment someone digs you in the ribs with his elbow to help him get forward. Everyone pushes. Everyone's in a hurry. Musicians bawl and gesticulate in front of the horn and the contra-bass that accompanies them. Soap merchants pursue you offering first-quality perfumes from Grasse. Porters staggering under the enormous loads they carry on their heads yell, "Look out!" when they are already on you. Newsmongers bawl themselves hoarse, calling out summaries of telegrams arriving from Spain. It is a crowd, a mob they could have no idea of in Paris. After sauntering around for several hours, my astonishment returned. I went to take out my handkerchief. It had disappeared along with everything I had in my pocket. At Beaucaire the ear is assailed by all sorts of languages and dialects. A handsome Catalan was trying to get me to come to a ball that evening, and it was undoubtedly while my pride was trying to understand what he wanted of me that I was robbed. Besides, you could hardly be robbed with less inconvenience. I found a handkerchief in a shop three steps away.

There are customs here that have the force of law. The linen merchants and the clothiers must lodge in the Grand Rue and the Rue-Haute by turns. The clothiers pay a much higher rent because they sell a rich merchandise. The linen-drapers are established quite close to the Rhone gate. The leather-sellers are at both ends of a certain street in which the Jews occupy the middle. The shops of the various commercial houses are not rented. Against the wall, in front of each shop, there are stalls covered with canvas. Small pedlars do business there.

The odd thing about this fair is the great crowd everywhere. The costumes are as varied as the languages, but what is most striking and lends a peculiar character to this labyrinth where the crowd teems is the number of big pieces of cotton cloth, making pictures of all colors and shapes, square, triangular, round. They float in the middle of the streets fifteen feet above your head. The merchants hang them from cords stretched between the houses. These cloth posters carry the firm's name, its home address, and its Beaucaire address. This is the way that the Catalan wholesaler learns that his friend, the Greek wholesaler, is at the fair, for it is useless to ask for an address in a crowd of people all strangers to one another.

These signs are amusing to look at. There are signs of beautiful red cotton with big white letters, some of jonquil with pretty Gothic lettering, others of green with red letters. These were hard on the eyes. This collection of colors has something oriental about it and reminds you of a ship decked out for a feast day.

As for mental activity, here is the chief characteristic: everyone is lively. Everything that can't be done quickly tends to disappear. The little town of Beaucaire can't hold all the merchants from Naples, Genoa, Greece, and all the southern countries. Luckily, on the river bank there is this vast meadow bordered with big trees, named the Ste Madeleine meadow, and I much prefer it to the town. A great many huts are put up there made of planks. Because it's very hot weather, many of the dealers prefer tents. In this way, streets, squares, and narrow passages are formed. Each one has a sign, the tool of his trade, and usually merchants from the same country gather in the same street.

After I had finished my business, my curiosity drove me here and there, and the first shops I saw were those of the soap merchants, the grocers, and the druggists of Marseilles. Further on, the perfumers of Grasse displayed their pomades and shaving materials, those of Montpellier their perfumes and liqueurs. I bought some of M. Durand's excellent Portugal water. As I went on, I found booths filled with figs, prunes, raisins, and almonds. Our nostrils were struck by a smell much stronger than it was pleasant, and we approached a street whose walls, thick and quite high, were made of onions and garlic. We fled.

We wanted to get to the Grand Rue. The cafés, billiard parlors, and places to dance are all there, and behind it, stretched out in a long thin line, are the jugglers' booths, the acrobats', the animal trainers', and those of the people who display wax figures of great men.

Legally the fair lasts only seven days from July 22 to the evening of July 28, but they stretch it out. The franchises, which were very considerable before the Revolution and made the Farmers-General groan, were first confirmed by Louis XI in 1463.

The happiest moment of the day is the *Ave Maria*, nightfall. Then there is a great hurry to shut up the houses, booths, and tents any which way. Generally each little merchant makes his bed on his counter and ties his dog to the side.

At nine-thirty the well-bred people go to the meadow and eat ices. Then instruments begin to tune up on all sides. Here is the Nîmes ball, there is Aix's, over there Avignon's. Each one goes to his local ball. The Provençal flute is always mingled with the violins and cellos and rises above them. The flute is not as good as the horn of the Bohemian musicians who embellish the Leipzig fair, but it is gayer. They don't think so much about the music as they do the dancing and how to enjoy quickly the life that is flying away.

But what makes the fun of the fair is all the young women from St. Étienne, Grenoble, Mâcon, Montpellier, Béziers, Aix, etc., who, for once in their lives, have made their husbands bring them to Beaucaire, and usually it is the year after their first child. A young woman who comes to Beaucaire wants above all to find some extraordinary pleasure. Do I dare confess, to the great detriment of morality, that no one takes anything seriously at Beaucaire except the non-payment of a bill of exchange? May I repeat what a pretty woman twenty-five years old told me as a fact more reasonable than any other? "You're sure never to see again the man you have had a moment of weakness for, where it would be something to think about in a little town when he would be continually under foot and might become an enemy."

Tarascon, July 28

BEAUCAIRE WAS CELEBRATED in the writings of the Troubadours. There the charming story of Aucassin and Nicolette was enacted. She was the adopted child of the Viscount de Beaucaire. This is the place to study the history of chivalry. Suddenly men took it into their heads to forget any really useful purpose and made women the judges of their merit. We have been cured a little too well of this amiable mistake of which fashion and Mr. Brummel are the last forms. To be noble no longer suffices. One must be *fashionable.*

The civilization so widely spread by the republic of Marseilles prepared for the reign of elegant and knightly princes who gave so many graces to the history of Provence. In 1172 Raymond V held full court at Beaucaire, and each knight strove to shine there by his magnificence. Raimbaud had a dozen span of oxen draw long furrows in the courtyards and the land surrounding the castle. In the furrows he sowed thirty thousand sous. (Each sou was sorth a franc today.)

Guillaume Grosmartel had all the dishes for his own table and the feeding of three hundred knights cooked over the flames of wax candles. This folly would have greatly surprised a Greek contemporary of Aspasia. Aspasia was nice, but she was not a good judge of merit. We are going back to the days of Aspasia now.

Raymond de Venoux had thirty of the finest horses he had bred burned before the court.

One day at Beaucaire we went up to that old castle so renowned among historians of chivalry. Nothing but ruins remains. Louis XIII had it torn down in 1632. From the top of the hill the countryside is quite pretty. The magnificent Rhone and the strange castle of Tarascon keep it from being commonplace. The Languedocians call the town *Bel-caire.* The two words taken separately mean "Beautiful Quarters."

Two things annoyed me among all the pleasures of Beaucaire, but I hardly dare name them. They are, first, the mistral, then, the fleas. I would a hundred times rather meet brigands on the roads.

We have a scholar at Beaucaire. He is learned but outrageously pedantic. He says he has counted three thousand words in Provençal that are not of Latin origin. "Dun" in Celtic means "elevation." We have preserved the word "dune." Hence the town names, Verdun, Issodun, Chateaudun. "Van" means "mountain," "dor" a current of water: the Durance, the Dordogne, the Doire. Here are some of the scholar's sentences: Ce *quai* conduit au *parc.* Sur ce *banc* je vois un *las* de *brocs. Fi* de cette *colle blanche.* All the words italicized are Gaelic and have remained in French.

But the great charm of Beaucaire was the society and friendship, if I dare say it, of Herr Sharen and his wife. I hesitate, I confess, to tell the following story. Aside from being a little racy, this adventure, which was for me the most interesting of the whole journey, seems very long when written out, and besides an adventure did not occur, and the story lacks the piquant word at the end. What you are going to read, then, will be, if you please, only an observation on a peculiarity of the human heart, and if it makes your virtue flare up, I shall say it is not true.

We, Tiberval and myself, spent some pleasant days at Beaucaire with the Sharens. Herr Sharen is a tall handsome German with an aquiline nose and fine blond hair very carefully done. He is a businessman, it is true, but he seems to be traveling more for pleasure than business. What we tried to do was to please Frau Sharen a little, the least of whose charms is a perfect beauty, but her face is so naive and at the same time so spiritual that you don't think of its beauty. When he sees Frau Sharen, a prudent man busies himself with only one thing, and that is trying not to become amorous. Her extremely dignified bearing is a help in this respect. One of our Beaucaire wits said that her movements are those of a great mind. Among her other bewitching attractions, Frau Sharen has the most good-natured smile I have ever seen. In a smile as pretty as this one there is a great spirit and, moreover, no possibility of malice. It is precisely this absence of any coldness that seems to me to be the adorable charm of the countries beyond the Rhine. This quality is even more singular in Frau Sharen in that she has a marriage portion of eight hundred thousand or a million francs.

What complicates the story is that Herr Sharen has a close friend, Herr Munch, a small nervous man with an elegant figure, elaborately turned out, who, ignorant as he is of most of our customs, yet has the most sparkling wit I have ever seen in a German. He also has a very pretty wife, a piquant brunette, proud of giving pleasure and, I think, a little silly. He is a businessman like his friend, apparently very rich, and he travels in the company of Herr and Frau Sharen. They left their home a year ago, a big town in Saxony, I gather, because they speak magnificent German, but they never say where they are from. The day after I was presented to this amiable German colony, some domestic trouble began. Perhaps Herr Sharen was jealous of M. Tiberval, a quite distinguished young Frenchman, acceptable in every way, and a friend of mine. But here is the odd thing. Sharen is not jealous on his wife's account. Tiberval was evidently paying court to that semi-princess with her silly pride and beautiful black hair, the dignified Frau Munch. The good German's jealousy was only too plain. There was great uncertainty with us, frequent councils of war, a redoubling of false gaiety, though not on my part. Aided by my gibberish German, I took the role of the good-natured man. I smiled little so as not to seem ironical.

Germans go crazy at the sight of what they call French irony. I pushed my anti-ironic pretensions to the point of sentimentality. *I quoted maxims,* all this to promote confidence. Vain hope. The day after the next, Munch and his wife went to Cette on what they said was a pleasure party while it is clear that to these good quiet Germans nothing can compare with the din at Beaucaire, which is gaiety itself in their eyes. Munch bought with delight all the books in the Provençal tongue he could unearth, and we talked all one night about the courts of love. There was a mystery, then, but for us, a complete impossibility of divining anything. If I had been master of my time, I would have sacrificed a fortnight. I was, at the bottom of my heart, so much in love with the appearance of goodness and simplicity of heart. "Appearance" is an injustice. No one is really good like a German. (Diplomacy is not in his line.)

A German throws himself out of the window. "What are you doing?" someone says. "I'm just acting lively." The word depicts the German politician. He thinks he is interested in being subtle, and he wants very much to imitate M. T——. You may judge the effects of this bizarre idea.

I left without being able to make any predictions about our two lovely Germans and their husbands, but I made Tiberval swear that he would write me the solution of the enigma if he ever found it out. Why is Sharen jealous of Frau Munch when he is so much in love with his own wife who is adorable besides?

I did not know how far Tiberval had gotten. As soon as his heart is scratched, he becomes impenetrable, but he was undoubtedly touched to the quick. Here is what I learned indirectly. He went into consultation with himself. He kept to his room even in Beaucaire and at last was able to appear without it looking too strange to take the waters at Bagnère a few days after the beautiful Germans, still intimate friends, had arrived there.

Four months later Tiberval wrote me a little six-line from Dresden, a curious brevity! The author was quite excited. Following his pledged word, he gave me the solution to the enigma, and in my turn I would like to give it to the reader without offending his highest sensibilities.

I would certainly abstain from revealing a fact like this if the parties were French, but Frauen Munch and Sharen live several hundred leagues from our frontiers, and, although their fortunes have wantonly overwhelmed them with all sorts of advantages, they feel a little fear at the back of their minds that they will be taken for gross, dull people. In the prime of life, enjoying with dignity a great fortune, having received from heaven frank and elevated minds, they arrived at Beaucaire, driven from Naples by the cholera. All this is easy to say, but this is the least of it. When they left their own country, they traveled together in two carriages. They had hardly gone a hundred leagues from Brixen to the Italian frontier when Munch, who has a most original mind, said to his friend, "You are making up to my wife. No, don't deny it. My dear friend, you are going to do everything in the world to betray me. Is this the way for boyhood friends to act, to deceive one another? On the other hand, are we going to have to give up this wonderful year-and-a-half trip we were going to make together? As for myself I couldn't stand the evenings alone, and without you I couldn't travel. But if you are going to try to cheat me out of my pretty wife, why, yours is charming, and perhaps I shall do everything I can to play the same role with her. We can make all the fine promises we like, but that's the way it will be. Circumstances seem to want to force us to please the wives of our intimate friends, and we will certainly be in a deadly mix-up when we return home. This will be a fine result of our trip, we who have been close since we learned to read in school. We are thirty leagues from Verona, and we shall get there tomorrow night. We will spend twenty-four hours there seeing the galleries and the antiquities. The next day we will leave that beautiful town. Very well, at the end of that day, let us change wives. Frau Sharen will call herself Frau Munch, and Frau Munch will call herself Frau Sharen. We must return through Verona, and just as we reach it on our way back, each lady will return to her lawful master. And never a word will we say about it!"

This proposal was made with unique good nature in the

presence of the two ladies. A complete silence of twenty-four hours followed. Only Munch dared say anything: "If your bourgeois ideas are opposed to my project, let us separate at once. But if, as true and noble sons of Germany, disdaining any lie that would make a coolness between us, we dare be sincere, let us go on with our noble journey into Italy."

In the end, that is the way it worked out, and I, who have greatly loved if not greatly studied these lovely German women, would undertake to say that they conducted themselves properly the rest of their lives. As for Tiberval, he got nothing although he was madly in love and very adroit at this kind of combat.

Nîmes, August 1

Since my trip to Beaucaire seemed to my father-in-law a signal act of devotion to the interests of the firm, I gave muself a few days' leave to see Nîmes, the Pont du Gard, and Orange.

Since you have to travel at night because of the great heat, I reached Nîmes at five o'clock in the morning, and I hurried to the Maison Carrée. What a bourgeois name for this charming little temple! In the first place, it isn't square at all. It has the form of a playing-card like all genuine antique temples. Its little open portico upheld by charming Corinthian columns stands out against the blue sky of the Midi. The other columns surrounding it are half-engaged in the wall, something that is not fashionable today. The whole effect is admirable. I have seen more imposing monuments in Italy but none as charming. It is like the smile of a person habitually serious. The mind is gently stirred at the sight of this temple which is only seventy-two feet long and thirty-six wide. Obviously it is smaller than most of our village Gothic churches, and what a difference in the number of things it says to the mind! And, further, it doesn't suggest the same things as the Gothic. The Maison Carrée is far from inspiring terror or even sadness.

The temples of the ancients were small, their circusses very large. It is the opposite with us. Our religion proscribes the theater and ordains that we mortify the flesh. Among the Romans, religion was a festival, and since it never demanded that its worshipers sacrifice their passions, rather it encouraged them to find an outlet useful to the fatherland, there was no need to gather the faithful together for long hours in order to engrave the fear of hell on their hearts.

Nîmes, August 2

A SENSIBLE MAN GAVE ME the real story of the murders committed in this part of the country and, to turn our minds from these black thoughts, told me, "Civilization is declining in the Midi because the officials are incapable and have neglected to condemn these murderers to death; but once the Midi saw what chivalry produced toward human betterment."

The exaltation of love, such a ridiculous sentiment nowadays yet one which reigned supreme in the poetry of Dante and Plutarch, was the principle of all chivalry. Provençal poetry called it "joy."

In the Spanish code, "joy" is enjoined upon knights as a duty. Thus, the sword of Charlemagne was called "joyous" or the enthusiast of love. Even today in Italian, *tristo* means a dull prosaic person, an enemy of all generosity, a being to flee from, almost a man to hang.

Provençal gallantry was established in sharply separated grades through which one had to pass successively. At first one was *feignaire*, hesitant, then *pregaire*, beseeching, then *entendaire*, a listener, and finally, *druz*, a lover. In Italian, *drudo* means the lover of a married woman.

August 3

(WRITTEN IN THE SHADE of one of the archways of the Pont du Gard.)

Orange, August 4

I profited by a clear moonlit night to go to the five leagues between Nîmes and the Pont du Gard. I was sound asleep when I got there at five in the morning. Faithful Joseph sent the horses on to the posting-station at La Foux and let me sleep. He made a campfire and some excellent coffee. A nearby goat furnished the milk.

You know that the Pont du Gard, only a simple aqueduct, rises majestically in the midst of a wilderness. The mind is thrown into an astonishment long and profound. The Colisseum at Rome hardly induced a reverie as deep.

The archways that we admire are part of the aqueduct seven leagues long that brings the water from the spring of Eure to Nîmes. It had to be built across a deep narrow valley. There is no sign of luxury or ornament here. The Romans made these astonishing things not to inspire admiration but simply and only when they were useful. A composition *for effect*, which is so eminently modern an idea, the mind of the spectator rejects at once, and if he is reminded of this craze, it is only to scorn it. The mind is filled with feelings it does not even dare articulate, much less magnify. True passions have their modesty.

Luckily for the pleasure of the traveler born to the arts, no matter in what direction he looks, he will see no sign of human habitation, any evidence of cultivation. Thyme, wild lavender, and juniper, all that grows in this wilderness, exhale their solitary perfumes here under a sky of dazzling serenity. The mind is left entirely to itself, and the attention is forcibly directed to the work before one's eyes. For the hearts of the chosen, this monument is such an event that it must have the effect of sublime music. The others will think admiringly of all the money it must have cost.

Orange, August 4

I STOPPED ONLY A HALF-DAY to see Orange. I found all the streets tented over because of the heat. This climate enchants me, but it would keep me happy for only about two weeks. I would say, almost like Araminthe, that it throws one into sweet languors.

I wanted to see the theater and the triumphal arch. The theater wall can be seen from a great distance, dominating the town. The arch, probably built in the reign of Marcus Aurelius, is admirably placed. It rises up on the dusty plain five hundred paces from the last houses of the town on the side toward Lyons. Its yellowish-orange tint stands out in the most harmonious way against the blue sky of Provence. This venerable arch is sixty-six feet wide and sixty feet high.

Lerbert, Abbot of St. Ruf, who lived in the eleventh century, says the arch was erected by Caesar, conqueror of the Marseillais. Today they call it the Arch of Marius, but there is nothing that can indicate either the period or the purpose of the monument. When this stately arch was raised to make eternal the glory of a great nation and its generals, who among them could have foreseen a time when it would survive almost complete without anyone knowing what its purpose was?

A guide took me around the big *cire*, which means "circus." This structure is on the slope of a mountain. It was a theater, not a circus. The mountainside was excavated to make the circular section where the spectators' seats were placed. You can still see the stumps of enormous columns. There were three rows of columns one above the other. The wall that cut off the semicircle of seats and constituted the base of the stage remains whole and makes a wonderful effect. You recognize the Roman manner at once. It is a hundred and eight feet high and three hundred feet wide.

It is hard to leave off pondering this wall, it is so large, so simple, so well built, so well preserved. It is adorned with two rows of arches and an attic story. In the middle is a large gate that was probably used as the actors' entrance. As with the Pont du Gard, the Romans everywhere give us a feeling of the deepest

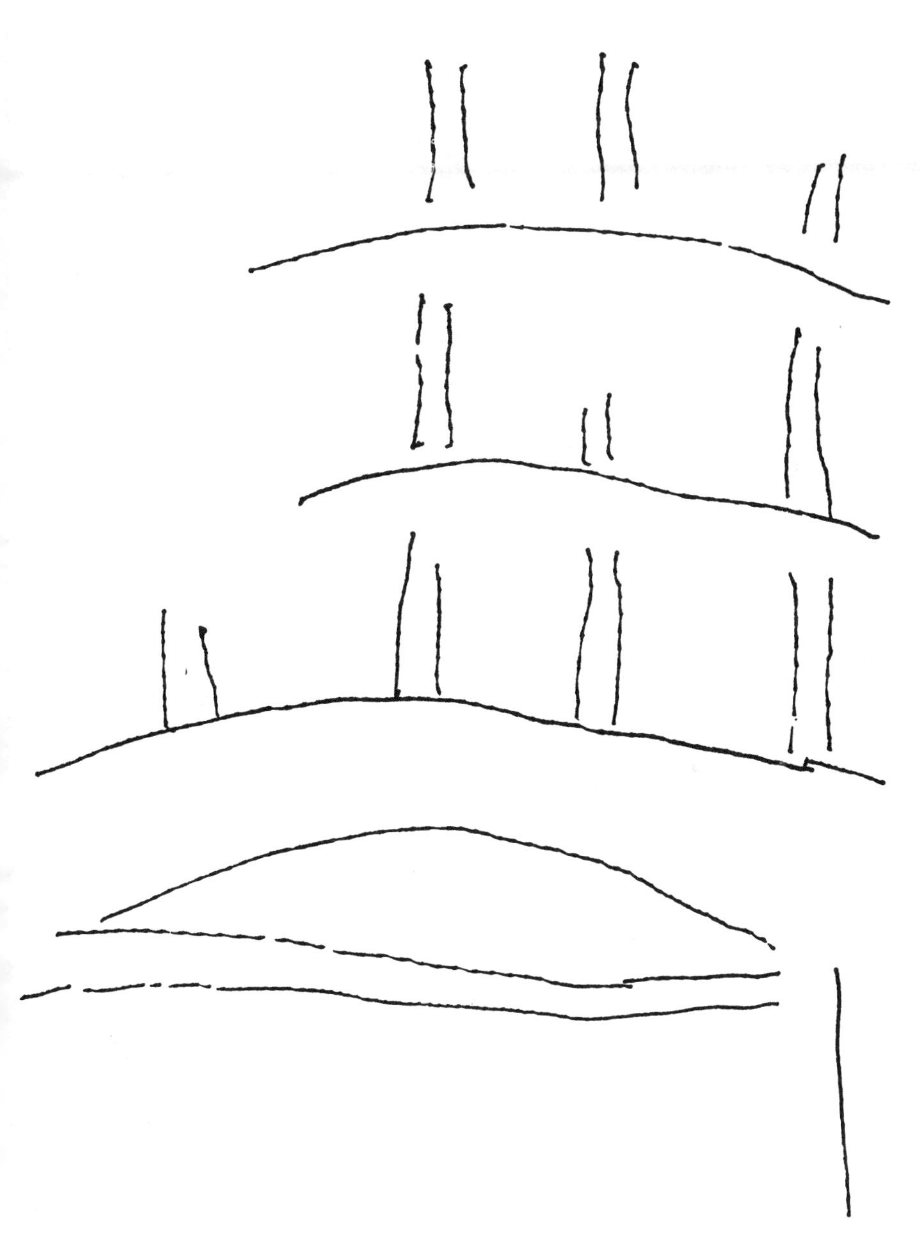

respect and the liveliest admiration for buildings intended for the simplest uses. This is the attribute of a great character.

Tullins, August 6

YESTERDAY AT VALENCE IT RAINED, and I was smoking a cigar in the hotel doorway as every good traveler must do who is trying to see and learn something. The proprietor came up and told me the history of the good wines of the region. The Bishop of Valence owns the vineyard where we get the sublime wine of l'Ermitage. He has let it out to a company who, beside the rent they pay, give him four hundred bottles of the finest quality on condition that he give none of it away. They undoubtedly fear comparison with the wine they put on the market.

I was discussing wines when I saw M. Buisson get out of the Marseilles coach. He is a dealer from Algiers who doesn't mind handling what little business we have there. He was on his way to Pont-en-Royans where he owns a textile mill. I offered to take him with me, and at five o'clock in the morning we left Valence.

On the way he told me some funny things about Algiers, where he was six days ago. Before the time of the wise Marshal Valée, we had been so boastful and so flighty that the Arabs firmly believed that the French were a miserable people, dying of hunger on the shore of the Mediterranean around a town not a quarter the size of Algiers which is called Marseilles. These French, think the Arabs, not knowing what was going to become of them, crossed to Algeria to steal cattle. They are, moreover, the silliest men in the world. One day they shoot their prisoners. The next day, naturally afraid that the Arabs will return, they overwhelm the prisoners with gifts. "The wisest thing to do, actually," said M. Buisson, "would be to kidnap fifty Arabs forty years old, take them to Paris, and give them lodging at the Invalides and ten francs a day. When they returned to the Atlas, they would tell what they had seen." At this point, our wittiness and our restless vanity have succeeded only in making us utterly scorned by the Arab gravity.

"The Emperor of Morocco," M. Buisson told me," is a Puritan fifty years old, ruling over a society of gloomy Puritans. Out of Mahometan humility he wears the same simple clothes as his subjects. What offends them most about the French is our frightful habit of stopping at a wall to satisfy a petty need."

"But that's English," I said.

"As far as gravity and this theatrical propriety go, the people of Morocco could have given points to the Methodists," M. Buisson said. "Although in 1837 the reigning emperor in Morocco has thick lips and the coloring of a mulatto, he is nonetheless descended from Mahomet and consequently nurses an infinite scorn for the Grand Turk, who is only a degenerate in his eyes, almost an infidel."

In spite of the extreme piety in Morocco, it is quite easy to get a man murdered for twenty-two sous, a peseta. The Moslem religion, fundamentally wise enough, has degenerated in practice like the Calabrian. The Moroccan mountaineers show exactly the same customs described in the Bible, which gives us our precepts of morality. They have introduced only one new custom: they have guns they make themselves.

The height of human felicity for a Moroccan is to own some horses, some guns, and some powder, a lot of powder. To do a stranger honor, they come galloping up and fire their guns, loaded with ball, two feet over his head. They don't intend too much malice. They always keep their guns loaded with ball in the interests of their own safety, and they know nothing about the use of a wad-extractor.

When a girl marries, they put her in a panier on a mule. They lead the mule into the middle of a field, and all the horsemen in the tribe ride up at full gallop and fire their guns between the mule's legs.

M. Buisson admires Abd-el-Kader very much, that young twenty-nine-year-old general who knows more about his trade

than our generals of fifty. He might become a great man. M. Buisson makes a great difference between the Arab who can be made to understand *his true interests* and the Turk, like Achmet, whom nothing can divert from an idea once he has conceived it. The Turk is very likely the most virtuous man to be encountered in the nineteenth century, and all this virtue is only a blind obedience to the Koran which he believes superior to any other book.

This African war will be able to instill some new ideas into French complacency which believes it knows everything. I had read a great deal in Volney that the French had no genius for colonization. There was not a single word of M. Buisson's that did not confirm this sad truth. He praises very highly four or five officers stationed in Africa who, if they are promoted, promise to make generals like those of '93. They have condescended to learn Arabic. There are frequent suicides, and it is usually young officers who blow their heads off. Life is appraised everywhere at what it is worth, that is, not much.

The businessmen established in Algiers give the French government seven hundred thousand francs a year for the salt at Arsew. It takes only ten hours to carry the salt by sea to Algiers. But a governor with a will of iron is the first requirement in this country. It is in *knowing how to will* that the Arabs make us look like fools, we who have only the advantages of an ancient civilization.

It struck six o'clock as I changed horses at St. Marcellin. I could still reach Tullins in time to sleep at the house of M. Guizard, the postmaster to whom M. Buisson had recommended me.

But before I reached Tullins I had a delightful surprise. Luckily no one had told me about it. I suddenly came upon one of the most beautiful views in the world. It is before you come to the little village of Cras as you begin to go down toward Tullins. Before your eyes a vast countryside worthy of Titian abruptly appears. In the foreground, the chateau of Vourey; at the right, the Isére, winding to infinity, to the horizon, to Grenoble. This broad river waters a plain that is most fertile, the best planted and cultivated, and of the richest verdure. Above the plain, perhaps the most beautiful France can boast of, are the Alps, and their granite peaks are outlined in reddish-black against the eternal snows which cannot cling to their slopes because they are too steep. Before you are the Grand Som and the beautiful mountains of the Chartreuse. To the left are the bold shapes of some wooded slopes. Anything boring seems banished from this beautiful region.

The mountain you go down from Cras is part of the Jura range which runs from Basle to Fontaneille, near Sault, in lower Dauphiné. I told the postilion that I was dizzy and wanted to get out and walk. Without saying a word, he walked with me to the bottom of the slope, thus nothing spoiled my pleasure.

Grenoble, August 8

I CAME TO GRENOBLE by way of Moirans and Voreppe. I am staying at M. Blanc's Hotel of the Three Dauphins, Rue Montorge, in Room No. 2 which was occupied by Napoleon on his return from Elba. My window looks out a wonderful alley of chestnut trees twenty-four feet high. They were planted by Lesdiguières, the emblem and the model of the Dauphiné character (bold and never duped). These beautiful trees are exactly in the center of town facing a beautiful mountain, and unfortunately they have seen their best days. They are more than two hundred years old, and a big branch comes down in every storm, but the finest of them, the one called "Lesdiguières," still holds up very well in spite of having been struck by a cannon ball on July 6, 1815, whose mark I went there to venerate.

The Constable Lesdiguières ruled Dauphiné all his life, and he did not let anyone come there and make trouble. He built the palace nearby, and the town bought it from his heirs. The Prefecture occupies a part of it today and pays a rent of six thousand francs. The Franquières house, a pretty place in the Renaissance style, was built by Lesdiguières as a lodging for his mistress, whose husband he had murdered, but he sent the celebrated advocate, M. Barral, to Rome to solicit absolution from the Pope.

I was afraid I was going to find those nasty sharp-pointed cobbles that keep you from walking in Lyons, but the Grenoblois are intelligent people. Already seven of their streets are paved with flat stones they bring from Fontaine, and in six years there will be no more pointed cobbles. The mayor of the town works twelve hours a day, and the municipal council is composed of intelligent men, most of them young and liberal. I wish to God that Paris was administered by these gentlemen! It wouldn't grow uglier while you watch it.

On the way to the Bastille you find yourself looking straight at the enormous peak of Taillefer. Below and a little to the left are the charming hills of Uriage and Echirole. At the right the plain stretches out to the Bridge of Claix with its magnificent avenue eight thousand meters long. The idea of building it was like one of Lenôtre's, to place it in the middle of wild mountains, and it makes a wonderful effect. By a lucky chance it is facing the new fort of Rabot, Captain Gueze's masterpiece of construction. I saw there some new drawbridges invented by this distinguished officer.

Grenoble, August 10

THIS MORNING I WAS WAKED UP at seven o'clock to go eat cherries in the fashion of Montfleury. It is an old custom, and at a former convent of noble women half a league from the town, its site is unique in the whole world. All the ladies who are staying in the country roundabout go early to this delightful little valley. The ladies from the town pull up in beautiful calashes. This makes for a charming morning. The peasants of the neighborhood in their finest clothes sell little bunches of cherries put up in bouquets and wonderful strawberries gathered in the woods on the slopes of the Grande Chartreuse.

Grenoble, August 12

THIS MORNING I WAS TAKEN to the chateau of Montbonot, which belongs to a learned and friendly man. The chateau crowns a pretty little hill that runs toward the Isére. It is undoubtedly the loveliest spot in the valley, but how can these things be described? I would have to take a high-flown epic tone for ten pages, and I have a horror of that. And the result of so much work would only be to bore the reader, probably. I have noticed that the beautiful descriptions by Mrs. Radcliffe describe nothing. They are like the song of a sailor that makes you dream.

I can say only to the traveler: when you go by way of Lyons, go twenty leagues further and see these marvelous sights.

From Montbonot I went down to the bank of the Isére to look at the site of an iron cable bridge for which I may supply some iron from La Roche (in Champagne). While I was at the workings, I heard about the strange suicide of a young Protestant girl of Grenoble. She had the finest eyes in Dauphiné, but she also had the reputation of being a little flighty, that is, on certain holidays she did not refuse to walk up and down with young men in front of her mother's shop. This was a great crime in the eyes of the sanctimonious people of the neighborhood who were already inclined to hate her because of her religion. As the sequel proved, there was nothing more innocent. Victorine was gay and lively by nature, known to everyone in the whole Trégcloîtres quarter. When she was happy, she got carried away easily. A young neighbor, a Catholic of a gloomy character, who at first found fault with her angrily, fell in love with her. In the beginning, she made fun of him; then she loved him. The young man's parents indignantly refused to let him marry a girl of such suspicious gaiety and a Protestant besides. The young people tried every possible way to bend them. Then they had the idea that next seemed the simplest, that of killing themselves. The day before the one that was to be their last, the young man took a hundred francs to the surgeon of the quarter and told him in these very words, "I am going to have a duel one of these days. If I should succumb, give me your word that you will perform an autopsy on the bodies. That is essential to the peace of *our* last moments. You are a sensible man, and in three days you will understand me. Remember, now, that I am counting on your honor, and it is honor that makes me speak."

The surgeon did not understand this kind of talk at all and believed that the young man had taken up his former mystical ideas.

These poor young things rented a room where they were found asphyxiated. The day before, the girl had said, weeping, "Some day they will recognize that I have always been good." Of that the autopsy of her body left no doubt. They found on her a touching letter. I saw a copy of it. Here is a sentence out of it: "I shall be forgotten as soon as I'm buried, but before this last forgetting of a young girl who was too unlucky, I hope they will say in all of Trégcloîtres, 'Victorine was perfectly good.' "

Memoirs of a Tourist

Grenoble, August 14

Grenoble has always been a place of war, and they have made a fortified town out of it. As a result it is the military who have absolute power over the closing of the gates, and this is a great bother to the poor traveler who has been detained. Yesterday evening both my postilion and I heard the bell in the big church of Grenoble strike ten in the distance. This meant that the town gates were being closed. With a cunning look and not a word to me, the postilion pushed his horses as hard as he could. We arrived at the Tréscloîtres gate at a gallop just five minutes after they had been shut. It was very hard to open negotiations with the porter at all, and in the end they led to nothing.

There was a dirty suburb nearby that made me think of insects. I backed away promptly and went to the inn at Gières to sleep. It is a big house on the road. I didn't stand on any dignity at all. While waiting for my supper, instead of keeping to my room which had oiled paper serving as glass in the windows, I went down to the kitchen where I heard a large group of people.

Often in these mountains, even in the middle of the summer, a little cool wind comes up in the evening that makes a kitchen fire very pleasant. No matter which way it comes from, this wind has just passed over high ranges of mountains which are covered with snow eleven months of the year, and it brings with it some of their cold. There were quite a few people in the kitchen, and I made out some young women laughing very hard and keeping a certain distance from a pretty fire of vine stems (stripped from the vine when they are cut in February), a brisk fire over which my supper was being prepared.

Heaven has given me the talent of making myself welcome among peasants. To do this you must talk neither too much nor too little and above all not affect a complete equality with them. In the end I succeeded yesterday evening, and I shuddered at ghost stories until one o'clock in the morning. It was a charming evening.

Vizille, August 21

Lesdiguières, that shrewd old fox, as the Duke of Savoy called him, lived at Vizille ordinarily and built the chateau there. There is a bronze equestrian statue of him in bas-relief above the main gate. At a distance the portraits of Lesdiguières resemble those of Louis XIII, but, as you draw nearer, the vacant and handsome face of the feeble son of Henri IV is replaced by the physiognomy, astute and smiling, of the great general of the Dauphiné, who was, moreover, one of the handsomest men of his time.

On the gate of a pavilion that he built in his park at Vizille, a bas-relief was called to my notice. It was of two fishes placed crosswise, perhaps a foot long; below, there was a severed human head. The Constable, having found a man fishing in his park, had his head cut off and this stone set above the gate. Such rulers impressed the minds of the people twenty times more than timid beings like Louis XVI.

When you find a bridge boldly constructed in the midst of the cliffs of these high mountains, you can be sure the guide is going to say it was built by Lesdiguiéres. If you see a well-laid-out street in Grenoble, it was built by Lesdiguiéres, and he made war all his life.

Grenoble, August 24

What I like about Grenoble is that it has the look of a town, not a big village like Rheims, Poitiers, Dijon, etc. All the houses here have four, five, sometimes six stories. This is most uncomfortable and doubtless not at all healthful, but the first condition of architecture is the display of power, and only the *comfortable vulgar* can be seen in the two-story houses of Rheims and Dijon. They say that all the facades of the houses in Grenoble have been rebuilt in the last twenty years.

Before the Roman conquest when Grenoble was called *Cularo*, it was set against the Bastille mountain and occupied the narrow stretch of land which is covered today by the Rue Saint Laurent and the Quai La Perrière. Gratian rebuilt it and gave it his own name, Gratianopolis, and "Grenoble" comes from it.

This evening when we returned from the promenade we found some light-red wine from Die, and we dined on *pogne d'herbe de Sassenage*. At a time like this the prudence of the Dauphinois forgets itself a little, and for several hours I was entrusted with, first, an account of the events of July 6, 1815 (Grenoble should have them placed on its coat-of-arms) and, second, the exact history of the clumsy persecutions directed against the anniversaries of that great day. These things seemed unbelievably awkward, and, if I told them, I would seem libelous. Also they killed any enthusiasm for authority.

Grenoble has a museum rich in beautiful Italian pictures whose description I suppress here. It has been placed in the upper part of the Jesuit church. After I had looked at the pictures and was walking at the southern end of the room, the guard opened a window for me. Astonished, caught up by the delightful view from it, I begged the man to leave me alone at the window and to go off a hundred paces and sit in his chair. I had a good deal of trouble getting this sacrifice out of him. He didn't understand what I wanted, and, a Dauphinois, he was afraid I was up to something. At last, however, I was able to enjoy one of the most charming views I ever saw in my life.

Noon struck. The sun was at its hottest. The silence everywhere was troubled only by the cry of some cicadas. It was Virgil's verse in all its truth, *Sole sub argenti resonant arbusta sicadis* ("Under the burning sun the orchard hums with cicadas"). A light breeze stirred the grass on the slope in the foreground. Farther away the delightful slopes of Echiroles, Eybens, of St. Martin-de-Gières, covered with their cool chestnut trees, spread their peaceful shade. Above, at an astonishing height, Mt. Taillefer's eternal snows made a contrast to the burning heat and gave a certain intensity to one's feelings.

Sadly brought back to earth by the museum guard, I went to visit the library, founded in 1773 by a man of superior intelligence whose name I have often heard repeated in Grenoble, M. Gagnon.* He persuaded his fellow-citizens to make up a subscription. He also gave quite a bit of money himself, and with it they bought a large library from the estate of a bishop who had recently died.

Le Pont de Claix, August 25

Very late last night I received a letter from M. C——, informing me that he had accomplished what I had asked him to do and that today, Sunday, at 10 A.M. I would find at Lafrey four peasants he had been so kind as to assemble. These peasants were witnesses, twenty-two years ago, at the interview between the battalion of the Grenoble garrison and Napoleon, who was returning from Elba. There was decided the fate of the finest, the most romantic undertaking of modern times. This battalion, sent by General Marchand, commandant at Grenoble, should have barred Napoleon's way at the point where the route is cramped between the big lake at Lafrey and the mountain.

Grenoble, August 27

At five in the morning, I left Grenoble in delightful weather, and at half past nine I was in the famous meadow strewn with rocks that stretches out from the big lake at Lafrey with its brook that runs out of the lake by the mountain to the right of the road that leads to La Mure. I admit I was childish. My heart beat violently, and I was deeply moved, but the three

* Henri Gagnon was Stendhal's maternal grandfather, as, of course, Grenoble was Stendhal's birthplace.—Tr.

peasants were not able to divine my emotion. (The fourth had not been able to come.) The ones who were there did not even once look sideways at me, since they didn't have enough enthusiasm for Napoleon.

After a hasty lunch at Lafrey we went several hundred paces along the road from La Mure. There, near a little wooden cross, we ascertained by some willow branches stuck in the ground the position of the battalion ordered by Gen. Marchand to block the road. It is only a two- or three-acre meadow. In front of the battalion was the lake and the mountain which comes down so close to it that there is barely room for the road.

I spoke very little. The peasants were talking among themselves, and luckily they didn't always agree. I had brought three or four bottles of wine along, and we sat down several times. I took care to be thirsty whenever I saw a doubtful point coming up.

"You can't have just a little stick here," cried one of the peasants. His eyes were shining. He went and cut from a big willow a branch twelve feet long that he thrust into the exact spot where Napoleon had stopped. Some day there will be a statue of Napoleon on foot, fifteen or twenty feet high, in precisely the uniform Napoleon wore that day.

Here is what he had done before he arrived there. The night before he had bivouacked with his little troop on a hilltop somewhere near La Mure. The real point of defense against him was the Ponthaut Bridge, a league to the south of La Mure, but this bridge was not occupied. Napoleon set out about ten in the morning. He took the ascent that leads to Lafrey and arrived finally at the culminating point where there is no room except the road between the mountain and the lake of Lafrey.

Here he saw the battalion of royal troops barring his way. France's fate and his own were about to be decided. For a little while he continued on the road that goes down toward Lafrey. Then he made a right turn with his little troop, entered the meadow, and occupied the position that will be marked by a statue some day. He had barely more than two hundred soldiers. Many had been left behind, but this little band were marching surrounded by enthusiastic peasants.

A quarter of an hour later he had reached the spot we marked with the big willow branch. Napoleon sent General Bertrand to the battalion of Royal troops. Bertrand found that the commander had been in Egypt and had even been decorated by Napoleon, but this brave man announced that since France now obeyed a king, he would fire on the enemies of the king if they advanced toward his battalion.

"But," said General Bertrand, "if the Emperor personally presented himself to you, what would you do? Would you have the courage to fire on him?"

"I would do my duty," said the major.

One of the peasants I questioned had been between the battalion's position and the one the Emperor had taken. He thought that General Bertrand tried to speak to some of the officers and even to the soldiers, who had been authorized to fire on him, but he did not succeed in making any of them move. He returned to the Emperor. Matters rested there for an hour, according to one of my peasants, and only a half-hour if the other two may be believed.

It is likely that General Marchand had picked the strongest men he had in the Grenoble garrison to make up the battalion and had given command of it to the officer who was the firmest and least likely to succumb to enthusiasm for the Emperor. But the soldiers saw their Emperor for an hour at short range. "If the whole battalion fired at once, he would fall, no doubt about it," said the soldiers, "and see how calm he is. He knows very well we won't kill him."

The likelihood of firing on the Emperor was so far from everyone's mind that the space between the battalion and the Emperor rapidly filled with peasants. They did not hide their enthusiasm, and they distributed the Emperor's pamphlets to the soldiers.

At this moment a young officer was seen arriving from Lafrey at a gallop. My peasants did not know his name but they supposed it was M. Randon, aide-de-camp to General Marchand.

Shortly after this, Napoleon came toward the battalion and uttered the words that are found in the official report, "He opened his riding-coat, according to the peasants, and had the courage to say as he uncovered his breast, 'If any one of you wishes to kill his Emperor, let him fire.' "

In front of the battalion was a small advance-guard of a few men. The A.D.C. gave the command, "Aim," then, "Fire!" One of the soldiers was in close range of Napoleon, and he aimed his piece. When he heard the command to fire, he turned his head and said, "Is it the major commanding me to open fire?"

"Fire!" repeated the A.D.C.

"I'll fire if the major tells me to fire," the soldier replied.

The major did not repeat the command. The soldier put up his gun.

That, I think, was the decisive moment.

The Emperor had continued speaking and was recalling the battles in Egypt, and the major was moved by his words and no longer opposed his approach. The Emperor, reminding him of some personal circumstances, embraced him. The soldiers of the Grenoble garrison were following every movement of the Emperor with eager eyes and, delighted at being freed from discipline, began to shout, "*Vive l'Empereur!*" at that moment. The peasants took up the cry, and it was all over. Tears were in every eye. In an instant the enthusiasm was boundless. The soldiers embraced the peasants and each other.

Seeing the turn things had taken, M. Randon, the A.D.C. to General Marchand, undoubtedly wanting to warn his commander, set off at a gallop toward Lafrey. Four horse grenadiers of the Imperial Guard galloped after him. The A.D.C. urged his horse at full speed, and he covered the terrible downhill slope to Lafrey like that. He went through Vizille at a gallop, always followed by the four guardsmen wearing the tri-color cockade. The whole population of Vizille were at their windows, and they understood nothing of what was going on. The A.D.C. went up the rise toward Jarrye, still galloping. He was about to be overtaken when a short cut occurred to him. It was a path not over two feet wide. The tired horses of the grenadiers refused to gallop down the narrow path, and the A.D.C. was saved.

Everyone knows the rest. The Emperor, marching toward Grenoble, met M. de Labédoyère with his regiment on the Eybens plain. M. Labédoyère, who had come from Chambéry with his regiment two days before, had been ordered by General Marchand to go reinforce the battalion at Lafrey.

The same evening about nine o'clock, the Emperor arrived at the Bonne gate of Grenoble. That day his soldiers had made thirteen leagues at the double. The weather was very cold, and the wind blew hard. An odd feature of the Dauphinois character is that, when strongly moved, these people seem to be merely thoughtful and attentive. Thus an inexperienced observer would have noticed nothing extraordinary in Grenoble that whole day. The soldiers executed the orders they were given smilingly. When they unlimbered their guns on the rampart at the left of the Bonne gate, the artillerymen said, "These guns aren't going to hurt anyone."

"It's quite simple. The powder is damp," answered the townspeople who surrounded them. They were discreet enough not to say anything, but their glances were in agreement. About nine o'clock the Emperor was seated near the Bonne gate, a pistol shot from the rampart. It was war, but no one had the notion of taking the shot that would have saved the Bourbons.

That day the Emperor had run a danger that has always been ignored, and, as there was some energy in this act, it had as its source a man of the people.

The Bonne gate was shut. It was hit several blows with an axe from the outside and also on the inside. Overwhelmed with fatigue, the Emperor entered the town and came to sleep in the room where I am writing this. At that time, the inn was owned by La Barre, a brave soldier from the Army of Egypt. He was ruined for receiving the Emperor with enthusiasm. I may remark that I have never seen a soldier of the Army of Egypt speak of Napoleon without weeping.

Whatever the people say about it who write history in more or less sonorous phrases without leaving Paris, there was no outward sign of enthusiasm that day in Grenoble while rapture that reached the pitch of delirium carried away the inhabitants of La Mure, Vizille, and the other places along the road or within reach of the road taken by the Emperor. Some peasants from these villages followed him up to the walls of Grenoble, thinking there would be a fight there. They feared for the Emperor, for he had not three hundred men with him.

In Grenoble there was only curiosity, apparently. It was somewhat like the July days in Paris. The lower class alone listened to their hearts without thinking of prudence. Many Grenoblois said to themselves, "The Emperor can be stopped at Lyons by the army assembled there or killed by some Royalist soldier's bullet, and if that happens, we will have military commissions here before two weeks are up." There were a few cries of "*Vive l'Empereur!*" under La Barre's windows, and they came from people of the lowest class. The next day about noon, Napoleon reviewed the troops in the Place Grenette. Again the enthusiasm of the soldiers contrasted vividly with the coolness of the populace. Many of them, however, forgot all prudence and listened only to their hearts. They were excited by the brave Apollinaire Eimery, the Emperor's doctor, born in Grenoble, who arrived with him from Elba.

I hadn't wanted to read the bulletin Napoleon issued about this affair until today. It is perfectly exact. Napoleon had no interest whatever in lying. And, since it had been a great and noble act, perhaps he didn't want to dirty it with a lie even though his interest as a despot counseled him to. Often the love which this great heart had for the Beautiful got the better of his interests as ruler. This was very clear on the 18th Brumaire. Often his contempt for his faithful and obsequious subjects crowding into the levees at St. Cloud showed in his fine, well-molded lips. He seemed to be saying to himself, "Is this what it costs to become emperor of the world?" And he encouraged this servility. Later when he was punishing the Jacobins and those generals who had some spirit, Delmas, Lecourbe, etc., he was acting from a different motive. He was afraid.

After the enthusiasm of 1815, the common people of France went to sleep for fifteen years, and the most ignoble selfishness reigned everywhere.

Fourvoirie, September 1

When the gate opened at four o'clock in the morning yesterday, I left Grenoble with two horses, one for me, the other for my guide. I didn't need a guide, for it's impossible to lose your way on a mountain road that always follows the bottom of a valley or climbs the length of a steep slope zigzag, but I am crazy about gossiping with guides. The hypocrisy of the last twenty years still has not penetrated the lower classes. All along the way I spoke of subjects peculiar to this locality, and I got the judgment of the people on everything. They surprise me sometimes, and they always interest me. In nearly every sentence I encounter a laughable ignorance, but their judgments are never influenced by low motives. This is the opposite from the way fashion dictates matters in good society.

I left the beautiful valley of the Isère by the little Corenc road. It goes up in the midst of vineyards for the length of the mountain that overlooks the north side of the valley. I could hardly tear myself away from this beautiful region I was seeing for the last time. I stopped often. After you lose sight of the Isère and the bottom of the valley, you are as if face to face with the famous Taillefer and all the high ranges of the Alps. You see a host of new peaks. They seem to grow larger the higher you go.

Through my opera glasses I made out perfectly the needles of granite crowning their summits whose slope is so steep it cannot hold the snow. It piles up at the foot. After stopping a long time, I said good-by to this beautiful valley of the Isère.

In the highly cultivated countries I know, the Scottish Lowlands and Belgium, the expensive ways of tilling the land, forty plows used in a field at once, suggest the idea of big, fine manufacturing operations but no solitude or rustic happiness whatever. Only a monstrous vanity can allow these farmers to apply to their present business the terms Virgil, Rousseau, and others have used about life in the fields and its simplicity. Nothing is less simple than a big agricultural operation. It is manufacturing whose capital instead of being in looms, for instance, or in linen as at Elbeuf, is in meadows and tillable land. Further, and it is this that spoils everything, you are forever disputing with the peasants, greedy, thievish, and poor. The Isère Valley, in spite of its extreme fertility, never gives me the idea of a factory but rather and at every moment that of a rustic happiness in a landscape of the most sublime beauty.

As you go up toward Sapey, the vegetation grows proportionately poorer. The trees become small and stunted. You meet peasants shouting at the tops of their voices and calling their team of cows by name, pricking them with long iron goads. These poor thin beasts pull wooden rafts to market at Grenoble: thirty or forty little beech-tree trunks, pierced by hatchet blows near the roots, are tied together by osier withes. These tree trunks with their butts carried by two wheels drag over the roads and ruin them. But how would you have the courage to prohibit this industry? This is the only way these mountaineers can get a little money and pay their taxes, the same taxes that built the useless Palais d'Orsay in Paris. I have depressing ideas. Actually our negroes in the colonies are a thousand times happier than over a quarter of the peasants in France.

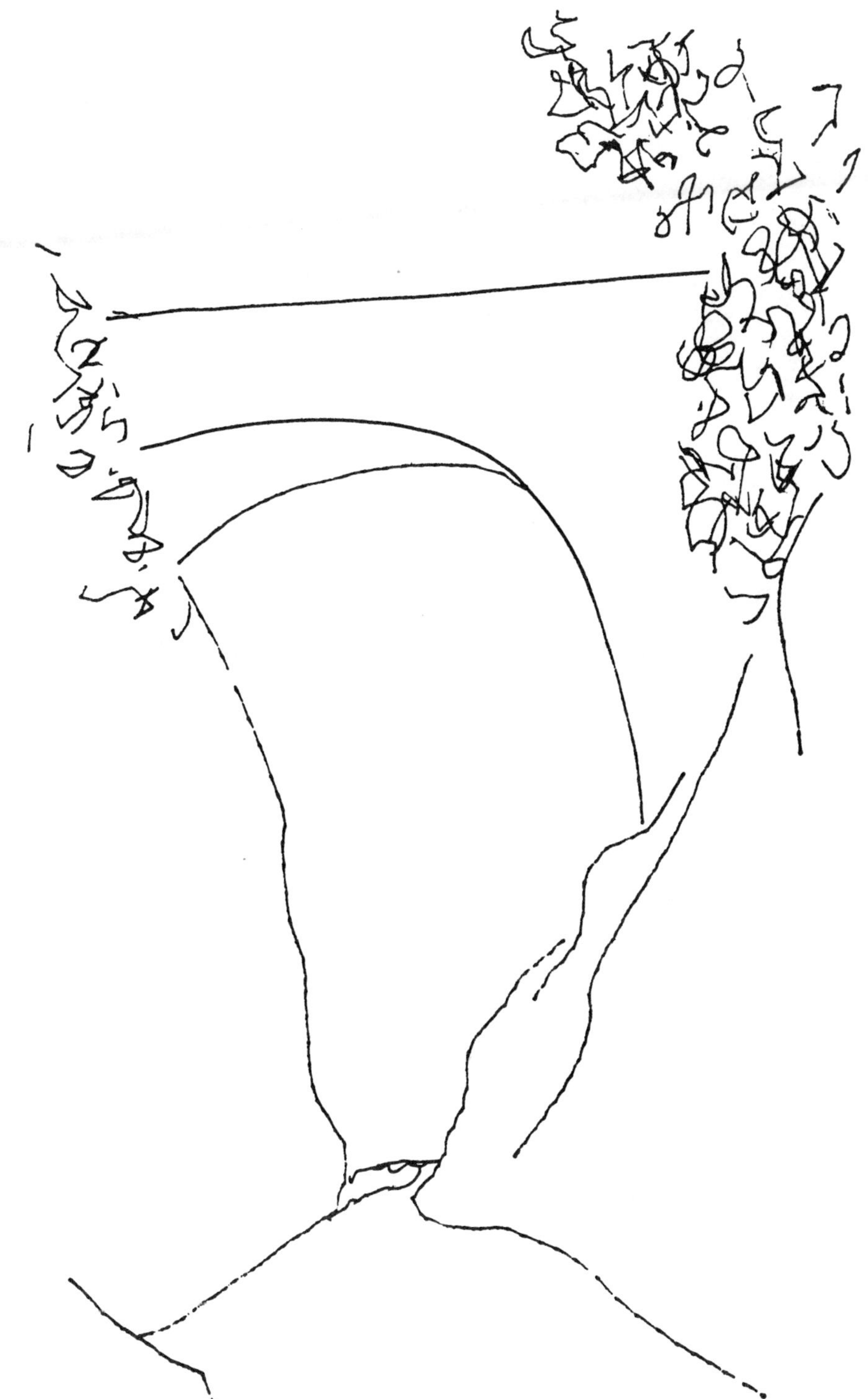

Fourvoirie, September 1

As I was coming into Sapey, the road was six feet wide, and I stopped to let pass a large party of Grenoblois who were climbing to the Chartreuse. I counted six ladies, all of them young. It takes courage for a woman to make that trip. Luckily I found I had met one of the young women and her husband at Montfleury, and I had a letter of recommendation to one of the gentlemen that I still had not sent him. The kind of gloomy wilderness we were passing through began to impress the imagination of these young women and allowed me to make the most of these claims.

We found some big trees as we drew near the high gorge where the Grande Chartreuse is situated, and almost at once the view became magnificent. An intelligent man, husband of one of the ladies, said, "That little pop was the cork of one of our bottles of champagne. All the wine's going to run over!" I pretended that this bracing air would give them horrible headaches if they didn't eat something, and they attacked one of the cold pâtés. It was a clever stroke. Their agitated nerves relaxed. We stopped under a big beech tree.

The narrow road we had been following since leaving Sapey was filled with stones half-rounded by rubbing. When it rains, the road is the bed of a little torrent, and these stones roll around in it. They made the frightened women's little horses stumble. They didn't say a word for some time, and they were not in any condition at all to enjoy the sublimity of the landscape. Our little halt gave them back all their youthful joy.

They were very gay when they got back on their horses, and we were all talking at once when we saw the Grande Chartreuse. It is not a very tall building, and it is finished off with one of those slate roofs that is itself higher than the building it covers. The Chartreuse was destroyed by fire in 1676. All that we now see is after that date and consequently very mediocre as architecture. If only the abbey of St. Ouen were on this spot or the monastery of Assisi!

M. N——, the prettiest woman's husband, is the possessor

of a superb beard and some learning that he shared with us a little too liberally. His chief merit is to distort the usual names of ancient personages. He doesn't say, "Clovis" but "Hlod-wig," not "Mérovée" but "Mere-Wig," and this has the advantage of leading to a dissertation on each name. I responded by speaking of "Virgilius" and "Késar."

It was in 1084, this scholar told us, that Bruno, born of a wealthy family in Cologne, and a scholar celebrated for his eloquence, determined with many of his friends to quit the world. He was then fifty-four years old. He presented himself to Hugh, Bishop of Grenoble, who had been a pupil of his. The bishop pointed out to him this wilderness of the Chartreuse. Here is the description given of it by Dom Pierre Dorland, one of the first historians of the order:

"Near Grenoble in Dauphiné there is a frightful spot, cold, mountainous, covered with snow, surrounded by cliffs and pine trees. Some call it *Cartuse*, and others the *Grande Chartreuse*. It is isolated, of great extent, but it is inhabited only by beasts and unknown to men because of the difficulty of access. And the ground is so sterile and barren that no one plants or sows. Bruno went to live in this place, and, since there was no cell there, he lived in a hole in the rocks."

Bruno lived in this place without writing any rule. His example alone took the place of it. Forty-four years after him, Guignes, one of his successors, wrote the statutes called "Customs of Dom Guignes." Here is a translation of one of the articles whose severe effects we were destined to prove: "We never permit women to enter our precincts, for we know that neither wise man, prophet, judge, God's host nor his children nor even the first model that left His hands have ever been able to escape from the caresses and deceptions of women. Let Solomon, David, Samson, Lot be remembered, and those who have taken women they have chosen, and Adam himself, and let it be well known that man cannot hide fire in his bosom without burning his garments or walk upon hot coals without burning the sole of his foot."

The Chartreuse is situated near Guiers in a very high valley at the foot of a still higher mountain called the *Grand Som* (the "Great Summit"). What a pity you do not see a beautiful Gothic building in this solitary and truly sublime setting! But here, if the mind is of an elevated nature, it must move itself. What would the mind of an attorney feel here? Ordinary souls have the beauty of the trees, the terrible and somber look of the rocks, and the sincere piety of St. Bruno.

Such was the talk of our little band as we went slowly on, and we were just catching sight of the Chartreuse when the Brother Servant, Jean-Marie, ran up full of alarm. He begged the women not to come any farther. He had undoubtedly been hearing their laughter and gaiety for some time. We stopped. A peasant turned up who told the women some funny stories about the horror that women inspired among the Carthusians. Apparently these stories were not exaggerated, for the Father Attorney who soon approached us had an air of utter stupefaction when he saw six women, and what's worse, all of them young and pretty. He told them that they would find accommodation two hundred paces from the monastery at the infirmary and that they must not dream of even approaching the gate. "In times past," he said with a meaningful air, "women were not allowed to cross our boundaries which were two leagues in every direction, but the Revolution seized our goods and still opposes the sanctification of our souls."

The Carthusian who was speaking to us in this way was a very handsome man of forty-five or fifty. Like the others he wore a robe of white wool, and, since there was a slight but cold wind, he kept pulling the hood of his robe up over his tonsure.

Do I dare admit that at this moment I began to find our visit quite silly? "What does thoughtlessness do to religion!" I said to myself. "Will it not be permitted these poor people, weary of men and the world, to flee their approach? They seek a refuge in a solitude at an astonishing height and among frightful rocks. All this does not suffice to arrest a curiosity which is both indiscreet and cruel. People will come to see how they look. They will come and make them think how ridiculous are the things they profess, perhaps remind them of the cruel afflictions they are trying to forget."

After the Father Attorney had gone, I said, "Ladies, if you will be kind enough to take my advice, you will set out again and stay tonight at St. Laurent-du-Pont. The younger and prettier you are, the more your presence here is a lack of delicacy."

"Alas, my dear sir," the learned and bearded husband said to me, "I see in you the noble delicacy and greatness of mind of the admirable Don Quixote and simultaneously his complete ignorance of matters here below. Your great mind is a little too much in the clouds. You forget the great word of our century, money. The Bourbons act here as elsewhere. The poor Carthusians cannot go pester them at St. Cloud, and they have done nothing solid for them. These poor monks get most of their living from their trade of innkeepers and the profits they make off travelers. We will each pay five francs a day. All the Bourbons have done for the Carthusians is to rent them at a low price the house, the fields that surround it, and the right to cut down trees to feed their three sawmills. They can also cut down enough wood to keep themselves warm. In this wretched state, they keep cows and chickens and sell the milk and eggs four months out of the year to people who are bold enough to make the climb up here."

I admit that his answer amazed me a good deal.

Jean-Marie led us to the infirmary. There were three big bare rooms. We were dying of hunger. They came to tell us that dinner was ready. It had the first of merits: it was abundant. It was fried carp, potatoes, eggs, and other simple things. We ate from a long, narrow, pine table set in one of the infirmary rooms.

Jean-Marie said, "Formerly we had ninety-two ponds, large and small."

As dinner was ending, the Father Attorney came to see us, and in his presence one of the ladies asked Brother Servant Jean-Marie for some coffee. The Father answered quite priggishly that there was no coffee in the Grande Chartreuse because it was a superfluity.

"But, Father, it seems to me that you use tobacco," answered this lively young woman.

"That is quite different. Tobacco has been prescribed for my terrible headaches."

I was hurt by the lady's tone; she was too right.

We hastened to follow Brother Jean-Marie who took us to the chapel of St. Bruno higher up the mountain, three-quarters of an hour from the monastery. This is the place where he founded the Chartreuse. Still higher, among rocks barren of vegetation is a little grotto where we men hoisted ourselves up, not without scratches. This is the place where St. Bruno stayed first. Returning, we found the Chapel of the Virgin at the half-way mark. The wild look of this place, so somber and so terrible, occupied us much more than the little monuments of men which were, moreover, done in a mean style. We hardly had time to examine this last chapel. An impetuous wind rolled up some big black clouds a pistol shot away from us, and we were afraid of rain.

As we re-entered the infirmary, a frightful clap of thunder made the bare rocks and the pine forest echo. You may imagine the effect on the ladies. The wind redoubled its fury and hurled rain against the windows of the infirmary as if it were going to break them in. "What will happen to us if the panes break?" the women asked. This was a sublime spectacle for me. We heard the wailing of eighty-foot pines as the wind tried to shatter them. The landscape was illuminated by an utterly extraordinary grey light. Our ladies began to be really afraid. Approaching night doubled the gloom of the countryside. The thunderclaps were increasingly magnificent. I went off by myself. I wanted to be alone, but the women called me back.

Soon Jean-Marie came and said we would have to go back in, they were going to close the monastery. We did not understand what he meant very well, and he did not explain, thinking that we knew the customs of the monastery.

The women's terror was at its height when the Brother said that all the men, even the husbands, must go sleep at the monastery and that the ladies had to remain at the infirmary absolutely alone. Now this building is easily two hundred paces from the other.

"But what will we do if robbers come and attack us?" one of the women said. At which Brother Jean-Marie said that if cries were heard and even if there were gunshots, nothing in the world would open the monastery door during the night. It would be a case of writing to Rome, he said.

At the word "gunshots," the poor woman became so frightened that her husband drew me aside and begged me to bribe Jean-Marie. I set to work. This brave monk refused me quite simply and, as it seemed, in good faith. I offered him as much as ten napoleons which he could use as alms if he had no personal needs. I got nowhere, and I went back to the ladies. They proposed to go back to Sapey to sleep, but when we consulted Brother Jean-Marie, he told us that it would be dangerous even for the men. "All the roads you took this morning are little ravines now, and there is half a foot of water in them. The water sweeps those round stones along with it. And your mules which are balky wouldn't want to go ahead, or they would obstinately take the sides of the road which are very slippery because of the rain. If the Father Attorney should order me to go to Sapey in such bad weather, I would go afoot and always walk in the middle of the road."

Two of the men declared they would spend the night in the woods, but this was positively refused. They insisted. "You oblige me to tell you, gentlemen," replied Jean-Marie, "that if you did, I would get twenty monastery servants, and we would come and shut up the infirmary, after we had turned the ladies outside with you, according to the rules. Why bring ladies to a place like this, anyhow?"

Finally, since Brother Jean-Marie was honestly pressing us, we had to abandon our poor traveling companions. We left them a pistol. We were very depressed. As we were going the two hundred paces that separated us from the monastery, we got wet to the skin, and we heard some really deafening thunder-claps. We thought of what they were suffering at the infirmary. When we arrived, we were each shown a very narrow little cell with a little bed of pine wood. In spite of the racket of the storm, we soon went to sleep, and we were sleeping soundly when we were waked with a start by a frightful clanging of bells and some thunderclaps that made the house shake. I have rarely had such a strange awakening. It was like the Last Judgment.

A monk came to invite us to go to prayer. My companions were in a very bad humor because of the way the ladies had been treated, and they did not want to get up. Myself, I followed him. Although it was mid-August, it was piercingly cold going down the narrow corridor.

There is nothing stranger or more dismal than the look of the church. They put me at the back near the main door. The Carthusians were in stalls, and they had a fence of planks in front of them, four feet high, so that when they knelt, I couldn't see them. In the midst of the most profound silence during the meditation, the thunderclaps began again worse than ever. How I wished, then, that I knew nothing of Franklin or electricity!

That moment was the culminating point of the terror. When I went back to bed about three o'clock, there were stars in the sky. The weather was superb, but it was terribly cold.

It was all the trouble in the world to wake up at eight. My companions had been with the ladies long since. I learned that they had had a very strange night.

Around two o'clock when the storm was still going on, the ladies thought that some robbers were trying to open their door. The most courageous of the young prisoners, Mme T——, who has such fine eyes, quaveringly asked, "Who's there?" No answer.

Can you believe that during this appalling storm there was a gathering of young fellows in the woods? As soon as the thunder stopped, they came to sing under the ladies' windows, the ladies being still terribly afraid, or at least they said they were. Before the young men began to sing, their footsteps were heard far away under the pines in the midst of this vast silence.

Around seven o'clock Brother Jean-Marie came and opened the double-locked door and very quickly withdrew. One of the women got up and put a lot of wood on the fire which they had been careful to keep going during the night. They had begun to wake up and talk among themselves when they heard the voice of someone in the antechamber. At the same moment their door was flung open with a loud crash, and they hid under the covers. To their great surprise, they heard the voices of men and women congratulating themselves on finding such a good fire. These strangers paid no attention to the women's hats hanging from all the nails which secured some branches of consecrated boxwood. The new arrivals were thinking only of getting themselves well warmed, when Brother Jean-Marie came to rebuke them and tell them that the beds that they saw were occupied.

At last the ladies were able to get up, and, as I arrived, they were served an excellent breakfast of potatoes, fried carp, etc. When they opened their napkins, they found some bits of verse, and the verses were actually not too bad. Maybe their authors lifted them from some old almanach of verse. The ladies attributed this attention to the same young men who had come to sing under their windows at four in the morning. Jean-Marie thought that they had hidden in St. Bruno's grotto during the storm. "Our dogs barked in that direction," he said.

Fourvoirie, September 1

Our ladies were very happy. They had just had two great emotions: first, terror; then, the keen enjoyment of tranquility and a good lively breakfast. One of the husbands who was very much in love with his wife or her intimate friend had the good idea of sending a man early in the morning to Fourvoirie, and he came back at eleven o'clock with some coffee. Out of courtesy to the Father Attorney, we didn't want to prepare the coffee in the house. We built a fire under some big trees, quite a distance from the monastery. Brother Jean-Marie brought us some excellent milk and served us with all possible care. This success was attributed to me, and it made me a personage.

The Father Attorney showed me a fine library. From the dust I saw on the shelves in front of the books, I saw that they were never touched. I was so simple-minded as to say, "Father, you should put some books on botany or agriculture here. You could grow all the useful plants that come from Sweden. This would amuse and interest you."

"But, sir," he answered, "we don't want to be amused or interested."

During the mass, at the moment of the Elevation, all the Carthusians fell on their hands as if they had been struck by a cannon ball. They disappeared all at once because of the little four-foot board fence. From our places at the back of the nave, we saw only the father officiating and the brother serving at the mass. Under the Restoration, the Duchesse de Berry came to the Chartreuse. Her rank of princess gave her the right to enter the monastery. Her prie-dieu and armchair were placed near the door. Her ladies remarked that not a single Carthusian turned his head to look at her.

We passed into a big room with quite a low ceiling where they have gathered together the portraits of all the generals of their order. The painting often lacks talent, but there are some strange faces. The same qualities and habits of mind can be recognized in men of very different strains and temperaments.

There is here some *simple* simplicity. To come at this idea by contraries, see the simplicity of the saints carved at Paris or among the Germans, to whom God give peace, imitating Raphael.

We were presented with a bill of five francs a day apiece, and, since we had learned luckily that the Carthusians sell an elixir, the gentlemen bought some of it. It is very dear and did not fail to produce some effect.

You know that the story which was the basis of *Les Liaisons Dangereuses* occurred at Grenoble. M. Choderlos de Laclos, an artillery officer garrisoned in that friendly town, took the plot for his novel from an event that happened before his eyes.

Les Échelles . . . 1837

THIS MORNING I WENT TO LES ÉCHELLES, quite a pretty market town which, I suppose, once got rich through smuggling. I had hardly arrived when they told me some wonderful ways of fooling the customs officers. For instance, an inn is established one end of the village. It is the last house on the street. It has a large garden running to the bank of the Guiers, whose course marks the frontier. Twenty mules ford this little stream and are unloaded at the kitchen door. The customs officers see no movement in the street. An iron plaque which decorates the bottom of the kitchen chimney is quickly lifted and all the mule loads are hastily thrown into a kind of cave which is behind the chimney. They let down the iron plaque again and make up an enormous fire. When the customs men arrive, five minutes after the mules, they find a group of happy peasants who ask them to have a drink. They hunt everywhere for the mule packs, do not find them, and end by taking the drink.

When the Army of Italy re-entered France after the peace of Campoformio, a restaurant owner, next to the covered promenade of Les Échelles, made his fortune by a rebus which charmed the soldiers and remained famous in this part of the country. He wrote on his door:

That is, "*Allons souper. J'ai grand appétit.**

Virien

From Les Échelles I went to see the admirable gorge of Chailles. I saw people fishing for trout in the Guiers which roars at the bottom of the cliff a hundred and fifty feet below the road. They use very long white horsehair lines, and when they pull out the trout, you see the poor creatures wriggling in the treetops. They give such a jerk when they pull out the fish that it is often very hard to disentangle the line from the branches. I gave my attention to the fishing and the interesting landscape, and it took me six hours to do the seven leagues from Les Échelles to Virien.

Chambéry . . . 1837

Chambéry has two monuments you would look for in vain in our French towns: a charming theater and a beautiful street with arcades on both sides. Suddenly I understood that I was near *la belle Italie.*

The first necessity for a town is to have a portico where you can walk undisturbed when it is windy or raining. What demonstrates to the least attentive the incredible and hereditary asininity of the mayors and magistrates of France is that the covered promenade is lacking almost everywhere. It is their

* "A" *long sous* "p." "G" *grand,* "a" *petit.*—H. B.

classic taste in all its stupidity. Instead of asking themselves, "What do we really need?", they say, "What have other towns done that's pretty?" They imitate the approved model. They would be terribly afraid of being hooted at if by some mischance they did something that was not a copy. The magistrates build a theater with colonnades as at Nantes or Bordeaux instead of a plain and simple covered promenade as at Dol in Brittany. But the columns of the street at Dol are all Gothic, which shows that this street was built during a period of good sense.

Varese in Lombardy, Brescia, etc., have excellent porticos to the right and left of their theaters, quite low porticos where the rain cannot penetrate no matter how hard the wind blows. A commodious place like this soon becomes a rendezvous for everyone who is bored and wants to amuse himself on a rainy day. Taverns spring up, luxury shops, bookshops, and you can go and spend an hour or two there when there is a north wind blowing and you are bored at home. But, it is objected, the Rue de Rivoli in Paris does not combine all these advantages. I know this very well. In the first place, the portico in Paris ought to be placed between the Rue Ville-l'Evêque and the Rue Montmartre so as to have the sun from noon until four o'clock. It should be filled with shops to rent, and it should, if possible, have a theater.

In the second place, the portico of the Rue de Rivoli is exposed to the west wind which blows five days a week, so that you get completely soaked when it rains. The porticos of the Bourse and the Madeleine are only blind and *classic* imitations of the temples of Athens, happy region that does not know our six months' winter. Since the death of the Gothic, French architects have never had the genius to invent a church adapted to France.

The Savoyard peasant is not sly like the Norman but prudent like *an honest man who is afraid.* The depths of his heart are filled with religion but not a *spiteful* religion, for his curé is also a Savoyard, that is, a good man at bottom. He is not like Tartufe; he does not teach him "to have affection for nothing."

On the other hand, the Savoyard peasant never acts thoughtlessly like the lucky peasant from the environs of Paris. He won't lift his hand unless he sees his way clearly, and he won't mix in any business if he sees in it any quarrel with the authorities, trouble with his neighbors, or any connection whatever with the Royal Carabiniers (the police).

The Savoyard peasant is excellent fundamentally. If it had lasted, the French Revolution would have given him the courage to dare.

Aix-les-Bains . . . 1837

As far as I can judge after a stay of less than forty-eight hours, it seems to me that the friendly inhabitants of Chambéry still deserve all the good that J.-J. Rousseau said of them.

It took us less than two hours to get to Aix. I was surprised at the number of carriages on the road, and, what doubled my admiration, all these carriages were filled with women highly decked out. When I got to Aix, I learned that today is Sunday, the day on which all the fine ladies of Chambéry come to Aix for the ball given by the people who take the baths. A crowd of handsome officers from the Chambéry garrison arrived at the same time as the ladies. One of them had a volume of Ariosto in 32mo. He mislaid it at the inn, and I was asked whether it belonged to me.

The waters of Aix are less *légitimiste* this year than in the preceding ones. I was hoping to catch sight of M. Berryer there whose wonderful talent sometimes makes the insipid sessions of the Chamber of Deputies bearable. I have noticed some very handsome crooks who have come from Paris and are winning heavily at play. One of them has to fight a duel tomorrow, and he has conducted his little altercation with a noble and knightly grace that enchants me. After all, it would be hard to find better company than these gentlemen's.

The ball this evening was charming. The local women have

a delightful bloom and at first sight a fascinating naturalness which, by force of art, is sometimes seen in the best society in Paris. Some provincial women, a very small number, it is true, have some naturalness of manner, but then they pass for fools among their acquaintances. At the ball I caught glimpses of two or three of the great ladies of France.

Geneva . . . 1837

THE ROAD FROM CHAMBÉRY to Geneva by way of Annècy is sublimely beautiful compared to the road from Paris to Montargis, Paris to Orleans, Paris to Troyes, to Chalons-sur-Marne, to Chartres, or to Amiens.

At last I saw again that beautiful lake, so vast and surrounded with such magnificence. From its contemplation arise ideas less serious, less sublime, if you like, but more tender than the sea itself. It was Rousseau who made the reputation of "his" lake, and this great man is still scorned or abhorred in most of the pretty towns around its edge. On the Savoy side, it's true, they don't even know his name. In the Swiss towns they abuse him every day, and I am glad of it for him. Considering only the interest of this great, dead man, it is better that he be abhorred. The more unjust people's feelings about him are, the longer will his glory endure. Machiavelli's name will survive perhaps as long as Montesquieu's. They have equal merit, but every rascal still hates Machiavelli furiously, and Montesquieu has been spared this. Also, he died rich, and the other in the greatest poverty.

As I always do in Geneva, I began by hurrying to the Promenade St. Antoine to see the lake. From there I crossed the town, and even before I got down to business and went to get my mail, I went to see the house where Rousseau was born in 1712. It has just been rebuilt. It is now a fine six-story house like those which daily help to uglify Paris. What consoles me is that I have often seen the little room with projecting beams where Rousseau was born, and once I found it occupied by a poor watchmaker who had a bad edition of the works of Rousseau and understood them. We talked for an hour about the *Social Contract*, whose chief merit lies, in my opinion, in its title. The workers of Geneva know how to reason in a manner which would seem to be above their station in Paris. They shock foreigners, especially titled foreigners. They are never obsequious.

I went to see the statue of Rousseau on the little island in the middle of the new bridge. It was a novelty to me. Honor to M. Pradier, the Genevan sculptor! He sees the Antique, but he also sees Nature. Among all his contemporaries, he is the man who sometimes does the best arm or leg. If his marble statues were broken up and buried and later only the fragments were discovered, no one would know what century to place them in, and they would be laid with veneration in some museum.

While I was considering this statue, a passerby stopped, and I struck up a conversation with him. He told me, "The twenty-eighth of June is Jean-Jacques' birthday. It is a children's holiday. About two thousand of both sexes paraded before the house where he was born. Then, going down the street to the lake, they laid at the foot of this statue the flowers they were carrying. As you may guess, sir, this holiday was not ordered by the government, but they placed no obstacle in the way. This year they even authorized three companies of militia to escort this immense file of children, two thousand! You may be sure that among them there were none whatever of the children of the gentlemen from the Height. (This is what they call the rich people who live in the high part of town, near the Promenade de la Treille. They are the aristocracy of the region.) It is the common people who celebrate the anniversary of the man who honored our country. All the Methodists who live on the Height cannot love this great man, but it's true they aren't openly hostile. The common people who know how the rich feel keep Rousseau's holiday to advertise the fact that he did not share their feelings."

As I left this fine fellow, a well-to-do working man apparently, I hired a boat, and in pencil I wrote down his answer, which I have just transcribed exactly. I much prefer this story to any I could pick up at dinner parties.

I can well imagine that many readers have heard certain peculiarities of Genevan customs spoken of—the matter of the patriarchal customs of the young girls. But this detail touches me and pleases me so much that I ask permission to tell it again.

Eight or ten little girls, seven or eight years old, gather together for work and play. This society will continue until the last survivor. Thus, ten years later, eight or ten young ladies gather at one of their houses one day a week, but on this day, the father, the mother, the brothers, and the other sisters each go to his own society, and these young ladies have their friend's house to themselves.

The society of the eight or ten young girls goes on until the moment when one of them marries. Everything changes then. The new bride presents her husband to her companions, and each one of them presents a candidate at the same time. They take a voice vote on each candidate, and the majority of suffrages decides whether he will be accepted or refused.

A young man receives a playing card, an eight of clubs or a jack, on which he sees written that such-and-such a young lady (whom perhaps he doesn't know) will receive him with pleasure on such-and-such an evening. He makes inquiries and discovers that he has been introduced by a certain young lady of his acquaintance.

Thus, after the marriage of one of the young friends, the society continues, but it receives young men admitted only after scrutiny. All is innocence and politeness, somewhat stiff perhaps, in these reunions where a woman strange to the society would not find a place.

Another thing, they give balls. When they do, the young lady in whose apartment the ball takes place invites the young men. As usual, on this day the mother goes out as well as the father and the grandparents.

Sometimes just at the end of the ball, you see the fathers come or, more rarely, the brothers to find their daughters or sisters. The young ladies no one comes for go home accompanied to their front walk by the young men of their acquaintance.

It is not hard to understand how easily love is born in the midst of such mild and innocent relationships. Then, it seems to me, it is the richer of the two fathers who seeks out the other.

A very odd thing in a moneyed town: it is not money that makes marriages here. I saw a dull young nobleman who had easily eighteen thousand pounds income marry a young lady whose dot was only a life annuity of five hundred francs.

As soon as a marriage is arranged among the grandparents, it is announced to the family and near relatives. From that moment the young lady can go out alone with her fiancé wherever she likes. At a ball, she dances only with him.

I well believe that if there were any drawbacks, Genevan prudence would take every precaution to keep them from a stranger's ears, but I am convinced that real misfortunes are as rare as can be in Geneva.

Nothing is rarer than to see an announced marriage broken off. Once twenty years ago an engaged girl danced with a partner other than her fiancé, and he took occasion to break the engagement. The young lady, who was very witty and very rich, was perhaps only moderately affected by the outcome.

Is it to Calvin that the Genevans owe this wonderful institution of young girls' societies? I am not intimate enough with any Genevan to dare question him on so delicate a subject.

Such a question is particularly shocking to a Frenchman. *In Paris it is the notaries who make the marriages.* This single fact which, in truth, is cruel exposes us to the jokes of all Europe and even to something more. What will be the counterweight to the attacks of love that overtake a young woman after two or three years of marriage when all the illusions begin to take flight?

Granted, the Genevans have all the British gloominess of manner; but at least they recognize in the evenings in their somewhat dull houses the woman they have chosen and loved in their youth.

Alas! The town that Voltaire hit off in a line is always like this: "All they do there is reckon up, and they never laugh."

I would have thought that people who inherited large fortunes would have been able to dispense with this reckoning-up. They have fallen into one of the very worst difficulties, English Methodism and all its mummeries.

The common people call them *momiers*, mummers, that is, Methodists. A young woman, fresh and pretty, comes into a salon. You think, you frivolous stranger, you Frenchman you, that she comes there to be pleasant and to agree that she is lovely. Alas, how far she is from such profane thoughts.

In the salon which is quite badly lighted, a gloomy silence reigns. Suddenly one of the ladies rises. She feels herself inspired, and this poor little feminine sprite, graceful, delicate, charming, begins to gabble some lines out of Chateaubriand, without the knightly varnish and the nobility of his turn of phrase, but "even when a bird walks, we see that it has wings."

When a woman preaches, she is always speaking of love. You recognize the sex of the speaker by the furious hatred for anything that brings to mind, no matter how remotely, the most innocent sensual pleasures. I have a fragment of one of these lady Methodist's discourses which I shall not write down because it is too depressing.

You know those pretty islands about which Cook and Bougainville have given us such amusing accounts, the islands of Tahiti? Some Methodist preachers have penetrated that far. Not only do the people no longer make love there—*the more love, the more joy*—but they are dying of hunger. These new Christians no longer cultivate the fields. The population dwindles. They are justified indeed, for such a gloomy life is hardly worth the trouble of planting potatoes to continue it.

There you have upper-class Geneva, and the upper classes set the fashion. Through imitating the Bible or what commentators say is the Bible, relations between the sexes have become very dull. The husband gets up at seven o'clock, works until twelve-thirty, comes home and eats dinner quickly so as to be at his club by two-thirty where he drinks a demi-tasse of coffee. He goes back to his bank or his factory and at seven in the evening hurries to his club where he spends the evening. He does not go home until ten or eleven o'clock.

I must agree that these clubs are perfectly organized with all possible good sense. First, you have complete freedom there; then, you have all the newspapers, any refreshments you wish, excellent wines. You see your associates there whom you see every day for twenty years and with whom you finally adopt the language and even the feelings of friendship.

Calvin is obviously Geneva's lawgiver. I have just seen the little window above a vault that is used as a passageway from which he preached to his people once or twice a week.

I shall add that I value Calvin very highly. He was undoubtedly worth more than the Roman priests of his time. From the beginning, without taking a vow of poverty, he always lived poor and he died poor. He formed a wise and moral people who still preserve after three centuries the imprint of an individual character.

What seems to me to distinguish Geneva is that there the two sexes see as little as possible of each other, and this makes me regret those good Jesuits who tell you: "Give yourself up to your passions. Be young. Do everything one does in youth, and then come to me and tell me your little sins. If you exercise some power in the State, let yourself be directed by me, and you may count on it that you will certainly have eternal salvation as well as the pleasures of this world. Believe especially that I can do you any little service very well."

Certainly Geneva has done a hundred times more for liberty and morality than Chambéry which has remained the faithful subject of the Jesuits and the Dukes of Savoy, but there is one question that astonishes and interests me profoundly: today where are they happier, in Geneva or Chambéry? Where would you want to be born? Notice the cheerful faces of the good Savoyards. As for me, having long considered it, utterly astounded at the conclusion I invariably come to, I declare I would like to have been born at Chambéry. Here are my reasons: they are undoubtedly less intelligent there, but they have better hearts. They hate less.

The Genevans are the leading money men on the Continent. In this line of work they have the first of the virtues, that of eating up less every day than they make. When they are young, their sweetest pleasure is dreaming of the day when they'll be rich. Even when they become rash and give themselves up to pleasure, they choose rustic pleasures that don't cost much, a walk to the summit of some mountain where they drink milk. Yesterday some of my friends went to the shore of the lake of Gers, some leagues above St. Gingolf.

It is not pure economics that makes them choose the pleasures they do. At the bottom of their hearts the Genevans are German and rustic. When he gets rich young, the Genevan buys a country house, and he does not, like a Parisian, prefer the one that is the best built where he can give dinner parties; rather, he chooses the one that has some beautiful trees that will make him *dream*. The Genevan's ideal is to drive a surrey drawn by a passable horse through a beautiful countryside, wearing a grey hat with a linen jacket.

I saw this evening that the Genevans have an antipathy, I would say an instinctive and furious antipathy, for French wit, and I do not in any way blame them for it. No matter what is claimed for it, French wit is in the end ridiculous to them. The songs of Collé, Panard, and Désaugiers put them in a fury. They have no conception of light irony, and they take it for malice. The Genevans place *Gil Blas* among the most immoral books. The thirty-six volumes of the *Memoirs of Bachaumont* make them grind their teeth.

In many ways the Genevan character approaches that of the English, but the resemblance is nowhere more striking than in the false estimate of irony. No more than the English can the Genevan mind follow the light witty dialogue of Regnard, the gayest comic author France has.

"What will you do, sir, with a churchwarden's nose?" is unintelligible to them. The profound satiric genius of Molière suits them much better. However, for both the English and the Genevans, true comedy is the charming comedy of Shakespeare who paints men as he would like so much to have them be. The melancholy Jacques is more agreeable to them than the misanthrope Alceste.

A man perfectly calculated to horrify the Genevans is Voltaire, who was so long their neighbor. He made a border for his garden on the right-hand side, a double row of Italian poplars which he called his *cache-Pictet.* In his eyes, M. Pictet was a representative of the Genevan genius, and as always happens between men of genius, the antipathy was reciprocated. M. Pictet was very learned and very estimable.

It can be seen that a good half of French literature is concerned with the opposite of the Genevan mind. It could be said that the basis of the French character, gay, satiric, mocking, rakish, chivalrous, flighty, escapes the Genevan entirely. On the other hand, what is pompous, reasonable, and sad, Nicolle, De Bonald, Bossuet, Bourdaloue, Abadie, goes straight to their hearts. They would love *Clarissa* if they heard she was no longer fashionable in Paris. Montaigne, Marot, Montesquieu necessarily annoy them very much. On the other hand, they love the reasonableness of Marmontel, Barthélemy, Laharpe, and all the dull *academic* writers. Our great ladies would be happy to become Methodists. They would be much less bored.

Isn't it glorious that a little town of twenty-six thousand inhabitants forces the traveler to devote three pages to describing its character? I would be very embarrassed if I had to write three pages on the character of the inhabitants of Lyons, Rouen, or Nantes. The curious who have seen Berne, Zurich, Basle, and I don't know what other Swiss towns soon clearly perceives what Geneva owes to Calvin.

I like the Genevan very much until he is forty years old. About that age he has very often laid by a fortune, large or small, but it is then that the main fault of his education appears. He does not know how to play. He cannot be taught to live in prosperous circumstances. He becomes severe and puritanical. He is ill-tempered with those who amuse themselves or seem to. He calls them immoral people.

A Genevan of fifty is more atrabiliar and disagreeable to all who are near him than a Frenchman of seventy. The older he grows, the more he loses his natural love for liberty; his hatred for the little people increases, but his head remains eminently logical, eminetly impervious to the pleasures of society, and he is touched only by decorations. I can't imagine why all the despots of Europe don't select rich fifty-year-old Genevans as ministers. As ministers of finance they would be capable of refusing money to themselves.

An Englishman told me that rich Genevans show themselves very fond of titles, crosses, and other monarchic baubles. He added that in New York merchants who go out driving of a Sunday choose by preference cabs with fine armorial bearings. In Paris a cab with arms painted on its doors would not be taken by any merchant going out for a Sunday drive. It would have an old-fashioned air. The bourgeois aspires much higher than the nobility. He wants to be in the fashion.

The Genevans have a way of doing business that is clear, precise, unrelenting, and it suits me very well. You have done, say, thirty thousand francs worth of business with a certain house. Everything is terminated promptly and fairly. After ten years you get a new statement. The company would beg you to observe that, at the time of the first negotiations, you forgot to reimburse them for seven sous postage. Proceedings like this petrify me, but I approve of them infinitely.

Geneva has produced more remarkable men than its neighbor, Lyons, a city of two hundred and four thousand inhabitants. The reason for this is that in Geneva, aside from the remarkable usefulness of the education given it by Calvin, the extreme love of money (1) gives a sound logic almost entirely lacking in France, especially in Paris. (Count the number of Genevan bankers who come to Paris with thirty louis in their pockets and are millionaires before they are fifty.) In Geneva (2), no matter how little talent you have of whatever kind, you know how to make a profit.

A watchmaker, for instance, who has the least little talent for writing cultivates it carefully and, at night when his shop is closed, hastens to write articles which he sells to the newspapers, or tales for young ladies, or an explanation of political economy, the Genevan science *par excellence*, or a translation of Ricardo, or a commentary on St. Matthew for every day in the year. There is, if you like, no intelligence in these books, but they are reasonable. They attain their objects perfectly.

A celebrated doctor, one who gets his patients well, once noticed that he was not very busy from three to six in the afternoon. He made it known that he could not be seen during those hours, and he began to work out some calculations on what were called around 1810 "State Papers" (the income) of different regions. In his three hours a day he made five or six thousand francs.

Would a doctor in any other town but Geneva ever had this idea? And if he had, would he have saved his patients? Logic is everywhere here, with the doctor as well as with the patients. While I am speaking of doctors, I must say that those in Geneva are admirable. (1) They condescend to question their patients. (2) They study their illnesses. (3) They don't try to be funny about them. (4) They don't take pride in the promptness of their decisions. In this they are far superior to the late M. Dupuytren and to many living doctors, witty fellows, who try to be funny with their poor patients. I don't believe any country in Europe has names that are superior to those of Prévost, Buttini, Maunoir, etc. The renown M. Jurine enjoys in Europe is well known.

In Geneva I know a doctor who is still young, the son of a well-to-do man, who likes his profession. He questions his patient for three hours before coming to an opinion, visits him four times a day if necessary before writing out his prescription, and finally he distributes among his poor patients what he gets from his rich ones. Unfortunately his own poor health has forced him to retire to the country.

About 1804 some Genevans started a newspaper, *The British Library*, which you could always open with pleasure when you were tired of the brilliant and empty verbiage of the French journalists. This paper was not markedly boring except when it talked morality. It wanted everyone to be happy in the Genevan manner. Since there is no bookmaking and no national literature in Geneva, this paper did not have to lie constantly to keep from making six mortal enemies every month. It never sank to cliquishness, that deadly affliction of literature and journalism in Paris.

How is a poor devil of a literate man in Castelnaudary to go about selecting new books that he must nevertheless buy? The reviewer who has just praised to the skies in a well-regarded newspaper the new translation by —— pats himself on the back before his friends for having gotten a passable article out of the flat productions which have cluttered his office for the past six months. But the translator is a friend of his proprietor, and, by means of his newspaper, he wants to get into the French Academy. He estimates that it will take four hundred laudatory articles spread out over three years. In a similar situation, I believe a Genevan would develop scruples *like those he has against sin* about deceiving his subscribers in an affair involving money, i.e., the purchase of a book.

In Geneva they say, "Such-and-such a man was put in prison; *since then* he went free." *Since then* is what they say for *then.* In the announcements of the *Gazette de Lausanne,* you find threatening notices addressed to young men who have been so bold as to seduce some girls who belong to the Republic or to the canton of Vaud. These amusing warnings are in the second person plural, "To you, François Monod, native of Montru, who after long and foolhardy frequentation had the rashness to seduce Jeanne Serang, etc., etc."

These warnings are the only amusing things I found in the Swiss newspapers. From them one can collect odd locutions from Swiss-French. You can often recognize the clear way of speaking characteristic of our excellent French of the seventeenth century, so superior to those "rhythmical" phrases so highly prized by our present Academy. A stiff person who pretended to the honors of literature would be ashamed to say anything clearly and vividly.

I am thinking of the ridiculousness of Academies because I dined today with a very amusing person, a Genevan scholar. This man really has an excellent memory, and it is right in his line of work. He can repeat exactly all the arguments of Montesquieu and Adam Smith, which once he learned by heart. He also knows a great part of Tacitus by heart, the best of Voltaire's verses, three or four thousand dates, and finally the names successively of all the sovereigns who have occupied the thrones of Europe since Constantine and Charlemagne down to Napoleon.

The pedantry of Parisian scholars is all in reticences and smiles of satisfaction. With exquisite politeness these gentlemen would have you understand that any discovery you tell them about cannot exist, because they have not elucidated it, or that it is something extremely ancient, forgotten, and out of fashion which they have explained a hundred times. Often when they find society too gay and free of speech, they preserve a dignified silence. Placed by the hostess around a tea table, if they are forced to break their silence, they don't address anyone in particular; they "profess" but with all the collegiate graces and all the reserve of the most prudent courtesy. On the other hand, the pedantry of the Genevan scholar is very positive and obvious. He irritates the indifferent and amuses the learned. His memory, which is not a ridiculous talent here, assures him that he will shine. He takes the floor on every subject and with authority. Since no one laughts in Geneva, he runs no danger. His face alone would pass for a spiteful caricature in Paris.

But let us pass over the exaggerated ridiculousness of feature and expression which comes from the absence of laughter in Geneva. It must be recognized that there is a great deal of learning in this region. There the five or six good works that appear in Europe every year are attentively read, and because the Genevans know languages, they read the good book that is published in London with the same facility as the one that appears in Berlin or Pavia; only if there is the least tinge of imagination in these books, the national character is annoyed, and the book is declared "light." I should like very much to see the first judgments they made on Montesquieu in 1755.

The logic which is so often lacking in their French neighbors the Genevans have to excess, or, rather, their minds enameled from childhood with the alleged morality people are paid to draw from the Bible, do not comprehend that logic is merely a universal instrument that serves to prevent deception. It applies to the interests of love, jealousy, or the most foolish passions exactly as it applies to the art of making 6 per cent a year buying and selling as a Frenchman makes 3 per cent. Logic does not prevent you from undertaking the responsibility of choosing the things that are true. It quite simply makes you see the truth in the object of your thought.

I have just met some charming women on the little suspension bridge before the Bastion St. Antoine. They are beautiful Germans with a serious intelligence in their eyes. Since the bridge was only four feet wide, I could see them very well without falling into those insolent glances with which the Germans so much reproach the French. The Genevan kind of beauty consists, when it is not purely German, in the chief traits of the Florentine, embellished by an extreme freshness. The fault of this kind of beauty lies sometimes in a heaviness of the chin and the wings of the nose, and an insignificant expression, that of a beautiful sheep who dreams. There is nothing superior to a beautiful Genevan of eighteen, but upon such a face where all gaiety is difficult, the mummerism makes frightful ravages.

I took a last walk on the road from Thonon. I found the following inscription on the gate of a little Gothic cemetery whose walls were crumbling under the hand of time: "The memory of the dead lives on in ruined monuments. There, sweet and clement at any hour, she speaks to bent heads."

Geneva . . . 1837

With great affectation one of the upper-class families has sent to England for a "serious" cook. Don't think for a minute that they want a cook who does not take the cooking lightly. What do gastronomic sensations matter to a family who is undertaking to restore in Europe the great monarchic and religious interests? No. They want a cook who never laughs. Try to believe this fact, O kindly reader!

Memoirs of a Tourist

Lyons . . . 1837

THE WAY HERE FROM GENEVA by the Fort l'Ecluse and along the Rhone might be called sublime if it were compared to those great flat bare lines of the country surrounding Paris. But it is not enough for a landscape to be interesting in itself. Eventually there must be a moral and historic interest. The Mozart of this kind of harmony is Livy in the country from Rome to Pozzolo on the Lake of Albano, for example.

Two leagues from Geneva I saw Ferney again. It is astonishing today how poor a house a man lived in who had an income of a hundred thousand livres in 1760, which would mean two hundred and fifty thousand in 1837, considering the increase of necessary luxury and the exigencies of a growing vanity. For it is not to the point to estimate the difference in sums of money mentioned in history only by the value of silver in the two periods. One must also calculate what would have been spent on luxury which was deemed unimportant in 1760 but the absence of which disgraces a man in 1837.

We judge very foolishly of Voltaire's position in the midst of the nearly legal regime his witticisms have obtained for us. During the first twenty years of his stay at Ferney he may have watched with anxiety every courier who galloped up the main road from France. Voltaire was certain he was hated by two of the great institutions of the state, the clergy and the Parlements whose cruel ignorance he had put on display. The Court would have been very happy to see this insolent poetaster *who was too much talked about* abused and degraded. Long before, the Keeper of the Seals had told him, "Be informed, sir, that if *Joan of Arc* ever appears in print, I'll see that you rot in the deepest dungeon." But *Joan of Arc* was soon printed.

If he were going to resist so much well-grounded hostility, Voltaire would have had to give up writing and make himself forgotten, but such restraint was beyond his powers. He was more horrified of being forgotten than he was of an eternity in the Bastille, and he launched a pamphlet every six months.

No one in France showed as much bravery as Voltaire. In vain he seized every occasion to pay a servile court to Marshal Richelieu and the Duc de Choiseul. His safety was lost if he were attacked. The day after he had been sent to prison, Messrs. Richelieu and Choiseul would have said; "But why didn't we do this ten years ago?" If he had seen him in prison, Richelieu would have made fun of him six months on end. Then he would have forgotten him. The clergy would have given benefices worth a hundred thousand livres to the sons and nephews of the magistrate who kept him in prison. The favorite would have been offered the nomination of two or three abbeys worth forty thousand livres income.

All these dangers were real. Even the coolest man could see them, and Voltaire had a childish imagination that magnified them a hundred times. His safety lay only in the foolishness and lack of accord among the all-powerful whom he was attacking. Worse, it was essentially the king he was offending. Once he had been thrown into the fortified castles of the Isles Ste Marguerite, he would have been there twenty years.

At Ferney they repeated the story they told me ten years ago. Voltaire, as a man of intelligence who was never understood by dense people, wanted to do everything himself. He drew with a pen the plan of the chateau he was having built. He had indicated the walls by a single stroke, but when the builders got to the second floor, all the rooms seemed small, and they saw that in the plan Voltaire had forgotten the thickness of the walls. My grandfather who went to see Voltaire at Ferney five times told me about the *cache-Pictet* poplars, and he believed the thickness of the walls was forgotten. Voltaire with his hundred thousand livres of quite real income thought two or three times that he was ruined, and he despaired like a child. His books were filled with little pieces of paper three lines wide and six inches long. On each was a word. When he wanted a fact, he climbed up to the top of the ladder in his library and quickly read the words on all the pieces in the volume.

Before you reach his chateau, you see a church in the avenue on the left and on the pediment the famous inscription *Deo erexit Voltaire* ("Voltaire erected this to God"). The great man's room is still in the state he left it when he went to Paris, hangings of embroidered blue taffeta, portraits of the King of Prussia, Mme du Châtelet, Lekain. Today they sell Englishmen the pen Voltaire used.

There is nothing more depressing than the lake and the town of Nantua, but it should have a kind of beauty when there is two feet of snow on the ground and the wolves are running over it. Then you could boast of being comfortable in a fine fur coat.

After I had been really annoyed at the customs-house at Bellegarde and had been so weak as to get angry, I had recourse to physical consolations. I drank a bottle of champagne to the health of that Marshal's first A.D.C. who gave himself the pleasure of beating the customs men with a stick.

I woke up at Miribel, a town well-situated in the mountains. Far below, to the left, I could see the plains of Dauphiné and the Rhone. I have followed this king of rivers as far as Lyons.

In the Middle Ages, after the barbarism of the tenth century, society was slowly reformed by the mingling of the Romans and the barbarians as society was reformed in Paris before our eyes by the mingling of the former upper class and the newly rich. In the eleventh century, this new society produced many things in France, among them Romanesque architecture which little by little was burdened with ornament. These ornaments, which added to its graces, ended by failing to please, and at the end of the thirteenth century, the bold and slender Gothic architecture came to be preferred. As for ornament, it was simple and severe at first. Slowly it, too, grew laden with ornament, and when its characteristic forms had disappeared under its accessories, fashion abandoned it in its turn. It was at this time that they returned to antique forms. This was the Renaissance of the year 1500.

Thus one might say that an excess of ornament killed these two architectures as excess of ornament and false delicacy was at the point of killing French literature at the end of Louis XVI's reign. Without the Revolution, literature would have descended to the astounding silliness of the later Roman Empire. The Revolution brought it to the energetic proclamations of the Republic and the speeches of Danton and Mirabeau.

Something of the sort happened to architecture at the death of the Romanesque and in 1500 at the death of the Gothic. In towns where there were Roman monuments, Romanesque architecture copied the Roman very closely. Thus it is understandable that the Cathedral of St. Lazaire at Autun is near the wonderful gates of Arroux and St. André.

There was also the influence of the materials. There, where a calcareous stone was found, easy to work, sculpture made rapid progress, while Brittany, which has only its blackish, hard-to-manage granite, had no sculpture. Compare the churches of Poitou with those of Brittany. Auvergne and Le Velay, rich in volcanic products of different colors had the idea of mingling the colors in their buildings, and, in the regions where they use brick, they had a great many mouldings.

The rich monasteries, the bishops who started building in the tenth century and followed the fashion of Romanesque architecture, were dominated by a new idea. *They were dreaming of the future.* They built with care. Vaulting replaced the wooden roofs. Later the heavy rectangular pillars were replaced by engaged columns, as can be seen at St. Germain-des-Prés. The side-aisles circle behind the choir, decorated with columns. Long abandoned, sculpture catches up. Statues, capitals, bas-reliefs are painted. Sculpture loads the saints and kings with magnificent vestments which, to the loutish peasants, are the surest signs of power and sanctity. It is still not a question of the *expression* of the heads or the gestures.

In Gaul as in Rome the churches followed one of four main forms: the basilica, the Latin Cross, the Greek cross, and the round or polygonal. *The basilica* has the form of a playing card. On the east side, it ends in a semicircle or *apse* near which the altar is placed. The *Latin* cross is the form of a crucifix. With the *Greek* cross, the four branches of the cross are equal, as in St. Genest at Nevers.

The facades are flanked by towers. They announce the metropolis from a distance, and in the eleventh century they could be used for defense also. Always notice in these buildings, seven centuries old, the circumstances surrounding them at their birth and the beliefs, so different from ours, of the men who built them.

The Romanesque towers, square at first, then octagonal, did not rise to a very great height. The Gothic wished before everything to seem bold, and it pushed its towers as high as possible. The roofs of the Romanesque towers were flat at first. About the twelfth century they ended in a pyramid.

Since the eyes and genuflections of the faithful had to be turned toward the Orient where the mystery of the Redemption was accomplished and from whence returned all the rich or holy personages of the eleventh century, the facade of the churches was placed on the west as at St. Germain-des-Prés, Notre Dame, etc. There were as many doors as naves.

The Romanesque artists considered the middle door as their master-work. Above it is a round window, very small at first, but by the end of the twelfth century its diameter is equal to or even larger than the middle door's. The facade is terminated by a pediment, but it is more pointed than the antique pediments.

Windows are rare in Romanesque architecture. In the middle of the transept a cupola was sometimes erected. It is the highest point inside the church, but if there were the cupola, the pillars had to be reinforced to bear this great weight.

The Romanesque architects observed that by giving a massive pillar the form of a bundle of columns or a bunch of asparagus, if I may be permitted this obvious comparison, the pillar seems lighter and less bulky. In time the Gothic architects put stilts on this idea which became the basis of their system of boldness.

The pavement of the choir was usually higher than that of the rest of the church. Usually there was a cave or crypt under the choir where lay the body of some saint when they had one.

In time the choir grew larger. Then the end of the church farthest from the door, the top of the semicircle, became the Lady Chapel, and the high altar was moved toward the door. Sculpture preached its language to all parts of the church. Above the main door one sees Christ surrounded by the Apostles. Above the side door, the Last Judgment, the Wise and Foolish Virgins, the Nativity, etc. Often among the sculptured decorations that overloaded all parts of the church, some can be seen which are ridiculous, even obscene. One finds more of that kind of thing in the eleventh century. The *conventions* have made progress. Hence our boredom.

In general, the sculptors are faithful to the great end of religion, to put the fear of hell into the barbarians. The chief subjects of their works are thus the tortures reserved for the damned. There are images of many animals the Crusaders had seen in the Orient. At St. Sauveur in Nevers, there are elephants and dromedaries.

It is curious to observe the capitals of the columns. They are called "historiated" when they are decorated with bas-reliefs of animate beings. In the center and the south of France all the capitals are historiated. In Alsace and the eastern part, historiated capitals are the exception. Some capitals can be seen elsewhere adorned with fantastic foliage. These are imitations of the Corinthian capitals. There is only one kind of capital recognized as being wholly proper to the Middle Ages. This is the cubical capital of Ste Marie du Capitole at Cologne. It was fashionable on the banks of the Rhine. Toward the end of the twelfth century (notice the date, which may be useful to your vanity) capitals with this fantastic foliage replaced those with bas-reliefs of men and animals.

In everything that was built under the sway of Romanesque architecture, the nave offered the appearance of solidity, and this look was even exaggerated. Much was sacrificed to obtain it. On the other hand, if a traveler going into a church is struck by the lightness of the nave, he may boldly assert that it was built during the thirteenth and fourteenth centuries.

These two styles have many common features. At first glance, one is struck by the breadth of a Romanesque church, which is great compared to its height. Neither the vaults nor the arcades are very high. The thick walls are supported by close buttresses. On examining the whole, one recognizes that empty spaces are fewer than the full. The columns are strong, often squat; the pillars massive. The engaged columns which in the Romanesque style climb up the walls of the nave to the springing of the vaults are actually interior buttresses. Finally, this passion for solidity allows the least possible space to windows. Would I be too bold if I said that this architecture through the idea of this solidity could lead people's imaginations to the pains of hell?

On the other hand, by a complete contrast, everything as far as the means go tries to seem light and airy in a Gothic church. On the outside, the height of the facade and the springing upward of its whole construction can be seen from far away. The buttresses themselves affect an air of lightness. As you go into this slender building, you are astonished to see vaulting suspended, so to speak, on columns of an appalling lightness. No more of the robust and heavy pillars of Romanesque architecture. They have been replaced by bundles of frail little columns.

The windows, so narrow in the Romanesque period, now fill the bay to the top. The mullions that divide them are so long and slight that, far from seeming to add to the solidity of the arch that surmounts them, you would be tempted to believe that they are supported by the glass. There is a gallery open to the light on both sides above the arcade. It replaces that somber little gallery of the Romanesque churches. It is impossible to conceive how the vaults of the whole building can be borne on such slender and elongated columns. The architects themselves could not conceive it. The architect of the charming church at Mantes, when it was time to take out the centering of the church he had just erected, took flight and went to Paris to hide. He left at Mantes only a nephew who was supposed to send him a horse to come back on if his church didn't fall.

For a long time the reader has, of course, known that the ogive exists in the *Emissary* of the Lake of Albano near Rome. The ogive is found in Nubia and America. All young peoples pass through the ogival stage. It is the easiest of all the arches to construct.

During that brilliant period of the Orientals, contemporaneous with our gloomy Middle Ages, quite frequent use was made of the ogive. In the castle of Ziza in Sicily the ogive figures in the windows and the doors. In France, on the other hand, the ogive appeared first only in the interiors of buildings, and, mark this well, it was used for solidity, not for ornament. The church of St. Gilles, which might be cited as the most finished example of the Romanesque style, has ogives in its oldest parts. Thus the ogive cannot be taken as the characteristic sign of the Gothic style, but it is found much more often there.

There is no exact measurement, no symmetry in medieval buildings. Everything grows out of feeling. When there are arches in a straight line, their breadths are rarely equal.

An odd thing: when the ogive first appeared, it succeeded in getting itself employed only in second-rate churches. In those that were built on a large scale with the aid of great riches, the semicircular arch was employed because it was considered the noble form. It was much more difficult to build, and for a long time, the ogive which has since seemed so proud a despot was only a makeshift. In the south, in the midst of its wonderful monuments of Roman architecture, the round arch was still fashionable, as the noble form, up to the middle of the thirteenth century. The ogive did not prevail until after the wily Louis XI, mocking the imbecility of Good King René, seized his lands and made the northern men supreme there, and they brought their own fashions into Provence.

It was the Gothic's good fortune to appear at the moment of the clergy's greatest power. With a few indulgences, an archbishop controlled thousands of workmen. During the eleventh and twelfth centuries, one thought only of providing for one's needs. There was neither enough wealth nor power for one to dream of magnificence. They built a number of small churches, but they rarely thought of raising those splendid monuments which are triumphs of pride.

In the fifteenth century, by contrast, it was by no means the fashion to build little churches. Princes, towns, even nations combined together to raise cathedrals. With immense wealth at its disposal, Gothic art boldly selected forms already in use from the Romanesque and perfected them all, in the sense that it made them serve its chief aim, which was never lost sight of, *lightness.*

The way the vaults of the Cathedral of Strasbourg were sustained in the air at a prodigious height even at the point where they reached the limits of mechanics and mathematical knowledge is still the subject of our astonishment. They increased the number of buttresses. They flung out flying buttresses on all sides. They did not hesitate to sacrifice the outside walls of the church at Bourges, for instance, to the effect they hoped to get inside.

Romanesque architecture loved jutting cornices. It stressed *horizontal* lines. These lines horrified Gothic architecture. In the cathedral at Coutances we see how every means was employed to fix the attention on the vertical lines. The architects of the fourteenth century strove to make the frontispiece like a pyramid. You are forced to forget any horizontal lines by a multitude of pinnacles.

As to decoration, the cathedrals of the thirteenth century

began by slightly modifying the decoration of the twelfth. By the end of the twelfth century they had already given up putting bas-reliefs of men and animals on the capitals of columns. They were using fantastic foliage.

Since it had great wealth to command, fourteenth-century architecture used foliage faithfully copied from nature. Oak and chestnut leaves were rendered with a truth and delicacy im-impossible to surpass. The long stiff statues of the twelfth century assumed grace and movement in the thirteenth. Sculptors began again to work according to nature, but the greatest variety in detail continued to be fashionable.

It was, then, in the fourteenth century that Gothic architecture reached its highest point of splendor. It shone forth then by the boldness of its plans, the skill of its execution of them, and by the delicacy of the work.

Lyons . . . 1837

One might say that the study of antiquities necessarily destroys a man's faculty of reasoning, so much so that scholars become simpletons, then pedants and Academicians (that is, they don't dare speak the truth about anything for fear of offending a colleague).

An expert on the ogive whom I met in Switzerland and who gave me the information for my sketch of this feature told me, "You have never seen anything beautiful until you have seen Notre Dame de Brou (in Bresse)." I never had the time for it (or rather, I never have had enough respect for difficulty overcome in sculpture).

Notre Dame de Brou is the last church inspired by the Gothic genius. It was begun in 1511. (Raphael, born in 1483, was then twenty-eight years old. Light was reigning in Italy. The Gauls were still in the shadows.) You may judge by a certain fact the patience of the workmen and the taste of the princes who paid them: everything that seemed hard to execute in *metal,* you find done in *marble* at Brou. There are vine leaves standing out three inches from the block of marble from which they were carved, and the whole choir, ninety-seven feet long, is of this kind of work. Could this patience, this more-than-monastic abnegation be allied to any genius at all? In another genre, this sublime patience supplied the talent to those *litterateurs* of the Academy whom absolute monarchy so much loved to reward.

This church took twenty-five years of work and two million, two hundred thousand francs besides, an enormous sum. What a difference it would have made to the reputation of Brou if some good genius had inspired the idea of asking Michael Angelo for a church plan or Raphael for two pictures! Instead of this they had sword hilts carved out of marble in basket-work. The statues are quite good. The sculptor, who knew his business, understood that statuary does not live except through the nude. After three hundred years, the nudities of Brou shock no one, and yet in 1832 the seminarians of Brou were scandalized, and the hammer did justice to everything that offended their chaste glances.

Since the boat for Avignon does not leave until tomorrow morning, I shall use the evening to see Fourvières again.

I went to the theater. As I never go to the Opéra-Comique, I had almost forgotten there was such a thing as a French counter-tenor, especially a high sharp voice like a woman's, yelling out a bravura tune and applauded enough to bring the house down.

I left the performance after ten minutes. How few ideas even the most famous composers have! The musical cliques must be even better organized than the literary ones. I don't know of any printed work that has made such a success with a comparable absence of ideas.

These French operas always remind me of a verse by Horace which undoubtedly I apply badly: *Non satis est pulchra esse poemata dulcia sunto* ("It is not enough that poems be beautiful. They must have feeling.").

Isn't music before everything a delight to the ear?

It is that feeling which this evening's music, imitated from von Weber, never had. The French are not specially ridiculous until they speak of music. Everything that Rousseau said eighty years ago was still perfectly true this evening.

The English government is the only one in Europe which I think is worth the trouble of studying. Everywhere else there is a despot, a nice enough fellow fundamentally but timid, taken in by pleasure, by his nobles or generals, filled with hatred and more or less imbecile. To justify this epithet which seems harsh at first glance, I shall say that I apply it here only to the art of governing. See the Duc de St. Simon, author of *Memoirs of the Court of Louis XIV*. Without any doubt it is worth a hundred times more than all its successors. St. Simon was a man of great intelligence. It was his opinion, however, that the royal power must grow incessantly. Now he was writing in 1733, just sixty years before 1793. Today it is obvious to the least experienced mind that in 1733 the royal power should have created a chamber of hereditary peers, composed of the five hundred richest noblemen. The unique task of this chamber should have been to examine and vote on the budget. As soon as the Revolution of 1789 occurred, this became impossible.

In this much more auspicious state of liberty into which the ineptitude of ministers has thrown us, it is only from events in England that we can make any conjectures about the fate the future reserves to us. I confess I have a child's curiosity about everything that happens in this country so slightly known to us.

Avignon . . . 1837

THIS WONDERFUL JOURNEY, sixty leagues in nine hours, gave me more pleasure the second time than it did the first.

I had some time to myself, and I went to l'Isle to spend the night and to see Vaucluse again. I examined the arch of triumph at Carpentras and its admirable bas-reliefs of prisoners, but you have to have an odd mind to like both things like that and the sonnets of Petrarch.

Aix-en-Provence . . . 1837

AFTER SEEING NOTRE DAME DES DOMS again and the Giotto frescoes in the Palace of the Popes, I left at nightfall for Aix. At last, as day was breaking, I arrived at the boulevard of Aix, decorated by the statue of King René. This pleasant spot is planted with old elms whose foliage this morning was all white with dust.

The finest houses in Aix are on this boulevard, but formerly they only barely gave on it, so to speak. Their facades and main doors were on little streets that ran into the boulevard, a well-understood practice that baffled scandal. Aix is a town of good society where the ladies have preserved their empire. Everyone knows that this street is adorned with three fountains. The middle one gives hot water.

At the beginning of historical time, the Salyes, a Ligurian nation, occupied the country around Aix. They offended Marseilles, and the Romans, allies of the Marseillais, attacked them. Sextius Calvinus, near the place where he overcame them, established a town called Aquae Sextiac because of its hot springs. Almost from the time it was founded, Aix was drawn into the bustle of Marseilles.

Alphonse, Comte de Provence and King of Aragon, took up residence there. This prince loved poetry and was himself a poet. He introduced the taste for light gallantry into Provence. From this arose the troubadours whose very name has become boring because so many dull writers have written of them.

The courts of love date from 1150, and life was very gay in Provence until France was united by the somber Louis XI. I learned all these details on the way to Tholonet, a charming little valley where there are some great trees, but the cruel mistral kept me from admiring them as I should have done.

To quiet one's conscience, one must take a look at the picture painted by King René who, it can't be denied, was an amiable man. He was a good man with neither character nor talent. So as to have the pleasure of making motets and mediocre pictures at his leisure, he let the crafty Louis XI blow all his states away. Provence lost her nationality, and she owes the loss to him.

From a distance I saw Mt. St. Victoire. It was on this spot that Marius defeated the Teutons. These barbarians, they say, left two hundred thousand of their dead on the field.

The location of Aix is fortunate. Backed by a hill, it faces south, and you are less bothered by the mistral than in all the little towns nearby. They still have there almost all of the happiness of the old regime and a society filled with wit, gaiety, and adventures.

In Aix one is counsellor to the Royal Court at the age of twenty-eight and no longer thinks of anything but amusing one's self. In Paris a counsellor to the Royal Court dreams of becoming Prefect of Police and barely considers the pleasures of wit. If he has some wit, he is afraid to joke about something or somebody who may become powerful.

I have been assured that in Aix a man's supreme happiness lies in having before his door two immense candlesnuffers. As soon as he has these candlesnuffers, he is respected by the common people and treated with the highest consideration in society. It must be realized that there were the nobility of the sword and the nobility of the robe in Aix. In St. Simon it can be seen what a poor role this second nobility played in Louis XIV's day.

Before the Revolution in Aix, only the nobility of the sword had the right to have their coaches or sedan chairs preceded each by two lackeys carrying torches; hence the candlesnuffers.

Of the nobility of the robe, only the First President and the Attorney-General had the *right to candlesnuffers.* The day when they could set these pieces of furniture before their doors was, in every sense of the word, the happiest day of their lives.

Happy the government which has such honors to give as rewards of merit, but in our own time, such things would be squandered and consequently rendered valueless; hence the weakness of governments. Instead of these gloomy political considerations, how can I give any idea of the charming little passions which animate the social life of this region? I liked Dijon very much, but I think Aix has the better of it. There is still a great deal of difference here in the respect given to the nobility of the robe and the nobility of the sword.

One of the most extreme contrasts I know between two towns so close together is between the social customs of Aix-en-Provence and those of Geneva.

People from the Midi make their fortunes in Paris only after excessive labor. Among them you find victims of this labor who have reached easy circumstances at the age of fifty after working fifteen hours a day for twenty-five years. What is prejudicial to the Southerner is the passion that bursts out when he speaks. In Paris work is only one of the elements of success and certainly the least necessary. The young man who courts fortune should know how to play on the vanity of the salons he frequents. He should be indefatigable, no doubt, but only in this way: he must arrive at the salons he has chosen at a suitable hour on the right day so that he never misses the "Tuesdays" of the aged lady whose protection he solicits. It is precisely in the salon of this lady that the Southerner is betrayed by the passion that inspires his words.

There you see the young Northerner, cold and thoughtful, who feels nothing but his desire to advance himself, get the better of the boiling Southerner, who is upset by the least little incident or beside himself at the slightest malice. He is always making mistakes that his rival, the young man from Lorraine or Picardy, overcomes. *His* coolness never fails him. Nature has denied him the faculty of being moved. He profits from this sterility of spirit as from a force, and he is right. Among the women of Paris, it is the greatest.

What stimulates the greatest antipathy in him is this Southern joy, this *brio* which gave me so much pleasure in Valence. The happy man who is animated by it, if he does not excite the liveliest sympathy, arouses the envy of intelligent people and seems vulgar to the rest.

If the Southerner succeeds in learning how to keep his mouth shut, he robs his enemies of all their advantages and soon makes his fortune. He has none of the nervous weaknesses of his rival, the young man from Lorraine or Picardy.

Marseilles . . . 1837

THE ROAD FROM AIX TO MARSEILLES ends by being abominably ugly, but a league or two from Aix there are some fine trees, one of which is called "The Tree of Villars." M. de Villars, son of the Gascon wit who won the Battle of Denain so opportunely, was only a man of pleasure in the widest sense of the word and a very coarse talker.

His father had made him Governor of Provence. One day, as he was going from Aix to Marseilles, he met the Intendant of the province who was going from Marseilles to Aix. Instead of pursing their lips at one another as the Prefect and the General of a department should not fail to do, they drove their carriages close together and tranquilly began to play ombre under this tree. M. de Villars lost three thousand louis.

About two o'clock in the morning, when I was about halfway to Marseilles and almost choked with dust, I caught sight of a very cool, very pretty little wood in a little valley that lay across the road, a miraculous thing among the arid slopes of Provence. In the summer there is nothing to this countryside but these burnt slopes and a vile dust that penetrates everywhere; I can always write with my hand on the sleeves of my riding-coat. Tonight behind this wood I caught sight of a chateau which belongs, they say, to M. d'Albertas.

Around three in the morning I was waked up by an atrocious smell. I saw some white smoke that climbed and descended on these frightful slopes, so utterly bare of vegetation. It was an artificial soda factory, the postilion told me.

I failed to see the beautiful view of Marseilles you get on arriving. I don't think I woke up until we were under the windows of the Hotel Bouches-du-Rhone, Rue de Paradis. It is a second-rate house, I agree, but I have a horror of a grand hotel, the fatherland of din and snobbery. Since I have resolved to keep a journal of this trip, even before I went to look up my firm's agent, I wrote down the preceding details, which are uninteresting in themselves and which tomorrow I should no longer remember.

Marseilles . . . 1837

The new agent for our firm's business in Algiers, an elegantly turned-out young man with, indeed, very little affectation, offered me his horse with such a natural politeness that I accepted it. Then, this morning about six o'clock, I went back down the road to Aix at a fast trot, forcing myself to look neither to the left nor right. When I was a good half-league past the Chateau-vert where, once upon a time, they served such good *bouillabaisse,* I turned my horse around. I let him walk, and I made my entry into Marseilles.

The local people call this point the Vista, the view *par excellence.* The place merits its name. In fact, the view is im-

mense and entrancing. At the right you suddenly catch sight of the Mediterranean. It forms a gulf here enlivened by a number of barques. The rays of the rising sun make the little waves sparkle on this tranquil sea, gently agitated by the morning breeze. The low rocks jutting out toward the sea make a right angle here to the shore you walk along and give a singular charm to the whole landscape.

I have often encountered these delightful views on the Mediterranean coasts. As this sea has no tides, it has few desolate aspects, so common on the gloomy coasts of the ocean. These shores are never spoiled by that half-league of sand and mud which, regularly, twice a day, appear to sadden the traveler and show him boats leaning dejectedly on their sides. Nothing is as pure and clean as the shore of the gulf of Bandol which I saw on my right as I returned to Marseilles this morning. A landscape that reproduced this view exactly would be called dry and unnatural in Paris.

Facing me I saw Marseille the magnificent, the Southern town *par excellence.* It is placed at the bottom of an amphitheater formed by those arid rocks like all of them in Provence, but at the foot of the rocks you see some dark green trees that mark the course of the Huveaune. On the right is the sea, and all the country surrounding Marseille on the left, at the foot of the rocks, is covered with little country houses of blinding whiteness which are called *bastides.** I think there might well be four or five thousand of them. Each one has its little garden, but the trees in this garden are barely more than eight or ten feet tall. The dazzling whiteness of these *bastides* and the fence-walls which are whitewashed every year stands out against the pale greenery of the olive and almond trees surrounding them. What keeps this little scrap of scenery from being dull is that the eye discovers plants every moment that we never see in Paris. I asked what those reeds were, a dozen or fifteen feet high, which grew in clumps along the main road. I was told they were *cane,*

* And still are.—Tr.

and they are used to hold up the low vine plants. There were many trees whose bright green leaves seemed varnished like those of the laurel.

When you go down the Vista toward Marseilles, the road is abruptly enclosed by two unending walls. Between them are so many mules, donkeys, carts, and swearing drivers that the cloud of dust keeps you from seeing and breathing. It is impossible to trot a horse through this disagreeable and hardly rustic scuffle.

At last I came to the triumphal arch which is on a height at the entrance to the town somewhat like the arch at the Etoile in Paris. On the right before you come to it, you pass the famous Quarantine Station which is the safety of Provence. From the triumphal arch, the eye plunges into the Cours, a magnificent boulevard planted with two rows of old elms. The Cours buildings are much lower than the arch, like the Champs-Elysées in Paris.

Before reaching it you go down a steeply sloping street. The Cours runs a little beyond the Canebière, the principal street of Marseilles. At this point begins the beautiful Rue de Rome which ends at an obelisk placed opposite the triumphal arch. The streets and the Cours are easily half a league long in a straight line. The Cours is lined by fine houses, and the populace swarms there. Suddenly you have the idea of a large city.

The people around you have a serious air and an incredible vivacity. They seem to speak only in exclamations. Their eyes sparkle. What is particularly striking is the astonishing transparence of the air. As I looked toward the obelisk which is at the Rome gate of the city, I thought I could get to it in ten minutes. Most of the lower-class women are busy knitting stockings of a dark *café-au-lait* color. They have a very nice leg for these stockings. They wear short dresses, and the pleats show that these are made of very heavy material. The younger women wear large silver hooks as a belt from which hang scissors on a silver chain. The longer the chain the higher the girl can hold herself among her neighbors. This is the one and only luxury of these lower-glass girls. These scissors, moreover, can be used as weapons against anyone who is insolent.

On the Cours the horses and carriages must go directly past the houses. Pedestrians are in the middle between the two magnificent rows of trees.

My horse and I, going along the street to the left of the Cours, were nearly hooked by the Toulon coach, and the driver didn't even cry, "Look out!" I find these lower-class Marseillais very coarse. Here you see the disadvantages of naturalness. It is not hard to tell that we are two hundred leagues from Paris.

I returned my new friend's horse to his groom, and, to keep from running the risk of getting angry, I continued my walk on foot, but I had scarcely taken ten steps when I was nearly suffocated by the dust that rose in great whirls from some antique carpets they were beating in the middle of the Cours in the part reserved for pedestrians. In Paris the police would certainly not allow a thing like that. A woman selling cakes for children got into a dispute with the men who were beating the carpets. The astounding dust they beat out of their carpets absolutely overwhelmed her little table full of cakes. Many shopkeepers, perched on their scaffoldings, took the woman's part. To defy them, the men beat their carpets all the harder. Breathing was impossible. I withdrew.

I have noticed that generally the women of Marseilles are pretty. They have a charming foot, and too much *embonpoint* never detracts from the grace of their bodies.

To the left on a hill that rises gently opposite the Canebiére, I caught a glimpse of some magnificent alleys of plane trees, the alleys of Meillan, along which were built many houses more elegant than those on the Cours. Many of these houses have gardens. The aspect of the whole thing is very gay.

After I had been driven from the Cours by the carpet dust, I turned right into the splendid street called the Canebière because long ago it was the sight of some field of hemp, which is called *canabis* in Greek. The Canebière leads to the port,* which is the shape of an elongated playing-card. The Canebière comes into the middle of one of the small sides. It is the headquarters of several hundred stevedores, a group who make themselves count in Marseilles. You see them loading ships or carts with the merchandise of every country. It is a cheering spectacle.

You have before you a crowd of little barques elegantly decked out in calico with red ornaments, and the owners all yell at once to offer you a little voyage on the sea, but you can't see the sea at all, and the port is more like a little lake cluttered with ships. Seduced by the cries and the round *and weather beaten* [*sic*] face of one of the old sailors, I told him to get his barque ready. I went into a little bookshop that offered its wares by the port. They sold me an octavo volume that smelled horribly musty, Gresset's *Méchant*. It is one of the plays I am most contemptuous of.

The old sailor took me out of the port while I was reading the *Méchant*. The mouth of the port turns to the right. That is why you can't see the open sea from the Canebière. The opening to the left toward Toulon is blocked by steep arid rocks, forming capes and islands on which there is not even a small tree. There is a project for cutting an entry on that side.

At the right, first there is the Ft. St. Jean, then a high bank called La Tourette from which there is a beautiful view. On the slope behind it was the old Marseilles Caesar laid siege to. It extended as far as a part of the shore now covered by the sea. Instead of Gresset's *Méchant*, I should certainly have had the *Pharsalia*, but I have less foresight than any man in the world. Beyond Ft. St. Jean is the Quarantine Station we skirted to the north an hour ago, passing the triumphal arch.

We went back into the port. It is perfectly safe and quite deep, but often it smells horribly bad from the Marseille sewers. I picked a bad day apparently. I remarked on it to my boatman

* Now the Vieux Port. Commercial traffic docks at Marseille Nord. —Tr.

with whom I had gotten on very well during our sail. He denied rudely and quite impolitely that his port smelled bad. It's possible that the Marseillais are not sensitive to a certain kind of bad odor. It's lucky for them.

My "patriotic" boatman, a word which in a certain sense means imbecile and sometimes wicked, grumblingly took me back to the Canebière. As we touched land, I very quickly forgot all these ideas. It was eleven in the morning, and I hurried about my business.

Marseilles . . . 1837

About the fourteenth year of the reign of Tarquin the Old, some six hundred years before Christ, some Phocians from Asia, either merchants or pirates, entered the Gallic sea and established themselves on the coast. Five years later there was a new expedition of which Simos and Protis were the leaders. They landed and advanced close by the lands of Namnus, king of the Segobrigiens, and asked permission to build a town on his borders. On that day the king was preparing for the nuptials of his daughter, whom, according to the custom of the country, he had to give to the man she chose at the wedding feast. Namnus told her to give some water to the guest with whom she wished to cast her lot, and she chose Protis who founded Marseilles.

The Marseillais needed courage to keep from being exterminated. They had to repel incessantly the attacks of neighboring tribes who were, most of them, Ligurian. They became friends of the Romans who were enemies of the Ligurians. The fable adds that they made public demonstrations of sorrow when Rome was taken by the Gauls and contributed to the mass of gold and silver the Gauls demanded from the vanquished.

For Marseilles to enjoy a lasting prosperity, it needed only to be an island like Venice. The beautiful customs of Greek civilization would not have been polluted by contact with the gloomy feudal government.

Ancient authors all agree in praising the sagacity of the Marseilles government. Its form was aristocratic. Six hundred senators called *timuques*, or "the honored ones," made up the council of the nation. A special committee of fifteen senators expedited public affairs, and three chosen from the fifteen exercised almost the same authority as the Roman consuls. Strabo informs us that, to be *timuque*, one had to have children and be the issue of a family inscribed on the role of citizens for three generations. This government continued until Marseilles was taken by Caesar. Reduced at that time to purely municipal functions, it still protected for quite a long time the welfare of Marseilles against the bad government of the Byzantine Empire. Tacitus says that Marseilles had made a happy mixture of Greek urbanity with Gallic temperance. When he wished to designate manners above reproach, Plautus called them "Marseillais manners."

As we have seen, the old Marseilles, besieged by Caesar, was built on the hill which extends from Ft. St. Jean to the triumphal arch. You could see the sea from the houses of this Marseilles, an advantage that the modern city is deprived of. The streets of the old city that still remain are black, rough, dirty, and very steep. There are so many wells there that they can't build sewers, and this gives rise to certain customs that actually can't be mentioned.

At the end of this district near the shore, I found the ancient cathedral, called in Provençal the *Major*. This is the oldest church of the Gauls. It is equally true that St. Lazarus, whom Christ raised from the dead, was its founder. He was driven from Jerusalem with St. Martha and St. Mary Magdalen, his sisters, Marcellus, their servant, St. Maximin, and other disciples of Jesus Christ because they preached openly that the Savior of the world had risen again. In a frail ship without sails or rudder, they were all exposed together to the fury of the sea, but a powerful hand was entrusted to lead them, and they fortunately reached shore at the port of Marseilles. St. Lazarus preached the worship of the true God whose worship replaced that of Diana, and her temple became the church of the *Major*.

The new city of Marseilles begins at the Canebière at the end of the port. The rich businessmen who had begun to build this district at the end of the eighteenth century paid the king six millions for the arsenal of the galleys. The galley-slaves were sent to Toulon at this time. The streets built on the arsenal land are straight, well paved, bordered with sidewalks, but they have no character. They resemble the modern streets of Bordeaux, Berlin, Petersburg, Vienna, Munich, etc.

It is fate. Everything modern seems to lack character. Everything precipitates us into a *boring* manner as if it were trying to.

Marseille . . . 1837

THE TOWN FOR PLEASURE, both of the mind and of good society, is Aix. Would it be credible that around 1820 the conversations there were so gay, so well-bred, and so shocking to our present prudery that I don't know if I have the necessary wit to recount them? Marseilles, so admirably located, is only a barbarous town if its manners are compared to those of Aix. You can be happy in Marseille but only through the primitive pleasures, hunting, tobacco, physical movement, and the absence of all discomfort.

In Marseilles, society is no use to a young man whatever, and he feels only its restraints. Even if he has a good head on him, he pays his court to merchandise, to insurance, and he is soon making five or six thousand francs a year.

On Sundays and during the week, he runs to a *bastide* to hunt, whenever he has a moment. Summers he goes bathing in the evening on the Faro. When the mistral is blowing, he goes to his club to smoke excellent Latakia tobacco and talk all the while very loudly with his friends. It is the end of the world if he appears at the theater for an hour, where, however, he has a season ticket, and even that hour he spends in the wings. In Marseilles, everyone who sits in the first row of boxes leaves the theater through a certain little door that opens at the end of the exit corridor, and the manager knows very well that if he closes that little door, he might as well close the theater, too. This is what the managers tell the police commissioner and prefects who, coming from Paris, are scandalized. Why impose Parisian annoyances on people who cannot taste the pleasures of Northern civilization?

After the play he goes out to enjoy the fine weather and promenade up and down the Canebière, smoking in the starlight. Nothing seems more bothersome to the young men of Marseilles, whose life we have just sketched out, than the proposal of going out socially as a habit.

I don't know whether I'm allowed to say that the *grisettes* of Marseilles are charming. They are not at all greedy, and they take an offer of money as an insult. A girl demands only love from her lover. To add to his good fortune, a commercial broker who was seen giving his arm to a girl of the class that wears the silver chains would lose all his business. It can be seen that everything combines to arrange a perfectly happy life for a young man in Marseilles, but this life is devoid of society.

There can hardly be a greater contrast than the actions and feelings of a young man in Marseilles to those of one in Paris. In Paris a young man can get ahead only through society. If he never misses a single one of Mme D——'s Tuesdays, if he is careful to speak only to women more than thirty years old, sooner or later one of the men who frequent the salon will come into some big position, and Mme D—— will compel him to give a little something to the young man who has never missed one of her "days" and never said an imprudent thing.

Even a vision of this kind of life would make a Marseillais grow pale. For him his life is all freedom and movement. He makes five or six thousand francs in and out of banks and by going to the two stock exchanges, for in Marseilles, as in Paris, there are two of them. The Café Casati serves in place of Tortoni's, but the Marseillais don't drink in cafés except with their meals.

"Do they take anything at your establishment?"

"Alas, they do, sir," is the reply at Casati's. "Sometimes they take the little silver spoons."

Under Napoleon the brokers did very little business.* The political opinion in Marseille is that the number of brokers has doubled since the conquest of Algeria. As I was asking for some more intimate details on the social habits of the neighborhood, a very handsome fellow, M. B——, answered me, "There are no deceived husbands in Marseilles because the streets are as straight as a string. When you are at the end of the Rue de Paradis, they can see you from the Canebière. There is never any crowd, any congestion in streets as straight as this. Everyone sees everything. There is only one family to a house. You knock. The cook comes up from her cavern and cries at you in the voice of a female Stentor, 'What do you want, sir? Monsieur is out. Madame is in her room.' The three neighboring houses hear your conversation with the cook, and if you have a youthful air, the ladies come to the windows. You are making a scandal, and the lady will have to tell her husband of your visit.

"In Marseilles everything is arranged for the husbands' benefit. They are the ones who make the laws. The women are their very humble servants. If you wish to submit to the bonds of matrimony, come to Marseilles to get married. Your wife will not torment you to buy her beautiful furniture, I promise you, and you will be as free as you are a slave in Paris."

In Aix, on the other hand, the doors of the mansions are immense, and there are never any porters at them.

* Stendhal knows, for he was one of them in wholesale groceries. It was a poor time for business because of the British blockade.—Tr.

Memoirs of a Tourist

Marseilles . . . 1837

INSTRUCTED BY THE LITTLE FACTS I wrote yesterday, I let myself be drawn into the pleasure of sauntering through the streets. Without any doubt it is the best way to spend one's time when one is far from Paris. I was struck by a hundred little details that I shan't forget.

In London a day spent visiting the curiosities of the Tower and the tombs in Westminster Abbey is deadly dull, and you learn nothing. These curiosities, these tombs somewhat resemble those to be seen anywhere. A day spent walking on the sidewalks of the streets leading to the stock exchange at St. James's reveals a thousand strange details about the social, or rather anti-social, habits of the English.

It is only in self-defense that I go to see provincial museums, the common Gothic churches, and everything that fools call "curiosities." What is curious to me is what happens in the street and does not seem curious to anyone else in the region. But what I observe there is difficult to describe. "The French language is proud," Voltaire said. (I don't dare repeat his remark.) But this great writer, having won over good society, was unable to foresee the miserable state of *stiff-neckedness* it has fallen into since. Ask for the catalogue of the bookshop that lends books in the Faubourg St. Germain.

I wandered over the hill this morning behind Ft. St. Jean to a place called La Tourrette. There was a grand boulevard there or at least a large space where they had had the good sense to tear down the houses. I was assured that the mistral forbade the planting of trees. Myself, I think they hate trees. You can see the sea very well, a hundred feet below. Old sailors were walking there whom I asked very gravely how long it would take me to go to Corsica if the wind was right. If you have a kind face, no more is necessary to lead to a long conversation.

Marseilles . . . 1837

I HAVE JUST COME BACK from the Sainte Beaume, a very tiresome drive. This sanctuary is twenty or twenty-five miles from Marseilles. That amiable Magdalen, to whom much was pardoned because she loved much, came, as everyone knows, to end her days in this grotto. These rocky masses which do not at all resemble those of the Alps recall the rocks, strange rather than imposing, which Leonardo da Vinci introduced into his pictures. The smallest fissures in the rocks surrounding the Sainte Beaume have bushes growing out of them. As we came to the top of the mountain, the neighboring summits abruptly permitted us to see the sea. The view charmed us as if the sea had been a thing unknown. This blue plain stretching to the horizon made a delightful impression.

My traveling companions were barely twenty-two years old. I was very much their elder. M. Corral of Mexico gave me a precept, never while traveling to associate with people as old as myself. This was all luck, and it turned out very well. I never saw such a gay party, and this gaiety which went as far as foolishness did not try to please anyone else at all or show him any consideration.

On the way back we were witnesses of a very jolly custom. When a village has to give a ball, which is called a *train* here, it puts up as prizes for the most tireless dancers some red-and-blue striped papers containing five hundred pins, stuck in the way they are in the shops of the little merchants. To proclaim the holiday and display the papers of pins, they send two of their handsomest young men to the neighboring villages, one playing the tambourine, the other the famous three-holed flute, and they send two of their prettiest girls besides.

This seems too poetic to be true. However, we saw this embassy of four people performing in the middle of the street.

The flute-player and the tambourine-thumper made a piercing racket, and two quite pretty girls, promenading with them in the middle of the street, displayed the papers of pins.

Marseilles . . . 1837

TODAY I PERFORMED what might be called some tourist chores. I saw a soap factory and a *chaix*, or wine factory. Out of wine, sugar, iron filings, and some flower essences, they make the wines of every country. A personage wrapped up in dignity assured me that neither litharge nor any injurious substances were used in the factory. I took that with a grain of salt.

I climbed up Notre Dame de la Garde, a barren and quite high mass of rock where once the sanctimonious people of the region desecrated a bust of Napoleon and massacred some poor old Mamelukes who had come from Egypt with the French expedition. I climbed up into a church steeple, and finally, to finish a day that bored me so much, I hired a barque and went to dine at the Réserve. It is a pretty house built on the little hill that closes the port of Marseilles on the left. There is a fine view of the sea from there which you can't see at all from the city.

In this way I ended the last day of my sojourn in this city. I have wound up all my business, but I am terribly tired. The double trade of businessman and tourist is too much. There is no more oil in the lamp and no longer the possibility of paying attention to anything.

Genoa . . . 1837

HERE IS AN ACCOUNT of the first pleasure trip I have allowed myself during the seven years I have been in irons. (No pun intended.)

I was dead tired in Marseilles. I needed at least twenty-four hours sleep. The French steamboat "Sully" brought me here in twenty-one and a half hours, and I spent a day seeing

Genoa. Tonight at midnight, after I had left the play, I slept all the way back to Marseilles. It is not out of egotism that I go into these details but to give some positive information to men pressed for time who, like myself, want to mix business with curiosity.

On board the "Sully" I did exactly nothing but eat and sleep. At five o'clock this morning in the most beautiful weather in the world, I woke up in the port of Genoa where I saw five or six bare hilltops and some little trees at the lowest points between them.

I put up at the big fashionable hotel, The Maltese Cross, where, as I might have expected, I lacked everything. They changed my room three times in the nineteen hours I stayed in Genoa, and the chambermaid didn't know where I was in the end.

This town is admirably situated as if in an amphitheater on the sea. Between the mountain, four times as high as Montmartre, and the sea, there was room for only three horizontal streets. One, the chief commercial street, is eight feet wide, and you can get good coffee there; another, behind the port wall, is abandoned to the lowest class of sailors; and the third, which is nearest the mountain and bears successively the names Balbi, Nuova, and Nuovissima, is one of the most beautiful streets in the world.

Its architecture is bold, all full of spaces and columns which recall those of Paolos Veronese or the decorations of the Scala in Milan.

When you come from the interior of Italy, this gay splendid architecture seems to lack gravity, but if you come from France, the eye, spoiled by the Place Bellecour, the buildings like furniture warehouses, and the other fine things of the Louis Quinze period, is astonished by the severity of the Palazzo Brignole and its neighbors. But this is a matter of feeling. At best I can only say to the reader, "Do you feel this?" Put it to the test. There is a vivid sensation to be picked up here. When I had wondered a full hour from palace to palace in this beautiful street, I looked for a café. They are all mean and ugly in Genoa, that city of money.

True to the character of Genoa, everybody here is ready to do you a service, *to make money*. My God, what a difference from the people of Naples, so philosophical and so indifferent to any idea of money! Also Naples has created a certain kind of music, that of the Cimarosas and the Pergolesis. When I was asking the way to the best café, an artisan left his work and offered to lead me to it. I accepted, despairing of finding my way through that labyrinth of streets four feet wide. He stopped me in front of the little door of a horribly dark café, made up of two dirty little rooms and a courtyard paved with marble. It was actually the café that was then in fashion. I was offered some milk even more aquatic, if possible, than the milk in Paris, and to make matters even more clear, my coffee was served in a scorching-hot glass it was impossible to touch. How different from the genial luxury of Milan and Venice! I left this tiresome café as soon as I could. I returned, however, several times during the day to drink the excellent "waters," especially the *aqua rossa* with five or six cherries at the bottom of the glass and, when it was hot, a delicious perfume of crushed cherry stones. This excellent and never-enough-praised drink cost three sous, and it quite reconciled me to the ugliness of the café.

This morning as I was following eastward to infinity the café street, I found first a little square and the great covered hall of the stock exchange. Next I came to the pretty Carignano church. To get to it, they had to throw a bridge across a street, and this was a sublime thing before the invention of suspension bridges.

This church, which would be a masterpiece of gravity and nobility beside Notre Dame de Lorette (on the Rue Laffite in Paris), is, I think, a Greek cross with a very high dome raised over the center. It is quite mediocre for Italy, but its location is admirable. As a site they selected a little hill that interrupts the general slope of the Genoese amphitheater toward the sea. It can also be seen from any direction, which is quite essential to the success of a church in this part of the country. When sailors are afraid of a storm, they must be able to see it from a distance. Then they make their vows to the Madonna they can see.

Politically speaking, what is astonishing is that a single family, the Sauli, I believe, built both the church and the bridge. I climbed up to the dome; it is the traveler's duty. Inside the church, I admired Puget's "St. Sebastian." It is this simple, vigorous style, never weakened by the imitation of the antique, that made me look with so much pleasure at his bas-relief of the Plague at Marseilles.

St. Sebastian is not at all a brilliant young man, an angel of beauty like the St. Sebastians of Guido which had to be taken out of the churches in Rome because they made the worshipers amorous. Puget's Sebastian is a vigorous young officer of thirty, which is more faithful to history. St. Sebastian was, I believe, an aide-de-camp, one of the Emperor Diocletian's colonels, and before the invention of powder a colonel had to be *strong*. The face is admirable, and it has a sincerity which, I think, disappeared from sculpture a long time ago. This particular aspect is also very likely to make you yawn like everything that is too noble. Puget has dared to give his Sebastian a belly, and this is a mistake. He has gone too far in his contempt for the "noblefiers."

After I left the Carignano church, I had to go see about my passport, and this is quite a business in Italy. I went to the Town Hall, where I was annoyed for three-quarters of an hour. In vain I kept saying to myself as a consolation, "These poor fellows are afraid of losing their jobs, and I'm sure they will lose them some day. They are unhappier than I am!" Besides I am convinced that the greatest pleasure you could give to minor passport officials in Italy is to get angry. A slightly ironic attitude is worth much more, and you must not seem to hear a word of their language. These renegades know very well that they are held in supreme contempt by foreigners and hated by their compatriots. Any anger you show pulls them away for a moment from the pleasant occupation of chewing on the contempt.

This Town Hall is a vast race-course of white marble badly used, and I had to go through every floor of it. Its mass is the only good thing about it. The building, at least the facade, should date from around 1760. In Italy then, as in France, poor Architecture was hard pressed.

After the passport, I went to drink an *aqua rossa* at my gloomy café, and from there I went to try to see three galleries of pictures in the main street. Since the owners have the good sense to live in the apartments where the pictures are, you have to stop in often. I saw some superb Van Dycks. How this painter must have pleased his contemporaries! What a calmly imperious air he gives his portraits! What progress he has made beyond the *natural manner* of Raphael's portraits! How well you see that these people have had the habit of being obeyed since infancy. Alas! why haven't we some Van Dycks to paint the officers of our National Guard in full regalia?

I saw a fine bust of Vitellius. It is the ideal grand seigneur avid of physical pleasures. A bust should render the habits of the soul, not the passions of the moment. About all we have in France is the bust of a man who feels he is being looked at or, still worse, the bust of a prince who shams dignity or tries out a simple manner.

I went to see the colossal statue in the garden of the famous Andrea Doria. From there I went up to La Villette, the delightful garden of the Marchese di Negro. He is a man of intelligence who, in spite of his rank, gathers around him all the talented men. The Marquis Gian Polo, as they call him, has astonishing verve and, in spite of his seventy years, composes very charming verse. I know no one in France to compare with him. He received me very cordially and made me eat some grapes in his Villette. A hundred and fifty feet below us, at the base of the Rampart on which La Villette is built, we overlooked the surrounding wall of canvas inside which some actors were playing comedy in full daylight and not badly. We could hear their voices quite clearly and follow the scenes.

Toward evening I went into the cathedral which is constructed of alternating bands of black and white stone. It is more bizarre than it is pleasing.

I took a hack and went to Albaro, a pretty town separated from Genoa by the valley of the Polcevera, I think it is. It is a river whose bed is three hundred feet wide without, at the moment, a drop of water in it, but, after a rain, it becomes terrible. A little to the left, going up the river again, you see the pretty house where formerly that amiable Lord Byron lived. His painted walls stand out against the pale verdure of the olive trees.

On the Marchese di Negro's recommendation, the Marchese N—— was so kind as to admit me to his garden near Albaro. The branches of the lemon trees lean out over the water, and when the wind blows down a lemon, it falls into the sea. This is impossible on the Atlantic.

Here is what can be said of the Genoese: I have been assured that there is little society here. A young girl does not read novels. She dreams of marrying a rich man. I think that the Genoese love only money. I am told that they also love their independence, which the English and Lord Bentinck swore to get for them when they took them over in 1814. They are counting on becoming independent again at the first convlusion in Europe.

You can't get out of a covered carriage before the theater here. When I objected, I was told that Genoa has very few streets where you could ride in a carriage. Whether she has or not, it is a major fault. Undoubtedly, during the rainy season (November and December), women come to the play in sedan chairs. Most of the streets in Genoa are very narrow, it is common knowledge, and the middle is paved with bricks set edgewise to make it easier for the mules which are the sole means of transportation.

At the theater we had *Il Furiosoa l'Isola di San Domingo.* It is a kind of *Misanthropie et Reportir*, only Meinau is young, and the poor devil went mad. He beats all the Negroes he meets in the forests of San Domingo with a stick and sometimes takes them to wife and falls at their feet. There was a duet that was quite nice as far as the words went. Il Furioso kissed the hand of a Negro who died of fear. What struck me was that the lady recounted how her seducer, who had made her leave the best of husbands, had been hanged. The music had the greatest kind of success, and it was flat, without ideas, and full of reminiscences.

On the other hand, the tenor who is Il Furioso and deals out blows with a stick to everyone has a very fine voice. He had been an apprentice abbé, and he lived or did not live on six écus a month (thirty-six francs). He threw his frock in the bushes and sold himself to an impresario at the rate of a hundred écus a month. Can you conceive how happy this young Italian is, who adores music and does not have to kowtow to anyone to make a living? In his profession of the abbé dying of hunger, he had to pay court to everyone. Now they pay his traveling expenses. He embarks in a *vetturino* and goes to sing in Venice, Turin, Naples, it doesn't matter where. The impresario makes money on him. In Genoa, he rented him out for twelve hundred francs a month. The tenor knows it, but he has such an aversion to what we call *cliquery* in France that he said in front of me that, after his first three years are up, he will sign a second contract with his impresario if he wants him to.

At Sea . . . 1837

We didn't leave until one o'clock in the morning. The weather is magnificent. A land breeze brings us the fragrance of lemon trees in flower. The sea is as smooth *come un oglio* ("as oil"), as the sailors say. We are coasting along a quarter of a league from shore. The number of country houses from Genoa to Savone is really incomprehensible, and most of them are palaces whose columns you can see from the water.

What a treasure is liberty! Genoa has made all this with a soil that does not produce anything to feed its populace four months of the year. This spectacle threw me into serious thoughts. This row of hills covered with palaces reminded me of England, that small, foggy, and infertile island which, for the same reason, has become the equal of France. With the same liberty from the year 1400 to 1790, France would have conquered it twenty times. I am glad that Napoleon did not understand the invention of the steamboat which they say Fulton offered him. From the exiles of all countries, he would have taken away liberty and the only sanctuary left them.

As we passed Savone, we heard the noise of a cattle fair. Every quarter-hour we found ourselves abreast of some fat town, all of them with an extremely opulent air. The churches were dazzling in the boldness of their architecture, always in the Palladian genre, never the Gothic. Its somber style is unsuited to this country. It would simply be the wrong thing.

At last we saw Nice, then the mouth of the Var, and suddenly the villages and country houses. The air of richness all disappeared. The coast of France is bare and sterile.

Toulon . . . 1837

I spent only a few hours in Marseilles. I found some letters that made me come to Toulon. The trip took nine hours.

At Cuges I examined the culture of the caper bush, a low-growing little plant, quite odd. The road, which is very lovely, wanders among bare and arid rocks like all those in Provence.

At last I came to Toulon, a pretty little town, slipped in between a high mountain and the sea. I admired a pretty street paved with bricks and planted with young plane trees. They make a charming effect and one that surprises me. I wound up my business in two hours. My agent here is a good fellow with all the Provençal candor. He took me to see the rope-walk, the shipyard, the galley-slaves, etc. These are sights of horrible drudgery, especially the last. I am persuaded that the people who showed us all this lie incessantly.

I had to go up into a ship of sixty guns. I pretended that I had never sailed so that I could hear something amusing, something unexpected. They told me about waves a hundred feet high. I caught a glimpse of some fairly erotic lithographs in the midshipmen's cabin, and I was very pleased with them, but I would have liked to see a volume of Montesquieu there also. What a *real* education you could give yourself in this profession! Without neglecting his duties at all and having only the courage to brave ridicule, a young naval officer could read, as one must read, twenty-five books a year. Returning to Paris after six years at sea, he could beat all the young men of his year. Can it be that even knowledge of their profession is ridiculous among these gentlemen?

A captain of a ship is quite different from a colonel. Almost always isolated at sea, he is general-in-chief. But, whatever these gentlemen say, theirs is not such a hard trade. They always know the terrain they fight on, and their soldiers always have their dinner, their beds, and their hospital with them. They have no garrison towns to be bored in, and, in peacetime, their chief enemies, the winds and storms, attack incessantly.

It would be hard to be more polite than the officers we met. There are no more of these theatrical sailors who say, "By Jove!"

Marseilles . . . 1837

Actually there is no longer any distinction between the professions in France. This grand young man with such a pleasant air who leans back in his chair in front of Tortoni's—he is an attorney. The only profession that still taints its man a little is that of the scholar. This little old man in the Versailles coach who looks with such satisfaction at his rosette of the Legion of Honor, who has such a self-satisfied and pedantic air, is necessarily a member of the Institute.

With few exceptions everyone in France is *affected* in direct ratio to his lack of intelligence, the amount of money, and the social importance he has.

A well-to-do man whose dress hits the happy medium between a wig-maker's and a retired actor's said to us one day, "A man is well-dressed if, when he has just left a salon, no one is able to say how he was dressed." It is the same with manners and I daresay with style. The best is the one that makes itself forgotten and allows the thoughts that it sets forth to be the most clearly seen, but there must be some thoughts, true or false.

Thoughts annoy fools who vainly try to comprehend them and whose literary habit consists in admiring the forms of style. A provincial who has become powerful says every book is badly written which has clear thoughts put down in a simple style, but pompous turns of phrase delight them. Messrs. Marchangy, Salvandy, and Chateaubriand are their heroes. A neologism wakes him up after dinner. He admires sentences of this kind, for example: "Winter is in my heart." "It is snowing in my soul."

Marseilles . . . 1837

As is not unusual in the Midi, I had a wonderful dinner at Toulon, which I ate heartily in the hope of going to sleep on the way back. I was wakened two leagues from Marseilles by a soft rain which is a blessing to the poor plants of Provence. They arouse a real pity in me.

From the Rhone to the Var, there are only arid little hills

to be seen covered with wild thyme. There is your real Provence. In the low places between the hills where a little moisture collects when it rains, you find some cultivation. Everything else the sun has burned up. Ask at some house for a little water, and they offer you wine. Water is brought from a league away and then only at mealtimes. At the moment there is none at all.

The chief merit of Algiers is letting us see our soldiers' heads cut off, but it has the secondary advantage of enriching Marseilles. For this reason, they are less jealous of Paris there than in Bordeaux. Also the great passion of the Bordelais is to get us to abandon Africa. If France could find a man comparable to Marshal Davoust, she ought to send him to Algiers for six years with a free hand, but if neither a Davoust nor a St. Cyr nor a Daru, the French colonizer will never do anything that is worth anything. Bold, imprudent, swept away by a moment of folly and the desire to play a part, a Frenchman will use up all his forces in a single day. The next day we lose heart. It is quite the opposite with the American. He would have already in the last seven years obtained some results in Algiers and done it coldly and reasonably. If it were impartial, it would be a curious story that an intelligent Englishman could write, M. Campbell for instance. His sole aim would be to have made one step in the knowledge of the human heart. We would see there the details of all the deeds of courage and folly, all the puerilities which the French have shown to the world since the court of Charles X had the whim of taking Algiers.

Nîmes . . . 1837

THE CAMARGUE VERY MUCH RESEMBLES ZEELAND. It is a country only about seven feet above sea level. It forms an island set between the sea and the two branches of the Rhone, an equilateral triangle, seven leagues long on each side. The edges of the island are very well cultivated, but unfortunately the center is lower than the edges. There ponds, salt marshes, and

fever are found. The Valcarès pond, the largest of them all, is five leagues in circumference. The immense stretches of uncultivated land are covered with cows and sheep that graze at liberty.

It struck one o'clock in the morning as I entered Arles. The sky was dressed like Scaramouche this evening. The night was very black, and I could catch only a glimpse of the part of the theater called "The Tower of Roland" and the obelisk. As you know, Arles has been the capital of a kingdom. It is deserted today but still preserves many monuments.

Caesar is the first ancient author who mentions this town. He had galleys built there in order to subjugate Marseilles. After it had enjoyed a moment of liberty, it was forced to recognize the sovereignty of the Comte de Provence in 1251, and in 1481 it was reunited to the realm of France.

In the market place I caught a glimpse of the obelisk of Egyptian granite. It is forty-seven feet high, and its pedestal fourteen. The obelisk was broken in a fall, and it is in two pieces.

The amphitheater at Arles has the look of a fortress. They built towers on the surrounding wall, and the amphitheater is filled with dingy houses. It is bigger than the one at Nîmes and could hold twenty thousand spectators.

I am assured that the Provençal tongue is nowhere spoken with more grace than in this town where I was unable to address a word to anyone except two sleeping postilions. All nuances are constantly disappearing in France. In fifty years there may not be any Provençals or Provençal language. I saw the same revolution at work in England, and they tell me it is the same way in Spain. Only racial differences will remain, modified by the climate. The people of Arles do not resemble those of Gap at all, and Gap is only thirty leagues away. When spoken by a young woman, Provençal admits the pretty diminutives of Spanish and Italian now driven out everywhere by *clarity*, this despot of modern languages. We must save time, and we must be clear before everything.

Formerly Arles had a costume quite like the one worn near Rome. The Revolution killed all originality of this kind when it made the trip to Paris easy.

Montpellier . . . 1837

MONTPELLIER IS A VERY PRETTY TOWN built on a knoll which gives a slope to many of the streets. This is, I think, one of its great advantages. You can see the sea on the horizon, four or five leagues away.

I took a three-hour walk through the streets. I found a great deal of gaiety and vivacity. There were some elegant houses. The town ought not to sadden the sick people who come here to seek such a rare combination of famous doctors and a fine climate. At bottom the great merit of Montpellier is in not having a stupid air like the other big towns of the French interior, Bourges, Rennes, etc. Montpellier is the birthplace of two great ministers who Napoleon was lucky enough to meet and to appreciate, the Counts Daru and Chaptal, men comparable to Colbert.*

Béziers . . . 1837

AFTER THE LAST RELAYS before Béziers, the country is pretty. This little town has a fine location on a height from which you overlook the Languedoc canal and a number of locks that go down to the Mediterranean. In rambling through the gloomy narrow streets, I recalled the sack of this town and the remark of the Catholic leader: "Keep killing. God will recognize his own." We are not so far from those times. Haven't we the remark today apropos of sacrilegious persons, "They must

* Daru, Napoleon's chief quartermaster, was a cousin of Stendhal. —Tr.

be sent before their natural judge"? And that other remark, almost as celebrated, "Only seven men are necessary to govern a department (one of whom is the hangman)."

This evening I was the object of an act of exquisite politeness on the part of the proprietor of the reading room. I was reading with great interest a brochure entitled *The Destruction of the Convent of Bajano at Naples.* I was alone in the reading room which closes at half-past seven. The candle was burning only for me, but the proprietor, seeing the extreme attention with which I read, waited until nine o'clock to speak to me about closing up. Notice that his candle was burning. That is a big thing in the provinces. I honestly didn't know how to prove my gratitude to this gentleman. I didn't dare risk a twenty-sou piece under the pretext of an expense made only for me. Theory tells me that I did wrong, but I would have been too ashamed if I had offended that amiable Languedocian.

Sijean . . . 1837

THE SUN WAS ABOUT TO RISE when I got to Narbonne, whose high tower I had been watching emerge in the dawn. This town interests me. Once at someone's house I met M. Fauriel, the French Academician who probably does the least lying and is the only one of the contemporary historians I have faith in. It seems to me that M. Fauriel told us that for a long time after Genseric had taken and pillaged Rome, Narbonne remained Roman in its customs and civilization. Julius Caesar and Tiberius beautified it.

I have seen the beautiful tower and some churches. I sacrificed an hour of sleep to curiosity. The country surrounding Narbonne is dry and desolate, worse than Provence. I am writing this at Sijean, waiting for dinner. In the manners of the inhabitants I find a singular difference. It is the Spanish character beginning to bite. The Spaniard has none of the bourgeois pettiness. He scorns to lie in the little affairs of life, but he makes up for it in his battle reports. However that may be, I esteem the Spaniard's private life very highly; I even love it. Like the Neapolitan, he finds it less trouble to wear a coat that is out at the elbows than to work fifteen hours a day like an Englishman to get enough to buy a new one. I swear I'm of the same mind. I still think very highly of the *Spanish silence*. Finally I adore certain scenes from their old poets.

Perpignan . . . 1837

I SEE THE CITADEL OF PERPIGNAN standing out against a clear sky in the distance. Part of the town is built on a hill. It was a very strong town once. The position it occupies is important to an army defending the French frontier. Perpignan pleases me infinitely, especially a certain bridge filled with Catalan merchants. They are a people absolutely new to me. The town is situated on the Teth. My agent's brother, a former officer, recounted to me the military events that happened near there at the beginning of the war of the Revolution.

The stock exchange, which is called the *Loge* as in Italy, is a pretty Gothic. After staying there four hours, three of which were taken up by business, I left for Port Vendre. This name, apparently so mercantile, has quite a different origin, *Portus Veneris*, "port of Venus," because of a temple dedicated to that goddess. It is a much frequented port. They embark for Algiers there. It is wretched, at least according to a vivid report, but the forts that guard it give a strange aspect to the whole.

I found some queer people there. They have been commissioned to buy iron, and they don't distinguish between the soft iron from Champagne and the short iron from Berry. These gentlemen will make some odd structures. However, I didn't complain at all. I was happy with my trip there.

I was told a very silly story. In the reign of Charles X, certain ministers formed the project without the King's knowledge of seizing one of the Spanish islands near Majorca. Why didn't they do it?

I have just committed a rank imprudence. My business was going well at Port Vendre and Perpignan, but it was going to take several days to finish it. I entrusted myself to a Spaniard whom I paid well and, against all ordinary rules, in advance, and I went to spend twenty-four hours in Barcelona. My guide thought I had very little money, which was true; I sewed some English banknotes into the lining of my frock coat.

I admired the beautiful cork forests and the greyish color of the trunks from which they had just stripped their precious bark. The hedges made of aloes pleased me very much. Actually everything pleased me. Is it unwise to be this way? The houses of all the villages had just been whitewashed, which gave them an extraordinary air of cleanliness and gaiety, an air precisely of what they are not. But, no matter. The sight of these rows of white houses in the middle of vast mountains covered with cork forests is charming.

Mataro, with its houses again perfectly whitewashed inside as well as outside, is situated on the shore forty feet above sea level, which gives it a fine view and makes a little town very pleasant. We were served a very heavy dinner. There were fifteen or twenty meat dishes for eight travelers, but all the dishes stank of rancid oil. We could not eat, and meanwhile we were dying of hunger. We tried to wash the meat in hot water and then eat it with vinegar, but it was impossible to remove the vile odor of the rancid oil.

During this sad experience, I was much amused by the appearance of the two servant girls of the inn. One of them was at least five feet, six inches tall, admirably well made with big eyes but a somewhat stupid air. On the other hand, there was nothing more malign than her companion, who also had a nice figure, charming hands, lovely black eyes, but she was four feet tall. These robust Spaniards watched what we did and understood nothing of our efforts. They took us, I think, for miserable Jews who didn't want to eat dishes prepared by Christians. We didn't understand one word of their language. The muleteers were off with their mules in a stable some distance away, and we didn't know how to get there. We were never able to make them understand that we wanted some eggs.

At last, seeing how we devoured our bread, the two servant girls ran out and brought us some excellent old wine called *rancio.* One of us discovered some fennel in the kitchen. It is like celery. We made a salad out of it with salt and vinegar and ate a lot of bread soaked in the wine which made us very gay and talkative.

The muleteer ran in suddenly, very frightened. He came to tell us we had to get away at once. Already we heard a big racket in the streets. They were shutting up the shops. They said the Carlists were only a quarter of a league away. We left at a fast trot on some very tough mules.

We camped about five hours' journey farther on. About noon the next day, we caught sight of the citadel of Montjuich that overlooks Barcelona. Two leagues from the city we rented a little vegetable cart from a gardener. We were worn out. In that equipage we appeared on the Rambla, the pretty boulevard that runs through the middle of Barcelona. On it is the inn of the *Cuatros Naciones* ("the Four Nations") where at last we found a dinner. It was a very keen pleasure.

After dinner we were busy getting our passports visaed. I wanted to leave for France again the next day. My companions, lively and resolute and consequently friendly enough but whose behavior looked very suspicious to me, did not seem any more interested than I was in making a long stay in Barcelona.

The police received us in an inquisitorial silence that augured badly for us, and when we left them, we went to buy some *pâtés.* I bought a bottle of Lucca oil and a piece of Parmesan from an Italian vendor. After that, free from all worry, I walked around the city, enjoying the delicious pleasure of seeing what I had never seen before.

Barcelona is, as they say, the most beautiful city in Spain after Cadiz. It resembles Milan, but, instead of lying in the middle of a perfectly flat plain, it backs up against Montjuich. You can't see the sea from Barcelona at all. This sea which ennobles everything is hidden by the fortifications at the end of the Rambla.

It must be observed that they preach the purest virtue in Barcelona, *the utility of everything*, and, at the same time, everyone wants a special privilege, an amusing contradiction. The Catalans seem to me to be in exactly the same situation as the French ironmasters. These gentlemen want just laws except for the customs law which has to be drawn to suit them. The Catalans demand that every Spaniard who uses cotton cloth pay four francs a year because there is in the world such a thing as a Barcelona wool rug.

The Spaniard in Granada, Malaga, Corunna, is unable to buy English cottons, which are excellent and cost a franc an ell, and must supply himself with the very inferior Catalonian cottons which cost three francs an ell. Except for that these people are republicans at bottom and great admirers of J.-J. Rousseau and the *Social Contract*. They claim to love *what is useful to all* and to detest injustices profitable to only a few; that is, they detest the privileges of the nobility *which they do not have*, and they want to continue to enjoy the commercial privileges which their turbulence once exacted from the absolute monarchy. The Catalans are liberal in the same way as the poet Alfieri, who was a count and detested kings but regarded as sacred all the privileges of counts.

I thought the Rambla charming. It is a boulevard arranged so that you walk down the middle between two rows of quite lovely trees. The carriages pass on both sides in front of the houses, and the trees are protected from them by two little walls three feet high.

I have a natural inclination toward the Spanish nation. That is what brought me here. I like the Spaniard because he is a character. He is not a copy of anyone. He will be the last original to exist in Europe.

In Italy everyone who is rich and noble is a copy of some great French lord, always trembling for fear of what they are going to say about him. The great Spanish lords we have glimpsed in Paris are not copies. As far as I can see, they need no reassurance whatever about their standing, and they care nothing at all for the opinion of the hundred well-dressed ninnies who gather at the neighboring embassy.

What wouldn't a great German or Italian nobleman do, first, merely to get into the salon of a neighboring embassy and, second, to cut a swathe there? The Spaniard goes there more out of curiosity, since he is in Paris, to see the monkeyshines.

I was burning to go see the Garden at Valencia. I'm told they have some strange customs there. The artisans work sitting down. Every Saturday they cover the inside walls of their houses with whitewash and paint the floors red.

From Barcelona the great problem was to get back into France. When we had made all our calculations, we ventured to hire a cart drawn by mules. My seven companions looked like emigrants to me. At least emigration goes on. Life in Spain is very unpleasant, and this state of affairs might well last twenty or thirty years more.

Several of my companions resembled Don Quixote perfectly. There was the same loyalty and the same lack of common sense in the way they came at certain subjects. The chords one must not strike were religion and the privileges of the nobility. With a great deal of wit and a charming vivacity, these gentlemen were continually proving to me that the privileges of the nobility are useful to the common people. What made me love them was that they believed it.

Just before we left, we went to drink some chocolate in the shop of a certain Piedmontese hidden away in a little street. I had procured twenty hard-boiled eggs at the inn. I had some bread, some chocolate, etc. In short, I was not going to be reduced to dining on bread soaked in wine that was one-third brandy. This doesn't sit well on the stomach.

My Spanish companions were much more intelligent than the ones I had on the way into Spain. For instance, I made it understood very politely that three hours a day talking politics seemed to me sufficient. With much pleasure they talked to me about their great dramatic poets, most of whom have guttural names abominable to pronounce. They claim that it is a real oddity that foreigners have not distinguished between such superior men as Calderón and Lope de Vega. They mentioned Alarcón and other names that escape me. In my opinion, all these poets have one great merit and one great fault.

Their merit is that their plays are in no way imitations, more or less elegant, of the masterpieces which have delighted other nations. Monarchic Spain obeys a sense of honor which is, if you like, exaggerated, but it is all-powerful there and determines the happiness or unhappiness of each man, and she has at no point imitated the tragedies by which Sophocles and Euripides sought to please the furious democracy of Athens. The plays of Fray Gabriel Telles, for instance, were written solely to please the Spaniards of his time and consequently expressed the taste and view point of the Spaniard of the year 1600. There lies their great merit.

The principal fault of these Spanish plays is that the characters are reciting at every moment a witty ode on the feelings that animate them and say none whatever of the simple and unwitty remarks that would make me believe they have these feelings and which, above all, would arouse them in me.

Speed of Spanish mules: each of them has a name, the Marquise, the Colonel, etc. The driver heckles them incessantly, "What, Colonel, you're letting the Marquise beat you?" He throws little stones at them. A young boy whose agility I admire, named Zagal, runs beside the mules to hurry them up. Then, when they begin to gallop, he catches onto the cart. This is an amusing trick. Occasionally, the mules throw their weight into the collar and gallop all together. Then we have to stop for five minutes because they always break one of the traces. This mode of locomotion, peculiar to the peoples of the South, is at once barbarous and amusing. It is just the opposite of English stagecoaches in which I have made a hundred and four leagues in twenty-three hours (from Lancaster to London).

Bordeaux . . . 1837

THE SOUTH OF FRANCE is in the same case as Spain and Italy. Its natural *brio,* its vivacity, keeps it from being "Englished" like the North. A man of the Midi does what pleases him at that very moment and not what is prudent. This man is not made for the civilization that has reigned since 1830: money and the shrewd and legitimate ways of getting it. Also he is jealous of the Northerners. He cries that they treat him like a pariah.

"But do you think of money every two minutes?" they answer him.

"You sacrifice wines to the interest of iron," he says.

There is no answer to that.

A good father who has a son in poor health augments his son's marriage portion so he can get along in the world. It must be admitted that this is not the way the government acts toward Toulon and Bordeaux.

In 1836 the Chamber voted a great many millions for canals and roads. Sixty millions have been allocated in the North whose discreet English character does so much to help it along. Only twelve millions have been given to the South.

What struck me, what shows very plainly that the Midi is not endowed with the grasping character it takes now to make and save money is that I saw no longer in Bordeaux any of those great commercial houses that I noticed so respectfully thirteen years ago when I was embarking for the colonies. Luxury, the lack of prudence, the sanguine Southern spirit, have eaten them all up. All the great commercial names of Bordeaux are changed. If it hadn't been for the troubles in Spain and America which have brought fifty millionaires here, Bordeaux would be in the physical and moral condition of Rennes, and yet Bordeaux is far from being the most beautiful town in France.

Elections can be corrupted by the awarding of jobs and crosses, but the *masses* cannot be bought. The Roman emperors could do this, but now it costs too much. The masses can no longer be seduced by an eloquent monk. Since the *Charivari* began publishing, the masses, actuated by their interests, steadfastly continue to make their voices heard, and in the end something will have to be done for the Midi, which will not be silent until it sees itself somewhere near the level of the North.

Between Montesquieu and ourselves, aside from the immense difference in genius, there is still a difference in point of view. What we see happening before our eyes every day, he barely regarded as a distant possibility in 1750. It is perfectly clear, then, that he should sometimes be deceived in his predictions. How many times have we not seen institutions, long desired and finally obtained with great difficulty, fail entirely of their aims?

Thus a society is formed, composed of Frenchmen of the greatest intelligence and education. They are charged with recruiting themselves, of choosing the better living writers, and yet to get Chateaubriand chosen, an order from Napoleon is necessary. It is not that they do not feel the merit of this great writer. They understand him only too well.

Montesquieu saw the world imprisoned in a religion and a monarchy which sent any dissidents to the Bastille. It was only his intelligence that told him things could be otherwise. We have seen them otherwise, and how many times have they not changed?

A young girl of Manosque, the most beautiful in that part

of the country, was selected to present some flowers to Francis I. The king seemed to be very much affected by her beauty. That night, barely disguised, he passed by her house and tried to see her. The girl felt that she would not be able to resist him. She burned the skin of her face with sulphur and made herself ugly for life!